Small Eden

JANE DAVIS

Printed and bound in Great Britain by Clays Ltd, Elcograf S.p.A., for
Rossdale Print Productions

Paperback ISBN 978-1-8380348-1-8

Cover design by Andrew Candy of Tentacle Design based on original
artwork by David Knights-Whittome, reproduced by the Past on Glass
and licensed by London Borough of Sutton Local Studies & Archives
Service; Photo of Yorke Stephens by Herbert Rose Barraud, published by
Carson & Comerford 1886 and licenced by National Portrait Gallery's
Portrait Picture Library, parakeet © Patrick Guenette @ Dreamstime.com
and hand-drawn figs by Geraria @Deposit Photos.

https://jane-davis.co.uk/

In memory of my father,

THOMAS MORE DAVIS

14 April 1935 ~ 4 April 2020

Also in memory of

LIZ CARR

Author, beta reader and valued friend

PRAISE FOR SMALL EDEN

'Like Thomas Hardy, Jane Davis shows the fatal consequences of chance and choices for her characters, people I cared deeply about.'

Jean Gill, author of Historical Fiction series,
The Troubadours Quartet

'With an eye for precise detail balanced by a sweeping imagination, this beautifully constructed book is built on deep foundations.'

J.J. Marsh, author of the Beatrice Stubbs Series

PROLOGUE

1884

When Robert passes the open door of the children's nursery, he sees his wife's face captured in a small halo of candlelight. The flame flickers and the halo shifts, revealing that she is bent over the boys' cot-bed, a hand laid over Thomas's brow. "I know," she's saying. "I know."

He stands in the doorway, unseen, and watches her. Freya is a natural in the role of mother while, as head of the house, Robert often feels like an actor miscast, knowing that his understudy would be more suited to the part. But as natural a mother as his wife is, Robert worries that the children will grow accustomed to her sitting with them until they fall asleep, and will not remember how to do it without her soft lowing and her lullabies. "Come down to supper," he says in a low voice.

Freya looks up. He sees now that she is anxious. "Thomas has a fever. I think we ought to send for Dr Stanbury."

The doctor won't thank them for disturbing his evening for the sake of milk teeth. Besides, they've been here before. When their daughter Estelle was teething she would get herself all hot and bothered. "Let's take a look at you, little man." (Here is a line Robert can say with authority.) He collects

1

the second candlestick from the mantel. The flame dances as he crosses the room to inspect his son. Thomas is grizzling, his skin pale with red blotches on his cheeks. His thumb is anchored in his mouth, splayed fingers glistening with drool. Robert crouches down to better see, and the shadow of his wife's head and shoulders rises up the wall, a dark guardian angel.

"Are your teeth troubling you?" At two years old, the boy already has his incisors. Robert prises Thomas's wet thumb from his mouth and feels along his gum – Freya's right, the boy's cheeks are livid. The moment Robert feels the sharp point of a tooth poking through, Thomas pulls away and whimpers. "There it is, right at the back. A molar."

He moves aside to let Freya feel. "Poor lamb," she coos. "There, now."

Lying beside Thomas, Gerrard is kicking the bedclothes just to watch the shadows he can make. He's the baby of the family, but with Freya in her sixth month and expecting their fourth, he won't occupy that position much longer. Four children under the age of four! If you could plan for such a thing, a gap of three years between each child would be ideal. But they agreed, they wanted a large family; Freya, because she came from one and misses it, Robert because he was an only child.

"Remember the sleepless nights we had when Estelle's back teeth were coming through?" Robert whispers. There is no sound from their daughter, whose bed is in the dark corner behind them. She's developed a miraculous capacity to sleep through most disturbances. "I'll fetch the Godfrey's Cordial. That ought to do the trick."

Joan glances up as Robert enters the kitchen. "Shall I serve supper, Mr Cooke?"

"Keep it warm for now." He goes to the scullery sink. "Thomas is having a bad time teething. Can you fetch me the

Godfrey's?" He washes his hands in the way his father taught him, methodically and up to his wrists. Hand-washing was one of the things Walter was fastidious about. A doctor, he was a firm believer in germ theory – the idea that poison could pass from hand to mouth – while his colleagues held fast to the view that bad air causes disease, and so flung the windows wide in all weathers. Robert's thoughts are fixed not only on the night ahead, but on Freya's coming confinement, the nine weeks during which she'll separate herself from the rest of the household to prepare for their baby's arrival. With three children under the age of three on their hands, Thomas particularly fractious, they'll need a nurse when the fourth arrives. It won't be difficult to find one, there are always women in need of extra income, but they have left it rather late.

Upstairs, Robert doses Thomas with a spoonful of cordial, and while Freya straightens Estelle's blankets he doses the baby. They'll be better able to deal with Thomas if Gerrard sleeps through. Robert makes a game of pretending to catch Gerrard's kicking feet, the boy giggling at his clumsiness. Their youngest is a sweet child. The most extraordinary eyes. They call them hazel, though by candlelight the colour Robert sees most clearly is gold.

Freya comes to his side, rests her head against his shoulder. "I'm so exhausted I could sleep on my feet. I think I'll have to turn in."

"What about supper?"

She looks down at her swollen belly. Her body has performed its miracle three times already. The fourth is no less wondrous to Robert. "Honestly, I have nowhere to put it. I need sleep far more than I need food."

Freya knows herself by now, knows the ordeal that lies ahead. He kisses her forehead. "Go and rest. I'll sit up with Thomas."

"You?" By candlelight his wife's skin glows golden, a match for her corn-coloured hair.

"Don't look so shocked."

"I'd thought to ask one of the girls."

Has she seen through him? "I'm perfectly capable."

"You'll fetch me if he gets any worse?"

"Of course I will." Robert says, though he has no intention of doing such a thing.

"Perhaps I should take Gerrard with me. To be on the safe side."

"Absolutely not. He'll keep you awake. Go!" He points to the door. "We'll be fine."

At eleven o'clock, the candle reduced to a molten stub, Robert measures out a second dose of Godfrey's. Exhausted and miserable, Thomas resists the spoon, turning his head this way and that. Seeing that Gerrard is still wide awake, Robert picks him up. With the boy's head over his shoulder, he pats out a gentle rhythm on his back. *I'm twenty-two years old, responsible for my mother and wife, and with a fourth child on the way. We need a bigger house.*

For Robert, it will be a restless night, constantly shifting about in the wooden rocking chair, trying to find the least uncomfortable position. His impression is that he's awake the entire time, but several times he hears a slight snore and knows it to be his own, or is brought to when his head snaps up from his chest. At an hour when darkness is absolute, Robert becomes aware of a noise he struggles to place. He fumbles blindly for safety matches and lights a fresh candle. Thomas is swallowing repeatedly, as if he's trying to rid himself of something. Robert wets a flannel with cold water from the wash bowl, lays it across his son's forehead. Three o'clock by his watch. *Stop feeling sorry for yourself. You've managed a day's work on three hours' sleep before.* Gently, gently he

4

blows on the candle's flame so that it dances a reluctant jig, the shadows following the flame's lead. "You try," he whispers. Thomas keeps his glassy eyes on the flame, but hasn't the energy to blow.

Robert determines to stay awake. At any moment Thomas might start crying and he won't have Freya disturbed. He covers his top half in a child-size blanket, pulling it up to his chin. At the first signs of light, heavy-lidded and stiff-limbed, he draws the curtains to better see. A tic springs to life above his right eye. Every blink is a chore. But he has steered them through the night and Freya will have had her sleep. He turns from the window to his son and sees – he *thinks* he sees…

He is *teething,* Robert insists to himself, and Thomas *is,* no doubt about it, but that is not all. Robert stands there gaping, appalled. *Dear God, please not that!* Then his fingers are struggling with the fastenings of Thomas's damp nightshirt, fumbling with buttons – dammit! – forcing them through too-small buttonholes – *What have I done?* – but finally Robert has the top three undone. Raised bumps, a red rash, no longer mottled, but angry. He lays a trembling hand flat. His son's chest is burning up, skin the texture of crushed shell. He feels a dredging kind of horror.

His wife arrives at the other side of the boys' cot-bed. In her nightdress, with her robe hanging open, Freya's shape is pronounced. "Gerrard," she says, not in greeting but in trepidation. Sure enough, Gerrard's cheeks bear the beginnings of a red rash. *There is produced a poisonous matter, which, passing from the diseased body, is capable of producing in another body a similar disease.* Robert's father had him recite this, yet when Freya proposed they sent for the doctor, when perhaps there was still time, he vetoed the idea. When she suggested they separate the boys, he said it was unnecessary. All because he didn't want to be like his mother, constantly assuming the worst, seeing danger where there was none.

And now Freya is reaching for Gerrard, about to scoop him up in her arms.

Robert's heart hammers at the bars of its cage. His arms shoot out in front of him. *"Stay back!"*

Startled by his voice, by his evident panic, his wife cowers. Her hands go to her belly, to reassure the child within who must be protected. Behind Robert, in her bed in the corner, Estelle begins to sob, the great hiccupping tears that come when she wakes to discover she's outside her mother's womb.

"I'll send for the doctor." Robert steers Freya away from the boys' bedside then goes back for Estelle. "Up you come, little lady." Her bed-warmed body is a weight in his arms. "It's all right. Here's your mother." He turns so that the girl can see Freya, but his wife cannot take her eyes from the boys in the cot-bed.

"Do you think it's…?"

"Hopefully not. But to be on the safe side, you ought to have Estelle in with you."

Freya would have stood in the doorway and kept vigil while Robert is elsewhere, but the boys will call out to her and she'll go to them – she won't be able to help herself – and so the door must be shut. And as Freya's view of her sons narrows, she cranes her neck, whimpering a small protest.

PART ONE
1870 ~ 1872

CHAPTER ONE

1870

If ever there was a day to take a risk, to dare himself, it is today. The boy – Robert is his name – wakes to the competing calls of blackbirds. Knowing only too well the feeling of being interrupted mid-sentence, he flings off his bedclothes and goes to the window. There on the branch of the apple tree sits one of the culprits (the bird is black, a male), eyes bright and hopeful, cocking his head to listen before opening his yellow beak in response: a burst followed by a chirrup. Sometimes all the bird does is open and close his beak, and then with a gulp in his throat. He isn't the attention-seeker the boy had him pegged to be, simply a herald of the new day. And what a day it is, the sky a shade frequently dubbed sky blue, but not seen for weeks, despite the season. His father promised: *The next time we're up early enough and the weather's fine, we'll go.* What's more, today is Robert's birthday, a day when he surely stands more of a chance than any other. He will risk his father's bark. He will even risk his mother's objections.

Outside his parents' bedroom door, knock ready, Robert pauses. He is too old, he's been reminded, to bound into the adults' room. He is a boy, not a puppy dog, and limits must be observed.

'These modern ideas, sharing,' Mrs Dwyer has said. 'It's bad enough that they...' She shook off the end of her sentence, perhaps something not intended for a child's ears. But occasionally, their housekeeper forgets herself.

Robert has learned a good many things from Mrs Dwyer, things he wouldn't otherwise know. He has learned, for instance, that as a doctor, living where they live, his father could be a rich man if only he'd stop giving away his time and his medicines. 'That they what?' he prompted.

'Never you mind. Just remember, you're old enough to entertain yourself.' With a flick of her dishcloth she batted him away. 'Your parents will make an appearance in their own good time.'

But time is wasting. Mrs Dwyer has already been up for a couple of hours, pattering from room to room, lighting fires, opening the front door to shake out the rugs. He could ask her for hot water, but all he intends is a quick scrub of his face, and for that he makes do with cold, standing at the washstand in his vest and drawers.

Dressed and as respectable as he's going to be, Robert presses his ear to the door of his parents' bedroom, hooking the shell of it with the curve of his hand to form a kind of receptacle – a receiver, if you prefer. The forefinger of his other hand makes a useful stopper for his other ear. Birdsong muted, he stills his breath, concentrates. No snore to suggest his father is asleep, but then again, no low murmur to suggest his mother is awake. There *must* be a way to hurry them along.

The blackbirds! They might be recruited as co-conspirators. Robert returns to his bedroom, hoists up the sash window, then tackles the window on the landing. The house fills with the chatter of birds: the do-re-mi, the cheep-cheep-cheep, the sequence of notes he thinks sounds like *pretty birdy*. Dare he open his parents' door? He must. Robert's fingers tighten around the brass oval. He squeezes his eyes shut, bites his bottom lip and twists to the right. A small click, nothing that would wake a sleeper. The boy pushes the door open a crack, willing the symphony to intrude where he cannot.

"Who's there?"

A single heavy thud then thunderous footsteps. Robert leaps back just as the door is pulled inwards. His father – Walter is his name, but it is not a name the boy ever uses – is tented in a white nightshirt. The version of his father he's accustomed to is the black-trousered, frock-coated, stiff-collared one. This is someone entirely different. "Am I needed in my surgery?"

The boy's heart pounds. "No, sir."

"Then why the devil would you wake me?"

"Sir, you said…" Behind his back, Robert's hands clasp and unclasp in an agony of their own.

"Well? Speak up!"

He raises his chin, prays he won't stutter. "You said that the next time it was a fine day and we were awake early, you'd take me hot air ballooning at Cremorne."

"Walter, you –" Two words and his mother's displeasure is all too apparent. She hardly needs add, *I hoped we'd heard the last of that.*

His father closes his eyes as if to shut out competing demands and objections and gives a low growl. When he opens them again, it is Robert he addresses. "What kind of a man do you think I am that you can –?"

"A man of your word, sir." The boy is shocked by his own impudence but it's too late to take it back. "I think you are a man of your word."

"Ha!" Walter turns his face towards Robert's mother (Hettie, another name the boy never uses), who is hidden beneath her own white cotton tent. "The young pup has me in checkmate!" The angle of his father's moustache often makes it appear that his mouth is downturned, so his mood is rarely

immediately apparent, but his voice tells Robert his gruffness was a pantomime. "What day is it, son?"

"The twenty-fourth of July, sir."

"Wait a moment." Walter aims the question over his shoulder: "Does that date mean anything to you, my dear?"

"Let me think now. The twenty-fourth…"

"It's my birthday." Robert pulls himself up to his full proud height. "I'm eight years old."

"In that case, you'd better have Mrs Dwyer put a pot of coffee on the stove – and tell her not to skimp on the beans."

The London his mother would have Robert know is one of palaces and parks, grand statues and stately monuments. Instead, the London of the boy's imagination takes its lead from his father's stories. When in a good mood, Walter makes an excellent tour guide. Places are accessible to him because of his profession. Places like the Royal College of Surgeons with its collection of human skulls. But he also knows a backstreet market which offers a selection of trousers whose previous occupants were hanged at Newgate. He has pointed out a discreet gabled frontage on Bishopsgate that conceals a magnificent banqueting hall, all that remains of the palace where Richard of Gloucester, later Richard III, lived at the time of the princes' disappearance from the Tower. 'Some say it was murder. Some even say,' Walter leaned closer, 'that he did the deed himself.' Robert's father knows of an ancient inn where Shakespeare's players performed while spectators heckled from the galleries, now earmarked for destruction, because London *must* have its railway. 'Change has only just begun, no doubt about it.'

Today, Mrs Dwyer's miraculous strong coffee has worked wonders. His father is particularly vocal as they approach Cremorne from his mother's preferred direction – via Cheyne Walk. (Less traffic. Fewer careering carriage wheels.)

To their left are evenly spaced trees and wooden railings. Rowing boats for hire point their noses towards the Thames, and beyond, gulls pick their way across the mudflats. To their right are red-brick houses, among them the handsome town house that makes his mother sigh at its elegant proportions. Walter has, on several occasions, pressed her gloved hand to his lips and said, 'If you like it, my dear, I shall buy it for you.'

And on several occasions she has narrowed her eyes and demanded, 'When?'

For the most part, there is room enough on the footway for Robert and his mother's rustling skirts, but the boy frequently hops down to join his father in the road. As he strolls, Walter offers up a slice of Cremorne's history, from what Robert assumes to be the distant past, given that it happened before he was born. "When Tyrell Smith took charge, he wanted to mark the beginning of his tenure with something few had ever seen. He billed the act he chose as *The Female Blondin*. You've heard of Blondin, of course."

Robert pipes up, "Yes, sir. He's the greatest ropedancer of all time!"

"Born on the same day as me. The twenty-eighth of February, eighteen twenty-four."

Robert's mother raises an eyebrow. "Is that so?"

"You thought him younger than me?"

Hettie protests: "I thought him older."

"You are the most terrible liar!" All the same, he seems pleased. "Blondin had recently outshone his competitors by attempting something no one else had dared."

"Crossing Niagara Falls!" Arms out, Robert walks the very edge of the footpath. *Imagine the deafening roar as the Niagara River ploughs over rocks, plunging vertically into the gorge below.*

"So you *do* know. A crossing eleven hundred feet wide, high above the rapids. As if that wasn't spectacular enough, he stopped midway to lie down on the rope. Then, to the crowd's amazement, he stood on his head."

His mother shudders. "I couldn't have watched."

"People are attracted to danger. What's more, they want it to be real."

"Not *this* person!" His mother's list of fears includes dark alleys, unpredictable horses, machinery, speed and above all, heights.

"Oh, they came for the sensation, no doubt about it. As Blondin walked blindfold, spectators happily wagered that he'd would plunge to a watery death."

"But he didn't fall," says Robert.

"No, he didn't. And Tyrell Smith would have booked Blondin for Cremorne, if the great man hadn't been embroiled in," his father winces, "*something* of a controversy."

"What kind of controversy?" the boy asks greedily.

"The kind that's probably unsuitable for an eight-year-old's ears."

Their walk has brought them to Cremorne Pier, where a steamer is pulling away, stirring and churning the water. Its cargo of high-spirited pleasure seekers traipse past in the direction of the gardens, but Robert is too distracted to pay them any attention. That *cannot* be the end of it. "Please tell, sir!"

His father defers to Hettie. "What do you think, my dear?"

Robert feels as if he may burst with the effort of trying to contain himself.

"Since I have no idea how the story ends, you'll have to be the judge."

"I suppose I must." His father strides towards the far end of the pier, then turns decisively. "Blondin was performing at Dublin's Royal Portobello Gardens when his tightrope snapped. Blondin was unharmed, but two of his assistants weren't so lucky. Sadly," Walter leans on the railings and peers

14

down into the murk of the Thames, "there was no water to break their fall."

"Goodness!" Hettie reaches for Robert's shoulder; pulls him towards her. He trips over his own feet in an effort not to tread on her skirts. "Was there no safety net?"

"Blondin refuses to work with one."

"That's arrogance!"

His father angles his head, as if considering her viewpoint. "He believes that if he plans for disaster, he'll attract it." Then he addresses Robert and Robert alone. "The tightrope was faulty, but that sort of thing leaves a bad taste. Tyrell Smith booked the next best thing, a woman who went by the name of Madame Genevieve – because, as everyone knows, France produces the world's best ropedancers. Madame Genevieve was to attempt to cross the Thames by tightrope, starting from the Battersea side."

Robert turns to the toll-bridge and counts: seven, eight, *nine* arches before the central point under which sailing barges pass, eight beyond. Quite an expanse, by anyone's standards.

"It was obvious, the best view was going to be had from the river. I was in a small boat." His father points in the direction of the turpentine works. "About there."

The boy fixes on the point, imagines himself in a rowing boat.

"I doubt Madame Genevieve's tightrope was as high as Blondin's, but you wouldn't have got me up there for all the tea in China."

"What about all the tea in India?"

"All right, clever clogs." His father pulls Robert's cap down over his eyes. "Madame Genevieve's tightrope was shaped like Brunel's famous suspension bridge." Robert rights his cap in time to see Walter demonstrate how the tightrope curved up and down. "At each high point was a narrow ledge where

Madame Genevieve could pause and rest, while evenly-spaced tethers pulled the rope taut."

Tight rope. Robert's mind makes new sense of the word. *Of course!* So delighted is he with his discovery, it's as if he's invented the word anew.

"Our first inkling that something was wrong was when Madame Genevieve stopped about two-thirds of the way across for what seemed a little too long. Our boat began to rock as people took to their feet in protest – they thought her reluctance was an act. But the danger was real."

Boggle-eyed, Robert demands, "What happened?"

"A whisper passed down the length of our boat: *'A tether's been cut.'*"

His mother flattens her hand just below the base of her throat. "Deliberately?"

"So it seemed. What looked like a tug-of-war team gathered on the bank and *pulled* the rope tight. With dusk fast approaching Madame Genevieve *had* to continue, but the second she stepped onto the rope it began to sway. Nobody dared breathe. Then came the terrible moment when Madame Genevieve dropped her balance-pole. As it crashed into the Thames an unholy hullabaloo broke out. Fortunately, Madame Genevieve's training served her well. She caught the tightrope in both hands. It swung wildly as she dangled there, but somehow she managed to lower herself into a boat. And the relief," his father pats his chest, "was enormous."

The boy can believe it. He finds he too has been holding his breath. But Walter claps three times, breaking whatever spell he had them under.

"Well, Signor Jacopo." He is teasing, referring to a boy-hood memory. A small monkey who used to parachute from a hot air balloon dressed in a scarlet hat and coat. "Enough excitement for one day?"

Good though it was, his father's story is hardly a substitute for a balloon ride. Robert is undeterred. "No, sir."

Walter turns to Hettie, as if to say, *I tried,* but Hettie grips the handle of her parasol and tightens her mouth.

CHAPTER TWO

1870

If Robert's father feels a connection with ropedancing because he shares Blondin's birthday, something similar is true of Robert and his fascination with ballooning. The boy was born in 1862, the year James Glaisher of the Greenwich Royal Observatory and the aeronaut Henry Coxwell made their ascent to thirty-seven thousand feet, the highest any human had ever flown. In the atmosphere's upper reaches, a man can freeze to death in ten minutes, but what is that possibility to a boy who, in winter, wakes to iced window panes, has experienced the itch of chilblains and believes he knows a thing or two about chattering teeth?

The party of three walk on – father, mother and boy. Outwardly, they look like any family on a day's outing, but Robert is acutely aware that a bad feeling is building between them, invisible, but powerful nonetheless. At any other time, his inclination would be to put a stop to it. He imagines his mother's face losing its tension as he announces, 'I've changed my mind.' How she'll suggest a diversion before he changes it back. A magic lantern display. The maze, perhaps. The talking mynah birds. *You like them, don't you?* But why should he? Why should he, when it is his birthday and his father made a promise?

As they pass between the pagoda and the New Hall, the boy feels a lift in his chest, a combination of excitement, wonder and nerves. *There it is!* It takes all his effort not to break into a run. There is something otherworldly about the balloon, as if it's visiting from a distant star. Though he'd never say this out loud, it seems almost to be alive. He senses its restlessness, how, in its tethered state, the balloon feels the pull of the sky. Robert cannot help himself. Despite knowing how terribly it upsets his mother, despite his father's anxiety at the thought of her distress, Robert wants this. More than he's ever wanted anything before.

On a previous visit – three years ago to the day – a tall-hatted, red-jacketed assistant had misguidedly offered Hettie a handbill. 'An exquisite new sensation.'

'*The Angels' View*,' she read aloud. 'How apt!'

'Can I tempt you, madam?' His moustache was of the luxurious type Robert particularly admired, his chin clean-shaven and deeply clefted.

'Isn't it terribly dangerous?' Robert recognised his mother's tone, the one that told him that her mind was already made up. Clearly, the man relished a challenge.

'Every possible measure has been taken to tame the danger. Our balloon is held captive.' He tugged on a thick guy rope. 'See for yourself.'

Invited to examine the tethers, Hettie checked each knot diligently. And although she couldn't fault them, she persisted, 'But what if one should work its way loose?'

'That's highly unlikely, madam.' His mother gave the man one of her looks. Robert crumples when she looks at him that way, but not this fellow. With great patience he softened his voice. 'But you're right to ask. Our aeronauts are prepared for every eventuality. The balloon has a hole at the bottom, which you can see quite easily.' Though they both followed the line of the man's scarlet-clad arm, only Robert's jaw dropped. Past the burners, he could see *inside* the mouth of the balloon, where stripes mimicked the sun's rays. 'That's where the hot air goes in. What you *can't* see is the vent at the top, which we open by pulling the cord, *here*. Heat the air inside the balloon and *voila!* it ascends. Let the hot air out and the balloon gently comes back to earth. It's as simple as that.'

Surely that must satisfy even his mother. Robert waited for her to reach for the clasp of her chatelaine bag – 'my indispensable', she called it; inside it, her calling cards, the lace-edged handkerchief embroidered with her initials, a Chinese fan and a small velvet purse. Instead she said, 'What about the heat source? Do you *really* use hydrogen?'

'Nature's miracle gas.' There was extravagance in the assistant's voice. 'The finest and most pure!'

'I've heard it's extremely flammable.'

The boy gaped. His mother had been reading again, arming herself with objections.

'If it were to come into contact with a naked flame, then certainly. But' – he winked at Robert to reassure him that everything was under control – 'no one will be smoking a cigar while I'm in charge.'

'If ballooning's so safe, why do I read about so many accidents?'

'You must bear in mind, aeronauts are constantly trying to outdo one another. They want to go the highest, to be credited with the latest scientific discoveries. In other words, they take risks I would never dream of taking. Today we rise with the ease of an ascending vapour, then we remain at the highest point for perhaps twenty minutes to take in the view. The whole of London laid out like a patchwork quilt!' Robert already knew London. It was the heavens that interested him. 'Then we bring you, ever so gently, back to earth.'

Up on tiptoes, the boy could hold his tongue no longer. 'Can we, Mother? Can we?'

But the man laughed, a great rumble of sound. *'You?*

You're too short to see over the basket. Go on, lad, up on the platform and see for yourself.'

Robert didn't wait to be asked twice. He charged at the steps. Apparently, the man had forgotten the compromises that being waist-high to adults entail. Robert hadn't for a minute imagined that he would look *down*. What was on offer was the Angels' View. He'd anticipated that he would look *up*, and it was up that he looked then. Up to the riggings, the hoop and the striped swell of the sphere. Up to the narrowest part of the balloon – the vent. Up to the bluest of blues, the clouds and the heavens beyond.

'I'll tell you what.' Down at ground level, the man beckoned. 'If air travel interests you, make your way to the pavilion. In ten minutes, Mr Delamarne's aerial vessel is due to take to the sky.' He offered Robert's mother another handbill. 'He claims it's the future, and if he *really* can fly from point to point in a straight line, he may well be right!'

'*The most celebrated dirigible manufacturer in the hemisphere*,' she read. 'Wouldn't you like to see that, Robert?' How urgently she willed him to agree, and the boy wanted the reward of one of her smiles, so he said, reluctantly, yes, he *would* like to see Mr Delamarne's flying machine.

The man seemed to sense his disappointment. 'How old are you, lad?'

To prove himself worthy, he jumped down the two final steps. 'Five, sir.'

'Come back and see me when you're eight.'

For three long years the thought of the Angels' View has been Robert's obsession. Though he knows there are words for a boy who thinks the way he does – stubborn, ungrateful, defiant – he will not give up his prize. Not when it's finally within reach.

"Tickets for the next flight! The air, like the earth and the ocean, has been subdued by science."

It is not the same scarlet-jacketed assistant, nor is it the same balloon, but at last Robert has a ticket in his hand. *For one ascent only. Le Géant. Not transferable.*

With a flourish, the assistant offers the second to his mother. "For you, madam?"

Hettie shuns the ticket as if repelled by it. "I shall keep both feet firmly on the ground, thank you."

Something inside the boy plummets, as if he has an anchor and it's dragging him down. Robert hadn't for one moment imagined that his mother would go up with them, but he'd pictured her waving her handkerchief, her face framed by auburn hair, by her bonnet and then by the halo of her parasol, growing smaller and smaller until he struggled to pick her out from the crowd. "Won't you watch, Mother?" he asks.

She shakes her head sorrowfully. Begins to walk away.

Walter bends towards Robert, pinning his arms to his sides. "Your mother's a little anxious." This is as close as he'll ever come to criticising her. Mrs Dwyer, on the other hand, has been more forthcoming. 'Keep your head down,' she's cautioned the scullery maid within Robert's hearing. 'Madam's up to her theatricals again.' Apparently his mother's flame-coloured hair colour is responsible for her temperament. Now Robert's father looks him in the eye. "I've promised I'll keep you safe, so you must do exactly as I say. Do you understand?"

The boy understands perfectly. He will be allowed to go up in the balloon, but he will not be allowed to enjoy it, not in the way he wanted. Already the swell of disappointment has found its focus in his bottom lip. He doesn't trust himself to say, 'Yes, sir.' All he can do is nod.

Ticket in hand, he hears Walter implore, "We'll be perfectly safe. The balloon's anchored fast." His father's voice is pleading, but pleading for what? Forgiveness isn't something you can ask for in advance. If it were, it would be spelled *foregiveness*.

"Yes." Her chin lifted, resolute, his mother gives a tight little smile. "Like Madam Genevieve's tightrope."

CHAPTER THREE

1870

The boy doesn't know the cause of his mother's anxiety. He has no idea she has struggled her whole life to mould it into something slightly more manageable. Constantly, she challenges her fears with logic, only to have them whisper: *The world isn't a safe or a kind place. Danger lurks; not only for you, but for your family.* Walter, her husband, has some idea. A scattering of facts, the few words that haven't snagged like barbs in her throat, a sense of something vast and bottomless lurking beneath them. Hettie, he might be surprised to learn, isn't much better informed than he is. What she has that her husband does not is the certainty that tragedy flows freely through her veins. Such is her family's curse, it may infect anyone she comes into contact with.

Life is already so fragile and precarious, Hettie has no desire to seek out new sensations to make her feel *more alive* or to watch people risk their lives in the name of entertainment. When others rhapsodise about skill and daring, what she senses is their barely-concealed desire to witness a dreadful catastrophe. Let us be clear. No relative of Hettie's has ever died while attempting to fly higher in the name of scientific endeavour or to go faster in the name of sport. When Hettie was conceived, what was described by her mother as 'the itch' skipped a generation, just as her grandmother's auburn hair passed her mother by.

Hettie's father was a man called Ernest Winstanley. Like Hettie's son Robert, Ernest had his head in the clouds from boyhood. Before he learned to talk, he would raise both hands above his head and his mother, Hettie's grandmother, would say, 'What is it you want, Ernest? You'll have to ask.' And so his first word was not 'mother' or 'father' but 'up'. Take the boy to the foot of a hill and he would scarper up it and proclaim himself king of the castle. But the boy became a teenager and the hills became fells, and as he inched closer to manhood the fells became mountains. When he'd climbed the highest peaks England had to offer, he packed his ropes and his ice axe and headed north to Scotland. His mother had no patience with these 'jaunts', as she called them, saying, 'Why can't you be content to stand in a valley and look upwards?'

'How can you be content to stand in the valley?' was his reply. The itch was in him and he couldn't help but scratch. The more difficult the challenge, the greater the victory.

'Don't mind your mother.' Ernest's father would slip into the shake of a hand whatever money he could spare. To his wife, he'd say, not without affection, 'You'll see, he'll give it up when he finds himself a wife.'

But Ernest found a wife who was sympathetic to what others thought was folly, because she too had been born with an itch. In the version of the story Hettie was told, Ernest claimed to have discovered her mother, Decima, on a Scottish mountainside.

'Discovered me!' she'd scoff. 'Why should you get the credit?'

'Had it been up to *you,* my mountain goat, you'd have walked straight past.'

Ernest had heard the walking party before he caught sight

of them. Decima's was the first human voice to invade his thoughts for some hours. So far, cud-chewing sheep and the odd lapwing had been his only company. There she was – *a woman mountaineer!* – complete with wide-brimmed hat, a high-necked blouse fastened with a brooch, a buckled belt cinching her waist, a plain skirt muddied about the hem and scuffed boots that might have been a man's, making her way down the rocky gully towards him. (This was the part of the story Hettie loved; the romantic part.) Ernest stepped off the trail to allow her to pass, the execution of this etiquette providing the perfect excuse to watch her descent. He thought Decima magnificent as she planted her walking staff. Such confidence! Two men he was soon to learn were her father and brother followed in her wake. To Ernest the men were incidental, though when, conscious of gawping like a halfwit, he said, 'Good day to you!', it was the brother who replied.

'A fine day for it.' There are no strangers at three thousand feet.

'You took the ridge route?' Ernest nodded towards a jutting rock.

The brother's feet were firmly placed. 'We did.' He occupied ground higher than his sister. His father, the king of this particular castle, had found handholds either side of the gully, his perch only affording room for the heel of a boot.

'Is it as narrow as they say?'

The voice came from the right. 'We lived to tell the tale.' The first words Decima said to Ernest.

'Your first time up here?' asked the brother.

Forced to look away from her – she must be a mirage, surely – he confessed, 'It is.'

'And you're alone.' The older man, the father, raised his voice to be heard from his high perch, like a preacher in a pulpit.

'I always walk alone.' Ernest wished he could communicate

to the woman near him that this wasn't because he was friend-less, but because he relished the way his thoughts flowed freely. 'I enjoy the solitude.'

'I envy you that.' She regarded him fearlessly and he felt a connection, or the beginnings of one.

Ernest didn't for one moment mistake Decima for a woman whose life was governed by the need to darn and sew, launder and iron, fetch coal and lay fires, but though she struck him as entirely free, the restrictions placed on that freedom told him she was unmarried – cause for hope.

'We're at the Clachaig,' said the preacher, 'if you'd care to compare notes.'

Ernest inclined his head. He was also at the Clachaig, for the simple reason that it was Glencoe's only inn. 'I'd like that.'

Ernest and Decima named their daughter *Aonach* after Aonach Eagach, the ridge linking Meall Dearg and Sgorr nam Fiannaidh. It was a place of jagged edges, tufts of dry grass its only punctuation, but it was the place that had brought them together. Before Aonach was teething, Ernest could resist the itch no longer. He resumed his solitary jaunts, heading first to Snowdonia and then back to Glencoe. Decima, proving herself as rare a person as he had first imagined, didn't say, 'Must you go?' or claim that she'd struggle to cope. Instead she said, 'This time next year, I'll join you.' Her eyes held a devilish glint. '*If* you won't object to my company.'

'Not one bit.' Decima wasn't a person who enjoyed the sound of her own voice. When they went walking together, an hour might pass without the exchange of a single word. Both enjoyed the unpolluted trickle of a mountain stream; the song of small birds that coasted on drifts of air. But Ernest also wondered if, by next year, Aonach might have a brother or sister, and Decima's trip might need to be deferred.

Because he was alone, nothing is known of Ernest's final hours. Whether his feet faltered on the awkward, sloping cliff-face or he lost his bearings in low cloud and succumbed to the drop from the ridge below Am Bodach. Decima didn't think her husband would have attempted to make his way down along the rim of Clachaig Gully. He knew better than that.

At first, the word 'death' wasn't mentioned. Ernest had 'disappeared'. But with a child to care for, Decima needed to deal in certainties. The reality was that her husband wasn't coming home. She had no choice but to square up to it.

Ernest's remains were never found, and that was perhaps as it ought to be. 'Better a mountainside than a coffin,' Decima said.

That Ernest's daughter was named after the very route that took his life was too much for the Winstanleys, so the child became known by her middle name, Henrietta (or Hettie, as she preferred when old enough to be allowed an opinion), but to Decima the ridge would always be the place where she met Ernest. This was the story Decima told Hettie each night after tucking her into bed, and when the story ended she'd say, 'When you're old enough, I'll take you to see the place you were named after.'

Even to a child, it was obvious that this promise was supposed to be a gift, something that shouldn't be shunned, but it opened up two terrifying prospects. The first was that Hettie would fall to her death, just as her father had. In her dreams Hettie often found herself lost in low cloud, and when it cleared – which it did with remarkable speed – she realised she was teetering at the edge of an abyss. She would wake, arms flailing, with a sense of impending catastrophe that lingered until, by night, the story came for her again, disguised as her mother's love.

The second prospect was that, while undertaking this arduous and holy pilgrimage, Hettie would stumble across her father's remains. Her mother had explained that there were people who practised 'sky burials'. They carried the bodies of their loved ones to the tops of mountains and laid them out where, in time, their bones would be picked clean. It was really rather beautiful, if you thought about it. The impression Hettie absorbed was that mountaintops were rocky wastelands littered with bodies in varying states of decay.

Ominous and ever-present, the threat cast a shadow over her childhood. Since her mother seemed incapable of detecting it, Hettie believed it was invisible, until one Easter when her grandmother came to stay. (This was Grandmother Winstanley, not Decima's mother, with whom they lived, because where else can a young widow go but home to her parents?) On this occasion, Hettie hadn't woken when she lost her footing; she'd landed at the bottom of a deep crevasse, to be cradled by her father's skeleton, his hollow ribcage stripped bare by buzzards, bones bleached white by the elements. And so she struggled against his embrace.

'Shhh.' It was not a man's voice but her grandmother's. 'You're having a nightmare.' To Hettie it would always be the other way around. She didn't have nightmares. They had her. 'What was it about, hmm?' the old woman coaxed. 'You can tell me.'

By then she'd recognised her grandmother's lavender scent and knew she was safe, but, 'I don't want to climb the mountain,' was all she could bring herself to say.

'And you shan't have to.' Her grandmother's voice was fierce: 'Not if I have anything to do with it.'

Hettie didn't know what passed between Grandmother Winstanley and her mother. All she knew was that the bedtime stories stopped, and she felt in their place her mother's disappointment that she'd given birth to such a timid creature. The nightmares were slower to depart, the images sketched by her mother and coloured with the vivid palette of a child's imagination. Her understanding was that by confiding in her grandmother those eight words, eyes squeezed tightly shut, she had forfeited the right to ask her mother questions. A drawbridge was pulled up, leaving her outside.

Grief is a strange opponent. For a long time, Hettie didn't feel her father's loss; after all, she had no memories of him. She couldn't recall the curl of his hair, the spacing of his clear blue eyes, the line of his jaw. Then, when she felt his absence, she learned that you don't simply grieve for the person who's gone, but for things that *might* have been. Her thoughts travelled long lonely corridors, questioning what her father valued more: his family or the mountains. She conjured up the moment when her mother held her in her arms and took her hand to make her wave her daddy off on what would be his final jaunt. 'Say goodbye to Daddy. *Goodbye, Daddy.*' If she hadn't forfeited the right, Hettie might have asked, 'Did Father love us?' but the only possible answer would have been, 'Of course he did!' and it wouldn't have been enough, because he had made his choice. It was the mountains he chose.

Marrying a doctor should have provided her with some kind of insurance, although it was not the only reason Hettie accepted Walter's proposal; she was not nearly as calculating as that. If the worst happened, and she always imagined that it would, a doctor would know what to do. She found she could rest easier by his side. At night her sleep was dreamless, and what a gift that was.

But then Robert arrived and Hettie knew the odds. One in six babies don't live to see their first birthdays. Her vigil was constant. Was he breathing? Was he too hot, too cold? When Walter was out on his rounds, she consulted his medical journals, realising there was more to guard against than even she had been aware. When her husband arrived home smelling of tallow and smoke and filth from the gutters, she knew he'd been east of Trafalgar Square, but could only guess at what squalor he'd encountered. People packed too tightly together, barely any ventilation, communal water pumps – polluted, more likely than not – and privies shared by multiple households. And as for the ailments he'd treated (tuberculosis, almost certainly; cholera, perhaps; smallpox, hopefully not). He always scrubbed his hands, but Hettie insisted he changed his clothes before sitting down to dinner or going to say goodnight to their son.

If she'd thought she would relax after Robert turned one, Hettie was mistaken. Even before Robert took his first steps she recognised that he'd inherited his grandfather's itch. Now, she could barely hold back her sense of dread. There was little she could do to protect Robert from himself. Instead her question was, *How long can I stop him scratching?*

CHAPTER FOUR

1872

Robert is ten years old when his father bids him to go and wait in his surgery, an instruction so unusual it brings the boy out in a cold sweat. He can't recall having been caught doing something he oughtn't to have done, but even ordinary things have upset his mother of late. The other day all he did was pull back the heavy curtain in the front parlour.

'Robert!' she'd shouted. 'Do you want to let all of London's soot and grime inside?'

He hadn't noticed her sitting there, in a dark corner. All he'd wanted was to let in a little daylight.

The book-lined surgery is where Walter receives patients who don't require (or can ill-afford) house calls. Mrs Dwyer casts a critical eye over those who come pounding on their door at first light, heavy-lidded after a night-time vigil. A man who arrives wearing work boots and gaiters may be left shivering on the doorstep, but a man with ink-stained fingers will be bustled into the warm and given a seat, perhaps even a cup of tea, while she goes to rouse the doctor. Walter holds the people of Grub Street – the writers, typesetters and printers – in high esteem, but both kinds of patients are the type to consult a physician only when Dr Collis Browne's

Chlorodyne fails to break a fever. Perhaps the poor desperate souls have tramped several miles, having heard that Dr Cooke said, 'Put that away,' when their neighbour offered him coins. Mrs Dwyer shakes her head, frustrated that reports of such kindness pass from mouth to mouth, allowing her employer's good nature to be exploited. Usually when it's too late for him to make a blind bit of difference.

'And, of course, the other doctors don't take kindly if they hear of it,' she tells Robert.

'But if the patients have no money to pay, wouldn't they be turned away elsewhere?'

'All I'm saying is it doesn't go down well.'

As the boy knows from school, being made to wait is a punishment in itself. The masters string it out and string it out, so it's a relief to get whatever's coming your way over and done with. All the same, his curious eyes wander. *The British Medical Journal.* Well-thumbed studies of anatomy. Buchan's *Domestic Medicine.* Dr John Snow's breakthrough study on cholera. Over there is his father's black bag, stocked with ointments, spatulas, splints, ready for any eventuality. On the table by the window are his tools of the trade: a pestle and mortar, a stethoscope, a microscope, bottles of medicine corked and tagged. And on the side desk where his mother writes her neat columns of figures, an unusual number of fee notes, skewered on a prong.

A hitch in Robert's throat: he cannot recall an unusually high number of patients that would account for them.

Robert glances into the hallway. No sign of his father. He crosses the room and thumbs to the bottom of the pile. The chits go back two months. This is not how things work. *'Any woman who keeps her own housekeeping book is perfectly capable of maintaining a set of business accounts.'* His mother transcribes details in the ledger, filing as she goes.

What can it mean?

Footsteps. Robert scuttles back in front of his father's desk, eyes front, hands behind his back.

"There you are." Walter closes the door with a click. "Sit yourself down. I've something to tell you."

Not the words he feared. 'Your mother tells me' or 'I've received a letter from your headmaster'. The boy sits, back straight. If not a telling-off, what might the alternative be?

"We'll be moving."

Delighted, he inches forward. "To the house in Cheyne Walk?"

Momentarily, his father looks flummoxed, then his expression clears. *Oh, that house!* "It was only ever a pipe dream. Surely you realised?"

But Robert didn't. He feels as if a despicable trick has been played on him.

His father's frown is almost an apology. "We're not, and we're probably never going to be rich."

You could be – if you made more calls to well-to-do widows. If you'd only listen to their descriptions of unspecified ailments and recommend a 'change of air'. "Then where, sir?"

"South of the river. A place called Carshalton."

Is he to be uprooted from all that's familiar? Away from the settings of his father's stories, his inheritance. Trousers worn by murderers, the princes in the Tower. And what about his hard-won freedoms? Streets he's only recently claimed, having countered each of his mother's objections? He'll stick to the main roads; he won't take any shortcuts or speak to strangers (the Italian organ-grinder hardly counts). He'd like to ask why, but why isn't an acceptable question. Instead he asks, "But what about your practice?"

"I'll need to stay in town to tie up a few loose ends."

A child isn't expected to have loose ends. What is it to his father that he's been waiting for the opportunity to win back his prize marble – the amber cat's eye – from Cyril Wharton? "And when will Mother and I move?"

His father doesn't meet his gaze. "Next week."

Robert's head swims. So soon? "What about school, sir?"

"It's all settled. You'll go to Cheam School."

He can hardly claim he'll be disadvantaged. Cheam has a reputation for being one of the best preparatory schools in the country. "Will I have to board?" So far he's avoided the need.

"I shouldn't have thought so. You could walk there in under an hour." Robert cannot tell if he's disappointed or comforted. Something of his confusion must convey itself to his father, because Walter says, "Perhaps I should look into it."

A fresh wave of panic surges, the thought of two hours' freedom being snatched back. "I can walk, sir. I'll manage."

"Well, then." His father slaps his thighs and stands. "A new beginning." But the tight smile on his face quivers and it occurs to the boy. This is some whim of his mother's. She has pestered and pestered until Walter caved in, knowing he'd never hear the last of it.

There is no one Robert can take his shock and resentment to except Mrs Dwyer. He clatters downstairs. When he enters the low-ceilinged kitchen the heat from the range is intense. Temperature aside, under normal circumstances Robert likes this place. Shelves of copper pots and pans are arranged by size. Each, he knows, emits its own distinct note when turned upside down and struck, something Mrs Dwyer tolerates, provided she doesn't have one of her heads. He needs no reminder to replace the pans in order, the handles all pointing in the same direction. To him they form a scale. Here, there is a place for everything, from the wooden salt box to used tea leaves.

Red-faced, Mrs Dwyer is standing at the scarred wooden table, stripping what remains of yesterday's roast mutton from the bone.

Normally placid, Robert barely knows what to do with this particular blend of emotions that spits and crackles like fat in a frying pan, sending the scullery maid scuttling away. He arms himself with a ladle.

Mrs Dwyer puts down both bone and knife. She wipes her greasy fingers on her apron, an operation that seems almost delicate. "So, he told you." Her expression is pained. She, at least, appreciates the enormity of what is being done to him.

"Why didn't *you?*" Robert slaps the round of the utensil into his palm. He'd be perfectly justified in bringing it crashing down on the tabletop.

Mrs Dwyer raises her eyebrows and keeps them raised. "It wasn't my place."

"I'm always the last to be told." Robert launches himself sideways into a chair, knocking a knee painfully.

"I expect your father wanted to be sure before he said anything. Sometimes these ideas come to nothing."

His words thicken with the effort of keeping tears at bay. "I won't know anyone."

"Nor will I. Not at first."

In his misery, Robert had forgotten that this isn't just a job for Mrs Dwyer. *His* home is also *her* home. The thought that there will be one familiar person, someone who's known him his whole life, provides the only comfort that can be clawed back from the day. "What do you know about this *Carshalton?*"

"I understand it's not far from Epsom racecourse. You like horses, don't you?"

Horses are a necessity. They empty their bowels onto the cobblestones and it's a constant battle to keep his boots clean. But Robert sees Mrs Dwyer is desperate to find something to make the hand he's been dealt a little more acceptable. "I suppose so," he sulks.

Robert will have cause to try to recall the precise words

his father used, and exactly what Mrs Dwyer said, but of one thing he'll be absolutely sure. At no point was it suggested to him that his mother was ill. That the move, the exchange of soot and grime for lavender and watercress, was for her sake.

PART TWO
1894 ~ 1895

CHAPTER FIVE

AUTUMN 1894

Out of the carriage window, Robert sees a sign that interests him. *Land for Sale.* Imagine not always having to factor rent into your budget. "Stop!" he shouts to his coachman, hears Abbots give the horses a familiar command, then alights.

"Everything all right, Mr Cooke?" Abbots' feet are braced and his whip hovers over the horses' flanks.

"Yes, thank you." Robert has come from his business over Mitcham way, where he specialises in medicinal plants. Camomile, white opium poppies, liquorice and mint, and of these the poppies have proved the greatest success. In a good year, each plant grows five feet high and produces seed heads as big as a man's fist. With the harvest in, Robert's thoughts have turned to expansion. For that he needs land, though it was Mitcham he had in mind. There isn't a single parish on which wholesale druggists rely more for their supplies.

A youngish man in a railway worker's uniform is unlatching the gate of one of the new cottages. "Excuse me!" Robert calls out, waiting for the man to turn. "The *Land for Sale.*" He points to the sign. "Is it the old chalk pit that's on offer?"

"That's right. Can't say we were unhappy to see the back

of it. The wife's glad to get her laundry dry without the stench of smoke."

Robert doesn't point out that the quarry was there first, that where the man's cottage stands the road used to be lined with double hedges of hawthorn and hazel, seething with insects, blooming with dog rose. The hedges were protected by ditches from which grew elms of considerable age, in whose trunks nuthatches made their homes in deserted woodpecker holes. This man has a right to live near the place he works, he supposes (close enough to go home for his dinner), but Robert cannot help but mourn the trees. "The site," he asks. "Does it still belong to William Reynolds?"

Interrupted by a high shriek, both men turn to see a trail of steam rise above the line of sycamores.

"On time," says the man with no small amount of satisfaction, though he has no pocket watch that Robert can detect. "As I understand it, the oldest son inherited."

"Inherited?"

"The old man died, oh, must have been last year."

Thrown by the news, Robert stammers, "I didn't know." When was the last time he'd been back to see William? *Long ago,* comes the shameful reply. "He used to let me play there when I was a boy." Profoundly moved by the memory, he reflects. It was shortly after his family arrived. At first, Robert had thought Carshalton a backward place.

"Play? In a place like that?"

Children younger than Robert had worked the quarry, boys whose parents couldn't afford to keep them in idleness or education. It shames him that he'd wished he was one of those barefoot boys, but he was only ever an interloper. "Perhaps it was more like unpaid labour. He'd have me haul barrows for him."

"Now, that sounds more like the Mr Reynolds I've heard talk of."

Robert finds himself wanting to stand up for old William, if only to say, 'He wasn't so bad.' He never saw William mistreat a boy – which was more than could be said of his schoolmasters, and Robert felt that William had sensed he needed a refuge from the playground insults hurled at him because he was an uppity newcomer who needed to be shown his place.

Robert turns to his coachman and, at much the same time, turns up the collar of his coat. "You go on, Abbots. I may be some time."

"Right you are, Mr Cooke." Abbots clicks at the horses. Impatient to be on their way, they need no other command.

Like the hedgerows, the chalk pit must have fallen victim to progress. Had there been no call for construction materials it wouldn't have been here in the first place, but keep it at a safe distance, where the smoke and the stench cannot reach the fine folk in their grand houses. Keep it on low ground where the sight of it can't offend. It was the same, Robert reflects, with the railway. No coincidence that the chalk pit and railway tracks exist side by side. Now the network of railways has been joined up and it's possible to travel to the metropolis by train, the benefits of living close to a station outweigh the inconvenience of hearing the whistle, the chug, the rumble. No doubt this land will be sold to speculators, divided into lots. Think how many workmen's cottages you could build, *here* and *here* and *here.*

Unbidden, his father's voice is there in his head. *Imagine if the farms opposite were also sold for development.*

Robert has been discovered, in this place he thought of as his. He turns to the freshly-cleared fields, dotted with clumps of lime. It would mean summer without sweet swathes of peppermint, and beyond, closer to the Wandle, the watercress beds. There'd be nothing to separate village from village, town from town. Eventually, Surrey would become an extension of London. It's a future Robert would hold back.

Walk with me, son.

Walter always preferred to walk, not because of the shortage of stabling in the city, or his concern that horse-dung was
always dumped in poor areas, but to undo in his mind with
each step what had been done to London's landscape during
his lifetime. Robert couldn't always see the boundaries his
father saw. A fragment of Roman wall. A milestone. A subtle
change of architecture – subtle because so often the new was
made to look old, so as not to stand out. Who'll keep that
knowledge alive now that the Walters and the Williams of this
world are gone?

No fence marks the perimeter. Robert follows what is
still an unmade track, carpeted with winged sycamore fruits,
littered with flints large enough to lame a horse. Here and
there, puddles muddy the way, but it isn't rutted by wheels as
it used to be when this was a working site. The grass on either
side has gone to seed: yarrow, dropwort and ladies' bedstraw
brittle and blackened. Grass may be all this soil is good for.
Even Mitcham's rich black loam needs frequent ploughing to
keep the soil fine and open, and twenty loads of well-rotted
manure per acre. But poppies – he scratches his stubble –
poppies don't mind poor soil.

If his father is with him still, Walter chooses to remain
silent. Did he know this place? There must have been casualties who required a doctor's services. You can't work with
explosives and heat without accidents.

Robert spots the first stray lump of chalk. He peels off
his kidskin gloves, stoops, picks it up. Over and over in his
hand he turns it, waking buried memories from slumber. He
pinches off an edge, lets go of the larger portion and crumbles
what remains between his palms. Small lumps like these,
the likes of which Robert sorted into size, were sold to local
farmers – Mr Pimms over at Batt's Farm (another William,
but fiercer by far) being one of the regulars who preferred it

to powdered stuff. From his crouching position Robert looks ahead to a grouping of alders and ash. Many a time he sought sanctuary beneath their boughs, settling his rump between their roots, his back against their trunks. For a moment – a moment so fleeting he doubts himself – he sees them, or shadows that resemble them. His shadow-sons. *The trees will stay.* Not his father, speaking to him from somewhere beyond, but a stray thought. The first stirrings of *something*.

Beyond the shedding branches, a scar is scooped from the white escarpment, the pit from which chalk was quarried. Here, the ground is laid with wooden planks, which wobble under the thin soles of his shoes. Perhaps they're the very same planks on which he wheeled barrows.

When Robert first came here, it was to investigate the noise. At the time he was smarting. A gang of boys had waylaid him as he walked home and had thrown him in the holly bush just beyond the juncture of the Wandle and Pyl Brook. The man he would come to know as William took one look at his dishevelled uniform and said, 'Studying history?' His voice was muffled behind a scrap of material tied over his mouth and nose.

'Yes, sir.' Robert hadn't expected the air to taste acrid, nor the intensity of the heat, hotter even than Mrs Dwyer's kitchen range.

'It was the Romans who taught us how to do this.' The makeshift mask was sucked in and forced out with each syllable.

Robert quickly made a mask of his own necktie. 'To do what, sir?'

'To burn chalk to make lime.' (*The old man,* Robert thinks, his chest rising and falling. He'd thought him ancient.) 'You know what lime is used for?'

'Plaster, sir?'

'Plaster, mortar, putty. Whenever you see a kiln, look for

the larger buildings.' Here, under stubborn tangles of bramble and ivy, are the kilns. A pair of redbrick igloos, hundreds of years old, but they did the job. 'This pit used to be attached to the Carshalton Estate. Course, these days, they bring chalk in from Dorking by train. And some o' those in the building trade choose limestone over chalk. But you have to dig deep for limestone.'

Larger quarries had their own internal railways, but here the chalk was dug by tools held in calloused hands and hauled by horses. A sheltered outcrop, ideal for a modest family-run enterprise. No one has worked the quarry for some time, that much is clear. The door to the coal shed is warped, its hinges rusted. Empty. Chalk might be out of favour, but coal will always be in demand.

Strange, this feeling of wanting to linger. Wanting something from the place – a little of old William's wisdom, perhaps. How was it that he understood when Mr Reynolds told him that the people from the big houses needed to be kept happy, so that the quarry could provide a service to those who worked the land? Why couldn't he apply the same logic to his father's practice? There was no shortage of poor who needed Walter's help in Carshalton and its surrounds. Agricultural workers, mainly, though a concentration of industrial mills with their waterwheels and chimneys line much of the Wandle. Corn, paper, snuff, calico, gunpowder, all are produced here. Add the gypsies and Cockneys who come to harvest the lavender, peppermint and watercress. The women who work the distilleries, extracting oils, drying, packing and selling perfumes, sachets and faggots.

You've heard of Blondin, of course.

"You're still here, then." Robert's eyes travel to the top of the escarpment, as if he might see the greatest ropedancer of all time crossing his line of vision on a thin wire above the scar of the chalk face.

He remembers his mother telling him how his father, too, had operated without a safety net.

Mother, mother, I feel sick.

Send for the doctor, quick, quick, quick.

But who does the doctor call when he falls ill?

It is twenty-one years since Walter passed away. It won't be too much longer before the balance tips and Robert will be older than his father ever was. His mother Hettie, whose health had supposedly been the reason for their exile, recovered, and it was never explained (nothing was ever explained) what it was she'd recovered from. Something else not to be spoken of, but swallowed whole like gristle on a piece of meat.

He stares ahead, the crisp white cliff-face a blank canvas. Imagine water stampeding, pooling in the basin that has been dug away with picks and shovels. *It would have to be lined.* He is thinking – of course he is – of the thing his father gifted to him in his will, something his mother knew nothing about. Described as a sculpture made of Coade stone, it was housed in a stable in nearby Wallington, storage provided in lieu of payment for medicine. Nestled among stray cartwheels and pitchforks, it looked out of place and yet perfectly at home. 'What is it?' Robert asked, when shown it.

'Neptune,' came the farmer's reply. 'Your father bought it at auction. Seemed a bit embarrassed about it if you ask me.'

'He must have been drinking.' Immediately, Robert regretted his flippancy. Walter rarely drank. He might have been called out in the middle of the night to attend a birth. Sometimes he was unable to save the mother or the baby, sometimes both, but at breakfast the next morning he would never let it show on his face.

Neptune came with a chariot and rearing horses, a complicated set of pipes and fittings. This was no ordinary sculpture. Robert had a growing sense that he'd seen it somewhere before. 'Did he say anything else about it?'

'Said it came from a pleasure garden. One of the grand ones that was closing.'

Something in Robert's chest fluttered. *Cremorne*. His father bequeathed him his writing desk, his pocket watch with its engraving to Robert's grandfather – things of use – but he also bequeathed him something of wonder: Cremorne's fountain. A message that life shouldn't be all be about work.

Perhaps, he thinks. *Perhaps.*

For so long, Robert's childhood has seemed like a riddle that needed solving. The people he thought he knew best became strangers, but parenthood – losing children, especially – lends a different perspective to actions, decisions, words that were said but, more often than not, unsaid. His mother was over-protective, but that's scarcely a crime. Lord knows, if he could turn back the clock. If he'd realised what it was when Thomas took ill with the fever. But really, all that was visible was the flush on his cheeks, and it was so like the flush that comes with teething. He dreams of them, his shadow-sons. Dreams of them playing in a garden. He'd thought it was heaven, and Robert has always thought that heaven and the Garden of Eden were one and the same. But what if he was wrong? What if it's a place he is supposed to *create*?

"Hot hot, all 'ot – yer reg'lar Irish fruit. Baked p'tato, sir?"

The heat from the man's fire-pot is not unwelcome. There's a hint of winter in the dying afternoon. Robert pauses to warm his hands. "Do you know of a Frank Reynolds?"

"Well, now, there's an awful lot of Reynolds."

Robert dips into his pocket for a coin.

"Very kind o' you, sir. This time of day, you might try the Greyhound."

Mrs Dwyer used to take him there to see the horses in their stables. The horses were named for those who made the news for one reason or another, and the housekeeper had a story to go with every name. Robert sighs. Save for a niece who lived somewhere in Tottenham, Mrs Dwyer had no family. He saw to her headstone. He was able to do that much for her.

In the straw-strewn yard, dressed in a shabby greatcoat, a man is feeding a handful of corn to a conker-coloured mare. Robert is about to enquire if he knows Frank's whereabouts when he pauses. Could it be? A life of toiling outdoors would have broadened his shoulders and ruddied his complexion.

Robert stops a few feet away. "Is that you, Frank?"

The man turns. His left eye is clouded over. A fragment of flint did for it. The eye was saved, but his sight was never the same. He remembers old William's words: 'He can see better out of his one good eye than you can out o' both of yours.' For a moment, Frank regards him blankly with his good eye. The horse continues to feed from his palm, lips moving, teeth churning, breathing small clouds.

Robert steps forward, offering his right hand. "Robert Cooke. You used to call me Whippersnapper."

Frank looks again, then, as if a key has been turned in a lock, he gives a hoot. "You're the Cheam schoolboy!" He brushes his palms together to dislodge the last of the corn, then grasps Robert's hand.

Robert can feel the strength compressed in that hand-shake. "It's a long time since I was anywhere near a school." He has a business, a wife and family. He keeps a house, a stable, servants. Yet there's still a residue of awkwardness, the sense of never quite belonging.

"Must be twenty years ago I last saw you."

It is more, but Robert doesn't correct him. There's something he must say. "I'm sorry about your father. I'm afraid I've only just heard, and quite by chance."

"He left quite a pair of boots to fill, I can tell you."

"He was always kind to me." Strange that Robert thinks of

his own father as he says this. How Walter crawled around on all fours with Robert riding on his back, or how he scooped Robert up and sat him high on his shoulders. The way his eyes lit up when he told stories about things that had happened *before you were even a twinkle in my eye.* Then, the day Mrs Dwyer told him he wasn't to disturb his father, who was feeling unwell. All evening she clattered up and down the stairs. Hot water, cold water, clean towels, fresh sheets. When she said they'd sent for a doctor, Robert's reaction had been, 'But my father's the doctor.'

Doctor, doctor, shall I die?

Yes, my dear, and so shall I.

"It's easier with strangers, don't you think?" Frank's good eye looks beyond Robert to the ponds, but when Robert glances in the direction of the other man's gaze, all there is to see is a row of gulls perched on the railings. "Easier to see what they might need from you."

Any response Robert could give would be clumsy. Instead, he rubs his hands together. "I don't know about you, but I'm feeling the cold. Perhaps you'll let me to buy you a drink."

Frank cheers at the prospect. "That's decent of you." He turns to the horse once more, shows him his hand, waits for the animal to nudge it, then strokes the length of the beast's nose.

"Yours?" Robert asks.

"Mine?" scoffs Frank. "We only ever had workhorses." On the way into the bar room, he stops by a noticeboard. "I'll tell you what you can do. Read the stakes for me."

Perhaps his good eye is long-sighted. "Epsom Races. In the morning –"

"Forget the morning. Tell me about the evening."

Robert scans the notice. "Here we are. *An alleged stake of five sovereigns each, with fifty sovereigns added, for horses that never won more at any time than eighty pounds.*" He goes to open the door to the bar room but Frank's hand is on his arm. "And the rest."

Robert relents. *"Three to start or the public money will not be added. The second horse to save his stake. The winner to be sold for one hundred and twenty sovereigns if demanded in the usual way."*

"Quite a thing, to buy the winner."

"It surely would be."

At the bar, the landlady, who Robert knows by sight, says, "We don't see you in here too often, Mr Cooke," and examines his coins closely. "Check everything, they say. There's counterfeit florins in circulation." A young woman (someone he doesn't know), is standing by, cracking walnuts, seemingly amused by the transaction. "They come from over Mitcham way. If I'm not mistaken, that's where your business is."

"You'll find my coin's good."

She scrutinises his face, then sweeps the coins into the waiting curve of her palm. "Away with you," she tells the girl.

By the time the sun sets over the ponds and the herons take to their high nesting places, Robert has established that he has the wherewithal to buy the Reynolds' land – he *can* create his small Eden.

"Pleasure gardens?" His wife is pacing, pacing. He can hear the rustle of petticoats, the curt clip of heels. "Have you taken complete leave of your senses?"

Robert has waited a week to break the news to Freya. Now he wishes he'd waited longer. "Rosherville Pleasure Gardens was built in a disused chalk pit."

He would not distress her, so he does not share his intentions. He doesn't tell her, 'I dream about them.' Thomas and Gerrard – who appeared robust, with chubby arms and legs, but then the flush of Thomas's cheeks, the red bumps on his chest – Gerrard's too – the swollen glands at their necks, and the shivering. The doctor came with his Epsom salts and his razor to shave their poor heads, but no amount of cool rags could soothe them. In the end it just seemed to be something to keep Robert occupied while Freya was instructed to keep her distance. (At least he'd insisted on that.) 'Change the rags,' Dr Stanbury said. 'See if they won't take a little broth.' He doesn't tell Freya and so she cannot ask, 'Do they look happy?' In his nocturnal world, his shadow-sons thrive. Thomas is already waist-high, Gerrard not far behind. They age at the same rate as their girls, their Estelle and Ida. He doesn't tell Freya that Thomas has lost a front tooth, or about the faces Gerrard pulls behind his brother's back. Superstition tells Robert he ought to be worried that he sees himself in dreams, but he can't regret this second life he leads, hearing the boys' laughter, watching the delight on their faces. And now he will create for them a place to play.

Instead he tells Freya: "It won't be on the same scale as Rosherville. That wouldn't be sustainable." He should have delayed his announcement until he had plans he could spread out on his desk and tenders that met with his accountant's approval.

She turns to him, her cheeks flushed pink, her face framed by a halo of hair that is not so blonde as it was when he first knew her. "And who do you think is going to come to your small scale pleasure gardens?"

Her anxiety isn't without good reason. Anyone with money to spend on leisure has larger gardens of their own. But Robert cannot allow his conviction to be shaken. This must happen. "Those from the Benhilton estate. Sutton Green. The new houses on Great Grennell Hill. Think how little entertainment this area has to advertise it."

"Theatre troupes visit," she protests.

"Twice a year. I remember our last visit to the theatre hall."

Freya smiles, half embarrassed. She toys with the pendant

that she wears on a choker and which sits in the hollow of her neck. "That dreadful yodeller. We went at my suggestion, didn't we?"

"If you can sell tickets for tripe like *that*, you can sell tickets for anything."

"There'll be entertainment?"

"Music on a summer's evening." He lures her in, with words, then with his arms. She smells of rosewater and lemon. "Theatricals."

It is clear there is much his wife would like to say, but she allows herself to be held and settles for, "I only hope you know what you're doing, Robert Cooke!"

All the permission Robert needs. He kisses her forehead, brings her hands to his lips, kisses one and then the other. He is light-headed, ropedancing without a safety net.

CHAPTER SIX

AUTUMN 1894

Hettie sits by the window, awaiting her daughter-in-law's arrival. "We must try not to watch the clock," she tells her parrot. "Not everything runs to schedule when you have young children."

Seldom caged, the bird (a walker and climber rather than a flyer) dips his head, fluffs out his feathers and turns a full circle. He (his name is Fairfax, for no particular reason) side-steps along his cast-iron perch and regards Hettie with hard, bright eyes, giving the impression of listening intently. Fairfax is black-beaked, white-faced, otherwise predominantly grey with the exception of his tail feathers, which are an extravagant crimson. Hettie has had him these last few years. Robert's reaction when introduced was to ask her what the devil she wanted with a parrot. It ought to have been obvious. She'd been a widow a long time, with only the creaks and groans of floorboards for company, only mealtimes to punctuate her daily routine. (She doesn't count the reading material she devours as a distraction: the newspapers, the pamphlets, the scientific papers and the novels.) Hettie learned to live with a husband's absence, as a widow must. What she hadn't expected was her son's absence, or to feel it as acutely as she does. Not once since Walter passed away has Robert suggested she might join his household. It feels as if a punishment is being meted out. Does she deserve it? Perhaps.

As Robert continued to glare at Fairfax, she'd answered, 'For the company.'

'A dog would have been more suitable.'

She bridled. 'I didn't want a dog.' In fact, she'd had in mind something considerably more exotic-looking. A bird bedecked in blue and yellow, not in the colours of a child's school uniform. But that's all Mr Haverhill had, that or a budgerigar, and to Hettie budgerigars seemed inconsequential.

There is no doubt that Fairfax has personality. He has enabled her to stop being so angry with Walter for abandoning her to face the world alone. 'Tell me this,' she used to say before the parrot's arrival to whatever empty room she found herself in, 'Do you think that in the years since you passed away, my life has simply carried on as it did before? Do you imagine that your coat hangs in the closet, that your papers are piled on the corner of your desk, that your black bag is packed?'

Now she says, 'Robert sees that I don't go without. But he works long hours. I don't see him as often as I'd like.' Hettie would not admit that, when they happen, her encounters with her son are brief, not necessarily fraught, but varying from vague to businesslike. She tries to engage him, but when she ventures, 'Tell me more about this physic garden of yours,' his response is, 'You know what I do, Mother.' After they say their farewells, Hettie is left to reflect that nothing meaningful has passed between them. As with her mother after the drawbridge was pulled up, so many opportunities have been missed. Robert is not to blame, she's the first to accept that, but hasn't the slightest notion as to how she might undo the damage. Her daughter-in-law Freya visits in her son's stead.

Where *can* she be? Another glance out of the window.

There goes Reverend Mears on his high-wheel tricycle. Thankfully he passes by without a nod in Hettie's direction. "I do hope nothing untoward has happened," she says to Fairfax. She thinks, of course she does, of her grandsons, such sweet boys. Hettie wondered for some time if Robert and Freya might try for another boy. (Other people seem to be able to recover from these things in a way she cannot.) Though Freya is still young, Hettie wonders no longer. "There you have it," she sighs.

Fairfax nibbles delicately on a scaled toe but lifts a wing at the same time, as if nonplussed. "Is that my cue?" She scratches his head, surprised as always by the softness and heat of another living thing. For a brief moment, it brings to mind how she would run her fingers through the short hairs at the nape of Walter's neck, against the pile, as it were. Yes, for a while, her husband had made her feel so safe. The bird's strange, almost reptilian eyes close over.

Her guest is settled. Annie brings tea. The teapot, the milk jug, the lidded sugar bowl, the cups and saucers, the teaspoons; all are arranged. Annie has been with Hettie long enough to know how she likes things. The girl makes a play of offering a cup to Fairfax, who nibbles at the scalloped rim and lifts a claw to ring out a bone-china chime. Hettie hopes he won't clack across the table as he sometimes does – *clack, clack, clack* go his toes – but Fairfax tires of the game and climbs away, gripping with beak then claws, beak then claws. On finding a perch to his liking, Fairfax promptly lifts his tail and relieves himself.

Hettie turns her attention to Freya, hoping to distract her. "Are you warm enough? I'll have Annie stoke up the fire. Annie…"

"I'm quite comfortable, thank you." Freya has on a half-sleeved tea gown. The pale yellow, a young woman's colour, flatters her flaxen hair. No, comfort is not what a woman expects from her clothes.

Annie nods and bows out.

"Well, then." Hettie straightens one of her new antimacassars. Now that her own hair is more white than it is auburn, the emeralds, teals and cobalt blues she used to clothe herself in drain her complexion. When the coarse white hairs began to appear, she still saw faded copper, but now there is a predominance of silver-grey. Less confident in her colour choices, Hettie turned her eye from the mirror to soft furnishings. She is pleased at how the turquoise-blue embroidered with pale green campanulas disguise Fairfax's 'handiwork', but Freya has not so much as mentioned them. She forces a smile, says, "I want to hear *all* of your news." She expects talk of Estelle's piano lessons and how beautifully Ida's handwriting is coming along – Miss Gifford at Benfleet Hall School really has worked wonders – things she can express grandmotherly pride in. Perhaps mention of Freya's family who hail from Leeds (her father is something in textiles), but is so large and scattered that Hettie struggles to keep track, especially of nephews and nieces who seem less significant somehow than the parents she has on occasion met, and the eight surviving siblings, most of whom seem to be interchangeable. But Freya's expression clouds. Life has taught Hettie that she cannot let down her guard, even for a minute. "What is it, my dear?" she asks.

The younger woman puts her teacup back on its saucer, a careful movement. "I don't like to come here and tell tales."

"No one could accuse you of that." Often, all Hettie gets from Freya is the bare bones.

"It feels like it sometimes. I know I ought to trust Robert's judgement, but I –" She silences herself by biting her bottom lip.

Hettie had thought Robert far too young when he married. To take on a husband's responsibilities at eighteen! But it was difficult for her to press the point. After all, she'd told Robert he'd have to be the man of the house when he was only twelve. "It may be my son you're talking about," she encourages, "but we're both women. I am only too aware that being a wife involves accepting one compromise after another."

"Do you know the old chalk pit?" Freya asks. "The one that backs onto the railway line?"

"I know *of* it." *This is quite unexpected, I must say.* "I can't say I've ever had cause to go there."

Peekaboo!

Hettie locates the parrot, high on the curtain rail. "Not now," she scolds, irritated to note that a doily is dangling from one of Fairfax's talons. He has entangled himself again. If William Morris has his way, the nation's drawing rooms will be stripped of Frenchified frills, but Hettie cannot be without her lace.

Tutt-tutt-tutt-tutt.

"I said *not now,* thank you." The last thing she wants is for Freya to clam up.

But Freya pays the bird no heed. "Robert tells me he used to play there as a boy."

"*Did* he?" Hettie slots this missing piece of history into place. She had sensed there was a some*thing* or a some*where*. He used to arrive home with his head full of stories – the kind Walter would repeat after talking to mill owners and farmers, not the type that are passed around the playground. And there was a smell of smoke about him – not woodsmoke or smoke from a coal fire, but something she could never quite identify.

"And now, out of some misplaced sense of nostalgia, it seems he's bought the site."

The news jolts Hettie from her reverie. "I can't imagine chalk soil will be suitable for cultivation."

"If only he had cultivation in mind." Freya's voice is a combination of incredulity and apology.

"What, then?"

"He plans to open a pleasure garden."

"A –?" Hettie is standing at a distance, watching a hot air balloon rise into the bright sky. She promised herself she wouldn't watch, but her son is in that wicker basket and she has an overwhelming sense that harm will come his way if she loses sight of him.

Long ago, she lost sight of him.

"It's not that I expect him to ask for my permission before he commits himself, but…" Freya breaks off to compose herself. "If there's one thing about Robert I'd alter, it would be his impulsiveness."

Hettie stares into her teacup. This idea is no cloud-castle. Robert will not be persuaded to change his mind. And for her part, Hettie must come to terms with uncomfortable truths. Robert intends to re-create the very thing he was denied; more specifically, the thing he thinks *she* denied him. Nobody's memories are perfect, Hettie understands that only too well. What is left is how you felt. How you were *made* to feel.

Freya's awkward smile betrays precisely how upset she is. "I can't help it. I'm not comfortable with risk." There it is, that deplorable word. "I imagine he inherited his reckless streak from his father." She reaches for a handkerchief.

"Not Walter. My husband was as steady as they come." It was hardly his fault that the feeling of calm he instilled in her when they were first married didn't last.

"Well, it certainly didn't come from you!" Her daughter-in-law pre-empts any detail Hettie might have gone on to share about her bloodline; how Ernest couldn't help but answer the call of the mountains. "I thought perhaps you might have some advice on how to deal with an impulsive husband."

"Try to steer him. It's all you can do." But how her son might be steered, Hettie has no idea. Robert inherited the itch from his grandfather, and all she's ever been able to do is watch. With nothing further to suggest, she decides to move the conversation elsewhere. "I must admit, I'm feeling a little impulsive myself." As she says this, her heart beats a little faster.

Freya looks a little alarmed. "Oh?"

A long time ago Hettie bolted the door to things she did not know. Now is the time to unlock it. Before it's too late. "I'm planning a trip to Scotland."

"Scotland? Why on earth would you do that?"

"I was named after a mountain and I've never seen it. Don't you think that's strange?"

The poor girl really does look lost. "Surely your name is Henrietta?"

"My middle name is Henrietta. My Christian name – if you can call it that – is Aonach." The name she so fastidiously avoided. The name that is embedded in her. It is the first time in many years Hettie has said it out loud, and with its utterance the name seems to lose a little of its hold over her.

CHAPTER SEVEN

AUTUMN 1894

Freya, who has Ida's hand in hers, shakes it sharply then leans to the level of her daughter's ear. "Eyes front. You don't want Reverend Mears to think you're not paying attention to his sermon."

"But the skull's eyes."

"What about the skull's eyes?"

"They're staring at me."

His forefinger a bookmark in his scarlet service book, Robert sits forward to better see the reclining sculpture of Sir William Scawen. The sculptor clothed Sir William in Roman robes, though the impression is hardly classical when he is also wigged and ruffed. The statue directs his gaze towards the choir loft, oblivious, it seems, to the skull he is balancing on one thigh, held rather too loosely, in Robert's opinion.

"Don't be silly," his wife tells their younger daughter. "The skull doesn't have eyes."

True, but it has blackened sockets. Robert has always found the effect unsettling. What's more, he has sympathy for Ida's inability to concentrate. All Saints' pews weren't designed for comfort and Reverend Mears is blessed with neither the thespian's gifts nor the showman's tricks. The clergyman fires an artillery of words at his congregation, buoyed up by the belief that hearing what wretched specimens they are is good for their eternal souls.

Robert feels the point of Freya's elbow. She mouths the words, *'Eyes front,'* her own eyes a stern grey blue. Before Robert complies, he sees Ida looking up at him. *'Eyes front,'* he mouths and winks. He grapples with belief as modern men must. Darwin foisted this on them. Outwardly there is no change. His neighbours look as they've always looked, but the seed of doubt has been planted. This life may be all there is. And if that is the case the dead are not waiting, they are just names on lichened headstones to be traced with fingertips. It hollows him out, the thought that he may never meet Thomas or Gerrard again.

Eventually the Reverend runs out of steam, restoring Robert's faith, if only a little. Familiar words resume and the service mumbles steadily towards the final prayers.

The Lord may have decreed that the last shall be first and the first shall be last, but at All Saints, Reverend Mears leads the way in his cassock and surplice. After the altar boys come the Carlisles, an old family with landowning, military and clerical connections, their history told on brass plaques and monuments on the stone walls of the church. White-haired, chins level, Mr and Mrs Carlisle look straight ahead, lest something be read into accidental eye contact. Next come the Colmans, the Surrey branch of the Norfolk mustard-seed growers. Baronet he may be, but Sir Jeremiah certainly isn't a man who thinks work ungentlemanly. The Jameses. The Benhiltons. Robert (who rents his family's pew because, God willing, he may in time inch forwards) files into the aisle, nodding to his opposite, Louis Spanier, a thickly-bearded professor of languages. Both men pause to allow their wives and children to go in front.

"Are you well?" asks Robert.

"Do you know who was the first to challenge the social order?" demands Spanier. "Jesus Christ, that is who." His mouth is buried so deep in brush and the dismal organ refrain loud enough that he gets away with it.

The professor and his family live at Hanover House, which straddles the boundary between parishes. The Spaniers had their pick of All Saints and St Nicholas's, but St Nick's is a modern monstrosity; a nice stone church of considerable pedigree was torn down to make way for it. To add insult to injury, its south porch is inscribed with the words, *How amiable are thy dwellings thou Lord of Hosts,* sufficient cause for any man to bear it a grudge, perhaps even to the extent of submitting themselves to Reverend Mears' sermons.

Robert emerges blinking into low sunlight, where the final formality of shaking the Reverend's hand must be observed. The professor already has his pipe out. Because of the time he spent studying in France, he is forgiven the odd eccentricity, though he causes great confusion by offering his left hand to be shaken.

Even as Robert bids Reverend Mears good day, the rector emanates disapproval. Whether it is for him specifically, who can say? Here is Mrs Mears. Many women part their hair down the centre, but none so severely as she. Still recovering from the professor's left-handed shake she refrains from offering Robert her hand, so in response to her austere, "Mr Cooke," he inclines his head. "My regards to your mother," she says.

Hettie and her maker had a falling out some time ago, and his mother being his mother thinks He should be the one to repair it. She comes only to tend Walter's grave, which he shares with Thomas and Gerrard. Robert's father didn't meet his grandsons in life. Only in death did they become acquainted. He thinks – of course he does – of the time Ida found Walter's gravestone and spelled out the letters of their surname.

'C-O-O-K-E. Mummy, three people have the same

surname as us. Walter Thomas Cooke, Thomas Wilfrid Cooke and Gerrard Stephen Cooke. Fallen asleep in Christ.'

Until then, Robert hadn't known that Ida could read. Freya reacted as if she'd been slapped, holding one hand to her cheek. It was his mother who crouched down.

'How clever of you, Ida. Walter was my husband, your father's father. And Thomas and Gerrard were your brothers.'

'Did I have brothers?' Ida asked.

'You did. They departed this life before you were born. Do you see the dates?'

Ida did see. 'I only missed them by two months.' And she traced their names, letter by letter.

On Doctor Stanbury's advice, Freya began her confinement before their boys were laid to rest. The doctor administered a calming draught, something he *hoped* would prevent her from going into labour prematurely, but he told Robert to prepare himself. If the child came now, it would not survive. Dispatched from Leeds, two of Freya's sisters – Edith and Hilda – arrived and took over, as women do at such times. Robert was cut off from his wife and her grief, and had no idea what to do with his own. Then, by the time Freya emerged from her lying-in…

A deep grinding sound draws his attention. The landlord of the Coach and Horses is rolling a beer barrel up the high street so he can minister to those who've taken to heart the Reverend's warnings against setting foot in a tavern on the Lord's day. Freya and Estelle walk past in the direction of his wife's group of friends. Robert watches Freya go. By the time she emerged from her lying-in it was too late to begin to talk about their sons. They had not the language for it. And, besides, their new baby was most vocal in making her needs known.

"Mrs Griffiths *and* Mrs Furbur," Ida sighs. "They will be for *ever.*"

Already they can hear the women's trilling. Robert smiles down at his daughter. "Shall we take a look in the churchyard and see if we can't find a lizard?"

Robert feels Ida's hand creep into his. "Come along, then." She is wise to him, this bright spark of a daughter.

Freya appears at the door of Robert's study. "A tennis court," she says and turns as if to go.

"A tennis court?"

"We discussed your project after church." She has rear-ranged her hair since this morning's service. No longer in the low chignon she wore to accommodate her bonnet, she has curled it into ringlets at either side of her face. "The one thing everyone would be prepared to pay for is use of a tennis court. If there were a club with tournaments, all the better."

In Robert's childhood it was unheard of for women to play sport, but the lawn tennis championship at nearby Wimbledon has helped reshape opinions. Women have proved themselves no less competitive than men. "Of course, a tennis court!" he agrees.

"If there's to be a club, we'll need more than one."

"Two, then." He adds to his list. "What about croquet?" he calls out – an afterthought – and then, craning his neck. "Do people still play?"

She's gone. No matter. On one corner of his desk he discovers a copy of *The Home* magazine, folded back so that an illustration of a tennis dress by Messrs. Debenham and Freebody is uppermost. Never let it be said that he can't take a hint. Freya shall have her dress.

He considers what he has so far: tennis courts (two) and a croquet lawn. For these, the site will have to be levelled, but since topsoil needs to be brought in, it may be a case of building up rather than taking away. A pavilion will serve as a café and clubhouse, in a design that gives a nod to the area's

Tudor heritage *and* the Arts and Crafts movement. A glasshouse too. It need not be large. 'Carshalton's Crystal Palace'. The idea brings a wry smile to Robert's face. Classical statues among chrysanthemums, yuccas and ferns. An orchid or two if he can source them.

There will be a bandstand on a central lawn, a place where music and theatricals can be staged on summer evenings. No garden should be without its planting. Roses to scent the air with Turkish Delight; honeysuckle and jasmine. And there must be areas where children can keep themselves amused out of sight of the adults. Robert closes his eyes, allows his second sight free rein. Paths will fork through the trees, forcing decisions (there they go, Thomas to the left, Gerrard to the right) and leading to secluded spots. Things to be discovered. Carvings of green men and goblins, lichened statues of Pan and Puck that give the impression of having sprung from tree roots. He hears it. Children's laughter: transient, fleeting, fading.

His gardens should have their own grotto. How much of the kilns are underground, and whether what is left of them might be adapted, Robert doesn't know. For the time being it feels like a possibility. A shell for a shellhouse, a design of dolphins, seahorses and mermaids in a mosaic of coloured glass and seashells.

And of course he'll have his father's fountain, a place where visitors can throw their coins and make a wish.

It won't be a Vauxhall or a Cremorne, nothing on so grand a scale – nothing that will attract as much controversy.

At supper, with the girls already put to bed, he returns to the subject. "I wondered about an aviary." He has in mind something white, octagonal, ornate.

"Do you know anything about keeping birds?" Freya asks.

He consults the ring-bound notebook in which he has sketched a pair of lovebirds. "I thought perhaps my mother might advise me."

His wife's gaze settles on the notebook. Only when it is back in his breast pocket does Freya continue, "She might," and dabs at her mouth with a napkin. "*If* she's here."

He smiles indulgently at her concern. "I don't think she'll be going anywhere, not for a good while yet."

"Then she hasn't told you."

"Told me what?"

"She's planning a trip to Scotland."

"Scotland?" He prongs a square of lamb chop, dips it in mint sauce. "What could my mother *possibly* want with Scotland?"

CHAPTER EIGHT

AUTUMN ~ WINTER 1894

After months of trying to keep the chalk pit afloat, all Frank Reynolds wanted was a fair price and a quick, clean sale. With the last of the papers signed, a toast is drunk at the Greyhound to mark the occasion.

"There it goes," Frank says as their tankards clash. "My short career as a landowner."

"You have my word," Robert tells him, his senior in years. "I'll put the land to use in a way that respects its history."

But when Robert gets up to leave, Frank asks, "Same time next week?"

The most valuable lesson Robert learned at Cheam School was that if a person wants to get ahead in this world, there are only twenty people whose approval he needs. There, those people were the prefects. *Warm the toilet seat, day boy! Spit-polish my shoes!* Indignities never quite forgotten. Everyone understands how the world works. You are either useful or you are not, and the moment you're not, you'll be dropped. Frank is no longer useful, but he offers a link to old William, and William to Robert's childhood. What's more, dammit, Robert enjoys his company! "Why not?" he says.

The air in the Greyhound's bar room is thick with warming smells. Woodsmoke, pipe tobacco, penny Woodbines and whatever stew is on tonight's menu. "I'm not sure I can stomach another lecture about treading a fine line between parkscape and wilderness!" Robert rolls his eyes. "I'm coming round to the idea of running a competition for the design."

Frank takes up his tankard and drains the dregs. "You'll get every young so and so who's trying to earn himself a bit of a reputation."

"That's what I'm hoping. The more publicity the better." The scent of hops – of resin and pine and citrus – rises up as Robert brings his mug to his lips. He isn't really a beer man. "Meanwhile, I'll start clearing the site. Get a feel for it."

"Can't work against chalk." Frank points to Robert's tankard. "Another?"

"I've hardly made any headway with this one."

Frank scrapes back his chair. "No rush."

He comes back from the bar with two brimming tankards, picking up seamlessly where they left off. "Thinking of clearing the site yourself?" Elbowed from his blind side, Frank turns to see who has almost spilled his pint of old and mild, a glare and a sharp word ready, but when he finds it's the barmaid he brightens, winking his good eye.

"I fancy I might roll my sleeves up," Robert says.

Frank looks scathing. "Show us your hands."

Robert holds them out, palms uppermost. To his own eyes, they look deeply creviced, the whorls of his fingerprints puckered, fine vertical lines running the length of his digits.

"When's the last time you held a shovel? Take a look at these. *These* are a working man's hands." Frank's hands are a landscape of their own, each callous a badge of honour. He has cut chalk since he was old enough to grasp a spade. He leans back and looks under the table at Robert's shoes. "Spats," he scoffs. "I'll wager *you* don't even own a pair o' work boots."

"A wager you'd win." Robert grins. He started his working life as an office boy. He filled inkwells, fetched files, ferried messages. It was a job that required a wing-tipped collar and polished shoes, things that at the age of twelve made him feel important. Though he's progressed to business owner, a pen-pusher he remains. Robert may know what needs to be done and the best way to go about it, but he's the man who does the deals and writes the cheques.

The fingers of Frank's left hand drum the tabletop. "I've the time if you think you could use me."

"I thought you'd be glad to see the back of the place."

"What am I going to do with myself?" Frank's face is plunged into shadow as he looks to the corner of the room. "We did things the traditional way. I was taught by my father and he was taught by his father before him." Generations of Reynolds worked that plot; now, everything they achieved will be erased. "There are fewer places for skilled workers in this world of steam-power. The whole rhythm o' life's changed."

Robert's business relies on mechanisation. The extraction of poppy resin can't be automated, but the process of distillation runs on steam, increasing output at a reduced cost. The quarry might have closed by the time his name was added to the deeds, but he's played his part in the story of progress. He's about to ask Frank if his brothers have found work, but Frank shakes his head wearily.

"Ventures like ours fall by the wayside – and I'm the wrong side of forty." Then he takes a sip and brightens. "But you're going to need someone who knows a thing or two about chalk."

Robert had men in mind, men in need of a wage, while Frank has the proceeds from the sale. But Robert knows what it is to be uprooted. He owes it to old William's memory, old William and his history lessons. A man who would share things Robert's mother was incapable of sharing. Having worn every emotion on her sleeve while his father was alive, she kept them under lock and key in the aftermath of his death and assumed that Robert – a child – would understand what it was she was holding inside. More than that, she expected him to be her consolation, and he couldn't. Not when she'd insisted they left the home where they'd been happy and come to the place that killed his father.

"I'd be glad of your help," Robert says. "Though it might only be short-term."

"You'll be impressed by how useful I can make myself."

"How much is this usefulness going to cost me?"

"Ten shillings a week seems fair."

Somewhere between the wage of an agricultural worker and a bricklayer. "I think I can see my way to that."

"And I've my two youngest. Good lads. They'll want four shillings apiece."

Robert's eyes widen. "I dare say. How old are they?"

"Eleven and thirteen. Do you have boys?"

In a blink, his boys' coffins. The size of them. At times like that, you stand outside yourself. How else could you do what must be done? Another blink and the vision is gone. "Girls," Robert replies. "You?"

"Four boys and a girl, but we've only the two youngsters with us now. I'll make sure you get a decent day's work out of them."

"I don't doubt it." They shake hands across the table.

"You drinking that?" Frank points to the second tankard he brought back from the bar.

The man can certainly hold his ale. "Be my guest."

Robert's new workforce arrives in the frost of an autumnal morning, a peach-coloured strip of light on the horizon, cockerels crowing at the edge of sound.

"This is John." Frank lays one hand on top of the taller boy's head, the one who's supposed to be thirteen.

Robert nods. "John."

John straightens his cap. "Mr Cooke."

"And this." The younger lad sidesteps Frank's attempt to ruffle his hair. "This is Gerrard."

There was no warning, but that's hardly Frank's fault. There are, of course, other boys called Gerrard, many other boys, but it is not *their* eyes Robert is staring into at this moment. It is a relief that this boy's eyes are not flecked with gold.

"Recent graduate of the National School. Mind you, Mr Bickford left the job o' teaching him his letters to Mrs Mears at Sunday school. Hands out o' your armpits when Mr Cooke's talking to you," says Frank, though Robert has yet to speak. How has this happened? After being kept apart when they most needed each other, when eventually he and Freya spoke about their sons, his wife vowed that their daughters would not grow up as she had, constantly compared to dead siblings and found wanting. Somehow since then, even speaking the boys' names has become taboo.

"Mrs Mears, eh?" he manages, then says to Frank, "I didn't think you were churchgoers."

"My father used to take the boys. Good for custom." Frank leans towards him, conspiratorially: "But I'm not a man who needs to have the errors of his ways pointed out. I'm all too aware of them –" he winks his good eye "– and much comfort they bring me too."

"Well, lads," Robert nods to the thigh-high grass, the weeds thick and woody. "You can see what we have to deal with."

No other instruction is needed. The boys take up scythes. How easily they've absorbed the skills needed for the lives they'll most likely lead. Robert catches himself watching them sweep the blades in arcs, transferring their weight as they go, taking the toppled grass with them, creating neat piles, stepping forwards with each return. Unable to tear his gaze away, he pretends to be massaging the small of his back (he has not yet learned to swing like a pendulum), wiping his forehead with a sleeve. The boys are so in tune with each other, it's as if one is the left hand, the other the right. They egg each other on, trading insults. Ratbag. Pigeon-liver. Halfwit.

When Gerrard asks, "D'you think that spider knows what its web will look like when it's finished?" Robert finds himself smiling. *Is a spider's web any less impressive than one of Brunel's suspension bridges?*

From time to time Frank raises his voice – "That's enough!" – and there is calm for fifteen minutes or so. Time when Robert can hear the sea-like swish of blades above the song of the blackbirds and robins. Unlike his own, the Reynolds' cuts are sure, close to the soil.

"Blade needs sharpening." Frank nods to Robert's scythe. "John, get over here with a good coarse stone and see to Mr Cooke's blade."

They are close enough to the railway station for the shriek of the guard's whistle to carry. Like startled hares, the boys emerge from their partial camouflage in time for the hissing of the air-pump, the pleasure of watching the engine – a breathing thing of coal and fire – pass cleanly under a glorious plume of steam.

"Boys," Frank says to Robert in admiration and apology. "But it won't stop them getting the work done, you'll see."

Robert does see.

He sees the way Gerrard turns to shout to his father, "Did you see it? Did you?" His unstoppable elation at everyday magic.

"I could hardly miss it, now could I?" Frank whistles through his front teeth, mutters, "Thinks his father's blind."

Robert turns away. *I'll never get to say these things.* But when this thought comes breaking and entering, his mind doesn't turn to his daughters. Estelle and Ida rarely intrude on his thoughts, but there is rarely a moment he is not aware of the Reynolds boys. It's not that Robert hasn't had close contact with boys. It is simply that the boys he imagined here, up to their knees in the skeletal remains of cow parsley, stopping at midday for bread and dripping, silhouetted against the chalk escarpment, were his boys. *Ours,* he corrects himself. Somehow, the girls – more of a mystery to him – seem to belong to Freya.

Days fall into a rhythm, easy for the Reynolds, but being on his feet all day and hard at it is new to Robert.

"Surely there are enough men in need of a wage that you don't need to pick up a scythe?" Freya asks.

But by tending the soil Robert feels he is absorbing the character of the site. When his palms blister, Robert drains the clear fluid and binds his hands so he can carry on.

"Robert, your hands!" says Freya when he changes his bandages, taking them in hers, turning them over. Her eyes betray her. She is thinking that she married a man who makes decisions, balances books, drafts advertising copy, distributes produce and pays wages. She didn't marry a labourer.

He thinks of how he laid a palm on Thomas's chest. He wouldn't be able to feel the crushed-shell texture now. Not with these hands.

Late October brings afternoons warm enough for them to remove their jackets. Both Reynolds boys are revealed, lean and smooth-skinned. Gerrard looks as if there should be no strength in those arms of his. Snappable, like twigs. When his vest rides up, each bone of his spine can be seen, the outline of his ribs, his skeleton on display, angular, awkward, coltish.

Then come squally days. Rain lashes down, wave after wave and, having shed their leaves, the alders and the oaks offer no shelter. Brims of hats and caps drip, hair drips. The taste of wet wool and sodden earth fills their mouths. Boots have no chance to dry overnight. It is miserable to ease one foot and then the other into clammy wet leather. But when Robert strips off sodden clothes at the day's end, the veins that stood out on his arms seem to have disappeared. His shoulders have lost their stoop caused by long days spent poring over ledgers, and his appetite is ferocious. Even his eyesight improves. At first when one of the boys shouted, 'See that bird?', the answer was, 'No.' Now with a quick glance he can tell if it's a meadow pipit or a dunnock.

When a man approaches him and asks for the owner, Robert must accept that he's no longer recognisable as being in charge. "That's me." He sets down the wheelbarrow, loaded with weeds and grass. "I'm Robert Cooke."

"Mr Cooke." Tall, spectacled and almost painfully thin, the newcomer tips his hat. "I beg your pardon."

"No need."

"I've come in response to your advertisement about the competition."

"Are you local?"

"West Street."

"Just around the corner! I'm surprised I don't know your face."

"We're recent arrivals here, but we live very quietly."

Very quietly, thinks Robert, *and not churchgoers.*

"Perhaps, if you've time to discuss what you have in mind…"

"I have a list." Robert pats himself down. "It must be in my coat."

"In the shed," says Frank.

"This way." Robert starts off in the direction of the old coal shed, the place where they now stow tools. And coats, apparently. "Mr –?"

"Hoddy. Oswald Hoddy."

Next, they dig. "'Portant to get to it now," says Frank, "Before the ground has a chance to freeze." It's tough going, the soil compacted. Tangles of fibrous roots are pulled free, flints picked up and a game made of tossing them into barrows. Gerrard hurtles towards Robert with his finds.

"Look what I've got!" A clay pot, a lead soldier, a piece of Dutch tile painted blue.

"That's enough now," Frank chides. "If you stop every time you dig something up, we'll never be done."

"Reckon this belonged to my grandad," Gerrard says of a wooden pipe. "Mind if I keep it, Mr Cooke?"

Where the boy's thumbs have rubbed the dirt away, there is the promise of fine grain. "By all means."

"I'm going to clean it up good and proper." Gerrard tucks the pipe into a pocket and goes away, light on his feet.

In comes the topsoil, cartloads of the stuff. This is spread over the ground, rolled, and readings taken with a spirit level. A blank canvas for Robert's small Eden, not a place from which people are cast out, but where they are welcomed. He consults his notebook.

"Know anything about laying a lawn for tennis?" Lately, Robert has found himself leaving off the beginnings of sentences. Freya has remarked on it.

"I know how to take care of a cricket pitch. Can't be too different." Frank stands tall, sniffs the air. "Mind, you've missed your chance this year. September would have been ideal for sowing. Oi!" he calls to his boys, pointing to a depression that can barely be seen with the eye. "What do I always say?"

They come to look, parrot sheepishly, "Second best isn't good enough."

"And what's that?"

They both look. Gerrard scratches his head. "Second best?"

"You know what to do, then, don't you?" They set to work and Frank grins at Robert. "Got to remind them who's in charge. Here," he offers his flask. "Have a nip of that." When he sees Robert's hesitation Frank says, "Keeps the chill out."

Not wanting to appear ungrateful, Robert takes the flask and swigs. *By God, that's rough.* "Is there a particular grass you'd recommend? Something hard-wearing."

Frank tips his head back, emits a sigh of satisfaction. "Rye's your safest bet, I reckon. Know where it'll go?"

"Not yet." As an afterthought, Robert adds, "The Reverend has objected. He had his wife speak to Mrs Cooke."

"Don't tell me. The good Reverend doesn't want tennis played on a Sunday."

"He doesn't want women playing tennis at all."

"With any luck he'll preach a sermon on the subject." Frank takes another swig from his flask. "Then you'll have them queuing."

In total, eleven men arrive with brass rulers and dividers. They pace the perimeter, their mouths moving as they count. Wise to this, the boys make a game of distracting them, John wheeling a barrow across their paths, Gerrard excusing himself and picking flints out of their way, so that the men lose track and have to start counting again. Robert lets it pass. But when one of them moves a peg to which a length of string is attached, a complaint is made.

Robert has words. "Which of you was it?"

Neither owns up. Well, neither would he. Nothing good ever came Robert's way as a result of taking the blame, and there were plenty of times when he was punished for something he hadn't done. But the point must be made. "Boys, this is serious. The measurements are the starting point. Unless they're right, the entire design will be out."

Frank approaches, his face like a bull's. "Boys, what have you done now?"

Gerrard swivels his right foot. "Someone moved one of the surveyors' pegs a couple of feet to the right."

"They were the surveyors' pegs? I thought they were the

lines for the tennis courts. They weren't true so I straightened them up."

"Are you going to dock his pay?" John asks, earning a clip round the ear for his trouble.

"Oi, that's enough from you. It was an honest mistake."

Dressing in a collared shirt and his favourite smoking jacket, Robert transforms himself each evening into someone whose education and lengthy apprenticeship wasn't wasted. Tonight, after a supper of boiled ham and parsley sauce he retreats to his study, where he pours a generous brandy. He feels as though he's earned it, but he worked no harder than the Reynolds and doubts they come home each day to the opportunity to bathe. It's unlikely they have clean clothes to change into.

Across the hall in the front parlour, Estelle is torturing herself with piano scales. Straight back, overlapping fingers, but then a sharp where there should be a flat, and back to the beginning she goes. Her perseverance is admirable, but it doesn't bear repeated listening. Robert shuts out the noise, seals in the warmth of the crackling fire and settles himself behind his desk (his father's before him). Awaiting his attention is the latest missive from Smithers, his Mitcham overseer. They are turning their hands to winter chores. Ivy and bramble removal, leaf clearance, dividing and replanting, and weeding, of course – weeds being the only plants that thrive in this temperature. Then there's the stable roof that's in need of repair. Robert double-checks the columns of expenses and finds Smithers' calculation correct, confirms that a consignment of chicken manure can be bought, agrees to the purchase of a new cart (second-hand, if the right sort can be had), writes a cheque for a sum that ought to cover everything. Only after he has blotted the ink does he turn to his other pile of correspondence.

Ha! The London, Brighton and South Coast Railway

company is looking to acquire plots for railway workers' cottages and has identified his site as suitable. Had he not stepped in, this is what would have happened. Terraces of cottages.

Ah, now, here we are. Farmer and Brindley's notepaper. Neptune and his dolphins have been cleaned, his frostbitten fingers replaced, his broken trident repaired, but the pipework is rusted and needs to be renewed. Would he like them to proceed? The price quoted is so astronomically high it is somehow meaningless. The fountain will be Robert's centrepiece. It will also be a fitting memorial to his father. He dips his pen once more, signing off the quote with a flourish that is a little more extravagant than usual.

CHAPTER NINE

WINTER 1894

Frank clears his throat. "The boys have something they want to ask. Go on. I'm not doing it for you."

They both stand there, barely able to meet Robert's eyes.

He addresses the older lad. "What can I do for you, Thomas?"

"He called you Thomas!" chirrups Gerrard, pointing and doubling up with mirth.

Robert's heart skitters. He's blundered. "Come along, Doubting Thomas, out with it!"

"Do you mind if we stop off a bit early today, Mr Cooke?"

"There's elephants." Gerrard cannot wait for his older brother to trip over carefully rehearsed lines. "The circus is passing through and the man said they're going to water them in Wandle Pond at three!"

Gerrard's excitement is contagious. "In that case, let's down tools at half past two. What say you, Mr Hoddy?" Robert calls over to the surveyor, who has set up a folding table for a desk on the newly levelled ground. His wiry limbs form sharp angles. He must be cold, though Robert has worked in offices that were colder than the outside temperature.

Busy with a ruler and a pair of brass dividers, he draws his spectacles down his nose and looks up. "I beg your pardon?"

"Have you any interest in coming to see some elephants?"

"I'd prefer to finish here, if you don't mind. Do you have any strong feelings about the trees?"

He does. In their shade, his shadow-sons are at their most real. "The trees stay."

"Yes, I thought so, too."

Robert can't quite fathom the man. He keeps intending to ask Freya if she's heard of the Hoddys, but it slips his mind.

Once dinner is over, the younger lad trots over regularly. "You'll tell us when it's time, won't you?"

"Don't worry, I'll tell you."

"It's just that I don't want to miss it."

Frank pulls himself up to his full height. "Don't use this as an excuse for idling. Mr Cooke has already said he'll tell you."

Gerrard hangs his head and slopes away.

"I shouldn't speak over you," Frank says. "But I promised you'd get a good day's work out of them."

"Not to worry." You forget sometimes. How young they are. How little excitement there is to be had.

"Have you ever seen an elephant?"

"I have." Robert leaves the site unlocked so that Mr Hoddy can finish his plan, though the sky already has a violet hue. He'll be lucky to squeeze another hour's work out of the day.

As Robert begins to walk, Gerrard trots to keep pace. "Where d'you see it?"

In London, Robert saw many elephants, bejewelled, sequined and trained to rear up on their hind legs, but he likes Gerrard's assumption of a solitary beast and so that is what he'll deliver. "At the Zoological Society. You might have heard of him. His name was Jumbo."

Gerrard gives a skip that betrays his father's lie. He cannot be eleven. He may not even be nine. "Wasn't he the largest elephant in the world?"

"Not too many questions, now," Frank growls a low warning, but Robert is enjoying himself. Curiosity ought to be encouraged. He tries to engage the girls. Ida is game, but all too often Estelle accepts his first answer.

"They'd have us *believe* he was the largest." A right turn under the railway bridge and they enter the narrow track between the railway line and the severe wall of the old manor house, now a girls' school run by the Daughters of the Cross. "He was only eight years old when I saw him, so he was still quite small – for an elephant."

"How small?"

Squeezed into the lead, Robert and Gerrard soon revert to single file to avoid nettles and brambles.

"Oh," Robert puts the flat of one hand on top of his head, "no taller than I am."

Sullen, John remains within hearing distance. "Told you they'll be big, pea-brain." Today's insult. Whatever *his* age, he's difficult to impress.

Enthusiasm undampened, Gerrard ignores his brother, turning a semicircle and walking backwards. "Bigger than a horse?"

Robert considers this. "Bulkier than a horse."

Backwards, backwards, with confident heels. "Like a cow?"

Robert holds his hands apart. "Wider. How big *these* elephants are will depend upon where they're from. If memory serves, Jumbo was from Africa, and African elephants are bigger than their Asian cousins."

"Look where you're going, now!" warns Frank.

Even at this hour, the Hope's customers spill out into West Street, breaking into raucous song.

In Westminster not long ago,
There liv'd a ratcatcher's daughter.

Frank hollers a greeting.

"Not stopping?" comes the reply.

"Later, p'rhaps." He raises a hand, chuckles, "I'll wager some of them'll go home with the milk in the morning."

Robert misses their evenings in the Greyhound, but Freya is right. A man shouldn't socialise with his workforce. (She would prefer it if he didn't work alongside them.) This outing, this is different.

"Recognise them?" Frank thumbs over his shoulder.

Robert looks back, frowns. "Who?"

He grins. "Two o' my brothers."

"What do they do with themselves these days?"

"What do your uncles do, Gerrard?"

"They're knackermen." Cheerfully, hands in pockets, still walking backwards. "They finish off lame horses and turn them into cat-meat."

"The new family business," says Frank. "Don't have the stomach for it myself."

It is the same story as they pass the Coach and Horses.

"More brothers?" asks Robert.

"That one's *my* brother!" says Gerrard of a man who doesn't look much younger than his uncles.

Frank grins. "I started young."

Past Richard Allen's tailor shop ("*A-ccout-re-ment* fitter to the Third Surrey Rifle Volunteers," reads Gerrard. "Pea-brain," says John). Past Preens' Wheelwrights and Timber Yard, past the weatherboarded houses (which is Mr Hoddy's? he wonders), the eighteenth-century water tower's distinctive silhouette comes into view. Left down Festival Walk and beyond the one-hundred-year old plane tree, they arrive at the first of two ponds – the one where the elephants will be watered. No crowd has gathered. Nothing as yet suggests this is anything other than an ordinary weekday.

"We must be early." Robert hopes the boys are not in for a disappointment. "Boys." He claps his hands, rubbing them together for warmth. "Where do you want to stand?"

"There!" Gerrard points excitedly towards the ford and the Greyhound beyond. "That's where they'll get into the water."

"I'd rather stay here," says John. "Watch them approach."

"We could make up two parties," Robert suggests. "You bide here, I'll go with Gerrard."

"That's very good of you, Mr Cooke. Mind you do as he says. And keep well back. Don't forget, they're wild animals."

The minute they are out of his father's earshot, the boy says, "They're trained, that's what the man told us."

Robert is moved to realise Gerrard is trying to reassure him.

Gerrard is not a boy who's capable of standing still. He lifts one boot, holds it above his opposite knee and fingers a hole in its sole as if rummaging about in a nostril. Robert clears his throat and, when the boy looks at him, nods *down*.

"I asked Mrs Mears why elephants have trunks."

Robert hadn't thought of it before, but if the Reynolds boys went to Sunday school, they must know his daughters. "And what did she say?"

"That it was God's design."

"She may well be right."

"My mother said it's so they can fetch things off high shelves." He laughs, the kind of laughter that is an invitation. "What I really wanted to know was, if you don't believe the world was created in seven days, does that mean God had nothing to do with it?"

Blasted Darwin again! "Isn't it possible that God set everything in motion and left nature to get on with it?"

"But then we might not have existed. Or *we* might have ended up with trunks." Again, that laughter.

Robert pictures Mrs Mears' reaction to the idea that mankind is accidental. "It depends whether you believe evolution was part of God's design."

"Any sign yet?"

Robert scans the road and feels a lift in his chest, but the dark lumbering beast in the distance proves to be the brewer's shire horses pulling his dray. "Not yet."

No, wait. Something has lured Miss Susannah Rotherham out of Holt's Library, a tall, thin building which is the closest shop to the ponds. Robert has fond memories of Holt's. It was at the stationery and bookshop that he spent what pocket money came his way on penny dreadfuls featuring Ernest Keen, who ran away from home and worked for a police inspector, and didn't Robert feel like running away too when he was first deposited in the back of beyond? Robert waits for Miss Rotherham's nod (she recognises him, even in his work clothes, but then she has known him a long time) and tips his hat.

By the time Robert looks back at Gerrard, the boy is leaning over the railing, his feet lifted clean off the pavement. "Not over the water," Robert warns. There must be strength in those twig-like wrists because they hold his weight. "Have you thought about joining the circus?"

"D'you think they'd take me?" Gerrard glances towards his father, whose gaze is elsewhere. Before Robert realises what the boy's about, he's upside down, hair hanging. The urge to grab the scruff of his jacket is overwhelming, but while Robert is still reaching out the boy's feet find the footway.

"That's the last time you pull a trick like that. I'm not going in to fish you out of the water."

It is clear the boy hoped for praise. "I've done it a hundred times," Gerrard sulks, kicking at the footway. "The pond's not even that deep."

"You've fallen in before, then?"

His reply is a grin.

"Well, *I* don't intend to find out." In fact, Robert knows full well. He ended up in the pond himself, must be almost twenty years ago, in a winter far bitterer than this one looks set to be. For two glorious weeks the pond was a skating rink. He was among a group of boys who, once the ice was past its best, tried to crack it with the heels of their boots, but he was the only one to drop himself up to his ears in it. Mr Woodman, who happened to be hanging carcasses outside his butcher's shop, came running and dragged him out by his collar. After Robert's gasping eased and he'd thawed enough for his limbs to burn, he bargained hard to stop Mr Woodman from telling his mother. A month of errands, it cost him. A month of sweeping up blood-soaked sawdust, plucking feathers from fowl and separating offal from innards. At the end of his sentence the butcher asked him, "Well, yob, what have you learned?"

The answer came easily: "That I don't want to be a butcher."

"Here they come." Robert nods. *At last!* Dusk is almost upon them.

Slight as a sapling, the boy juts out his neck as if he's leaning out of the carriage of a train. "Where?"

Mr Gardner emerges from his saddler's shop in time to see a man on horseback followed by the largest and most impressive of the elephants. The bull. There is no crier. No call of *Hold your horses, the elephants are coming*. Robert feels Gerrard step closer, the distance between them narrow. The boy is quiet. Robert senses that he's holding his breath. A tug on his jacket sleeve: he finds that Gerrard has a hold of it, his knuckles proud and white. Robert watches his face for the pleasure of seeing the drop of his jaw, the way he looks up to make sure Robert is seeing what he's seeing. "He's big." The boy breathes wonder into those words and they freeze in the air.

Robert drinks in every nuance of Gerrard's expression before looking for himself. "Bigger than you imagined?" He experiences a sense of something ancient and majestic. You'd think a beast of its size would lumber, but there is a grace to its slow, ponderous movement. It comes, unhurried, feet testing the road. If Frank's hands are calloused and lined, they are nothing compared with the bull elephant's trunk. It curls back on itself, snake-like, his tusks more weapon-like than Robert remembered.

Only when they are swallowed up in its shadow does Gerrard speak again. "One of his *legs* is bigger than me."

"See!" Robert finds himself pointing. "The animal behind has his tail in its trunk."

"As if they're holding hands!"

It was the same when Robert saw them inside the big top, when the whip snapped up clouds of sawdust and the crowd cheered as the beasts ran in circles.

"You should get an elephant for the gardens."

"I don't think we could have an elephant roaming loose."

"You'd keep it in a cage. Just overnight."

"And in the daytime?"

"Children could have rides on it."

It seems so simple. The idea that you could do that. Robert remembers his father telling him there was once an entire menagerie above a shopping arcade on the Strand. Lions, tigers and a bull elephant called Chunee, all kept in iron cages. But for the occasional roar, the quill-pushers blotting their ink at street level wouldn't have known they were there.

And then, towards the back of the procession, with a second man on horseback bringing up the rear, one of the smaller elephants turns its head towards their conversation, drops the tail of the animal in front and stops. There is a moment when it blinks at them both, takes them in, one species examining another. Robert watches as the boy recognises the beast's intelligence, knowing for the first time that he is part-animal and that the elephant knows this too; realising that the creature in front of him is not just a spectacle, but something that *feels*.

The horse's hooves are restless, but undeterred, the elephant takes a step closer. Robert puts one hand on the boy's shoulder. There's a noise of air being dispelled, a snort rather than a sneeze. Its trunk sways like a second creature, strange and separate. The tip explores the footway, then moves to Gerrard's leg. The boy's shoulder tenses under Robert's grip. He remembers now. Chunee, who'd been so tame he was hired to play various parts on the stage, eventually became violent and had to be shot. In a voice that isn't quite his own, Robert cautions, "Stay as still as you can."

"It tickles." The boy grins up at him, not at all worried, and while Gerrard's head is turned, the trunk crawls to finds his face. The boy looks alarmed, but the elephant breathes in through its trunk, then tucks the end of its trunk inwards, bringing it to its mouth.

"She likes you." The man on horseback kicks his heels and prods the elephant's flank with the iron end of a pole. "Come along, mush, get a move on."

"There were six elephants," Robert tells his daughters, both in identical tartan dresses in a heavy brocade, "all having a lovely time. They have a way of taking in water with their trunks, then using them as hosepipes. They suck up the water and drink, and when they've had enough they offer it to their friends." He looks over the tops of his daughters' heads and sees Freya framed in the doorway. He is smiling as he says, "I was just telling the girls that I've come from the ponds. We saw the circus elephants being watered there."

"So I heard. Girls, could I have a quiet word with your father?"

"Ow," Ida protests, but that's the extent of it. He cannot read Estelle's expression as she files out of the room. Perhaps she wasn't waiting for his return in the way he imagines. Perhaps she's glad to be excused.

Freya turns to close the door and remains there for a moment. While she has her back to Robert, he remembers Gerrard saying, 'When the elephant looked you in the eye, did it feel as if he *recognised* you?' That was exactly how it felt. The thought absorbs him as Freya turns to face him, her chin held high.

"Is everything all right?" he asks.

"No, Robert, everything is not all right."

He waits, because she clearly has more to say. 'What do you think it's like to be an elephant?' Gerrard asked, reminding Robert how he himself once wrestled with such urgent and important questions.

"Annie delivered a letter." Freya thrusts out one hand, in it an envelope. "She tells me your mother plans to go ahead with her Scottish trip in the new year."

Robert tears open the seal, scans the first page. *I will take the West Coast Route as far as Carlisle and then the Glasgow and South Western to Glasgow, where a carriage will meet me. Would it be taxing you too greatly to ask that you accompany me as far as King's Cross?* When Robert had said, 'What could she possibly want with Scotland?' it was not his mother's choice of destination he was questioning. (He has never been tempted himself, having read that it's a country of extremes. Extreme weather, extreme temperaments and extreme beliefs.) It was why she – who wouldn't contemplate his suggestion that she get herself a lapdog because it might want occasional walking – should suddenly take it upon herself to travel the length of the country. And in winter, too! *I am assured that although I will have to purchase several tickets, I need not change trains. It is the locomotives that are changed.* Moreover, the prospect doesn't seem to daunt her.

"How could you?" his wife erupts.

As a reaction to the letter, the explosion is so uncalled for that Robert finds himself on the verge of laughter. "My mother's a grown woman. Why shouldn't she go to Scotland if she wants to?"

Quick colour flares in Freya's cheeks. "I'm not talking about your mother!"

He blinks. The single sheet of the letter sags.

His wife's cheeks may be flushed, but her words are unflustered. "You've barely seen the girls these past few weeks. You haven't so much as asked how they're getting on with their schoolwork, and when you finally give them five minutes of your time, it's to tell them that you've taken someone else's children to see something *they* might have liked to see."

A frown tugs at Robert's forehead. It's ludicrous that he should have to defend himself. "I didn't elect to go on an outing. The hired hands wanted to go and suggested I tagged along. After all their hard work, it would have been churlish to decline."

"Can you hear yourself?" Raising her hands, Freya looks as if she might block her ears with them if she could. "Do you realise how that sounds?"

Robert opens his mouth to speak, but his wife is there first and knows exactly what she wants to say. "You thought the Reynolds boys deserved a reward, but what about your daughters? Do you ever give a thought to how hard they work – in the hope of a word or two of praise from you?"

The truth is that Robert barely thinks of the girls' lessons and pursuits as *work*. In his mind, Ida has only recently progressed from tearing chapters (invariably the last ones) from his mother's novels and scrawling on walls. Her latest preoccupation is the violin, much to his relief – though he may have a change of heart if she can't expand her repertoire beyond *Twinkle Twinkle Little Star*. He would be surprised to learn that Estelle's high school has a chemistry lab.

Any remaining defensiveness ebbs as Freya's anger turns to regret. "If only you'd sent word, I could have brought the girls to join you."

He can't imagine how that would have worked. He doubts Freya would have allowed Ida to join Gerrard and him at the railings or Estelle to join Frank and John at the far side of the pond. And where would Freya have stood? "If you'd let me continue," he forges blithely ahead, and it's a foolish thing to do, a ridiculous tone to take, but he doesn't want his wife to think him uncaring, "you'd have heard me tell the girls that I've bought tickets for the circus."

"For all of us?"

"Of course. We'll go as a family. A pre-Christmas treat." He'll throw money at the problem if he has to.

"When?"

"Tomorrow. I pick up the tickets tonight."

"I thought the circus was moving on tomorrow."

"So it is. I've had to purchase tickets for Cheam, but Abbots will take us and it will feel like more of an outing."

"Tomorrow, then?"

"Tomorrow."

Freya doesn't take her eyes from his as she reaches for the door handle, pulls it towards her and calls, "Girls, you can come back in. Your father has something rather exciting to tell you."

He can see from her glazed expression that she doesn't believe him, but will allow this charade to play out – forcing him to make good his promise.

CHAPTER TEN

JANUARY 1895

London is busy – far busier than Hettie remembers. The concourse at King's Cross is a carnival of noise and movement. Trolleys laden with luggage and mailbags. The smell of freshly baked bread and the less savoury amalgamation of horse-dung and unwashed bodies. *There is nothing to be afraid of,* she tells herself. She has her son by her side. Two decades have passed since the city was struck by garrotte-mania, victims of pickpockets left lying unconscious in the gutter. Two decades since a mother and her two daughters were found dead in a hansom cab, the cabman unaware that his other fare – a gentleman and well-dressed – had poisoned them using a concoction laced with prussic acid. Not to mention the human remains found floating in the Thames inside a carpet bag. Pitiless crimes, and such great indifference to them, except as fuel for newspaper headlines and fodder for street-ballads. Hettie wondered that people could go about their business as if nothing were wrong, while these atrocities played on her mind until she could no longer think straight.

Until something inside her head came apart.

Her husband had gripped both of her hands and looked

her in the eye. 'You *cannot* carry on like this, Hettie. I won't allow it.' It was then that she realised: the colleague Walter had examine her, who'd spent what felt like hours mapping the contours of her skull and measuring the distance between her eyes (whom she'd heard use the word *hysteria*), might have recommended he have her put away. The alternative – the prescription for so many women's maladies – a change of air.

A whistle shrills. A low swoop of wings. Instinctively, Hettie cowers. It is only pigeons, she realises, startled from their steel perches under the glass roof. She's back amidst the clamour, the press and trodden toes of unfamiliars. Who *are* all these people, shoving elbows, shouting about their wares, lifting their toppers?

"This is your platform." Robert speaks at the top of his voice to make himself heard above hundreds of other raised voices. Somehow he grabs the attention of a porter. "Do you have your ticket?"

Does he honestly think she might have lost it? He saw it being written out at the counter. But Hettie pats the reticule hanging from her wrist. "I have it here."

"And you *will* keep an eye on your belongings," he cautions as if she is a person who cannot be trusted to think for herself.

She wonders now what was real, whether she controlled her thoughts, or they her. Didn't she manage to set aside her anxiety after Walter died? It took a supreme effort, but she did it. For Robert's sake.

"You needn't worry." As she turns to her son, her gloved hands somehow collide with his. The awkwardness of trying to make it appear intentional, a slight squeeze, and it comes to her: his tiny hand wrapped fast around her forefinger, stubbornly refusing to let go. How Walter had tried to prise away the delicate digits with their near-transparent fingernails so that she could go down to supper, and she'd said, 'Don't. I'll sit with him a while longer,' because it had been the most precious thing in the world. He was so dear to her, she would have done anything, *anything* to keep him close to her, and safe. "Anything valuable is sewn into my pockets," she says.

The hissing of steam.

"In that case…"

She remembers – how vividly she remembers – kissing each of his dear little toes.

The porter ushers Hettie to a carriage. Two men are already seated. She would be more comfortable in a women's only carriage, or a carriage where other women are present, but cannot see her way to saying so without causing offence.

She nods a greeting. Both men reach for the brims of their hats. The older of the two soon has his newspaper back at full mast. Hettie used to be the sort of woman a man removed a hat for. Increasingly, she feels herself becoming invisible, to men at least. Women still notice. They take note and they judge. *But you can't have it both ways.*

"You'll be more comfortable with your back to the engine, madam." The porter indicates the side the men are occupying and coughs discreetly. The men gather their belongings and move to the seats opposite.

"Much appreciated," Hettie says to her companions. With as little fuss as possible, she settles the dark green tweed of her cloak and travelling dress around her. She risks a glance at the man with the newspaper. *Not even a hat-tip.* He is close enough that she can read the back of his copy of The *Times. We offer false teeth with a 5 year guarantee! Feather bed cleaning and purifying service our speciality.* Here's something. An advertisement for a photo-stereoscopic exhibition. She has read about how they're done. Two photographs are taken from slightly different positions but when viewed through a special instrument, they merge into one, giving a depth of perspective that resembles real life. The exhibition runs until

February. Perhaps on her return journey… Hettie shakes her head to dislodge this stray notion. She's not the type of person who sees a newspaper advertisement and thinks, *yes, I shall*. One cannot change one's nature.

She steals a glance at the other man, who has his leather bag – the kind Walter used to carry – on the seat beside him. (She rather wishes her cases hadn't been stowed on the roof so that she might place them on either side of her.) Hettie feels rather more predisposed towards this second man, who discreetly tucks his pipe into an inside pocket. Perhaps it's not that she's invisible. Perhaps the men would prefer to have smoked. Hettie would have preferred to read her novel – *Lady Audley's Secret* – but fears that she'd be judged, as surely as if she herself was a bigamist, or condoned such behaviour.

"Any person not intending to travel on the train, please disembark now. Please disembark now if you do not intend to travel on the train."

It cannot be helped. This is the carriage the porter showed her to. And better two men than one. The train hisses and shudders and they are moving.

Fifty miles an hour or more. Hettie is hurtling towards her destination. No, she is not the one who is doing it. She is *being* hurtled, leaving behind everything she knows on the long, straight track; at the overcrowded station, in her exchange with her son, whom she dearly loves but cannot reach; in Robert's carriage that delivered them to King's Cross; in Annie's fussing as Hettie bade the girl goodbye at the front door; in the final glancing inventory she took of her parlour, as if she might in the space of a fortnight forget where everything belongs; in the words she said to Fairfax, to whom 'goodbye' means nothing. Is she making a terrible mistake? What does she really know of Scotland? She has read her Henry Buckle, and he has a very low opinion of its inhabitants. A superstitious people, he calls the Scots, who've clung to a belief in witchcraft. Buckle blames the weather. Storms and mists, peals of thunder reverberating from mountain to mountain, echoing on every side. Annie helped her pack, picking out her warmest winter clothes. To travel in spring would have been far more sensible but Hettie knew she would lose her nerve if she delayed. 'I doubt your umbrella will be of much use, ma'am. A strong gust will have it inside out,' Annie said. 'Then I'll leave it with you.' Hettie thrust it at the girl and Annie took a step backwards before reaching for it gingerly, as if expecting it to attack. Thus, Hettie is on her way, without an umbrella, to a place where she has been warned it will rain non-stop.

How can Hettie trust her eyes? At this speed everything in her line of vision swims, shades of blue, green and brown barely taking on forms. It rather reminds her of the time she was hypnotised, the moment before she went under. She'd had so many thoughts running loose inside her head that surrender came as a relief, just as Walter assured her it would. He'd hoped something the hypnotist said would cure her. But Hettie's thoughts woke with her and ran amock, just as before. Now there is the sickly-sweet smell of silage. Her mind travels in strange directions, taking half-remembered routes, stopping at unlikely ports of call. Buried clues blindly claw their way to the surface.

Plunged into sudden darkness, she finds it hard to tell if her eyes are open or shut. Hettie clutches her reticule tighter to her lap. She remembers Walter once telling their son about the construction of tunnels. How two teams of men would work from either end, the idea being that they would meet in the middle. Except it didn't always work out. Sometimes the teams would miss each other. She and her mother used to communicate by much the same method and with similar results. And now the same is happening with Robert, and she has allowed it.

'What did the workmen do when they realised they'd missed?' Robert had asked his father.

'They had to start all over again.'

'And what happened to all of the half-dug tunnels?'

'They're still there.'

A sigh tears its way out of Hettie's chest. Inside her are so many abandoned tunnels she has lost count.

CHAPTER ELEVEN

JANUARY 1895

Robert settles on a blind selection process for his design competition. He has Freya take delivery of the entries, instructing her to number each one, then after the closing date she seals a list of the corresponding names in an envelope.

In the end, Robert selects his winning entry on the strength of the drawings for the buildings. The land he has come to know, but the nature of the structures he might lay foundations for has evaded him. Here they are. A charming T-shaped cottage will sit on a raised area to the left of the gardens: a chimney at its heart, steep roofslopes, dormer windows facing north and south and deep overhanging eaves to offer shelter from the elements. Occupied by a gardener-cum-manager, it will double as his ticket office. There is to be a splendid half-timbered pavilion where refreshments will be served to those watching the tennis, an ornate glasshouse and a wrought-iron aviary. Although the buildings will be set wide apart, common design elements will lend the scheme a symmetry, a flow.

It doesn't yet strike Robert how accurately his vision has been interpreted. The gardens took shape in his mind, and now they are here on the page. A sufficient number of alcoves and arbours to balance the long, straight rose walk. Sculptures placed sometimes in opposition, sometimes in collusion, with the placement seeming to say exactly what he wants it to say. If the designer has added creative flourishes here and there, they are entirely in keeping with Robert's specification.

Satisfied he's made the right choice, he gives the fire a good prod and shovels on a few celebratory lumps of coal, then summons the girls to his study. He means to show Freya he has taken note of what she said about paying his daughters more attention. "I've chosen the winning design," he announces once they are assembled.

"For the gardens?" asks Ida.

"For the *pleasure* gardens," he says. "Here, tell me what you think." An invitation for them to come around to his side of the desk. He remembers the few times his own father allowed him this rare treat; when he sat in Walter's chair, his forearms on Walter's armrests, surveying the doctor's domain. The leather-topped desk, the inkwell, the fine nib of the fountain pen, all at his disposal. How important they made him feel.

Estelle's face is solemn – too solemn, he thinks, for a child her age. She doesn't come first, as is her privilege, but pushes her sister in front, one hand on each shoulder. Her step is heavy as they arrive at Robert's side. She wishes it to be known that she's here under sufferance.

Immediately, Ida has her hands all over the plans, an adventurous fingertip tracing the main path. Robert fights the urge to tell her not to touch. "I should like to live there," she says of the cottage. "Then *all* of this would be mine," she says of the gardens.

"So you approve?" he asks.

Ida nods an emphatic *yes*.

"And you, Estelle, what do you say?"

She shrugs. Her hair has been styled in much the same

way as her mother's, parted at the centre and brushed back from her face. Instead of being piled into a bun, it has been plaited. Two titian ropes hang to her shoulders, each tied with green ribbon. "I haven't seen the others."

He laughs awkwardly. "The decision is already made, I'm afraid."

"Then why ask what I think?"

Sutton High School, with its forward-thinking atmosphere, has instilled in Estelle a greater confidence in her own opinions, but this indifference cuts through him. Freya does not so much as say, *Don't take that tone with your father.* Robert is on his own, his ground uncertain. "I thought you might be interested in finding out which of the gentlemen has won."

"I haven't met any of the gentlemen."

She has made her point. To her, they are just a list of names. Meaningless. The moment that was supposed to be shared has dulled like a pair of spectacles fogged by a breath. Robert turns to his younger daughter: "You'll help me, won't you?" Ida might still polish it with a clean cloth.

A child young enough to want to please, she is owl-eyed. "What do I need to do, Daddy?"

She's still his little girl, hair worn in ringlets, her dress smocked. "The winning design is number six. What you must do," he reaches into his desk drawer and withdraws the sealed envelope, "is open this and read out the name that appears beside the number six."

Ida takes the envelope, her movements reverent. She seems to understand his intention – that they share in the excitement – but struggles to get her small fingers underneath the seal.

He would like to say, 'Here'; to break it himself. Instead, he offers her an exquisitely carved ivory-handled letter opener, something the girls have been warned not to touch, not because they might break it (it is too robust for that), but because of its value. "Perhaps you'd like to borrow this."

"Thank you, Daddy!" Properly equipped, Ida makes short work of the task. She sets the letter opener down where Robert can reach for it and hold it close, then pulls out a folded sheet. "Number six." She hesitates, turning to her sister. "I opened the envelope. Would you like to read out the winner's name? You'll do it so much better than I could."

Robert is touched by the gesture. Ida lives in her sister's shadow. She has so few moments to truly call her own, yet she's prepared to relinquish this one.

"Father didn't ask *me*," Estelle answers spartanly.

Robert detects a wobble in his younger daughter's bottom lip. If what she's been told about the natural order of things is true, then this temporary promotion will have to be paid for. "Number six," she repeats. Her eyes scan the page, finding their destination. "Miss Florence –"

Miss? Robert's forehead furrows.

Suddenly animated, Estelle reaches over her sister's shoulder to pluck the sheet from her hands. "I've changed my mind. I *will* read the name." Ida's expression turns to dismay; her eyes follow the sheet that was to have given her a fleeting moment of glory. "Miss Florence Hoddy." Estelle's expression is triumphant.

The surname is familiar, but surely Oswald was the surveyor? Robert looks to his wife, who is smiling.

"Well, well." The first words Freya has spoken since entering the room. "Eleven entrants and you chose the only woman."

CHAPTER TWELVE

JANUARY 1895

Hettie arrived at the Clachaig in darkness, but standing in the courtyard she felt enveloped by a presence which could only have been the surrounding mountains. After a long day's travelling, she could barely summon the energy to struggle out of her dress and petticoat. It amazed her, as she lay in the sag of a mattress softened by many bodies before her, that one could begin the day in Surrey and end it here, in what she imagined to be a volcanic wilderness.

Now she will see the truth of it. She draws back the curtains, clears the window of its morning fog. She has expected everything to be hewn from rock, but it is neither as dark nor as forbidding as Horatio McCulloch's oil painting – the only image of Glencoe she'd seen. Nor are there peals of thunder reverberating from mountain to mountain, as her guidebook warned. Low in the glen, a heavy mist softens the tumbled edges of crags. Cloud encircles the stark weather-carved creases and wraps itself around castellated crests. It is the mountaintops she looks to now. Snow-capped as they are, they appear to be on the brink of eruption.

Hettie grew up knowing the uncertainty of being the daughter of a young widow, living with whichever relative would take them in, be it Decima's parents or one of her uncles. After her mother's bedtime stories ceased, she told Hettie little more until, towards the end as Decima lay in bed, readying herself to be reunited with Ernest, her tongue was loosened by laudanum. 'The moment I heard that your father hadn't returned from his climb, I drew a line. Nobody – not a soul – knew what it cost me to draw it. There it was, even before they sent his things back to me.'

Hettie swallowed down a queasy feeling. 'What things?' For a moment she imagined that his knapsack had been found.

'Oh, luggage he'd left at the inn where he was staying.'

This came as a relief. Left to their own devices, as Hettie knows only too well, facts have a habit of rearranging themselves.

'I decided there and then that you weren't going to grow up with a grieving widow for a mother. And you didn't, did you?' Decima reached for Hettie's hair, pulled free a strand and wove it between her fingers.

'No,' Hettie stammered, astonished to be hearing such secrets. The truth is that, until she was herself widowed, Hettie didn't give her mother's suffering much thought. The lengths she must have gone to in order to ensure Hettie didn't see her swollen eyes. Tears fell all these years later, and Decima's pain seemed so raw.

It had always been just Hettie and her mother, but Decima made it clear she'd had no intention of living like that. 'The truth is, I was furious with your father. We were supposed to be a family.'

'We *were* a family.'

Decima frowned at this. 'You were meant to have a mother *and* a father. I did the best I could. Mealtimes, bedtimes, routines. And I *tried* to keep him alive for you. I tried to paint pictures.'

Pictures Hettie had done her level best to erase, believing they were something to fear. Her childish understanding was that her parents' story was a love story. As an adult, Hettie realised how very brief their time together had been. Decima married Ernest, bore him a child and was widowed – all within the space of two years. They barely had time to get to know each other, let alone fall *out* of love. If her mother's priority was that Hettie should have a father, she might have remarried, and yet she hadn't. This wasn't something Hettie would ever have dreamed of saying, but realisation ambushed her, something it was possible to voice: 'You didn't climb again.'

'I could hardly have gone off on my own, leaving you to wonder if I was coming back.'

She is here now.

This, then, is the place that enchanted her father away.

After a brisk flannel wash, Hettie pins her hair in place. The white hairs are less inclined to be tamed than the faded copper. She turns to the question of what to wear. The innkeeper's wife, she noticed, wore more than one woollen skirt. She'll wear a second skirt under her tweed. There is no one to tell her she's in danger of looking like a servant. It will be heavier, but at least she'll be protected from the cold.

Downstairs she heads, to find a flickering fire and a place set for breakfast. Her surroundings are rustic, but hardly as uncivilised as people would have had her believe. She holds her hands out to the flames, rubs them together, then takes her seat.

"Ah hope yir no disappointed by the view, Mrs Cooke." The innkeeper's wife sets down an enormous plate of food. Hettie thinks the woman said her name was Aileen, but when they met the hour was late and her accent strong enough for Hettie to wonder if she was speaking another language.

"No, no." At any other time, she might be daunted by the size of the breakfast – sausage, bacon, kidneys, two eggs, and *is that fried bread?* – but she ate little yesterday, fearful that travelling on a full stomach would make her nauseous.

The woman points out of the window. "The mist will hae cleart by the time ye've finished here. The clood, I'm no sae sure aboot. Were ye warm enough last nicht? Comin' fae the sooth ye'll feel the difference."

That last part, Hettie has no trouble in grasping. December in Surrey was mild. Ida brought her yellow primroses she'd found blooming under the hedgerows, but before they had wilted, a steep drop in the temperature delivered freezing fog. "Perhaps another blanket, if you can spare one."

"'Tis nae truckle. Is there anythin' else ah can dae fir ye the noo?"

So much for barbarism and witchcraft, a national character shaped by barren soil and constant warring. "I don't – I don't suppose you keep old guest books?"

"How auld?"

"Going back fifty-four years."

The good woman raises her eyebrows. "Ah'll hae a look aboot, see whit ah can find."

"Thank you."

"And whit're yir plans fae the day? You'll be wanting tae see the waterfalls, ah expect."

Hettie has been mistaken for an ordinary tourist, which is fine. She doesn't want everyone knowing her business. She isn't altogether sure she knows it herself.

Hettie had thought it would be enough to stay in the last place her father had stayed, but after a day by the fire with her guidebook, she finds she wants more. This is the rugged landscape of her family mythology, and somewhere out there is her father. Her mother too, because wasn't Decima here first, with her walking staff and a feather in her hat? Strange – and not a little unfair – how Hettie's father always comes first to her mind, not the mother who was at her side all those years. But Hettie is a woman alone. Alone in a village, a woman is judged. Judged for failing to remarry (Why? What's wrong with her?) Judged for lingering too long in one place. Here – so far, at least – no one has passed judgement. Being alone ought only to mean she has no one to answer to! And so in a pair of stout shoes that haven't seen service for some years, and then only on flagstones, Hettie steps away from the sanctuary of the inn.

Cold – the chill damp feel of it – immediately makes itself known in her upper arms and around her ankles, where fewer layers protect her. A bullying wind funnels up the valley, whipping at her face, carrying pinpricks of sleet in its wake. She holds on to her hat. A short excursion, then. Hettie strikes out on a frost-fringed track, which she takes for a path, but it is difficult not to feel dwarfed by the sheer vastness of her surroundings. Imagine anyone being able to reach such distant summits!

When several nervous sheep give her a wide berth, Hettie reflects that she may well be on a sheep track. One could walk the entire day, she imagines, without meeting someone she might ask. Her guidebook is of little use. What good is it to know about the massacre of the MacDonald clan? She might easily turn an ankle or slip and lie undiscovered for hours. And wouldn't she look a fool?

Defeated and deflated, Hettie hopes to return to her room unseen, but the innkeeper is in the yard chopping a fallen tree, and the inn's entrance is on his far side.

The thing to do is stride past, but to say nothing would be ill-mannered, so she nods and says, "Good day, Mr Imrie."

He looks up from his task. "Guid day, Mrs Cooke. If yir aff travelin, ye'll need a travelin stick." He picks a branch from a pile, discards it; selects another. Holding it upright, he closes one eye and looks at her, then marks the bark with a thumbnail. "Aboot thair shud dae it." His axe makes a clean cut. "Huv a go o' this."

It comes to just below her shoulder. "Perfect." She tries to sound as if she is a person who knows about such things.

"Ah'll jist tak the bark aff." Before Hettie can protest that there's no need, he uses the sharp edge of the axe to start stripping it away. "Ma guid wife tells me ye wuz asking fir auld visitors' books."

"I was, yes."

"May ah ask why?"

"My father was staying here when he met his end."

"Is that right? Whit wuz his name?"

"Ernest Winstanley."

"Mebbie one of the auld boys'll mind um." The pale wood exposed, Mr Imrie runs his hands over it, checking for rough edges, trimming them deftly away. "Shall ah ask?"

Anyone who remembered him would be old by now. But you'd have to be hardy to live in these parts. "That would be most kind."

"Here ye gan." He plants the staff in front of her.

Hettie tries it and finds she is rather pleased. "It's a thing of beauty. Thank you."

"Yir welcome."

"I – I don't suppose… No, not now. You're busy."

"Ask awa'. Ah dinnae bite."

"I wonder, do you have a map I could borrow?"

A second sojourn, then. Hettie locates the path that will take her into the valley, crossing the meandering Coe. Stick to that and even *she* cannot get lost. It is shameful how long Hettie has been cooped up. The same four walls. Her view from the parlour window, dissected into leaded diamonds. Waiting for someone to pass by, so that she might rap on the glass and raise a hand in greeting. Worst of all (what an admission!), she's been her own gaoler.

Consulting the borrowed map, she is unable to locate a peak by the name of Aonach Eagach. "Damnation!" she allows herself. She should have asked Mr Imrie, but she didn't want to admit how poorly prepared she is. Then out of the corner of her eye she sees a blue hare like an apparition, forelegs raised, poised, alert to her unexpected presence.

"*You're* not lost, are you?" *No, and neither am I*, Hettie resolves.

She strays further, planting her staff, crunching through frozen grass. All the while, she looks about, keenly and with wonder, turning full circles to better see how the landscape slots together. What can be responsible for the dark patches that slowly traverse the trough of the valley? *Oh!* Hettie is in her fifth decade, but until this day she hadn't realised: clouds cast shadows!

Her eyes follow pathways up the steep terrain, paths her father might have taken; she tries to memorise the shapes of the peaks, some conical and mossed; others tumbled from stone on which nothing seems to grow. At home, Hettie read Mr Lyell's essay which theorised that the earth is far older than estimated, maybe even hundreds of millions of years old. Seated in her plush velvet armchair, she'd pooh-poohed this as outlandish, but not now. Perhaps some mountains *were* created in an instant by earthquakes and eruptions, but here Hettie senses the work of a gradual, grinding process, the Earth ancient, reaching back into the deepest recesses of time.

"Snaw's comin," says Aileen on Hettie's return. "Wance the road's blocked, ye wilnae be gaun anywhere in a hurry."

Good, she thinks, and the thought surprises her. "Would you have room for me if I need to extend my stay?"

"Plenty o' room. Thir's nae one else comin."

CHAPTER THIRTEEN

FEBRUARY 1895

The prize-giving is arranged, an occasion that must be made the most of. How best to 'talk up' his pleasure gardens is never far from Robert's mind. He had intended for the event to take place at the old chalk pit, imagining a photograph of his wife and daughters, prettily dressed, handing over the cheque. Instead, he's been asked to attend an address opposite the West Street water tower. Like most of the local businessmen, Robert has a tame journalist at the *Sutton and Carshalton Chronicle,* a shrew of a man called Loax who has a taste for mint humbugs which he keeps loose in his coat pocket. He and his photographer agree to meet Robert there, with the photographer's paraphernalia. Robert would have preferred it to be a family occasion – after all, the gardens will offer family entertainment – but Estelle declined, and not even the offer of a new dress could persuade her. Freya has declared that she and Estelle will have an outing of their own. They are to call on a friend who has taken delivery of a two-wheeler bicycle. 'It will be good for the girls to each have the attention of a parent for the afternoon.' *So be it,* thought Robert. Best not to have Estelle's scowl ruining his photograph.

Before setting off with Ida, complimenting her on how ladylike she looks in her coat with its fur collar and matching fur muff, he cannot help but notice that Estelle is wearing a new dress, and her hair, though styled with the same severe parting, is softened by a few curls; a single plait of hair coiled at the nape of her neck. "You look very charming," he says, and doesn't think he says it begrudgingly (in fact he thinks the style of dress inappropriate for a girl of thirteen), but the look Estelle gives him tells him more effectively than any carefully-selected words that she doesn't care for his opinion.

There is only so much ground a man should relinquish in his own home, but Robert holds his tongue. This is one appointment he would not be late for. And the matter needs consideration. Estelle must have had her mother's approval. The dress didn't make itself.

Freya (in the claret-coloured silk velvet and lambswool coat he gave her for Christmas), is busy with Ida, asking if she's had her cod-liver oil.

"Yes, Mother."

"And have you brushed your teeth?"

Ida draws back her lips, exposing her gums and teeth, then opening her mouth and breathing a *hah!*

"That's quite uncalled for," her mother says. "A little modesty wouldn't go amiss."

The house they alight in front of is weatherboarded and painted white, a feature that binds the row of cottages and houses together. Each has a distinct personality, some grand, some far humbler, punctuation marks squeezed between established sentences. The winter rose threaded through the trellised porch is well-established, but the doorknocker is a new addition, fashioned in the shape of a fox, complete with head, front legs, paws and tail. Robert knocks, three distinct raps of brass on brass, at the same time looking down at his daughter. His bones cry out when he sees her gold-flecked eyes, so like Gerrard's.

Though I know not what you are, twinkle, twinkle, little star.

Footsteps and the rattle of a chain. Robert clears his throat. "There's no need to be nervous. Just be yourself."

"I'm not at all nervous," comes her reply.

The door is opened by Oswald Hoddy. "Mr Cooke." He prods the nosepiece of his spectacles. "And you must be Miss Cooke." As he looks beyond them to Loax and the photographer, his smile dissolves. "I didn't realise…"

"I thought the occasion ought to be commemorated," Robert says.

Mr Hoddy glances over his shoulder. "My sister isn't accustomed to being photographed." His voice is low. "Perhaps you'll give her a little time to get used to the idea."

Here is clarity. "So your *sister* is our winner?" Only now that Robert can see the black pinpricks where Mr Hoddy's beard will break through does he acknowledge the direction his thoughts had taken. Had Miss Hoddy attempted to hoodwink him by disguising herself as a man?

"I simply acted as her surveyor. This moment belongs to Florence and Florence alone. Won't you come in?"

He stands aside, pointing the way down a corridor so dark and narrow that their arrival at the rear of the house comes as a violent explosion of light. Robert squints, raising a hand to shield his eyes.

"Hello, Miss Hoddy," he hears Ida say, without waiting for any kind of introduction. "I liked your drawing very much. The cottage especially."

"Oh, I'm so glad!" The voice within the glare is as clear and bright as the bells that summon the faithful to All Saints.

"Was it from a dream?"

Robert wonders that his daughter can see. All he can determine is an outline, someone seated in front of the window, haloed by the low winter sun.

"I don't paint dreams, as far as I know."

That is not quite true. He is beginning to realise that she painted his.

"*I* draw," Ida says.

Robert thinks of the spoiled wallpaper. It seems a boast too far for Ida to call her scribblings 'drawing'.

"And do *you* draw what you see in your dreams?"

"Sometimes I do."

"Isn't it strange that so often we see better with our eyes closed? Logic would have us believe it should be the other way around."

"Have you drawn many gardens before?"

"Only ours."

Robert, who has been blinking back his temporary blindness, finds that the white impressions on his retinas are dulling. When he takes down his shield of slatted fingers, Miss Hoddy's face is turned away from him. It is her neck he notices first, how slender it is, the fine fronds of dark hair escaping their pins.

"It's very pretty." A step closer and Ida's nose will be pressed against the glass.

"It will be prettier still in the summer. If you look, you'll see it has a lot of paths, so that my brother can wheel me about without causing himself an injury."

At the mention of wheels, Robert's eyes flit to Miss Hoddy's rattan bath-chair. *His winner is an invalid.*

"Why does he wheel you about?"

"Because my legs don't work."

Miss Hoddy's legs, he sees, are covered by a tartan rug. Little wonder she left the surveying to her brother. Robert, too, seems unable to move, not even to open his mouth and tell his daughter not to stare.

"What happened to them?"

He can remain silent no longer. "Miss Hoddy, I must

apologise for my daughter's forwardness." His voice is tinged with embarrassed laughter, a father's indulgence.

Ida turns to him, devastation written on her face. She has done exactly as he asked. She has been herself.

Miss Hoddy reaches for Ida's hand, as if she has more of a right to it than he. She gives Robert a bold look. "Why apologise?" A fine face, not pretty – her cheekbones are too pronounced for that, her chin too square – but most certainly handsome. Skin, pale in the way of those who spend their days indoors. Younger than himself at a guess, but old enough to be referred to as a spinster. "It was a perfectly reasonable question." Gently, Miss Hoddy pulls his daughter closer, until she is standing between the chair and the windows, where she tells her, "I had an accident. I was hit by an omnibus and my legs were damaged."

An image rears up at Robert. *Two horses, eyes wild, ears pinned back, whinnying, snorting, panicked. The conductor pitched from his running board into the road.* He prays Ida's imagination is not as vivid as his own.

"Goodness," Ida says, clearly impressed.

"They tell me I was pulled underneath the wheels."

Ought this much be said? Freya would be horrified.

"Did it hurt terribly?" his daughter asks, her expression earnest.

"Actually – and you may find this hard to believe –" Miss Hoddy breaks off to laugh, as if she herself struggles "– I have very little memory of the accident. I was visiting friends in Mile End, that I *do* know." She tells it as if she's relating the story of an everyday outing. "We were to have seen a performance of operatic arias." Miss Hoddy pulls a face and, delighted, Ida giggles. "So I was spared that, I suppose. I remember that a street-vendor was selling Persian Sherbets – I'm rather partial to Persian Sherbets, aren't you? – so I went to cross the road. I wouldn't have stepped out without looking, because I was always most particular about crossing the road."

"The driver took the corner too tightly," Mr Hoddy says so quietly it can only be meant for Robert's ears, though his anger is undisguised.

"There was a flash of green and gold, and I have a distinct memory of looking up and seeing an advertisement for Lipton's Teas. They told me I was unconscious and must have imagined it, but that's what stuck in my mind. Lipton's Teas. I was lucky to keep my legs." She smooths her rug. "They give me no bother. I have no feeling in them."

Ida's eyes are wide. "Nothing at all?"

"Nothing."

"I'm glad they don't hurt. It's a very grand chair you have."

"I call it my chariot. See these handlebars?" Miss Hoddy grips them.

"Yes." Ida basks in the attention.

"My brother Oswald pushes me, but *I* steer."

"Florrie's in charge." Time skips forward a second. *He calls her Florrie.* "Mind you, she always was." There is pride in Mr Hoddy's voice.

If, as her title suggests, Miss Hoddy was unmarried at the time of her accident, the chances are she will remain so. Robert looks about the room. Oswald hasn't mentioned a wife, and there are no signs of children. *So this is how they live.* Brother and sister. Miss Hoddy was painting before their arrival. The evidence is all about. An easel, her palette, various brushes in jars of milky turpentine, squeezed tubes of oil paints. A useful pastime for someone who spends her life sitting down.

Ida is gripping one of the handlebars. "I should like awfully to try it."

"Ida, I hardly think –"

Miss Hoddy cuts across him (it is her house, she may do this). "How's your back today, Oswald?"

Her brother puts his hands to his waist, thumbs pointing to the front of his torso, fingers pressing into the small of his back. "Not too bad, all things considered."

"Strong enough to push one large person and one smaller person?" She pulls her Paisley shawl tighter.

"I should think so." Robert sees Oswald discreetly walk to a side table, wrap his hand around a bottle of blue-pigmented glass and pocket it. *Laudanum.* No doubt he's strained something.

"It's high time I took a turn around the garden. You won't mind sitting on my lap, Miss Ida?"

"If you're sure I won't be too heavy."

"I'd have no way of knowing." Miss Hoddy gives another laugh. "I suppose it's very cold outside."

"Terribly," agrees Ida.

"Be a dear, Oswald, and fetch my hat. The fur one." She returns her gaze to Ida. "That way we'll match. And perhaps I should have another shawl. As for you." Ida again. "We'll have to navigate the steps down to the lawn before you climb aboard."

Believing himself unobserved, Robert turns his attention to the canvas on the easel. It is as if he's looking out of the window. A sidestep, a slight bend of his knees, and Robert identifies the cyclamen from the foreground of the painting by their dusky pink. He transfers his gaze from the real plant to the painting, back and forth – the detail on the variegated heart-shaped leaves is truly remarkable.

"Well, Mr Cooke?"

Caught out, Robert returns to the purpose of their visit. "What of the prize-giving?"

"Do you know?" The smile Miss Hoddy gives him has a curt quality that might even be disappointment. (Should he mention how much he admires her cyclamen?) "I had quite forgotten."

"Oh, but you mustn't," Ida insists. "I've been practising the lines Father wrote for me."

"How clever of you."

"I have them here." Ida tucks one hand inside her fur muff to make sure she hasn't lost her piece of paper. "Sometimes I use my muff as a pocket," she explains.

"I imagine it makes an excellent hiding place."

"Oh, it does! I could give you the prize in your favourite part of the garden."

"That will be by the sundial. It's tucked away in an alcove cut into the hedge, and the hedge is evergreen. I imagine the photographer could make something of that. What say you, Mr Cooke?" She looks at him and he feels that, in that single time-stopping glance, she is taking in all the minute details of his face. "Will that do for the newspapers?"

Robert wants to protest that, had he known, he would never have dreamed of imposing upon her. But what's the use? The competition was a publicity ruse, the prize-giving no different. Even now, Robert's thoughts are straying to how Loax could make something of the story of his mystery winner and her self-sacrificing brother. "That would be fine, I'm sure," he contents himself with saying.

The photographer appears less than certain. His challenge is to control the exposure and the low sun will be in his eyeline. But Robert isn't expecting perfection, just something from which a woodcut can be made.

"Ida." Robert reaches inside the pocket of his sealskin coat. "You had better take the envelope."

She does so with great reverence.

Miss Hoddy watches. "You have an enchanting daughter, Mr Cooke."

"The credit for that goes to Mrs Cooke."

"I'm sure it does."

Crestfallen at this compact summing up, Robert opens his mouth, to say what he isn't sure, but already Oswald is pushing his sister through the French windows. With the bath-chair lined up at the top of the steps, he lays down three planks, one for the front wheel, two more for the back. Down they go. (Little wonder he strained his back.) Ida almost dances with excitement before climbing onto Miss Hoddy's lap. And Robert? Robert is excluded.

"Are those pear trees?" his daughter asks.

"How clever of you to notice, and in winter too. I never minded what kind of house I'd live in, but I always wanted a garden large enough for pear trees."

CHAPTER FOURTEEN

MARCH 1895

By the fireside at the Clachaig, the day's exertions make themselves known in Hettie's hips and knees. She hears her name – her given name – spoken out loud and turns to see two men poring over a map. She glances at their country boots. Trousers tucked inside socks. Mountaineers, the first to arrive since the thaw made the road passable. (It is only these last couple of days that Hettie's been able to venture out again.) And they're talking about tackling the ridge. But one cannot simply approach two strangers, not without knowing who they *are*.

"Are ye a'richt thair, Mrs Cooke?" Aileen stands behind the bar, drying glasses.

"Fine, fine."

"Is it the young gentlemen ye wir wondering aboot?"

"I –"

The innkeeper's wife calls out cheerfully. "Mr Grey, Mr Douglas. Mrs Cooke here hus something she'd lik' tae ask ye."

The men look up from their pots of ale. They are young, Hettie sees. She cannot say how young, exactly. A labourer can look old at twenty, but Mr Grey and Mr Douglas aren't labourers, that much she knows simply from the fact of their being here. One – a clean-shaven young man wearing a pair of small wire-framed spectacles – stands. In Hettie's day, a moustache was considered a sign of manliness. Any man capable of growing facial hair did. "How can we help you, Mrs Cooke?" he asks.

"Gentlemen." When normal rules do not seem to apply, Hettie is unsure how to conduct herself. "Do please sit down, Mr –?"

"Mr Grey. And this is Mr Douglas."

Hettie is struck by the second man. The combination of tousled blond hair and deep brown eyes. "Mr Douglas." She inclines her head.

"Won't you join us?" Already, Mr Grey has pulled out a chair. This isn't what she had intended, not at all, but having disturbed them it would be awkward to refuse, so she sits.

"I couldn't help overhearing. You're planning to tackle Aonach Eagach. Do you know it?"

"This will be my fifth time up there," says Mr Grey.

Mr Douglas attempts to flatten down his hair. "My third."

Something her grandmother said: *a man will pursue a goal relentlessly, while women are more concerned with how their activities affect others.* She will not ask if there is a Mrs Grey or a Mrs Douglas waiting at home. "I'm struggling to get an idea of it from the valley," she says.

"You would, I'm afraid. The ridge doesn't come into view until you've climbed Am Bodach. See here." Hettie tries to memorise the route that Mr Grey traces on his map. From the inn, up the valley, then cutting across the contour lines. "Was there something in particular you wanted to know?"

"It would sound terribly morbid if I were to explain." Already, Hettie understands that the tapestry she wove from a few threads of knowledge is only a shadow of the truth, and she feels – feels very deeply – that she's duped herself. All those wasted years!

"Try us."

Anywhere else and the request might feel like an intrusion, but Hettie senses that here she can be freer with facts, fragmented as they are. Perhaps wild places give a person permission they have never before been granted. "I'm on something of a personal pilgrimage. It's where my father met his end."

Mr Grey's expression falters and it is left to Mr Douglas to say how terribly sorry he is.

"There's really no need. It happened when I was an infant, so I never actually *knew* him." Hettie has been told that he stood a head taller than any other man in the room. That he was a fine baritone. But there is far more she doesn't know. "Mr Imrie has kindly asked around, but anyone who was here then has long gone." She is appalled to find that her eyes are pooling. "I've left it too long."

"Let's start at the beginning. What *do* you know?"

"Only that he set out from here and didn't come back."

"Conditions change so rapidly." Mr Grey's spectacles make him look endearingly earnest. (Perhaps it's also the fact that his upper lip is exposed.) "Even the most experienced mountaineers can be caught out."

"My father knew the terrain. My mother too."

"Your *mother?*"

Decima made so little of her own achievements, although by the time Hettie might have been old enough to take an interest, her mother's memories must have been tainted. "They met on the mountainside. She was on the way down as he was on his way up, so the story goes. I was named after the place and it's taken me all these years to pluck up the courage to visit."

"Well, that settles it," says Mr Grey. "Come with us on the first part of the trail."

"That really is most generous." Hettie finds herself flustered. "But you'd find me terribly slow."

"We'll happily go at your pace. It will be far easier to answer your questions when you can see what we're talking about."

"You're sure I won't inconvenience you?" She puts this to Mr Douglas. He ought to have a say in the matter.

She's surprised to find sympathy in his brown eyes. "Not at all, Mrs Cooke, not at all."

As she steps into the yard the following morning, the skin on Hettie's cheeks tightens. She breathes in the chill, feels its passage down her windpipe and into the bellows of her lungs. Early light flattens the landscape, stripping it of colour. Looking up Hettie sees the moon, pale, but still high in the sky. *How old are you?* she wonders. *Older than the Earth or younger?*

Mr Grey touches the peak of his tweed cap. "Shall we?"

The men's walking poles have pickaxes for heads. The ends of her staff are bluntly sawn-off, but she's glad of it. Were she not there to slow them down, Hettie has no doubt that her companions would be pushing off as if punting in shallow stretches of the Thames, setting the items hanging from their belts clanking like cowbells. Hettie tries to find a little extra speed. "Can you tell me what it's like up there?" Her words fog the crisp thin air.

The men trade glances. Thinking of her father, no doubt.

"Please. Don't censor yourselves on my account." Hettie no longer believes in skulls and bones. Had she come here as a child, she would have realised that her ghoulish conjectures weren't tethered to reality.

Mr Grey begins tentatively. "It's a version of Britain few experience. Our sort are fairly small in number."

"And what sort is that?"

"Those with restless feet."

Hettie muses, "I like that." In that moment, she understands what she wants from this trip. A sense of her father's faint imprint. The trace he left by walking himself into the landscape. She knows not what form it will take – if form is the right word. Spirit or energy might be more appropriate.

"It doesn't take long to gain height; the sky appears to be closer than the earth, and the valley floor is far below." Mr Douglas takes off his cap and smooths down his wayward hair. "The first part of any climb is all about the valley. The greens deepen somehow. You begin to get a sense of how the glacier shaped it."

"Then, as you climb higher, you can see how the waterfalls join together to become the River Coe." Mr Grey plants his walking pole and points out a distant cascade. "Higher still, you can see over the lower mountain ranges and, from there, the view opens up. Layer upon layer upon layer."

As they resume their walk, Hettie falls into a steady rhythm: breath, heartbeat, motion. Each step inside the imprint of one of her father's footsteps. "And the ridge? Exactly how narrow is it?"

Mr Grey holds his hands (the pole in one) about ten inches apart. "Wide enough for your feet but no more, with a nine-hundred foot drop on either side."

Hettie seems to hear it. A skitter of loose rock. Decima might so easily have tripped over the hem of her skirt. *Weren't you terribly afraid?* The question Hettie would put to her mother, were that possible.

Mr Douglas is looking at her, concerned. "Sorry, you did say…"

She checks her feet and finds them still on solid ground. "No, no. Please, do go on."

"I'd only tackle the ridge on a fine day. It's a different beast in mist."

"And if the weather should change while you're up there?"

"The sensible thing is to turn back, but if you're beyond the point of no return…"

The point of no return. Moments pass, during which Hettie listens to the tame sounds of the valley. The metallic clank of her companions' toolbelts. The distant bleat of sheep. "I feel giddy just thinking about it. I don't know that I'll ever truly understand the appeal."

"To be honest, the fear is part of it. The idea that I'm testing myself."

"That I understand, but why repeat the experience?"

"The same reason the Bible tells us Satan took Christ to a mountaintop and showed him all the kingdoms of the world. It's a view like no other."

The Angels' View, thinks Hettie. Not something she's seen for herself – or is ever likely to.

Mr Grey stops and turns. "Come with us. Just high enough to give yourself a view of the valley." From the startled expression on his face, his impulsiveness seems to have surprised even *him*.

"Oh." Hettie looks to Mr Douglas, whose resistance to the idea appears to mirror her own. She's a woman whose feet must be firmly rooted. Accept the invitation and she'll have to rewrite her own history. "I couldn't."

"The path isn't vertical, if that's what you're imagining. The first part is surprisingly gentle."

Mr Grey isn't horned or cloven-footed, but he is a tempter nonetheless, and this seductive landscape is most certainly the wilderness. The pull of it is undeniable. Her mother walked these mountains and one of her new companions seems to think she is capable of doing the same. If Hettie doesn't do it now, she never will. "I will come with you and look at the path," she says.

CHAPTER FIFTEEN

SPRING 1895

"I don't believe it!" Robert says over the top of his letter.

"What?" comes his wife's reply from across the breakfast table.

"My mother's extended her stay in Scotland – again!" At first it was snow that delayed her return, and that was understandable. Were it possible (which he doubts), travel in those conditions would have been ill-advised.

"Does she mention for how long?" Freya pushes a small amount of scrambled egg onto her fork.

"Just that she'll write again when she's settled her plans." Robert is paying rent on a property that, but for a parrot, is standing empty. Not to mention wages to a housemaid whose time is spent mostly on leisure.

Freya dabs the side of her mouth with a napkin. "I doubt it's a journey she'll want to repeat. It makes far more sense for her to stay as long as it takes to conclude whatever business she has."

"You think she's there on some kind of *business?*"

"Honestly, Robert, you can be so *literal*. All I meant was whatever the purpose of her trip is."

Yes. Yes, he can see that. "I just wish she'd let me know."

Had she told him, he could have found tenants. Not one of the women in his circle is behaving as he expects.

Freya inclines her head towards the letter. "She *is* letting you know."

The fact that his wife is right doesn't prevent a fizz of irritation. "I had a mind that when I went to collect her from the train, I would ask her to come and see a shipment of exotic birds." His man has a consignment of ring-necked parakeets. They're most attractive, apparently.

"For your chalk pit?"

It vexes him, the way Freya says it. As close to Robert's heart as the project is, it's also a serious proposition. But, of course, Freya does not *know*. He has not told her. "For the pleasure gardens, yes."

"I have also received a letter." She pushes an envelope across the table. "From your Miss Hoddy."

Robert feels a slight pull in his chest, as if a tiny cog has been turned. He hasn't heard from Miss Hoddy since the prize-giving. Not a word of thanks for the prize money, or the photograph he subsequently sent. It has been difficult not to feel slighted. And now she writes to Freya. "What does she have to say?" he says airily, as if he doesn't care.

"Apparently Ida made quite an impression. She's been invited to join Miss Hoddy to paint. One afternoon a week is the proposal."

"Lessons?"

"Why don't you read it?" Freya nods towards the envelope. Miss Hoddy's elegant cursive is exactly the kind one expects of an artist. "There's no mention of Estelle. It places us in a slightly awkward position."

"Miss Hoddy can hardly be expected to extend an invitation to someone she hasn't *met*." Robert teases a morsel of food from a gap between his teeth. "Besides, it's Ida who's shown an interest. Estelle will understand."

"No one in the parish seems to know much about the Hoddys. I find that strange, don't you?"

"Her brother told me they live very quietly."

"But you must have formed an impression. What sort of a person is she?"

Words come to him. *She's paralysed.* But that is not who Miss Hoddy *is*. Or if it is, then she's much more besides. "I can't say I spent long enough with her to form an opinion." Robert's opinion may be incomplete, but he intends to add to it. At the Hoddy residence, while the rest of the party took another turn of the garden, Robert went back inside and turned the pages of Miss Hoddy's sketchbook – one page, then another. What he saw there, the ordinary everyday things of her scaled-back world, the things she chose to draw and paint, amazed him.

"How old would you say she is?"

"Oh, mid to late twenties."

"And she lives with her brother, whom you already knew?"

"He's a pleasant enough fellow."

"And it's just the two of them?"

Robert thinks himself back to the bright room at the rear of the house, how it has been turned into a miniature garden, almost a glasshouse, the kind of thing a woman would think of. "There must be a housemaid, I imagine."

Freya lays down her cutlery. "Do try, Robert. I need to know how to respond."

"From what I saw, she appears to be a fine artist. And Ida would benefit from any kind of activity that forces her to sit still."

"What I'm asking," Freya looks uncomfortable, as if he's forcing her to say something that shouldn't need to be said, "is if you saw or heard anything that might suggest it would be *inappropriate* to accept."

"I can't think why it would be inappropriate."

In the roll of her eyes is the question, *Must I spell it out for you?* Freya leans towards him to hiss: "Her relationship with *the brother.*"

"I hardly think…" Robert is appalled by what's being insinuated. Oswald is devoted to his sister, but anything beyond that? No. And yet Robert didn't see a housemaid. Perhaps Oswald does perform all of the small ministrations Florence requires – washing, dressing and the like – but that needn't mean anything. He would say it now – *She's paralysed.* Because then Freya would judge that Miss Hoddy must be harmless and her brother a man who has sacrificed his own happiness. But that really would be a betrayal – of both of them. "Why not take Ida and call on Miss Hoddy? See for yourself how the two of them are together."

"Yes, perhaps I shall."

Robert wonders then. Has he said the right thing? If his wife and her circle don't know about Miss Hoddy, it's because she's deliberately kept herself to herself. The offer in this letter is quite a risk. He would not have Freya tell her friends as they sip from delicate china that her daughter visits poor paralysed Miss Hoddy, as if those visits were acts of charity, something Ida should be commended for.

But Ida *is* to be commended, he realises. She met Miss Hoddy while she was seated in her invalid-chair and saw only the artist.

Amid a confusion of emotions, Robert pushes on the table edge to see himself to his feet. "I must be on my way."

"Where to today?"

"The gardens." He stoops to kiss the top of his wife's head.

"It's just that I thought…" He can guess the direction his wife's thoughts have taken, but he waits to hear them. "You haven't been over to Mitcham for weeks." Her voice has an imploring quality.

Robert always resists when told he *ought* to do something.

He aims for a cheerful tone. "What is the point in employing an overseer if I'm forever staring over his shoulder? If I were there, all I would do is agree to Mr Smithers' recommendations."

"So what makes your chalk pit different?"

There it is again! If Freya could see the work that has gone into it, the ingenuity. This week he and Frank lined the basin from which chalk used to be cut, and when Robert mentioned that Neptune would need to stand on a flat surface, Frank sketched out a wooden frame. 'We'll pour concrete into it and allow it to set.' Given the sizable invoice from Farmer and Brindley, Robert is rather regretting that he didn't ask Frank if he knew anything about pipework. The man would most likely have shaken his head but, within half an hour or so, he'd have come up with a workable solution.

That aside, it's a simple enough question. "It's no different," he tells Freya. "I'll get the business up and running, then hire someone to take charge."

CHAPTER SIXTEEN

SPRING 1895

i

Hettie sheds her old skin, discarding it on a mountainside. Not the seductive high ridge that claimed her father, but perhaps the rocky gully where her parents met, Decima coming down as Ernest was going up. Iain (now that they are just two, she has been persuaded to drop 'Mr Grey,' and she is plain Hettie) is as good as his word. He goes at her pace, assuring her that they'll turn back the moment she says so, but the valley reveals itself in more hues of green than names have been invented for, and the rocky layers in an abundance of graduated greys. She has climbed as far as the April snow line, sighted a golden eagle, tasted mountain thyme. Possessed by a childlike desire to declare she's on top of the world, Hettie thinks there *must* be a better way to describe it. Her thoughts take her back to the advertisement for the stereoscopic exhibition – two images taken from slightly different positions which, when viewed through a special eyepiece, merge to create one dynamic image. The landscape has a depth she never knew existed, never *would* have known had she stayed safely in the valley, making gentle forays from the inn. Though Hettie's heart pounds, though she feels flushed when she pauses to take in the view, or to brush the palm of her hand over a moss-covered rock, she quickly recovers, finding herself ready to continue.

"Time to head back?" Iain asks.

"Oh, no!" So determined is she that Iain laughs. Hettie, always so reluctant, has discovered that she too has restless feet. Perhaps here, words are unnecessary. There's a spiritual aspect to walking that she hadn't anticipated. The rocks themselves are possessed of spirit. For the first time in as long as she can remember Hettie is at peace, with herself and her surroundings. Here one can observe the daily rotations of the heavens. It is possible, even, to believe in God.

ii

Seated in the light-filled room at the back of the Hoddys' house, Freya listens to Miss Hoddy making suggestions about Ida's drawing of a blue jug.

"Don't try to force it to be something it doesn't want to be," says the artist.

Ida frowns. "What do you mean?" Exactly what Freya would have asked.

"If you study something long enough and don't try to dictate what you think it ought to say, eventually you'll find it speaks to you. Does that make sense?"

Impatience rises up within her – *for goodness' sake, it's a jug!* But her daughter nods enthusiastically, ringlets bouncing off her shoulders, as if this advice *means* something. Ida sucks on her bottom lip, staring intently at the jug as if it might become something else. Something more, or otherworldly.

Why did no one think to tell her? Freya can hardly blame Ida, but surely it must have crossed Robert's mind. Clearly

Mr Hoddy – who immediately invited her to address him as if they were familiars (she did not reciprocate) – Mr Hoddy expected her to know, because he said nothing. And when he showed them through to the room where Miss Hoddy paints – a well-apportioned room that could be made so much more of were it cleared of clutter – naturally Freya looked to see why their hostess didn't stand to receive them. A discreet glance was all she intended. She took in the bath-chair, the tartan rug covering Miss Hoddy's legs. Perhaps Freya's eyes lingered a moment longer than was seemly, because, when she met Miss Hoddy's gaze, the look Miss Hoddy gave her was almost challenging, and so they have started out on the wrong footing.

Ida, of course, was already under Miss Hoddy's spell. It has been *Miss Hoddy* this and *Miss Hoddy* that since she first met her. It must be said, the pair are entirely natural with one another. Ida is sweetly attentive. She even allows it when Miss Hoddy asks, 'May I?' and makes a new line slightly outside the one Ida has drawn. Were Estelle to do this, she'd never hear the last of it. When they talk, their heads come close together. They express wonder in and laugh at the same things. Occasionally, Ida oversteps – 'When did you know you wouldn't walk again?' – but she always receives a reply. Freya wonders what Miss Hoddy would consider out of bounds. And there, of course, lies the difficulty. One cannot be certain what rules are at play.

The fact is, Freya's blood feels fidgety. Invited to sit, she was effectively excluded, and not only from the conversation. Perhaps she would have declined had she been offered drawing materials, but Miss Hoddy wasn't to know that. Her gaze drifts from the cobwebbed mouldings at the corners of the ceiling down to chaos: squeezed tubes of paint, irregular piles of sketchbooks. How can people live like this?

"Would you care to take a turn around the garden, Mrs Cooke?"

Freya starts. Her palm flattens itself against her breastbone. Under it, her heart is jumping.

"Oh, but you must," her daughter advises. "There's the most beautiful secret spot, just by the sundial."

"Actually, Miss Hoddy," Freya says, not knowing when another cue might present itself. "I think we've taken up quite enough of your time. Ida, if your jug hasn't spoken to you yet, I think we can assume it isn't going to." She cannot say who looks more astonished: Ida or Miss Hoddy. Freya thinks back to what she's just said. Perhaps it was beneath her, but it cannot be undone.

Miss Hoddy is the first to speak. "I assumed, that is to say, I *hoped* that you'd stay for afternoon tea." She turns to smile at Ida, something that simply ought not to be done. "Oswald and I always have a little treat at about four."

"Oh, Mamma, can't we?"

The thing now is to extract herself. "I'm so sorry, your invitation didn't mention refreshments. I'm afraid we're expected elsewhere."

"Another time then." Miss Hoddy reaches for Ida's hand and squeezes it. "You'll come back to see me soon, won't you?"

"I'd like that very much." Ida's voice says that she doesn't know if she's allowed to commit herself; that if she doesn't come again, it will be because her mother has forbidden it.

"My brother will show you out." Miss Hoddy makes no pretence of false cheer. Freya senses that maintaining an expression of neutrality is proving difficult. "Oswald. *Oswald!* Are you there?"

"*Coming!*" He arrives with shirtsleeves rolled up to his elbows. Freya pretends not to notice the dusting of flour on the dark weave of Mr Hoddy's trouser leg, evidence of the sweet buns or jam tarts he's been making.

"Mrs Cooke and Ida are ready to leave."

"So soon?"

"I'm afraid so." Freya reclaims her daughter, circling her shoulder with an arm, pulling her towards her. "Ida, aren't you going to thank Miss Hoddy?"

Ida makes herself small and hunched, the way she does. "Thank you." She is a storm cloud and, once they are alone, she will burst.

"No, thank *you*." There is such reverence in the way Miss Hoddy says it that Freya wonders if she's ever used the words to their full effect. The thanks are entirely for Ida, and the way that Ida's expression calms suggests that this is how they are received.

Outside the garden gate, Ida, who usually has to be reminded not to drag her heels, marches several paces ahead, showing that she knows full well they are not expected elsewhere. It was a lie, and what's more, it was shoddily done. Freya, who is known by almost everyone living in each of the white weatherboarded houses, and thinks she can see curtains twitching, has lost. Ida will never be entirely hers again.

CHAPTER SEVENTEEN

SPRING 1895

i

February's hard frost penetrated deep into the soil, and early March brought a blanket of snow. Finally, it is warm enough to sow grass seed for their lawn, but first they must rid the soil of weeds. The whole area is dug and raked, and chemicals are liberally applied and left to take. Then fertiliser is dug in. Robert's hands blister anew, each pillow of fluid a reminder of why he normally pays people to do work of this kind for him. Finally they scatter the seed, each concentrating on his own area. Within hours, the need for bird scarers becomes apparent. Gerrard runs about, hollering, whooping and flapping his arms.

Robert and Frank stand and watch him.

"I suppose we ought to have some kind of netting," Robert says, but it is a large area to net.

"Ah, the boy can let off steam a while longer."

"Get him a slingshot," suggests John.

ii

Hettie stands in the courtyard outside the Clachaig and hugs herself as Iain supervises the loading of his luggage onto the carriage.

"Well, Mr Grey," she says as he walks towards her.

"Well, Mrs Cooke." Iain's rope is still slung about him. He offers his hand to be shaken, but Hettie does not shake it. She takes it in both of hers.

"I don't know how to thank you."

"It was my pleasure." He smiles, and she likes that there is no moustache to obscure it. "Really."

They stand there, looking at each other.

"If you should ever find yourself in Surrey..." The likelihood of this, Hettie imagines, is slight. This was Iain's last sojourn before he takes up a position as assistant rector in a small parish in the Midlands. Their paths crossed here, in Glencoe. This isn't just farewell. It is goodbye.

"If I do, I suspect I might not find you there."

"Oh, I'll be heading home soon enough." Hettie's old life is waiting, like a threat. The smallness of it, the pettiness. She pictures herself sitting in an armchair with her embroidery sampler, stitching her days together, playing another game of solitaire, the keeper of her hearth, but little more. She will put off her return a little longer. Just a little longer.

iii

Delivery after delivery. Wood, bricks, clay tiles, sand and gravel. Frank opens a hemp sack, shakes his head, says, "Would you credit it? Lime." The bricks have a deep red hue. Frank passes them from hand to hand as if weighing them. He asks the brickmaker where he gets his clay from, how long the bricks have been fired for. Each night after supper, Robert tots up his column of outgoings, double-checks his calculation, arriving at the same figure. The numbers don't lie – he's spent more than he budgeted for, but this is to be his sons' memorial. He won't cut corners.

Even so, the numbers are never far from his mind – numbers are what he's good at. Nor is the fact that Freya is right: he's neglecting his business at Mitcham. It is not a case of *needing* to be there. it is a question of the workers' morale. But Robert resists even his own conscience, telling himself it's important to be here when the foundations for his cottage are poured. And for that, they need a run of dry weather.

Robert keeps a keen eye on The *Times's* meteorological column. Smithers would know. It is Smithers who decides when the skins of the still-ripening seed heads should be scored. A time carefully chosen so that rain and wind won't spoil the milky-white poppy tears before they dry to a brown resin. Each pod scored in shallow upwards strokes, one eighth of an inch apart, three or four times over two to three days. It's a laborious process, all done by hand. No, Robert will not miss the poppy harvest. That gives him a window of two months. *"Wind south south-west to west north-west moderate to fresh, some showers. This may be the best we can hope for."*

Frank is scathing. "Forget your west by north-west. I've worked outside my entire life. I know how to watch the sky."

"And what does the sky tell you?"

After a few moments of pacing, hands behind his back and looking upwards, Frank returns to Robert's side, grins. "That this may be the best we can hope for."

Cement, sand and stone. Robert gives the word and the builders begin to mix.

The walls. Robert will wait until the walls are up. Two shadow-sons are by his side, watching. He tells them things his father told him. How the Egyptians cut stone to build the pyramids. *Quarry workers carved a shallow groove into the stone, then they placed wedges of dry wood into the groove and poured water on the wood. The wood expanded, splitting the stone.*

Gerrard doesn't stand by and watch. He rarely stands still. The boy's curiosity extends to how things are put together. From man to man he goes, wanting to know how their jobs are done, tilting his face in concentration as they demonstrate. To an outsider (or an interloper like Robert) the process looks crude. There is no automation. Wood, cut into equal lengths, is raised by hand. The workmen's shouts rise high above the sound of passing trains, and two days later the house has its framework, ready to be faced with brick. The builders try Gerrard with a hod and see how many he can carry. After a growth spurt the boy is several inches taller, his limbs reed-like and angular. What Robert assumed would cause Gerrard an injury simply makes him stagger, and when Gerrard staggers the foreman puts a stop to it. "I don't want any breakages!" He unloads the hod, brick by brick. "You! Let me show you how a wall's put together. In each course, we alternate the headers and stretchers, see?"

Beside Robert, Frank comes to a standstill. "The grass has taken nicely. You might want to be thinking about one o' those mowing machines." He inspects and then sucks on a thumb. "Absolute buggers, those roses. They'll look a treat when they're trained over the arches, mind." Then Frank nods towards the bricklayers: "Flemish bond."

Robert assumes it's the mortar he's talking about. (The lime is for the mortar, that much he does know.)

"I've decided I'm going to be a builder," Gerrard announces, his hands and the sleeves of his jacket ruddy with brick-dust.

His brother is scathing. "It was a train driver yesterday."

"Don't you discourage him. It's a good trade, son." Frank whips off Gerrard's cap and ruffles his hair. "A man needs a trade."

Might I have been happier working with my hands? Robert wonders. But a man who works with his hands – even someone like Frank, who can see dimensions in his head – is irredeemably working class.

Frank continues to watch the builders. "What will you do once the gardens are open?" he asks. "Manage them yourself or have someone do it for you?"

"My wife has appointed herself president of the tennis club. As for the rest…" It's the question Robert has avoided. "Would you be interested in staying on?"

"I'd have to think on it."

"Of course."

"I could be a kind of caretaker, keeping the gardens looking tidy, seeing to repairs, and I can do sums in my head quick as anything. Only thing is… I don't write so well."

"How about the boys?"

"They write. But," he looks straight ahead, "I couldn't tell you what any of it says."

Frank doesn't read. Of course he doesn't. He asked Robert to read details of the stakes for the horse-racing.

"Gerrard!" Robert calls and the boy comes running. Robert reaches into an inside pocket and retrieves his notebook and a pencil-stub. "Would you write a note to remind me to order more sand?"

The boy looks from Robert to his father and back again. "You want me to write you a note?"

"Don't answer back. Mr Cooke's told you to do something, now do it."

The boy takes the notebook and pencil. He squats down so that he can rest the notebook on a knee. Scores a line after the last entry. "How much are you after?"

"Two of the large sacks."

Robert accepts the notebook back. *I could just go and place an order for you,* he reads to himself. *I would only be gone for half an hour.* Gerrard's no fool, that's for sure.

"That's it?" the boy asks.

"That's all for now."

"Well?" Frank asks.

"Between them, I'm sure John and Gerrard could deal with the takings."

"Now Mrs Reynolds, she might be open to helping out with the refreshments. Course, it might help if the caretaker actually lived on site. In case there's an emergency."

"You'd like to move into the cottage?"

"I'd need to give notice on ours."

"You might want to wait and see it finished. Mrs Reynolds might not think it suitable."

"She'll think it's suitable, don't you worry."

That evening Robert tells Freya, "I've decided to take Mr Reynolds on as a caretaker."

"Oh, I *am* glad." She pulls him into an embrace. "Now your poor hands will have a chance to heal."

He'll wait and see Neptune craned into position. The fountain will be Robert's showpiece. It is important that he's here to see it switched on.

Fortified by brandy, Robert spends his evenings playing around with slogans, attempting to capture the essence of what he hopes the gardens might come to mean to others. Everyone deserves beauty, the time to pause and dream a little. Again and again, an image of Adam and Eve presents itself. The world's first outcasts, arriving, the wrought-iron gates flung open in welcome. *Cast your cares away.* Not quite. *Cast away your cares at Cooke's.* Better. Smithers writes that the poppies seem set to do well again. If the weather carries on as it is, they should flower in early June. He's had the usual enquiry from Ballantyne about first refusal, and buyers are lined up for the seeds and the oil. They could go to auction but why upset regular customers, especially such reliable payers. Why indeed?

Approached via a broad, verdant expanse and a stepped path, the cottage stands alone, to the left of centre of the gardens. As Robert surveys the scene, it strikes him how right it looks. He stands under the eaves and flattens his hands to the brick walls – solid and true, he has made them a reality. He cranes his neck to better examine the wooden struts, each exactly as it ought to be. It isn't just that the building is perfectly proportioned, though that must be part of it. From the sheltered porch with its black and white tiles – perhaps a bench should go here – he can visualise the rest; the tennis courts are already marked out, the concrete slab on which the pavilion will sit has been poured. And there is the beginning of the path that will meander through the alders and oaks, where his Thomas and his Gerrard will stumble on hidden sculptures.

"Mr Cooke?"

Caught up in thought, Robert hadn't heard anyone approach. The speaker is a woman in middle age. His first impression is that there's something of Mrs Dwyer about her. "Good day to you, madam."

"Mr Reynolds said I might take a look inside."

"Am I speaking to Mrs Reynolds?"

"For my sins. That is, being Mrs Reynolds, not speaking to you." She's endearingly nervous.

He alters his view of Frank to accommodate the person standing in front of him. "I'm delighted to meet you at long last. Shall I show you around?"

"Thank you all the same, but I doubt I can get lost."

Now he's seen her for himself, Robert is in no doubt as to who makes the domestic decisions. A man who spends his evenings in taverns and has a taste for the horses needs a wife who is both enterprising and thrifty. "Be my guest." An afterthought. "Tell me. Have the Reynolds family ever lived on this land before?"

"Mr Reynolds has slept off a few hangovers in the coal shed in his time." She colours. "I prob'ly shouldn't tell you that, you being his boss."

Robert smiles at her indiscretion. "From what I remember of his brothers, I doubt he was the only one." Yes, he decides, she'll be an asset.

CHAPTER EIGHTEEN

MAY 1895

Robert checks his watch. His consignment of parakeets will arrive by train not an hour from now. The birds are Indian, supposedly, though he suspects his birds have never seen the sub-continent. Robert can still remember goldfish being considered foreign. Mrs Dwyer was always most particular about calling them *Chinese* goldfish, even when several British generations were swimming in the Wandle.

For once, Estelle shows an interest, asking, "When do you collect them?"

"They'll be on the quarter past nine train." The thought amuses him. "I can make something of that. *From India by ship, from London by train.* What do you think?"

Estelle wrinkles her nose; shakes her head.

"I'll work on it. Why don't you come with me?"

She turns to her mother. "Can I?"

"I don't see why not. Your piano lesson isn't until eleven o'clock."

"Both of you girls," Robert is quick to add. Ida shouldn't be left out.

Freya raises her eyebrows, pretends to be put out. "Am I not included in the invitation?"

"I thought this was your day for church flowers."

"They'll have to manage without me. Gloves and bonnets, girls!"

Robert had no idea that flower arranging was something that could be dropped. Ridiculous though it seems, he hasn't told Freya that one of Frank's lads is called Gerrard. The right moment hasn't presented itself. What to do? He has promised the Reynolds boys that they can see the parakeets into their new home. Formal introductions may not be called for, but he can hardly avoid calling Gerrard by his name.

Or can he?

His wife's mood is light, a little rebellious, as they set out. He and Freya sit facing the horses. "I don't imagine you counted on so large a party," she says.

"At this rate, there'll be no room for my cargo." This excuse, at least, has the advantage of being true. "You may find yourselves walking back home, I'm afraid."

Opposite, Estelle and Ida rock side by side.

"Why should *we* walk? The parakeets can fly!" Ida's left hand is gloveless. Robert notices how she tries to hide it as if it, and not she, is in disgrace.

Freya smiles. Is he worrying unnecessarily? For all Robert knows, one of her friends' sons is called Gerrard and she has found her own way of coping.

"I can carry a cage on my lap." Ida smooths out her skirt, forgetting herself for a moment. (To be out in public with only one glove!)

"You'd be swamped." Robert turns from his daughter to his wife. "And I've no idea how clean the cages will be." He winces.

"In that case, girls, we'll do as your father suggests."

Robert feels his shoulder muscles relax. He *will* tell her. Later today, he'll tell her.

But Ida is not finished. "The cages will be small. Birds come in pairs."

"Not all of them," Estelle corrects her. "Fairfax doesn't."

"Fairfax is different. He's a parrot." Ida looks devilish as she hunkers down in her seat. "Besides, he *has* a pair. He has Grandma."

"Small or large," her mother says curtly, "if the cages are dirty, I don't want you touching them. Now, sit up straight, Ida. And don't think I haven't noticed."

"When is Grandma coming home?" Estelle asks. Robert wonders if by changing the subject she is trying to deflect attention from her sister and her missing glove, or if she knows his mother's extended absence is a sore point and wishes to pick at a scab.

"Soon," he says, though her letters haven't been specific, and when he called on Annie to see if she'd heard (he was passing and has every right, since he pays both the rent and her wages), the girl was no better informed than he. He fears he may have been sharp with her, a by-product of his frustration. That and the feeling she was not alone in the house.

As the carriage makes its final steep approach and sways to a halt, a train can be heard pulling away from the station.

"We've missed it!" Ida laments, as her opportunity to wave to the driver disappears in a flurry of steam.

Robert sits forward in his seat. "That's because you made me late."

"Never mind," Freya says. "At least we won't have to stand about waiting."

The engine's hiss gives way to a contrasting sound: squawking, high-pitched and competitive.

"Goodness," Freya looks alarmed, "Is that –?"

Goodness, indeed! No wonder the birds were so reasonably priced.

Estelle smirks. "It sounds like Ida practising her violin."

"That's unworthy of you," chides her mother, but Robert detects a slight glint of conspiracy.

Ida responds by nudging her sister with the toe of a boot.

"We'll have no more of that, young lady." Freya wags a finger.

Robert alights, then reaches up to assist his wife and daughters, in that order. In her impatience Ida hurls herself into his arms. "What about your mother?" Words are wasted. The minute he sets Ida down, she runs through the gate in the picket fence and onto the platform.

Freya will not raise her voice, not in public. "That child must learn, she can't just go hurtling off!" She lowers her voice further. "I *had* hoped that school might instil a little discipline in her. Benfleet Hall was so good for Estelle."

Boys are never criticised for having high spirits, Robert thinks. But it strikes him: his high-spirited sons live only in his imagination. The truth is, he has few memories of the boys. The loss was not of Thomas and Gerrard's histories, which were painfully short, but of their futures, and that loss will fill all the days of Robert's life.

He forces a smile. "It's not every day that a consignment of parakeets arrives." But as he sees his wife safely down Robert grimaces. "Good God, the noise. It's relentless."

Finally comes Estelle, reluctant to have her hand held by her father. Robert cups the underside of her elbow. Only once does her weight come to lean on him before her feet find the footway.

Mr Kedge, the stationmaster, touches the brim of his cap. He's a man who never looks entirely at ease in uniform. Today the wings of his collar are adrift. "Special delivery?"

"I'll have them out of your way in no time," Robert says with some embarrassment. If anything, the racket is louder still.

There is merriment in Freya's eyes as she tucks her hand inside his right elbow. "I'm sure they'll settle once they're in their new home."

He is almost ready to laugh at himself, if only to uphold the pretence that his purchase isn't a disaster. "I'd hoped they might sing!"

Their heads are close, close enough that he can feel the brush of her breath on his earlobe. "Ida plans to teach them to talk."

The cages are rectangular, three of them, neatly stacked. Not the gleaming cages of Robert's trip up to the city, they are a little rusted and sorry looking. While in transit, they had a covering of dark cloth that has seen better days (no doubt giving the birds an impression of dusk rather than night). The boy who accompanied them from the dealer has folded it back so that Robert can inspect his purchase. Drunk on daylight, his parakeets are encouraged by the sight of treetops into small forays – they cannot quite be called flights. He begins to count: there should be four birds to a cage. When they realise their way is barred, the parakeets move about by beak and claw, just as his mother's parrot does.

"They're pretty enough," his wife remarks to the boy. "What kind of green do you call this?"

He tugs off his cap and holds it behind his back. "Lime, madam. Like the fruit."

"I don't think I've ever seen a lime."

"Well..." There is something of the birds' restlessness about him, as if he too would fly away if he could. "That is the colour. In my country, very great number. It is quite a sight when a flock streaks across the sky."

"Imagine the racket a flock makes!" says Freya.

Ida is using her gloved forefinger as a counter.

"Do you make it twelve?" Robert asks. He himself, has only managed eleven. The darned things refuse to stay still.

"All present and correct, sah!" she says.

'Enthusiastic breeders,' the seller called them. 'You won't need more than a dozen, allowing for a couple of casualties, though they'll happily survive a British winter. They can live up to thirty years.' *They may outlive me.* 'And I'll throw in a month's supply of seed to sweeten the deal.'

"And this is the feed?" Robert grabs hold of one of the two jute sacks.

"Allow me, sir." The boy unties the sack and holds it open so that Robert can dig inside. He lets a handful run through his fingers. It is seed, certainly. More than that, he can only hazard a guess.

The infernal squawking! Perhaps Gerrard's suggestion of an elephant would have been wiser. There is no rule that says the larger the animal, the more trouble it will be.

His wife startles: "What did you say?"

Robert looks at Freya's parted lips, sees the way she clutches her parasol and his heart stutters. "I beg your pardon?"

"You mentioned an elephant." In her eyes, his slip is reflected back at him. He mentioned more than an elephant.

"Simply that caring for one large animal might be no more ridiculous an idea than caring for a dozen parakeets."

Ida is up on tiptoes in her excitement. "You haven't bought an elephant, have you, Daddy?"

But his wife, his wife looks away.

CHAPTER NINETEEN

JUNE 1895

The blunt sounds of the woodcarver's mallet can be heard all over the site. Robert's shadow-sons will have their green men, their Pan, their Puck. Frank is now constructing the bandstand. ("I built the coal shed when I was still a boy. How hard can it be?") With his lips pressed around a row of nails, a hammer in hand, he kneels on the roof and picks out the next terracotta tile. The glasshouse is filled with palms, ferns and potted citrus trees. There is no flash of insight. It is a gradual dawning as the gardens take shape. No one could have drawn Robert's vision exactly as he'd imagined it unless they'd seen inside him, seen him for who he really is. And yet Miss Hoddy didn't meet him until *after* she submitted her design – and he's far from certain that the impression he created was favourable. It remains a conundrum, a riddle that refuses to be solved. Robert must know more about this woman who sees with such clarity but has no difficulty in painting herself out of the picture. He will call on Miss Hoddy and invite her to see what he's made of her design.

His hat is in his hands. "I wanted to enquire how Ida's visits are going."

Miss Hoddy – there is no invitation to call her Florence – is at her easel. She doesn't set aside her brush. She wasn't sitting here idly, waiting for him – or anyone else – to call. She doesn't ask, *You don't mind? Won't you take a seat?* Instead she weighs each of Robert's words: "To enquire how Ida's visits are going."

Repeated back to him, they sound ridiculous. "Exactly," he says.

"You didn't think to ask *Mrs* Cooke?" Miss Hoddy angles her head; closes one eye and uses her brush to take a measurement. Robert is very aware of the nape of her neck; the soft wisps of hair that refuse to be tamed. "If I stop, the light will change and the piece will be ruined." Without turning her head, she has read his mind. Freya calls Florence *your Miss Hoddy*, but this woman is so entirely her own person, it's impossible to imagine her belonging to anyone.

He looks out to the garden, finds the shaft of light, sees how it is interrupted by the branches of a pear tree. Already she has the tree and the box hedge, and there – there is the sundial. (The scene comes back to him, the prize-giving, Miss Hoddy choosing to look at Ida rather than the camera.) With only a few fine brushstrokes she captures the slant of the rays. Light, filtered through leaves, dissected by branches. Perhaps, Robert thinks, it will never fall this way again. "Don't stop on my account." He stands hat in hand until it seems more awkward not to speak than to say something. "Ida seems to be enjoying herself," he ventures.

With just the slightest sound from the back of her throat, Florence adds a dab more white to the yellow ochre she's been using. Such subtlety. The light on the canvas is as real as the light in the garden but, come sunset, the canvas will not fade.

"How would you feel if I were to ask Ida to sit for me?"

Air forces itself through Robert's nostrils.

"The idea amuses you?" She glances at him, the briefest moment, catching him smiling and uncouth.

"The idea that Ida might be persuaded to sit still." Would it be acceptable to put his hat down? Miss Hoddy can hardly object if he puts down his hat. He clears his throat. "That sounds like something Mrs Cooke would want to be consulted about."

"Your wife doesn't like me." She doesn't look at him. Apparently she has no interest in seeing how her words land.

"Does she not?" Robert, too, has sensed this.

"No." Miss Hoddy is matter-of-fact, not seeming to care one way or the other, or caring only for her painting.

"I don't think she likes me terribly much either." He is thinking of how he said to Freya, 'It isn't the boy's fault.'

How her lips tightened and she avoided looking at him. 'No one is suggesting that it is.'

'I can't not call him by his name.'

When he went to put his hands on her shoulders, she shrugged him off. 'No. No you can't.'

'Tell me what to do.' But she didn't have an answer, and still he is not forgiven. They live their lives edging around things that cannot be said, the hurt emerging occasionally, unable to comfort each other.

"She doesn't like your *project*."

This observation brings Robert back to the moment. That Miss Hoddy would put it so bluntly takes his breath away. "Did she say so?"

"She didn't need to. Also," she looks about her, "she disapproved of my room." This judgement, as something *earned,* appears to please her.

"With or without saying so?"

"Without. She *glared* at my clutter."

"Ah," he says. "Mrs Cooke has perfected the disapproving

glare. I give her plenty of cause for practice." If it is a betrayal it is surely a small one, intended only to lighten the mood.

"Why are you *really* here, Mr Cooke?" The finest of brush-strokes, dragging rather than painting. What was opaque becomes translucent.

"I've been meaning to call on you."

"Then this is a *social* visit!"

"I wondered if you might like to come and see what I – that is to say, *we* – have made of your design. I thought you might have some final suggestions."

"So it's my professional eye you're after?" A darker shade now. Robert sees that this is what was missing. All that was missing.

"Yes." He has been moving the brim of his hat through his hands the way the parakeets navigate the bars of the aviary. "I mean no. No."

"You weren't thinking of inviting a photographer or two?"

Robert cringes to think back at his presumption. But to have put a stop to it, to have said, 'Perhaps we don't need a photograph after all.' What would that have implied? "Just you. And your brother if he'd like to."

"How are the paths?"

"Very flat. You might," he suggests, intending to be gener-ous, "like to bring your easel."

"This is my view of the world." Her voice is severe, as if she's repeating something she has been told over and over again and has begrudgingly accepted. "*This* is what I paint."

"Of course," Robert says, though he thinks her quite wrong.

"You think me accepting." She says it plainly and with great dignity. "I've had to reckon with the loss of the life that used to exist for me."

There is no reply Robert can give, so he bows his head and says nothing.

"Ida tells me that your parakeets make quite a racket." Her voice is transformed, as if his daughter's name makes all the difference.

He clears his throat. "Worse than peacocks."

"Will you speak to your wife about Ida? I wouldn't paint her face. I can see how Mrs Cooke might object to having her daughter's portrait hanging on someone else's wall."

"You sell your work?"

She turns to him, eyes ablaze. "How else do you think we live? Charity? A rich benefactor?"

"I –" He feels himself turned inside out. Miss Hoddy is not accepting. She is provocative, defiant. It would be vulgar to ask – indeed, it's none of his business – but Robert hopes the prize money has made a small difference to their circumstances.

She (*Florrie, Florence, Miss Hoddy,* he's confused how he ought to think of her) doesn't expect a reply. The corners of her mouth curl into a smile. "You thought my painting was a nice little pastime, didn't you?"

She has him. He'd admired her work. Known it to be good. No, *good* sounds so patronising. Here, in front of her easel, Miss Hoddy isn't crippled. (Is there no better word than that?) She has all the movement she needs. What Robert means – what he *really* means – is that her work wouldn't look out of place in the Royal Academy. Not that the Royal Academy admits lady members. They prefer battlefields to botanicals.

"The view would be of Ida's back. I would have her at play. Perhaps here." She points with the fine bristles of her brush to the left of her canvas, leaving the tiniest dab of yellow in the grass. A buttercup.

"It's for *this* painting?" Freya will know about the society for female artists. She went to one of their annual exhibitions. Robert makes a mental note to ask, then perhaps he can make a suggestion that might actually be of use.

"A commission. From a Mrs Griffiths." Miss Hoddy says the name as if it is caught between her front teeth.

"I know her." One of Freya's circle. Church flowers and parlour-gossip.

"She wanted something green. To match her wallpaper." Miss Hoddy adds another rebellious touch of yellow. Now he sees. They aren't buttercups. Mrs Griffiths' verdant lawn is to be blighted with dandelions. "You know, arsenic is used in the compounds that give green wallpaper its colour."

"And poppy juice in paint."

"Really?"

He is pleased to have finally impressed her. "I wonder, would you consider a small commission from me? It wouldn't be a painting."

"What would it be?"

Easier by far to show her his sketches than to attempt an explanation. He digs in his pocket and pulls out his notebook, opening it to a double page. "A design for a bill-poster to advertise our Grand Opening." He is rather afraid she will ridicule his attempt.

"Mr Cooke?" She nods at the notebook in his hand.

"Oh, yes." Robert shifts his weight from one foot to the other, more nervous than he ever was handing in an exam paper. Miss Hoddy raises her eyebrows, but they settle again.

"You see how much in need of help I am."

"You might have recruited Ida, but the couple are clearly Adam and Eve, and these are the gates of the gardens. Can I ask what message you're trying to convey?"

"In what way?"

"In all the obvious ways! Are you coming down on the side of the creationists? And if not, are you mocking them? Or is it that the gardens are intended for sinners? Because from what I've heard about your Reverend Mears, I can't imagine that would please him."

Robert can hardly tell her he'd thought to create an Eden, so that his shadow-sons have somewhere to play. He swallows. "Can't it simply say that the gardens offer the community a taste of Paradise?"

She appears to consider this, then hands the notebook back. "This isn't the kind of work I usually take on."

"Your name need not appear."

"And it's difficult to estimate the expense because I have no idea how long it will take me to get right. You might be better off making enquiries elsewhere."

"I won't quibble over your bill, if that's your concern."

"How long would I have?"

"A month."

She eyes him. "You'll speak to Mrs Cooke about Ida?"

"I will."

"In that case, I'd better accept your invitation to come to see the gardens. When will they be least busy?"

CHAPTER TWENTY

JUNE 1895

"If the gardens are intended for everyone, the Grand Opening should be on a Sunday." Mrs Reynolds settles her expression. "Not everyone gets their Saturday afternoons off."

Seated in the pavilion, they are sampling a selection of Mrs Reynolds' cakes. Freya didn't think she'd be able to bear the heat from the kitchen range, and it would have been presumptuous to suggest they use the parlour. Besides, it's easier to discuss how the pavilion will be laid out when they can see the space they have to work with.

"Take my Dulcie. She finishes work at two, but she must have a note from me if she's to come home for the weekend." Mrs Reynolds removes the fly-cover from a plate of sticky buns. "Try these and see what you think."

To watch Freya contemplate eating is to be aware of every instruction she was ever given as a child. *Show a little restraint, Freya. One should never give the impression that one is starving.* "Would you mind cutting me a piece?"

Mrs Reynolds places her knife.

Freya winces. "Smaller, if you don't mind. But a Sunday won't suit everyone." She takes a slice of the bun, placing it on her plate. "Our girls have Sunday School."

In private, Freya has expressed her view. She doesn't see how they can attract the *right* sort of people if they admit *everyone*. Admission by invitation was her proposal, but Robert needs bread-and-butter customers. 'That's why there's an entrance fee,' he explained, though he cannot deny a feeling of betrayal. He created this place for his sons, and now the gates will be opened to the public. To Freya, he says, "I think the girls could be allowed to miss a week."

"In that case, it might be a kindness to have a word with Mrs Mears."

It won't be well-received. The Reverend is fond of reminding his congregation that no one can serve both God and Mammon. "Tell me, Mrs Reynolds," he says. "What would you think of if I were to mention Adam and Eve?"

"Now you've put me on the spot."

"Please," Robert persists. "I'd like to hear what you have to say."

She looks uncertain. "I'd have to say the Garden of Eden."

"Anything else?"

"Well, there's the story about the apple, obviously."

"The fall of man!" Freya says. "*That* will be the Reverend's objection, if he objects at all. But, really, I don't see *why* he would. We're offering an alternative to the taverns." Freya appears to consider the subject closed. "Tell us more about your daughter, Mrs Reynolds. What does she do?"

Mrs Reynolds presents the plate of buns to Robert. "Dulcie's done ever so well. She has a position at Peter Robinson's."

"My mother used to take me." He reaches for the nearest piece of bun. "I liked to watch the miniature railway running overhead, carrying change for the tills."

Freya picks up her morsel between finger and thumb. "You must be terribly proud of her."

Mrs Reynolds stands back and waits for their verdicts.

"Very light, but the icing…" Freya wrinkles her nose. "It's a little sweet for my palate, I'm afraid."

"I was thinking of the children."

"Oh, in that case…"

Mrs Reynolds looks to Robert, who says, "I rather like the icing. Is that lemon I can taste?"

Visibly cheered, Mrs Reynolds offers him the plate again. "Finish it. It will only go to waste."

Next comes ginger cake. Pre-empting a request from Freya, Mrs Reynolds cuts it into dainty triangles.

"Now that is… Oh, that's awfully good. Do try it, Robert. And your daughter, she lives in?"

"All of the staff do. They're ever so strict. Of course, we don't see her as often as we'd like, but that's the way of things. Young people have their own lives, don't they?"

Dark treacle, spiced molasses and rich. "Mmm." Both women wait for him to swallow so that they can hear what he has to say. "Delicious," he mumbles.

Freya turns to Mrs Reynolds. "Then that's settled. Buns for the children, ginger cake, and we must have scones."

"Plain or fruit?"

"Plain, but with cream and jam."

"I have just the thing. Two dozen jars made from last year's blackberries."

"I rather think it ought to be strawberry," says Freya. "My sisters are so very fond of strawberry. They'll be coming all the way from Leeds."

Robert finds himself in the role of peacemaker. "Why not give people the choice?"

"Blackberry and strawberry," says Mrs Reynolds, but then Freya has the final word.

"If there's to be a choice, perhaps we should also have apricot?"

Smithers writes that the poppies are an impressive sight should Robert care to view them. *Heads as big as a man's fist.* The challenge now is to harvest the resin before the crows make off with the seed heads. Robert dips his nib in the ink, writes: *If conditions are favourable, do not delay on my account.* He agrees to Smithers' estimates of the number of extra hands needed, the same rate as last year, scarers included – *purchase more clappers if needs be* – and asks to be informed of any labour shortages, though this is unlikely. The gypsies migrate to Mitcham for their annual fair and remain for summer work. The poppy harvest is labour-intensive, but nothing is wasted. First the resin scraped from the seed head is bundled into balls and wrapped to prevent drying. Then the seeds are harvested and cold-pressed to extract oil or sold as a raw ingredient. Once the resin and the seeds have been extracted, what's left of the head and stalk – the straw – is crushed, powdered and sold as poppy tea. Every part of the plant has its use.

Personal invitations go out to the select few, embossed and printed on good card. Armed with brushes and buckets, John and Gerrard are instructed to paste bill-posters on any flat surface they can find. "Cover whatever's there already, if necessary." The boys make the most of what, to them, is a small rebellion. At Gerrard's insistence, Robert goes to see what they've done for him at the railway station. "Mr Kedge didn't even come out to ask what we were up to!"

There is barely a brick on the bridge, neither the straight outsides nor the curved inside, that hasn't been plastered with Adam and Eve, their modesty covered by roses and ferns, Miss Hoddy's trees, her parakeets. Miss Hoddy told him hers isn't the first depiction of Adam and Eve to feature members of the parrot family.

'Their call was thought to sound like *Eva-Ave* —Eve and Ave Maria.'

'Without meaning to contradict you, I doubt you could find an unholier racket than our parakeets.'

Robert wanted a bold statement, and now he has one. Miss Hoddy can distance herself from her artwork, but he cannot. His name is writ large for all to see. He thinks better of venturing closer. That way, if Mr Kedge asks if the display was his doing, he can claim ignorance and offer to take the posters down immediately.

The final week, the Reynolds boys traipse from door to door and shop to shop with handbills. Gerrard blasts away on a penny trumpet, so that he can announce himself.

"But we're not selling anything," John protests as they parade past the smithy, the haberdasher's, the cheesemonger's.

"We're selling *information*," Gerrard says. "Coming to the Grand Opening?"

Outside the butcher's, Mrs Haydon looks up from the mess of bloodied sawdust she is chasing into the gutter. "Grand opening of *what?*" All the cue Gerrard needs.

"A taste of Paradise here in Carshalton, but without Saint Peter asking what you've been up to."

"The boy's got the patter," Frank says when they report back on their progress. He, too, has done his bit, distributing handbills at each of the village taverns; reassuring his beer-drinking pals they'll be in no danger of becoming dehydrated. Robert has ordered a dozen barrels of beer from Nalder and Colyers.

"More's the pity," sulks John, picking up a shovel and getting back to the business of digging holes for the last of the bedding plants.

"It's strange, a lad of his age so set against alcohol," Robert remarks.

Frank grins. "Sometimes I wonder if he's mine."

On a fine morning, Robert has Abbots bridle his horse, Buzzard, and rides the three miles to Mitcham. It's Buzzard's first outing for a while, but his ribs need only a gentle nudge.

At first, the horse's movement under Robert is like the gentle swaying of a boat. They take the holloway bordering common land, passing under a canopy of horse chestnut. The morning is alive with the call of cuckoos and doves, the *rat-a-tat-tat* of woodpeckers. Then comes the one-two-one-two beat of the trot. If it is some time since Robert has used his riding muscles, it is longer still since he looked over the top of hedgerows. Gone is the large-scale lavender growing of his boyhood – plentiful fields of purple in satisfying straight lines. Instead, aniseed, rhubarb and an abundance of mint, the air laced with its clean scent.

He passes the domed tents of the gypsy encampment, a canvas shanty town. The same families come year on year, except that each has its new babe in arms, swaddled, with each family to one tent. Beyond, the fairground booths are under construction.

While he is still looking, half a dozen cows come charging off the common, tails in the air, pursued by a dark cloud of flies. Buzzard whinnies; his ears go back. Robert bends forward to whisper: "Poor things have been bitten." The feel of horse hair under his palm, Buzzard's dark, rooty smell. "There now. I'll not let them get you." Half-submerged in the Three Kings Pond, the cows switch their tails until the pests disperse.

The chimes from the clock tower are ringing out the half hour when Robert rides into the farmyard, greeted by the rich smell of ripe manure. At Cooke's, they mix it with what's left of the peppermint after it's been stilled. After passing Buzzard's reins to the stableboy, he goes to the cool stone office to find Smithers, who repeats much of what was in his last missive: "The weather was kind. Even the crows were polite – more polite than they've been in recent years."

"Take a little credit for yourself."

Smithers passes him a letter. "Ballantyne wants to know if there's any movement on price."

"Every year he tries this! He knows full well that imports are cheap for a reason."

"How would you have me reply?"

"You've enough on your plate. I'll do it." Robert pockets the letter. "How's the camomile crop?"

"Ready to harvest in a fortnight."

"Have you all the labour you need?"

"There's never a shortage once the schools close for the summer."

"And a penny a pound's still fair?"

"That should do it. Shall I gather the men?" Smithers says 'men', though Robert has women working for him. Always has.

"If there's nothing else that needs my attention."

"Not that I can think of."

"In that case." Robert holds out one arm, indicating that Smithers should go first.

Smithers rings the handbell, then has the first youngsters to show their faces run to the far fields to fetch those who are out of earshot. Robert paces idly, pleasantly, his hands behind his back. He may look back on this time as an experiment. It is possible he can run *both* businesses at a distance.

The farmyard begins to fill with the men, women and children, a tinge of summer sun on their cheeks like red apples. On seeing him, they touch the peaks of their caps, nod their heads, and Robert nods in return, waiting until they have assembled.

"All here?" he asks Smithers.

"All here," the overseer agrees.

"My apologies for the interruption – and for my absence these past few months. My attention has been taken up by a new venture, and it's thanks not only to Mr Smithers, but to each and every one of you that this has been possible. It's not every employer who is so fortunate in his workforce. And so, as a small token of gratitude, I want to extend an invitation to you and your families to the Grand Opening of Cooke's Pleasure Gardens. I have some free tickets if you'd like to come and get them." His fanfare is met with murmurs of approval. "And if you're able to help spread the word, that would be much appreciated."

"How many for you?" Robert asks and, as each gives a number, he imagines the mouths that his business helps feed. "All keeping well?" and "How's the family?" he asks.

"Is it all right to take one for my sister?" says Hilda. "She was here for the poppy harvest and she'll be back for the camomile."

"She has family, does she not?"

"A husband 'n' four youngsters. I'll take some handbills as well."

Robert counts out five more tickets.

"Oh – oh, I'm sorry, Mr Cooke." Mortified, Hilda holds the bills at arm's length. "Excuse me, but I couldn't ask no one to put these up."

His Adam. His Eve.

"No matter," he says.

CHAPTER TWENTY-ONE

JULY 1895

After supper Hettie lingers in the bar room at the Clachaig. She must give it all up and go home. The sky and the light. The lichened rocks. The wide open space. The clouds casting their great reaching shadows. The spreading strata, layer upon layer upon layer and the accumulation of it all, perfect, wild, perpetual.

"This is fir ye," the innkeeper's wife says as she approaches Hettie's table. "Ah thought ye looked as if ye could dae wi' some hoat milk 'n' brandy." Aileen sets down a pottery mug.

"Thank you, Aileen."

"Yir last nicht wi' us."

"I can't remember when I've enjoyed myself more. You've made me feel so welcome."

"Ah dare say yir kin'll be glad tae hae ye hame. They'll hae missed ye."

"Perhaps." Her son who is rarely able to make time for her. A daughter-in-law who is dutiful but dull. Grandchildren, then. The elder who barely makes the effort to stifle her sighs, thinking wistfully of places she'd rather be. The younger, at home in any setting, but a whirlwind of rushing and tumbling. "My parrot will have missed me." Hettie hopes that in saying it she doesn't sound too self-pitying. There *are* things to look forward to. The Grand Opening of Cooke's Pleasure Gardens, to begin with.

"Ye hae a talkin' burd?"

"Not talking, but good company all the same."

"Ah wid hae thought you'd hae a dug, an ootdoor body like yirsel'."

Hettie laughs, a loud *Ha! An outdoor body.* She, who'd never imagined she might find in herself one iota of Wordsworth's wonder at the natural world. The fact is, it is quite unnecessary for Satan to make an appearance, telling Hettie that all she sees can be hers. She's already earned it, walking herself into the landscape, feeling the burn in her muscles, the press of her corset, muddying the hem of her tweed skirt. She has been present, entirely and in each moment, doing nothing more than putting one foot in front of the other. In Glencoe, Hettie has reclaimed a belief, not necessarily in something or someone, but in possibility. In mystery. It is her secret, something tourists who stay in the valley will never know about – hers and Iain's and her mother's and father's. The peace within her is something Hettie has never previously known. The question is, can it survive the journey south? "I don't suppose…" She may be clutching at straws but ask she must. "I don't suppose you ever found the visitors' book."

"Ah'm feart ah can't help ye there, Mrs Cooke."

"Never mind." And she doesn't. "My father's been more alive to me here than ever before."

"Then ye foun' whit ye came fae."

And not just my father, Hettie reflects. Decima has taken her place in Hettie's thoughts alongside Ernest. They're inseparable now. There was a moment only yesterday. Hettie had climbed a gully and, as she felt for her next handhold, she had such a strong sense of her parents, she had to catch her breath. It didn't matter if here was the place they met, or if it was another place. The important thing was that it was real to Hettie, the moment when two people meeting accidentally recognise something in each other. Yes, she found what she came for.

CHAPTER TWENTY-TWO

JULY 1895

The marquee is set up on the lawn; twenty yards wide, thirty long. Down the middle are the boards people will dance on, on each side the tables and chairs where they'll take their refreshments.

Robert feels a nervousness he hasn't known in years. Good nerves, he tries to convince himself as he reaches for his watch chain. Fewer than five minutes have passed since he last checked the time. They've done enough. It *has* to be enough.

He takes one final stroll, checking the day's schedule. The Punch and Judy show, the children's treasure hunt, the tortoise races, the fire-eaters and jugglers who will move among the crowds. At three o'clock, the tennis match – the courts are pristine, Robert notes with satisfaction. Freya has persuaded the Baddeley brothers to appear. After their performance at Wimbledon they are hottest ticket in town. Herbert Baddeley beat Reginald Doherty in the semi-finals, only to lose the championship to his twin, Wilfred. Freya won't disclose how she pulled off this small miracle, but there could be no better endorsement for their tennis club. The programme describes the match as a 'friendly' but between brothers as competitive as these, there's bound to be rivalry.

The music hall star Miss Annie Adams will perform at four thirty and again at six. Retired she may be, but her star still shines bright. Garlands of flowers and bunches of lavender have transformed the bandstand into a stage fit for the queen of serio-comic vocalists. And between appearances, Miss Adams has agreed to officiate at the switching on of Neptune's fountain.

A winding detour takes Robert through the trees, their lower branches strung with Chinese lanterns. As he passes, he trails one hand on the broad trunks in the way he feels his sons would have. Ivy inches upwards towards the pale sunlight. Here is Pan with his pipes. Puck who owes much to John Lough's muse.

Festivities will conclude with a grand firework display. He pictures, for a moment, two boys, a year between them. It is only possible to see their glowing faces because each traces in spitting silver cinders from a penny sparkler the letters that spell his name, giggling at the wonder of it, for the few magical minutes it lasts. He's a mass of contradictions. This is the last time the gardens will be truly, exclusively theirs.

Robert wants crowds.

He does not want crowds.

His gardens are going to be a great success.

And that success will destroy his small Eden.

Several green feathers litter the floor of the aviary. What Robert mistook for annual moult is apparently an act of mutilation. As he unlatches the door, there is a flurry of wings, the squawking he'll never quite grow accustomed to. The parakeets stir up a green tornado, a flash of green feathers with contrasting yellow and grey undersides, like the silk lining of a jacket. Robert seldom ventures inside. Under the soles of his shoes, the floor is gritty with empty husks. It's a texture he struggles with. The association.

He stoops to pick up four bright plumes, fans them and tucks them into his breast pocket. Ever since Freya attended a lecture on how egrets are slaughtered for their plumage, she wavers on whether it's acceptable to wear the feathers she already owns. The lecturer said it mattered not whether the bird from which a particular feather came had suffered, because the practice of wearing feathers makes it more likely that other birds will suffer. Then he sees it: the poor shunned creature has worked its way into a corner. A sleek head of feathers, but its tail is threadbare, plucked by members of its own species – no less cruel than man.

Footsteps, running. Gerrard is barrelling towards the aviary. The boy's mother hasn't let him put on his new red waistcoat yet – doesn't trust him to keep it clean – but his hair has been flattened, comb marks still evident. "The tortoise man's here. I showed him where to set up."

"Good lad. Do we still have the cages the birds arrived in?"

The boy opens the door a crack and sidles in. "As far as I know." Two parakeets fly from their high perches. Gerrard bats away talons that would sink into his scalp, his focus on the huddled bird. "Poor little blighter." He squats down, knees together, feet splayed apart. He holds out a finger, making a clicking noise. "Are the others still picking on you?" He strokes the bird's neck, as tender as can be, but this parakeet has no resistance. It rocks under the slightest pressure.

"We should separate him," says Robert. "Will you see to it?"

"What'll we do with him?"

"It depends how happy he is on his own."

"I could take him." This isn't one of Frank's reluctant suggestions. Gerrard wants this.

"You'd better ask your father."

"It's my mother who'll need persuading. Can't get used to the racket, she says."

"Take him to the cottage for now. Assure her it will only be until we find him another home."

Dressed like a bookmaker at the Downs, the tortoise man has marked out lanes and is edging his racetrack with bunting. For the life of him, Robert cannot remember the man's name. "I trust you have everything you need," he says as he approaches.

The man straightens up, hands in the small of his back. "All ready for the Carshalton Derby." The buttons of his bright yellow waistcoat are straining.

"How will you work this?"

"The standard betting system. Win-only or each way."

"And if none should finish?"

"Oh, we have some very strong contenders. And plenty of lettuce."

At noon, Robert returns home for a change of clothes. He'd feared he might find Freya brooding. Only yesterday a letter arrived from her sister Edith. Both she and Hilda have come down with a summer cold and they won't be able to attend the opening after all. But instead of brooding she's buoyant, putting the finishing touches to her costume. Her tennis dress is blue check on white, the bodice cut to her figure and over it a jacket of plain flannel in pure white.

"I thought to myself, what's the point in trying to compete with a famous music hall star?" She turns a full circle so he can admire her. "Miss Annie Adams should be allowed to shine."

Granted, Miss Adams is almost as famous for her extravagant costumes as she is for her voice, but Robert sees what his wife is about. Freya has set herself the challenge of collecting fifty signatures for their tennis club. There will be no clearer signal that she was responsible for securing the Baddeley brothers' appearance. "It looks well on you," he says.

"Do you think so?" She seats herself at her dressing table and turns her face to better see her hair in the mirror.

Robert stands in front of the full-length mirror, buttoning his scarlet jacket. His thinking was to look like the man who showed his mother the hot air balloon, but he fears he looks more like Signor Jacopo, the parachuting monkey.

"Let me look at you." Freya brushes his shoulders, her busy-ness bringing him back to himself. She sits his silk top hat on his head, hands him the silver-headed cane he has had for some time but which has seen little use. "Oh, yes," she says.

All of the roles that scarlet has taken in his life, none of them good. Black would have been the better choice. "You don't think it too vulgar?

"Not at all! It's *quite* the thing for the master of ceremonies."

On his return, Mrs Reynolds corners Robert to tell him Miss Annie Adams has commandeered the pavilion for her preparations. He should have anticipated it. It is not a problem, he assures her.

"But the teas," she frets.

"If people want their teas before her performance, they can use the tables in front of the pavilion."

Miss Adams can be heard warming up her vocal cords. Not anything that might be called singing. An elongated *Ah* that soars from a great height to the depths and back up again.

"My Dulcie made up her honey-water to her husband's instructions. Ever so exacting, they were."

"I'm sure she did an excellent job."

They both listen, neither commenting.

"Honey protects the throat from injury," Mrs Reynolds says. "That's what he said."

Humming follows. This at least has a tunefulness, reminding Robert of the wistful vibrato street musicians make when playing the saw. In between arias come great gasping, lung-filling breaths. When the humming is replaced by a sung, *Ah,* they both nod, as if this is what they expected.

With oiled hair, deep-set eyes and tidy moustaches, the Baddeley brothers are as alike as Freya described. They may have spent their entire lives swapping places when it suited them, in schoolrooms, on centre court and in the chambers where they practise law. They shake hands and remove their sports jackets. Shirtsleeves neatly folded up to their elbows, ties tucked inside their shirts above the third button.

A tennis ball is bounced. One brother seeks the other's opinion. It will not do: another, please. This is not Wimbledon. A little buffoonery is permitted. Three balls are rejected but, as play commences, the spectators' laughter mutes until the *pop-bop-pock* of racquet hitting ball carries over what conversation remains.

Cane in hand, Robert moves among the crowd, every inch the proprietor, ensuring that his visitors have everything they need – preferably things that have to be bought and paid for. He looks about, searching among faces for a Carlisle, a Colman.

"Don't know what to make of it. If Cremorne couldn't turn a profit, what makes Cooke think he'll fare any better?"

But you're here, aren't you? He sets his face into a smile. Under his topper, Robert's hairline already itches with sweat. The afternoon is going to be a scorcher.

"Roll, bowl or pitch! Three balls a penny! You knock 'em down, we pick 'em up."

The girl who had been selling paper windmills outside the gates is now inside. She has stopped a couple with a child – a boy – and asked him to blow. When the windmill spins and blurs, he reacts with delight, demanding, "Again! Again!"

"I think it's well-placed. The reason London's pleasure

gardens failed is that as the city expanded land became a valuable asset."

Precisely! He tucks his cane under his right arm, tips his hat and…

What in heaven's name?

There is Estelle. Not with her mother or sister, but with a young man.

Confound the Reverend and Mrs Mears who choose the moment to make an appearance, Mr Mears in his usual wideawake hat and cloak, Mrs Mears a severe black crow. Robert's extravagant jacket seems to cause them discomfort. "Reverend. Mrs Mears." He touches the brim of his topper. "Do excuse me, I must –"

He cranes his neck. It is not just any young man Estelle is with, but John Reynolds. *As we forgive those who trespass against us.* In the new waistcoat Robert supplied, hair slick with pomade, he cuts a fine figure.

His daughter is smiling, her eyes downturned, a little coy, and John – he is not doing anything he can be criticised for. Nonetheless, Robert recognises what he's stumbled upon. Two young people in the process of discovering that the laws of attraction pay no heed to ordinary conventions. Robert is not so old that he doesn't remember how it was. How, when her eyes darkened, he knew they darkened for him and, with that knowledge, time ceased to exist. Though, at the time, the intensity of the charge in the air between them was excruciating, what he feels now for the experience is a kind of nostalgia. But this is his daughter and she's drawing attention to herself. "John!" he calls out, striding towards them, his hand holding his cane raised.

Eyes startled, Estelle looks up. The hollow of her throat is flushed.

Bop-pop-pock.

"There you are!" Beyond this, Robert has no idea what he

might say. It cannot be – they *must* realise this. "Would you mind taking over on the gates?"

Far from being embarrassed, John says smartly, "Right you are, Mr Cooke."

"And ask Gerrard to tot up the receipts, if you would." He turns to his daughter. So often of late Estelle's expression has been brooding. Were the circumstances different, it would be a pleasure to see it so unguarded. "I thought I'd find you watching the tennis." No doubt her mother made the same assumption. Freya would never have permitted Estelle to go about unchaperoned.

"I tried." She seems a little uncertain of herself, as well she might. "But I couldn't follow the rules."

"Don't you have any aspirations to play?"

"I think I'll stick to croquet."

"And where *is* your mother?"

Estelle nods in the direction of the pavilion. Freya is easily identifiable in her tennis outfit, daringly bare headed in a sea of bonnets. "Will you walk with me?" he asks his daughter.

Estelle shakes her head. "I'm on my way to find Ida. She's joined the treasure hunt."

It is just as well. It would be more difficult to tell his wife he's just averted disaster – he will use that exaggerated term jokingly – had Estelle agreed to accompany him. "In that case," he tips his hat, "I wish you luck in trying to steer your sister clear of mischief."

The next time he sees Estelle, she will be playing croquet with Ida, taking such childish joy in it, Robert will try to convince himself he was too hasty in his conclusion. That he witnessed the precise moment the pair bumped into one another and Estelle, only too aware that she was alone, was uncertain whether or not it was proper to acknowledge John.

"*A dozen native oysters, best quality, only three pence a dozen.*"

As Robert heads toward his wife, sounds from the tennis match reach him. Collective gasps and cries of *Oh!* He is surprised that Freya would abandon her front row seat. This, after all, is her moment of triumph. But there she is, holding court at one of the tables in front of the pavilion. Cucumber sandwiches, crustless and cut into soldiers, scones, clotted cream and a choice of jams. Mrs Reynolds and her daughter have seen to it all.

"Do you remember the last night at Vauxhall? My goodness, if you must go, let it be in a blaze of glory."

Today's commentators are very sure of themselves. He'll show them. (Already he is thinking this, losing sight of his shadow-sons.)

He makes a beeline for Freya's table, ready to remind her lady friends that the fountain will be switched on at five o'clock sharp. Then he will draw his wife aside and make her aware of Estelle's and John's blossoming friendship. (That's how he'll put it.) Who would have thought it would be Estelle who needed to be kept on a tight leash!

"Yes, a lady designer. A wonderful artist." Freya sets the tea strainer on a cup and pours. The role of proprietress comes naturally to his wife. She's always ready with the small talk that remains a mystery to him. "Such a pity, to have designed the gardens and then to miss the opening."

A pity indeed! Miss Hoddy ought to be toasted and cele-brated.

"Is she unwell?" one of the ladies asks, keeping half an eye on the tennis. Something inside Robert unsettles. He main-tains his smile and pretends to be looking about for someone. Not Estelle. In this moment, for all he cares she might have decided John was worth the risk and followed him through the crowd.

"Not unwell." His wife's voice is hesitant. He can see nods of encouragement while she tries to give the impression that she isn't sure if she ought to continue. "But it's difficult. When you're confined to an invalid-chair."

Despite the afternoon heat, the skin above Robert's elbows prickles into goose pimples.

"It was really quite tragic," his wife confides. "But you've probably already heard…"

"*I* haven't." The speaker looks to her companions and sees that they haven't either. In their world, information is currency, and his wife has something they want.

It is as if Robert is watching the scene unfold through a window. He ought to rap on the glass and interrupt, but *I haven't,* thinks Robert, willing the clinking of teacups and lemonade glasses to still, the applause from the tennis match to abate, so he can better hear what his wife has to say.

"Before her accident – it was dreadful."

Before and afterwards. Words that will be repeated in front parlours. Words that are beyond reproach.

"Of course, she doesn't talk about it, but from what I can gather she was dragged underneath the carriage –"

"Oh!"

Once again Miss Hoddy is knocked to the ground. *A sickening confusion of hooves and wheels. A wildness in the horses' eyes, their nostrils flared. Beads of sweat stand proud on Miss Hoddy's waxen forehead as she looks to her friends for reassurance that it is not so bad, not nearly as bad as she thinks.*

"It's a wonder she survived. And before, she'd been engaged to such a promising young man."

Who has Freya had this from? Not Miss Hoddy, of that Robert is certain. But Ida, Ida might have asked a bold question and been rewarded with an answer. *Yes, I was engaged once, a long time ago.*

"He was overseas when it happened. Chile, or somewhere like it, somewhere mountainous." Yes, yes, mountains. "He started out as a shipping clerk but, within a few years, had his own mining business and secured several lucrative government contracts. In his leisure time he documented the country's bird and insect life. Some of the specimens he brought back are housed in the British Museum, I'm told. He would have married her – he was that sort of person."

"Oh, I'm sure."

They are all so very sure. The tragic tale will spread by word of mouth, evolving a little with each telling. The fiancé may start his working life as a tea taster in Mincing Lane before setting sail to China to seek his fortune. He may be a humble plate engraver for the printing industry, before a minor royal enquires about the die plates he produces in a Hackney back alley.

"It was she who broke off their engagement. One assumes she wouldn't have been able to give him children."

Oh, Freya, this is beneath you. It is pity that keeps Miss Hoddy – who has more right to be here than any of them – confined to her own home, painting only what she sees from her window.

"She lives with her brother. Also unmarried."

"It must have been dreadful for everyone. Quite dreadful."

If you knew, he wants to say. But what is there to argue with? Chances are that Oswald *would* have put his skills as a surveyor to fuller use, would have married and had a family of his own, had it not been for –

"And her young man? He married, did he?"

"Oh, yes. He and his wife have several children, so you see, she did the right thing by him."

"Still, it can't have been easy."

"She really is the most marvellous artist. Ida – my youngest – goes every week to paint with her."

Robert turns away, unable to trust what he might say. *That's right, claim for yourself a role as a patron of the arts.* His dream, everything he wanted this place to be, everything Miss Hoddy designed it to be, is sullied.

But.

It can't be. He must be mistaken.

This woman walks with a stride that is a match for any man's. Dressed in travelling clothes, her hair more white than auburn coming loose, and using a branch as a walking staff, she is an apparition. And yet somehow...

His mother holds up one hand and calls, "Robert!" then heads towards him, unperturbed by the family groupings, the children with their toffee apples and cones of fudge, the waiters in their buttoned waistcoats, the fire-eater who pedals backwards and forwards, backwards and forwards, on his unicycle. She seems not to care how anyone reacts to her. "Look for the red jacket, they told me, and here you are!"

"You're back." This, Robert finds, is all he is capable of saying. Part of him would like to demand, *What have you been doing all this time? Did you not think we would worry?* Part of him would like to usher her to somewhere she cannot be seen, to say, *Take a look at yourself.*

"Freya wrote to tell me about your Grand Opening."

"Freya *knew* you were arriving?"

"Don't fuss. I *told* her not to tell you. I knew your time would be taken up."

"But I could have sent Abbots with the carriage."

"You did." She smiles as if she's said something awfully clever. "But this is marvellous!" Her face, he sees, is noticeably thinner but her eyes are gleaming. "I feel like a bead in a kaleidoscope!" She laughs, turning a full circle. When Hettie is facing him once more, she reaches for one of the brass buttons on his jacket. "I know what this is." He wonders for a moment if she has somehow done what his wife has not: imagined his shadow-sons here, in this place. Hettie has always had strange insights. "I watched." There is a tremor at the corner of her mouth. Robert knows now that she sees the scarlet-jacketed assistant. "That day. I watched you and your father go up in the balloon."

"You –" This is not their way. Speaking like this. But she *watched?*

"I couldn't help myself." There is no artifice here. "It was cruel not to have told you. Can you forgive me?"

She'd said she wouldn't watch – that he couldn't ask it of her. Is this revision better or worse? As a parent, Robert knows he wouldn't have been able to stop himself.

"Don't feel you have to answer." She swipes away a tear. "And now," her expression changes again, "I must explore. I have to say, I can't quite take in all that you've done here." She turns away, leaving him open-mouthed. This cannot be another thing that they brush under the carpet.

"Not by myself," Robert says. "I had help."

She turns. "Ah, but you *made* it happen. *You.*" He's astonished she doesn't think his gardens are a frivolous endeavour. "I don't suppose you'd like to give your mother the grand tour."

Robert checks his pocket watch. It is almost time for the fountain to be switched on. He looks to the bandstand and catches a glimpse of Annie Adams coming down the steps, fluttering a fan against her décolletage. Her husband Henry follows behind, fussing about the hems of her skirt like a bridesmaid. He could invent an excuse. But there are far worse things than having an eccentric mother. "Come with me." He offers his mother his right elbow and she hooks her hand inside. "Do you remember the fountain Father left me?"

It is gone eleven by the time they persuade the last of the lingerers to leave. The gates are padlocked, empty bottles lined up, deckchairs stacked. Time to count the takings. Robert supervises John and Gerrard, separating the receipts from the gates and the refreshments, so he can analyse where his profits come from. Writing up the chits from which he'll write up the ledger.

"You have a neat hand," he compliments Gerrard.

The boy shrugs. "Not much point in writing if you can't read it."

I'll teach him bookkeeping, he thinks. Single and double entry. Balance sheets. Bills of exchange. A good bookkeeper is never short of work. And as Robert knows himself, there is no better way to discover which local businesses are profitable. To identify those you might want to invest in.

Freya shrugs him off, sits up in bed. "Show me your hands."

Robert submits to her fussing. His skin has blistered and healed, toughened by hard and satisfying work. Proof that finally he is more than the man who writes the cheques.

This is precisely what his wife sees, but her reaction isn't pride. "We must do something about this." She slips out of bed in her nightdress and goes to her dressing table to fetch one of her potions. "You'll be mistaken for one of your workers."

He laughs. "Would that be such a terrible thing?"

Using her thumbs, she begins to massage cold cream into the part of his palms between the base of his fingers and his lifeline. "I shouldn't need to answer that, not after today's triumph. Do you know? I really think we caught the attention of the right sort of people. I only hope they won't hold your mother's appearance against us. What can she have been thinking of? She looked as if she came straight from the train."

CHAPTER TWENTY-THREE

JULY 1895

i

I t is not just calling cards that begin to arrive.

"Here's another." His wife's eyes gleam as she reads from the next letter on today's pile. *"My Dear Freya, Will you permit a very old friend to express her extreme gratification at the well-deserved success of your Grand Opening? I had been waiting anxiously to see the results of your endeavours and they did not disappoint."* Unable to keep the triumph from her voice, Freya raises her eyes for Robert's reaction. "I do think Minnie might have addressed the letter to you."

Whatever doubts she had about the pleasure gardens appear to have evaporated. Robert cannot allow himself to be quite so excited. With the exception of the mayor, not one of the twenty people whose circle he hoped to infiltrate – local dignitaries, captains of industry, men of consequence – had attended. "Women are rather better at this sort of correspondence," he says. "You will keep a note of anything I can feed to the press, won't you?"

"The notices *are* rather good." Scissors out, Freya is ready to clip columns for her scrapbook.

Receipts would have been higher still had Robert not erred. He rented the tortoise man a plot when he ought to have negotiated a share of the profits. Who could have anticipated that the races would draw such a crowd? But that was where their bread-and-butter customers felt most at ease. Even the saintly Reverend Edward Mears placed a bet – and on the Lord's day!

Freya snips at the air. "You *will* set aside some time to make house calls, won't you?"

"Organising the tennis tournament takes priority over social calls."

"I meant to mention, we'll need trophies. One for the gents and one for the ladies."

The seed of Freya's idea germinates. "We'll announce that our aim is to produce the next lawn tennis champion. Someone fit to compete at Wimbledon."

"Cooke's Tennis Academy." Freya basks in the notion. "I think perhaps the ladies ought to be taught by a woman and the gents by a man, don't you?"

He drops off his advertisement at the *Chronicle's* offices. Loax scans the copy.

Could you be the next lawn tennis champion?

Simply put, lawn tennis offers everything croquet does and more. Equally accessible to both sexes, it is a game that may be played by two persons (one against the other) and called a single match, by three persons (two against one) and called a unicorn match, or by four persons (two on each side) and called a double match.

Lawn tennis is the most fashionable pastime for young ladies and gentlemen seeking the intimate social pleasures of outdoor recreation. Join us at Cooke's for a mixed double match.

Racquet and ball hire available.

He stamps the sheet of paper and puts it in his tray. "Present it as news and you won't have to pay."

"There isn't any more news about tennis. You've already written up the Baddeley brothers' match."

"Use your imagination." Loax pops another humbug.

ii

Gerrard blinks in the darkness. Tall stories drift up the staircase. Mr Cooke and his father are increasingly animated as they sit on the bench under the eaves. His father is putting it away. The particular laugh Gerrard associates with his drinking grows steadily louder. How is he supposed to sleep?

A sharp scrape brings him to. The Huntley & Palmers biscuit tin being pulled out from under the bed. A clatter of coins. He pretends not to know about his brother's haul, but when you live in such close quarters, secrets are impossibilities. If Gerrard were to say anything at all, it would be, 'Mind our father doesn't see that,' but he holds his tongue. If he doesn't poke his nose in, perhaps he'll be rewarded.

He grips the blanket so that John doesn't steal it all for himself. More money passes through Gerrard's hands than he ever imagined existed. He writes it all down in the way Mr Cooke showed him, accounting for every farthing. That way, Gerrard reckons it's safe. What he'll do when Mr Cooke stops collecting the takings every day he doesn't know. It is just him doing the counting now, sitting in the quiet pavilion, out of temptation's way (and by that he means his father's). John is out the gates the minute Cooke's closes (before, if he can get away with it), doing whatever it is that earns him his silver coins.

iii

As he arrives at his mother's house, Robert is light-hearted. His position on the Parish Council has been confirmed. Now he can ensure that Cooke's is firmly established as a fixture on the social calendar. Already he's volunteered to host the harvest festival. Today he and his mother may even return to the conversation they abandoned. The question of forgiveness. Not that the adult Robert thinks there's anything *to* forgive. A person cannot help the way they're made. Even as a child, he understood that his mother was someone who needed to be treated with delicacy. But he *would* like to hear what she thought as she watched him go up in the hot air balloon.

She receives him dressed in a simple shirtwaist and a plain skirt, and with her stout shoes on her feet.

"Weren't you expecting me?" he asks.

"Of course I was. You sent word."

"But you're dressed to go out."

"And so I will. Later." Oblivious to the point he's trying to make about her attire, she asks, "What's that you've brought me?"

He has newspapers tucked under his arm and carries with him the smell of fresh ink. "A few pieces about the opening. The *Chronicle's* column about the Baddeley brothers has already brought us a flurry of interest." As Robert looks about his mother's parlour it strikes him that he doesn't feel, as he has so often in the past, that he's stepped inside a cage.

"Oh, that's wonderful. Put them on the side table and I'll take a look." Robert goes to the table, but finds it covered with bric-a-brac. "But, first, I must tell you. I met your Miss

Hoddy."

Robert pauses in his search for a free surface. "You *met* her?"

"Ida told me about her visits, so I called on her."

"Without an arrangement?" He *might* call on his mother without sending a note, he supposes, but he's never taken that liberty.

"Do sit down."

Robert jokes with Freya that the chair directly opposite his mother's brings him under too much scrutiny. He prefers the wing chair a little to her left. Before sitting he checks the seat, as he is in the habit of doing. More than once he has come away with parrot's mess on his coat tails.

"She really is a most remarkable person, don't you think?"

He slots the newspapers between the cushion and the armrest. "I do." What's surprising is that his mother does too.

"To begin with a blank sheet, then bring it to life. To sit there and watch her paint was a rare privilege. She *looks*. She told me she spends a long time looking. It's the same scene she paints over and over again, but each time she finds a different starting point."

"I didn't realise that."

"I understood what she meant, I understood completely. I spent several months at the Clachaig and saw people come and go. They asked me why I stayed so long, walking the same valley day after day."

"You were *walking* all that time?"

"Not *all* that time. Snow kept me inside for a fortnight and then I was a little nervous of the ice. My point was, I may have followed the same route, but it was never the *same*. One day the sun would be soft and the greens pure, but the mountains would lack definition. The next it might be misty, and my eyes were drawn to the foreground – the small details you might miss on any other day. The clouds are never the same clouds, and they cross the valley, and their shadows somehow helped shape it. I never tired of it."

Robert cannot recall his mother ever being so talkative. Sometimes all she says is, 'Tell me your news.' But she's seen the results of his labour, and for the first occasion in some time, she has news of her own.

"When I told Miss Hoddy about Glencoe, she had her brother fetch a great pile of her sketchbooks. I don't mind admitting, I was a little daunted. 'Take your time,' she told me. She didn't stop what she was doing. She carried on painting."

Robert finds himself nodding. It was exactly the same when he called on her. "I take it they weren't just sketches."

"Watercolours, mainly, though some had clearly started life as pencil drawings. And there it all was. The seasons unfolding, the light changing, the flowers. I felt a little guilty for spending less time with some of the paintings than others – I worried she might be able to hear how quickly I turned the pages – but I found reasons to go back and forth. When something spoke to me, I wanted to understand how she'd done it."

She's marking the weeks and months of her confinement.

"She told me that she wants anyone who sees one of her paintings to feel that she stumbled on the scene for the first time. The beginning of a painting is quite deliberate – thought goes into every stroke – but at some point the brush takes over. It seems to know what's right, that's what she said. And so that's how I tried to look at each painting. I tried to find her starting point."

"And did you?"

"No! Part of her skill, I imagine, is rendering it invisible." For a moment, his mother looks distant. "One of the paintings I particularly admired was a self-portrait. She'd painted the reflection of her own face, looking back at her from the greenery of the garden. It was as if she were outside, looking in. Quite extraordinary." Her eyes come back into focus. "I think she'd be the most marvellous portrait artist, but she tells me she doesn't paint portraits."

"No," Robert says, sadly.

"I asked if she painted every day. 'It's the reason I get up,' she said. And that shamed me."

He shifts in his seat. "How, exactly?"

His mother gives her fingernails an impatient appraisal before she turns her attention to him. "I have spent too much time indoors, alone and frightened."

Does she expect him to challenge her, to insist, *You weren't alone*? But he can't detect a note of blame in her voice.

"I've taken time for granted, not really caring how much more there would be. And, of course, all along, I've had the use of my legs."

"You didn't say that, I hope!"

"Certainly I did. Miss Hoddy doesn't need to be shielded from her own reality. A person ought to be acknowledged, and that includes the challenges they face and how they manage to overcome them. Besides, how could I tell her how much I admire her while avoiding the differences between us?"

Robert has admired Miss Hoddy's work, but to tell her that he admires *her*. Such an admission might be misunderstood. And as for referring to… it's ingrained, the avoidance, that same instinct that causes him to rein Ida in. "But you always told me…"

"Told you what?"

What exactly had she told him? "Not to stare," is all he can come up with.

"Well, of course one shouldn't *stare*. But neither should one look the other way." The expression his mother adopts is curious rather than critical, as if to say, *How could you not have understood?* "I think it's intentions that are important, don't you?" She smiles, giving him the opportunity to redeem himself by agreeing, and he doesn't disappoint her.

When Robert thinks on it, Miss Hoddy didn't give the slightest indication that she minded Ida's questions. If anything, she seemed relieved to have someone speak so frankly. "How did she reply?"

"With a question. She asked me how it felt to be outside again, after all this time. And I told her I wasn't sure. You see, in Glencoe, there is so much space. Indeed there is nothing *but* space. It gives you an incredible sense of your place in the world. Here, it's quite different. Miss Hoddy summed it up very nicely. 'Here, there are people who would put you in your place,' she said."

Imagine. Imagine if Robert had persuaded Miss Hoddy to attend the Grand Opening and she'd heard what he heard. Then, almost as an extension of this thought, *Imagine if her young man had married her out of pity. That* was why Miss Hoddy broke off her engagement, not because it was the *right* thing to do, not because she wouldn't have been able to give a husband children, but because she didn't want pity from the person who was supposed to love her. And perhaps she didn't want to have to live with people saying how *good* her husband was for keeping his promise. How *kind* he was.

"I told her that what I'm most afraid of – more than the noise and the chaos – is of falling back into my old ways. 'Dawn,' she said."

"Dawn?" Robert finds himself repeating.

"Since you persuaded her to leave the house, she's been visiting the gardens each day at dawn."

Can this be true? "But the gates are locked at that hour."

"The younger Reynolds boy lets her in. Gerrard, I think his name is." How easily his mother uses his name. If she once had a grandson of the same name, it was not this boy. "Oswald leaves Florence to it for an hour or so."

He blinks. Struggles back to the moment. "But how does

she –?"

"Manage? Gerrard, of course. She likes to watch him feed the birds."

It strikes Robert. There have been no interruptions, no flurries of wings. His mother has addressed him and him alone. He turns in his chair, looks about. "Where is your parrot?"

"Fairfax? He's gone to stay with Miss Hoddy."

She has beaten him to it. He'd had a mind to offer Miss Hoddy their injured parakeet. "But you loved that bird."

"The arrangement may not be permanent. It's to see how they get along. The main trouble will be the paints. We don't want him making himself ill."

Robert bristles. "The main trouble will be the damage he'll do to Miss Hoddy's commissions!" He only has to look around his mother's parlour to see the results of the bird's destructive curiosity.

"If he can't leave them alone, I shall have him back. It was she who offered."

This conversation leapfrogs from one thing to another. How is a person to keep up? "Why should she have made such an offer?"

"I told her it wouldn't be fair, leaving him on his own so much of the time. I don't intend to spend my dotage staring at these four walls. That is my decision."

Her *decision*? But one thing at a time. If his mother has been making a nuisance of herself, he must put a stop to it. "How often have you been back to see Miss Hoddy, Mother?"

"Oh, let me see… Every day apart from Tuesday, I think."

"Every day?" No, that is too much. Oswald can hardly tell unannounced callers his sister isn't at home.

"I'm sitting for her. Didn't I say?"

Pressure is growing in Robert's chest, an impatient nagging. "No, you didn't." But really, what is his objection?

However resourceful she is, Miss Hoddy must be lonely. And if his mother, now that she's undergone this dramatic transformation, is a willing companion, who is he to deny her that? More than this, it seems she's been invited – and he has not. She is no longer *his* Miss Hoddy (the label that vexed him so), she is Ida's and his mother's.

"It's fascinating to see yourself the way someone else sees you. Not just the imperfections we try to hide, but things we've never even noticed. I suppose that's the mark of a true artist. To uncover what was previously unseen. No, I'm afraid I rather lost track on Tuesday. I followed the Wandle and ended up in Mitcham, would you believe?"

"Mitcham?" The room feels stifling, airless. Robert loosens his necktie.

"Mr Smithers brought me back, and by then it was rather late for house calls. It was good of him, don't you think?"

"I had no idea you were acquainted." It is no longer an impatience in his chest, but a sharp, needling pain. Is there no part of his life his mother hasn't infiltrated?

"Oh, we weren't. I'd never seen your farm before either, but I asked for directions to the Cooke place. Since you weren't there I had a mind to press on to Merton to see Mr Morris's silkworks. But Mr Smithers offered to act as my guide, and really he was most accommodating. I have to say, I was surprised how much land is given over to poppy-growing. I wonder, do you have any plans to diversify?"

"Diversify? Why would I do *that*?"

"Well, if the Christian Union and the lawmakers have their way, salicin will become the new laudanum."

A line quoted directly from a pamphlet! Robert pushes himself to his feet. "Salicin won't become the new anything. It's been in use for centuries." His mother also stands. "The trouble is, it doesn't suit everyone. And if – *if* – the Christian Union succeeds, Britain's ties with the India-China trade will be severed, in which case *our* crops will be in greater demand."

"There you have it. I imagined you'd given it a lot of thought." She follows him to the door (Annie is nowhere to be seen) and hands him his hat. "Your father certainly thought opium perfectly safe, and I didn't think twice about dosing you with Godfrey's Cordial when you were a baby."

No more of this. Robert doesn't need anyone to sell him his own produce. "Until next week," he takes his leave.

"You'll see me on Sunday. I thought I'd join you at church."

Any other time and Robert would be relieved to hear this. His mood is such that he doesn't care to ask what has brought about this change of heart. "Sunday, then."

"Mr Smithers seems very capable, I must say. Between Mr Smithers and the Reynolds, you certainly have surrounded yourself with good people."

Good people, he thinks as he marches down the garden path. *Good people!* He starts out in one direction, each step a jolt. Then Robert about turns. Impatience in every limb, he strides back the way he has come. For several blessed days he thought that he and his mother had arrived at a new understanding, that he no longer had to be the small boy, worried that whatever he wanted would in some way cause her heartache. Now, suddenly, she's meddling in every aspect of his life. *Diversify indeed!* But it was Freya who first showed him Dr Bull's *Hints to Mothers,* a pamphlet highlighting the dangers of opiates in the nursery. One of the women at church had given it to her, perhaps ignorant of the nature of his business, but more likely not. *Of course* he doesn't agree with the practice of dosing up babies so that they sleep all day, he told his wife, but yes, he's aware it goes on. Working mothers have little choice but to leave children for hours at a time, so they doctor their gripe-water. And it's not *just* the poor. Mothers read the labels that say *Infant Preservative* and *Soothing Syrup.* They think that 'purely herbal' and 'natural ingredients' means that products are safe. Though it *was* chilling to read about case after case of infant deaths linked to over-use.

As many as a third of infant deaths in industrial cities.

And he, who has buried two sons.

But even Dr Bull didn't condemn the use of opiates outright. *They are medicines,* he wrote, *and like any medicine, ought to be prepared by pharmacists.* The trouble is, Robert told Freya, that until recently any Tom, Dick or Harry could operate a pharmacy. And hasn't he been vocal in his support for an overhaul of the system?

As for adults, they're capable of making their own decisions. Freya wasn't suggesting that *she* shouldn't take her 'women's friends' when she needed them, was she?

Well, then.

The market will not dry up, despite Dr Bull, despite the Christian Union and despite his blasted mother, because British men and women don't like to be told what they can and cannot use to relieve their ailments. As for those who use opium for recreational purposes, that's their own lookout!

Five blinkered minutes later, Robert finds himself outside the Hoddys' house, staring at the latticework of the clean white porch, not quite knowing what business he has being there. He removes his hat, smooths down his hair. Miss Hoddy is blameless, that much he *does* know. His mother will have introduced herself – 'I believe you know my son' – and politeness will have dictated that she reply, 'A pleasure to meet you.'

He feels more in control now that his blood is no longer charging about his body. If Oswald were to appear at the front door with a 'Won't you come in?' Robert would politely decline. But, still, he waits a moment longer.

It's better this way. Whatever urgency he felt has evaporated, and there was nothing he would have been able to articulate without sounding like a spoilt child. Better that he tends to business.

First, there is one thing Robert must do. He visits the local pharmacy. The polished mahogany is scrupulously clean, deep shelves occupied by gleaming jars of whale oil, calomel, camphor, drawers of powder with metal shovels, neat rows of boxes and tins and corked glass bottles. He scans past smelling salts, galvanic oils, Holloway's Ointment. Here we are. Sydenham's Laudanum for dysentery, camphorated tincture of opium for asthma, vinegar of opium, opiate clyster. Exactly as it always has been. "Good day." He touches the brim of his hat and backs out of the door.

At the gardens, he finds the gates unmanned. Frank and the boys must be busy elsewhere. There is no perfect solution. They have settled on displaying a notice with the price of admission and directing people to the 'ticket office'. *Please retain your ticket ~ you may be asked for proof of payment!* Robert heads for the cottage to seek out Gerrard and discover how much of what his mother told him is true.

"Anybody home?" he calls through the open door. He tries to respect the Reynolds' privacy, venturing only as far as the porch, where he's passed several pleasant evenings discussing with Frank how they can ensure fragrance on a summer's evening and colour the year round.

"In here, Mr Cooke! Is it Mr Reynolds you're after?"

The air tastes of bread fresh from the oven and the hot metal of baking trays. "Actually, no. It's Gerrard."

"He'll be cleaning out the aviary, I expect." Mrs Reynolds wipes her forehead with a sleeve. Like Miss Hoddy, Mrs Reynolds doesn't stop what she's doing simply because he's made an appearance. He wonders if she ever stops. "Here, let me wrap up a few of these rolls for you to take home." She is already busy with the greaseproof paper.

"Aren't they for the pavilion?"

Tentatively, Mrs Reynolds ventures, "Yes."

He hadn't thought it necessary to keep track of stock. Mrs Reynolds lets him have a list of what she needs, and he places the orders. At another time he might let it pass, but not now, not today. "I know you mean well, but ingredients bought for the gardens must be accounted for."

She shrinks into herself. "I only thought because it was you…"

"The gardens *have* to pay for themselves. That can't happen if we start making exceptions."

Head bowed, eyes downcast. "I understand," she says, quelled.

The discomfort in the room is as tangible as the heat from the range. Robert looks about, at the shelves, at the larder door. "Do you have sufficient storage to keep your own supplies separately?"

"I'll manage, I'm sure."

At the door, he turns. "I hate to think of food going to waste. If something isn't saleable, give it to your family, by all means." He sits his hat on his head.

Outside again, Robert closes his eyes briefly. Badly done! *No,* he corrects himself. *It needed to be said and now it's out of the way.* The next time he sees Mrs Reynolds, he'll thank her for her hard work and put any unpleasantness behind them.

Gerrard is in the aviary. He stands talking to a bird whose wiry talons are wrapped around his finger. "Off you get." The boy brings his digit parallel to a perch, but the stubborn bird clings tighter. "Off, you little blighter, I've a lawn to mow!" The bird plumps its feathers and fans its tail.

Robert imagines Miss Hoddy with a hand up to the wire mesh, perhaps holding a sunflower seed to tempt the birds closer. "I hear Miss Hoddy is very fond of the parakeets," he says.

"Oh, she is!" Gerrard's mouth falls open as he realises he's been tricked into saying something that perhaps he ought not to have said. "Mr Cooke," he stammers. "Have I done something wrong?"

"Not at all. Miss Hoddy comes early in the day because she doesn't like crowds."

"I don't charge her." Gerrard grimaces. Robert has known boys like him, boys who own up, hang the consequences. Robert had not been one of those boys. He wasn't nearly so brave. "It wouldn't feel right."

"I wouldn't expect you to." It strikes him that after what he said to the boy's mother, his message must be consistent. "But you charge everyone else?"

The boy's grin is sudden and mischievous. "Double if they look as if they're from London. After I've had the entrance fee, I follow them around and make sure they order their teas and buns." And with a jerk of his arm, he tricks the parakeet into flight.

"And where is John?"

Gerrard turns his back and picks up the bucket of sawdust. "He'll be about somewhere, I expect."

CHAPTER TWENTY-FOUR

AUGUST 1895

Robert is passing by the cottage when Frank approaches him. "Can I have a word?" he asks sheepishly. His good eye is bloodshot.

In the summer months the hour between five and six is considered most suitable for exercise. It is ten to four and Robert had thought to take advantage of a brief lull before the rush. "Can it wait?" he asks. "I'd thought to show my face at home."

Frank's face suggests not. When Robert steps up the path and moves towards the bench under the eaves, Frank gestures to the open door. "I'm afraid it concerns our John."

Robert swallows. "John?" He hasn't allowed himself to dwell on the tableau he witnessed, of John looking at his daughter. Just a look, he'd convinced himself. Now he recalls the flush in the hollow of Estelle's throat.

"Do sit, Mr Cooke." Mrs Reynolds pulls out a chair at the kitchen table. "Sit."

All around are signs of industry – bones are being boiled for stock, dough prepared and balled for morning rolls, boots paired and polished – but Frank and his wife wear the downcast looks of guilty schoolchildren.

Mrs Reynolds tucks a stray hair into her cap. "I'm afraid John spent last night in the cells."

The relief! For a moment Robert thought... He is not sure what he thought, but it was not this.

A gruff involuntary sound comes from the back of Frank's throat. "I've been dragged into Sutton nick before now. Humiliating, it was. All I'd done was stop to watch a quarrel, thinking I might need to step in."

Visibly agitated, Mrs Reynolds frowns at her husband. "The thing is, the constable doesn't seem too inclined to let our boy out." Her eyes tell of the image she has of police cells. Vile-smelling places full of every ne'er-do-well that's been had up on a night charge. All of the Toms who'd quarrelled with policemen, the Dicks who'd got up a row and the drunken Harrys. "We wondered if you might see your way to vouching for him."

"Did they say why he was taken in?"

"He's been spending his evenings riding the train to London and back," says Frank. "Playing draughts for money."

Robert looks from Frank to Mrs Reynolds. "Was there any suggestion of cheating?"

"Not him." Mrs Reynolds is adamant. "He's always been skilled at the game. He won money from city gents, that seems to be the crux of it."

As a man who regularly places bets, Frank wouldn't have been in any position to criticise even if he'd known what John was up to. He might even have encouraged him. "A simple bet between two men," Robert says. "That's hardly a crime."

Frank folds his arms across his chest. "The authorities don't seem to look too kindly on it."

"Not in the face of complaints, they don't!" Mrs Reynolds widens her eyes.

"It makes no sense. Why pay up and *then* complain?" John is just one person, as tall as his father, but without Frank's bulk or strength. "He *was* operating alone, was he?"

"What do you mean?" Mrs Reynolds asks defensively.

Robert picks his words carefully. "He didn't have a second – to take care of his winnings?"

Frank's mouth tightens. He understands Robert's meaning: someone who made sure the city gents coughed up. "No," he says but waits for Mrs Reynolds' careful nod before continuing: "The only other thing they told us is that John only buys the one ticket but rides there and back several times."

"It's hardly picking pockets. All right." Robert winches himself to his feet. "I'll see what I can do."

"Thank you, Mr Cooke, thank you!" Mrs Reynolds ushers him out. She has such confidence in him, he would not be the person to tell her that her boy must go before the magistrate. "Gerrard said he felt awful, lying to you like that."

Taken aback, Robert turns. "When?" but he knows, even before Mrs Reynolds answers.

"He said you asked after John and he told you he didn't know where he was."

"Tell him I'd have done the same for a brother of mine."

On his way towards the gates Robert nods to a good number of people – faces he knows. There are few strangers in a place the size of Carshalton. He greets Professor Spanier, who sneezes and reaches for a handkerchief.

"I am here under sufferance."

"A touch of hay fever?"

"An allergy to Mrs Harvey Carlisle, perhaps."

Robert turns, gapes. Carshalton's matriarch is approaching, unhurried, upright. From a distance, with her white hair covered by a bonnet, she might easily be mistaken for a younger woman. But she wouldn't wish that, because she likes to believe she's earned her position, as so many people born to wealth seem to. Is she simply curious, or could it be that Cooke's is now the place to be seen? He turns back to the professor, intending to remark that the Carlisle's grounds must be twice as large as his gardens, but the professor has scuttled away.

A woman who rarely smiles, Mrs Carlisle does not do so now. "Mr Cooke." Her clipped salutation offers no hint of what will follow.

Robert grabs for his hat. "Mrs Carlisle." He is used to her avoiding eye contact, and it is strange to find himself held in her steel blue gaze. "What an unexpected pleasure." Should he apologise for his worsted wool jacket and work boots?

"Your rose walk is a treat." Still no smile. "Would you be so good as to convey my regards to Mrs Cooke?"

"How kind of you to remember her. I'd be delighted." *Freya will wish to call and leave her card. Imagine, if that were to lead to an invitation!* But Robert is getting ahead of himself. Unless he resolves this business with John, it will all come crashing down before it has even begun.

Outside the gates, several private carriages are waiting, drivers stretching their legs and enjoying a smoke. He might be taken more seriously if he were to arrive at the station-house by carriage, but in the time it would take Abbots to ready the horses he could be on his way. A decision, then. Robert marches the same route he took each day as a schoolboy, passing the juncture of the Wandle and Pyl Brook, the holly bush. To keep any hint of scandal out of the papers will be his priority (Loax can be bribed, but there'll be others). Then the question of what to do about the Reynolds – he couldn't possibly keep them on.

Slow down. There is no suggestion that John has broken the law.

That will be his assumption. Robert must present himself as a person who's accustomed to walking into station-houses and demanding the release of innocent employees. He strides up to the counter. "I understand you have a John Reynolds in the cells." His nostrils twitch. Even in the front office, a stench of slops and unwashed bodies pervades.

"We do, sir. Know our young gambler, do you?"

"He's in my employ." The lack of a carriage is one thing. It would be easier to be self-righteous in a stern suit than a collarless shirt. "I've already lost a day's work. On what grounds are you keeping him here?"

"On the *grounds* that he's a mouthy young so-and-so who'd benefit from a couple of nights in the cells."

"If he objected to being brought in without good reason, he's perfectly within his rights."

The constable leans forwards, anchoring himself on his elbows. "It's one of those grey areas, isn't it?"

"What is?"

"Gambling." Said with a sneer.

"A wager between two men is perfectly legal."

"As the law stands it may be so, but as to whether it's *moral...*"

Is the constable trying to bully him into offering a bribe? "Given the reason for the young man's detention – obtaining money by fair means in a game of skill –"

"Draughts," the constable smirks, but Robert will not be undermined so easily.

He grits his teeth. "I wouldn't want to have to notify your superiors that you attempted to extort money from me."

"Who mentioned money?" The two men stand there looking at each other, long enough for Robert to wonder if he's damaged John's chances. But the constable narrows his eyes. "I'll fetch him for you."

Left alone, Robert pinches his nostrils shut and breathes through his mouth. He has no desire to remain here any longer than is absolutely necessary.

John is brought out in handcuffs. He's dishevelled, but Robert can see no sign of mistreatment. If a lost night's sleep is the worst of it, he'll have escaped lightly enough.

The constable fetches a bunch of keys from a drawer. His mouth is close to John's ear as he says, "I'm obliged to inform you that if you're caught gambling on railway property again, young man, you'll be banned from the trains."

John inspects his wrists, massaging their soft insides. Robert, sensing that John is warming up to say something, takes his arm. (Hard and muscled, no longer a boy's arm.) "Thank you, constable. We won't be troubling you again."

But John is spitting anger. "Taking bets isn't against the law."

"Perhaps it isn't," the constable says, "But the railway is in private ownership, and they're not obliged to sell you a ticket."

Robert has John most of the way to the street door before the younger man shakes him off. "I should like my money." Robert hadn't thought this far ahead. Naturally John feels aggrieved, but carry on in this hot-headed manner and he'll land himself back in the cells. "I won it fair and square."

"I don't have your money, son."

"Then who does?"

"You'll need to ask at the railway station."

John takes in the constable's smug expression, then without another word turns and walks out of the door. Robert remains. He has no doubt that the stationmaster has *some* of John's winnings – fifty per cent of it, he imagines. "I hope that's what the record shows," he says.

Robert lengthens his stride to catch up with the boy. "John!" He dodges an open-mouthed street-hawker, not waiting to hear what he has to offer. "John! Are you hurt?" By now, he's a little breathless.

Nothing.

"My house is at your disposal if you'd like to bathe before seeing your mother." He flinches. *Not such a good idea. Estelle will be at home.*

John maintains his pace. "I don't know how many times I have to repeat this. I've done nothing wrong."

"Which is exactly what I shall say if I'm asked."

"No one need hear about this."

"John, Sutton's a small town with two local newspapers and not enough crime to keep its journalists happy. I'll do all I can, but a groundless arrest is quite a story."

That brings the younger man to a halt. He puts his hands on top of his head and turns a full agonised circle.

"It won't go against you, I'll see to that. It might even help get your winnings back."

"But there won't be any more where they came from."

"How much *did* you win?"

On the move again, and fast. "Excuse me, Mr Cooke, but I don't see that it's any of your business."

Robert tries a different tack. "Why the trains?"

"I got talking to a man who put himself through law school with what he won from playing dominoes on the trains. I thought, *Why not draughts?*"

"What do *you* need money for?" Once the question is out, Robert realises he's afraid of the answer.

John turns to him, scoffs. "I don't want to be a groundsman all my life."

"You're not thinking of law school?"

"I'm thinking of business."

As if that's an occupation in itself! And yet Robert had no particular leaning towards poppy-growing. It was simply that he had a family to provide for and saw there was more money to be made than he could hope to earn from bookkeeping. Is Robert's difficulty that self-help usually involves hard graft and, while perfectly legal, John's gambling seems like an attempt at a shortcut? (The other shortcut, emigration, seems unlikely in John's case.)

"What I said…" Not quite contrite, John's tone has lost its accusatory edge.

"Go on."

"There's nothing wrong with what you pay me." John shrugs. "It's just that it all goes to my mother."

With four wage-earners in the household, surely Mrs Reynolds must be able to spare him a few coins? "I don't suppose it would help if I were to speak to her."

Daggers.

"I thought not." Perhaps there's another way. A kind of bare-faced cheek. *Play Cooke's Champ at Your Peril.* "I'm curious. How do you decide whom to approach?"

"I go to first class and look for anyone reading The *Sporting Times.*"

A sure sign that someone's not adverse to a bet. But John is not only smart, he's hot-blooded. Something that needs to be kept in check. "Your mother says you're a skilled player. Just how good are you?"

"You have to give the odd game away, otherwise no one will play you."

If it could be kept separate from the tennis and limited to the evenings, it might even become a lucrative sideline. "What if I were to allow you to use the pavilion for your games? It would have to be above board."

"I'd keep my winnings?"

"Seventy-thirty in my favour. But I'll cover your losses for any games you have to give away."

"Fifty-fifty."

"Not when I'm already paying you a wage. But you'll be free to set the bets. Think it over."

CHAPTER TWENTY-FIVE

AUGUST 1895

The Cookes are going up in the world! An invitation to one of Mrs Carlisle's famed dinner parties. Access to Carshalton's inner sanctum.

Freya hums as she considers her detachable collars and cuffs, the contents of her wardrobe. *Altered. Refurbished.* "This, perhaps." *Re-trimmed.*

It's said that when you've earned a regular place at Mrs Carlisle's table, she presents you with a set of cutlery engraved with your name. "You must have something new," Robert insists.

She consults her dressmaker. Nile-green silk, richly embroidered with white silk and beads. There are fittings, adjustments. A week later, a delivery, boxed and wrapped in layers of delicate tissue. Robert is pleased to see Freya so happy, confident that she won't let him down.

The evening arrives, and with it, stirrings of trepidation.

"You don't think the sleeves too bold?" Freya stands in front of her mirror, fussing at them. They are puffed, larger than her normal style, an aspect that delighted her when she first tried on the finished gown.

"Not at all!" Robert hopes he sounds convincing. He doesn't know the first thing about ladies' fashions.

"It's not nearly so complicated for men." She plucks at some other barely discernible detail. "All you need do is replace your frock coat with a dress coat."

If only that were true. Robert has chosen a coat with a traditional collar over one with a roll collar, a single-breasted waistcoat over a double-breasted waistcoat (cut low, of course), a boiled shirt with a winged collar over one with a straight-standing collar, mother of pearl studs over enamel with gold, a white piqué bow tie over black, patent-leather button boots over pumps, and after all this, the only item he's absolutely confident about is his top hat. In that, he had no choice.

The carriage rocks. Freya pulls at the fingers of her white satin gloves. "What if I should call someone by the wrong name?"

Robert stills her hands with his own. "You won't. You've spent your entire life preparing for this opportunity." But the evening has taken on the mantle of a test. There's every reason to be nervous.

Outside, a row of gleaming carriages. Freya cranes her neck to look. "We're not late, are we?"

He checks his pocket watch. "We're in perfect time," he assures her. Tardiness is the kind of thing that can limit a person's ascent through the social firmament. They decided on arriving fifteen minutes before dinner is to be served. It seems that other guests decided on thirty.

Robert sees Freya down and slams the carriage door behind him. He and his wife know Brandries Hill House in the way that all but a privileged few do, from a distance. The Palladian mansion once belonged to Sir Francis Baring, founder of the bank of the same name, who made his money in the usual way (sugar production in the West Indies). Robert allows himself a moment to stand on the terrace and look out over the panorama. Were it still light, he would see a bowling green, a patchwork of deep green watercress beds and purple lavender fields.

"It's difficult to tell where the grounds end and the fields begin," he remarks.

Freya leans close. "You're assuming the Carlisles don't own the land all the way down to the Wandle."

They cross the courtyard, where men in livery taking the night air speak among themselves in low voices. "Breathe," he advises Freya. She'll be less anxious once she's inside and has assured herself that her sleeves are right for the occasion.

The vestibule is as dwarfing as a cathedral's nave. Robert's eyes range up the marble staircase to sparkling chandeliers and gilded-framed portraiture. He feels the lightest nudge of his wife's elbow, realises he's gawping. His gaze bypasses the alabaster goddesses stationed in individual niches and an array of potted palms to alight on an elephant's foot, a repellent thing stuffed full of parasols and walking sticks. A trigger that jogs his memory. Something he heard about Mrs Carlisle's father having cultivated a taste for hunting from his time in India, perhaps a suitable topic for conversation.

An impeccable butler shows them to the blue drawing room. (How many drawing rooms can there be?) Robert pauses to allow Freya to go first. It would hardly do to arrive side by side.

"Mr and Mrs Robert Cooke."

He sees Freya tense and looks for the reason. Their hostess is also in green, perhaps not Nile-green, but dark green, bottle green, green nonetheless.

Mrs Carlisle's eyes steel. "Mrs Cooke." She makes a great play of greeting them, but it is unmistakable. "Do look at us, both in the same colour."

Heads turn.

Eyes rake Freya, the newcomer, the social climber, a northerner from what little they've heard, up and down, up and down, and Mrs Carlisle all the while smiling. "And doesn't it become you, my dear?"

Confidence visibly dissolving, Freya opens her mouth to respond, perhaps a compliment about Mrs Carlisle's gown.

"And Mr Cooke." Something gritted about the way she uses his name. A hard 'k'. "How wonderful that *you* could join us."

"It was kind of you to include us both in your invitation." Under her gaze, he remembers – how could he have forgotten? – that Mrs Carlisle's father was found dead after a shooting party. Lying there, still clutching his double-barrelled gun, and no way of knowing which of his company fired the fatal bullet.

"Do make yourselves at home." In the tide of her gesture, they are swept towards the centre of the room, where dry sherry is offered.

"I'm mortified." Freya whispers, chastened, the words that might have saved her unspoken. "Should I have made it my business to find out?"

"Who would you have asked?" But the answer seems obvious: Mrs Carlisle's dressmaker. All the comfort he can offer is his own near-blunder. "I almost mentioned her father."

"Robert!"

"We must make the best of it." He looks about. "Do you see Mr Carlisle?" Their host is known not to be at ease with social gatherings. If his wife allowed it, he would correspond with the world only by letter.

"Over by the fireplace," Freya barely moves her mouth, "with Sir Jeremiah Colman."

Ah, yes: white moustache merging into muttonchop whiskers, his chin clean-shaven, Mr Carlisle stares at his shoes like a child receiving a dressing-down. There is no possibility that Robert will catch his eye.

Freya angles her head to Robert's ear, the first fragile signs of a recovery. "Goodness, Sir Jeremiah does appear to enjoy the sound of his own voice."

Something about a visit to Stonehenge, from what Robert can hear. How after he chiselled off a modest souvenir some hawker calling himself a caretaker demanded that he hand it over. Naturally, he refused. And what did Sir Jeremiah see later? The scoundrel selling stone fragments, no doubt the very ones he had confiscated! Perhaps Mr Carlisle prefers the company of someone who doesn't require anything from him. Sir Jeremiah may be an angel come to stand guard.

The Benhiltons are here, and several racehorse owners Robert knows by sight. He sips his sherry, alert to anyone who might acknowledge them.

"Isn't that –?"

"Mr Berkeley James," he confirms, inclining his head. The owner of the manor that lent its name to the Oaks, which passes through his estate en route to Epsom Downs.

The Cookes are the youngest couple by quite some margin. Back on the bottom rung. *Spit-polish my shoes, day boy! Go and warm the toilet seat!* Things you think you can't do that you suddenly discover you can – and more besides. Robert finds himself repeating eagerly, "No, we haven't been introduced before, but of course, I know *of* you."

He is able to make an exception for the mayor, who attended their Grand Opening and greets them amicably. "Cooke's gardens are a wonderful facility for the community to have at its disposal."

At her most charming, Freya says, "We were *so* grateful you were able to find the time to come, your Worship."

"My dear Mrs Cooke, you cannot imagine what a relief it was to leave politics behind for a few hours." A bell sounds; high, bright, pristine. The mayor turns his head. "Ah, we're about to go in."

Robert excuses himself and seeks out Mrs Benhilton,

whom he is to escort to the table. "Mrs Benhilton." He makes a small bow and presents his arm.

She is in apricot, her dark glossy hair elaborately curled and piled high. If she's disappointed to find herself paired with him, she is most gracious about it. "So few opportunities to meet new people." As if she has forgotten entirely that the Cookes sit three pews behind her in church.

The rustle of silk, the gleam of varnished shoes, dazzling silverware, candelabra alternating with floral arrangements, crystal bowls overflowing with candied fruits. Too much of too many things vying for attention, and the glory of it all multiplied by carefully placed mirrors. Reactions among the bright constellation of Carshalton society are restrained. Such dizzying opulence is apparently nothing to remark upon, so Robert withholds any comment he might have made.

Mrs Benhilton locates her place holder. "Here I am."

Surprised to find his card positioned to the right of his hostess (who is seated at the end of the table) and opposite Mr Berkeley James, Robert hesitates. *Do not sit down in a place of honour, lest someone more distinguished than you has been invited.* "Well," he says discreetly as he helps Mrs Benhilton with her chair. "I wasn't expecting this."

She turns her head away from Mrs Carlisle. "Newcomer's privilege."

Not all newcomers, apparently. Freya's seat is some distance from Mr Carlisle's. Robert wonders if her card has been moved. A punishment for the dress, perhaps. Surely if she's guilty, he is equally culpable?

Under the tablecloth Robert peels off his gloves. He hadn't realised he would be under such close scrutiny. If he could, he would communicate to Freya how grateful he is for her ministrations this past fortnight to ensure his hands neither look nor feel like a labourer's. *Gloves on his lap. Starched linen napkin on top. Bread roll to the left of his place setting.* He looks to Mrs Carlisle, whose neck drips with diamonds, desperate not to miss any opportunity, however small, to make an impression. People refer to her as elegant, and she is undeniably so, but was she ever beautiful? She is engaged with Mr James (something about breeds of horses). Robert keeps half an ear on the conversation Mrs Benhilton is involved in (a new bronze the British Museum has acquired). At last Mrs Carlisle tears her bread roll in two (her almond-shaped fingernails may be the most elegant thing about her) and Robert does the same.

It is only after the soup bowls are collected and the wine has been poured that Mrs Carlisle addresses him: "Mr Cooke, we heard about your mother's adventures."

"Oh?" Robert enquires in what, to his own ears, is an exaggerated manner. His formerly reclusive mother strides about like the Wild Woman of Borneo and is fast gaining a reputation as the village eccentric.

"Last Sunday, after church." Not a smile, but a slight upward curl of the mouth. "Will you tell the story or shall I?"

A story? Silver cutlery stills.

Ignoring a twinge of disloyalty Robert says heartily, "You should tell it. I might introduce a little bias – inadvertently, of course."

"Well, since you insist." She addresses the table. People who might introduce the Cookes to influential people, should they so choose. "The good Reverend Mears rather outdid himself with his sermon. I can't think of a single parishioner he didn't damn for all eternity," Robert is quick to join the enchanted laughter, "but, as everyone filed out of church, he and the good Mrs Mears were there as ever to shake each of us poor sinners by the hand."

"Fearless of the threat of contamination." Robert immediately regrets his interjection. It might suggest a presumed intimacy with his hostess.

"Quite," Mrs Carlisle says. "Your mother, if I recall, has been somewhat... *irregular* in her attendance in recent years."

Pinned by her stare, he struggles for words. "In all fairness, before her travels, my mother very rarely left her house." There can be no illusion now. Robert is Mrs Carlisle's latest performing bear, claws trimmed, teeth extracted and chains attached to rings through his nose so she can tug on them whenever she wants him to dance. And dance he does. "Now it's the opposite. We can't keep her within doors." He defers to Mrs Carlisle. "But I'm jumping ahead."

"A little, perhaps. The Reverend said to her, 'We're delighted to see you, Mrs Cooke,' and Mrs Cooke – Mrs Cooke senior that is..."

"Oh!" Her cheeks two bright spots, Freya waves away the distinction.

"She replied, 'A most informative sermon, Reverend. I had no idea my soul was in such grave peril. And *beer* will do that, you say?'"

Another burst of laughter and Robert, knowing what is coming next, stretches his mouth into an even wider smile.

"'Does the Lord hold equally strong views on sherry?' she asked."

"Good God, I hope not." This from someone to Robert's right.

It is Freya that Robert feels for. Fashionable society had, at last, seemed within her grasp.

"At which time *Mrs* Mears decided to intervene, saying, 'Forgive me. I was under the impression that you no longer believed.' To this Mrs Cooke replied, 'I found it rather easier to believe in God in Scotland. You really must go.' And Mrs Mears said, 'Thank you, but we have no need for Scotland. We are already firm in our belief.' This was the *precise* moment the landlord of the Coach and Horses set down his barrel of beer, and on seeing him, Mrs Cooke said very sweetly, 'Do excuse me,' then called out, 'I'll take a pint!'"

The small part of Robert that craves an audience silences the larger part that hates it. "To my mother!" He raises his wine glass.

"Goodness, is that true?" Mrs Benhilton asks, after drinking a toast.

"She downed the lot." Robert's jaw aches from the lantern show of mock bonhomie. "It was her first taste of ale, and she assures me it will be her last."

"Tell us, Mr Cooke, what is it we hear about this new festival of yours? I understand you promise feasting under the stars."

"It's actually a revival of an ancient Roman festival in honour of Neptune, the god of water. But – and I imagine Mr James already knows this – Neptune is also the god of horse-racing."

"Do you hear that, Mr James? Mr Cooke says that Neptune is the god of horse-racing."

"Quite so, Mrs Benhilton. Neptune Equester. It's where the word *equestrian* comes from."

"Well, I never!"

At her most convivial, Freya says with a cultivated sunniness Robert admires, "I do hope you'll join us, Mr James."

"Madam, if it has anything to do with horses, I'd be delighted."

He had not imagined for a moment... Robert glances at his hostess. *Should he extend the invitation?* But there is no need. If Carshalton's Best and Most Prosperous say they'll attend, Mrs Harvey Carlisle will claim her place at the head of their table.

The mood during the ride home is reflective. Between husband and wife it is understood. This is not friendship (people like Mrs Carlisle have no need of friends), this is *patronage*, but they can still benefit from it. The food too rich for his constitution, indigestion will keep Robert awake, with guilt for company. (He allowed his mother to be the subject of a joke!) He looks sideways at Freya who is faring no better than he. She will be thinking about her dress. The Nile-green dress. Perhaps it can be dyed.

Now that Robert has Carshalton's senate to impress, recreating ancient Rome seems a far greater challenge. "If I were to say 'ancient Rome' to you, what would you think of?" he asks Estelle at breakfast.

"An amphitheatre."

He turns to Ida. "And you?"

"Mosaics."

"Chariot racing."

"The forum!"

None of this is cheering.

"The guests will be in fancy dress." This, from Freya. "They'll provide the scenery." She has consulted the fifth edition of Debenham and Freebody's *What to Wear at Fancy Balls*. "As host, perhaps you should dress as Bacchus, god of wine and the harvest."

He studies the illustration. A cloak. A crown of vine and ivy. "I'd better grow a beard," he concludes miserably.

Outside the gardens, Robert encounters street-sellers. Hot eels in halfpenny cupfuls. A potboy with foaming cans of beer. Mutton pies. He is nettled to find John on the gates. "You didn't think to see them off?"

"I tried to, but I don't have your authority."

"You can't stop us provided we stay outside," says the pieman in response to Robert's demand that they leave.

"You're on my land, and I can."

"Where does it say so?"

"Everything up to the railway workers' cottages is mine. It's a place for carriages to set down our visitors, it is not here so that every hawker in Carshalton can take a bite from my profits." He waits for them to disperse, then says to John, hackles half-raised, "No one comes in with food or drink they've bought outside."

"But then they might *not* come in, and we lose the price of admission."

Damnation, the boy's right. "Are we more expensive than the street-sellers?"

"No, but we don't carry the same range."

"I am *not* stocking jellied eels. All right. Let me think on it."

In answer to the question about ancient Rome, Frank says, "Get me some stone and cement, we can build a ruin easily enough." But there are still the ordinary chores: winter pansies to be sown, iris and daffodils to be divided, geraniums and delphiniums to be sheared off just above ground level, slugs to deter. Visitors won't want to visit a building site, but neither will they expect to see weeds among the foxgloves.

"We don't need to build it *all*. I'll make a sign," Gerrard volunteers. "Give the buildings new names and leave it to people's imagination."

"Frescoes," says Miss Hoddy when he calls on her on his way home. "For the walls of the pavilion. Ida and I will work on them. We won't even charge you."

"That's very generous of you."

"Isn't it?" Already she is sketching. "Tell me, will there be chairs or will your guests recline on cushions?"

On Sunday at All Saints, while Reverend Mears works himself up into a righteous frenzy, Robert stares at the statue of Sir William Cawen, dressed in his Roman robes. *You are not so very convincing.* The skull stares back at him.

"Mr Cooke!" Mrs Carlisle calls from her carriage window in a way that only someone whose status is assured can. Should Mrs Carlisle ever fall from grace, she'll have little in the way of manners to fall back on.

He takes off his hat (he has only this minute put it back on) and faces his tormentor. "Mrs Carlisle, Mr Carlisle." Mr Carlisle is in profile. "Good day to you both."

"A week to go. I trust your preparations are well underway?"

He tries to visualise Mrs Carlisle reclining on cushions, Mr Carlisle feeding her grapes, then dismisses the idea. "We're hard at work constructing the forum." He exudes all the confidence he can muster. "Even as we speak, columns are rising along the rose walk." An outer wall surrounding the bandstand, Frank assures him, will give an impression of a ruined amphitheatre. He hopes the honeysuckle and the jasmine – the evening flowers – won't be past their best.

"Mr Cooke." She pulls on his chain, beckons him closer. "I would like your assurance that I shall be the only Roman empress."

What she is really saying is *Your wife will not come as an empress.* Of that, he has no fear. Freya has decided on the Roman goddess Diana. (How will Mrs Carlisle like that?) But *other* empresses may arrive at their gates. Would Mrs Carlisle have him turn *them* away?

"In return, I will offer you the use of my cook and kitchen staff. I take it you were going to use caterers?"

The slightest drop of his jaw. Simple but plentiful fare is how he has priced the event, and Mrs Reynolds is more than capable. It is far too late to change strategy. "That really is most generous, but –"

"You may send your menu up to the house with instructions for what you would have Cook prepare. The dishes will need to be finished on site, of course. She'll let you know what equipment she requires."

"I –"

"And I hope you will understand, but Cook prefers to source her own ingredients."

What choice does Robert have? He bows his head and grieves at the loss of a little more of his self-respect.

"The gardens were lit to mimic the stars in the heavens. As carriage after carriage rolled into the Approach, guests were welcomed by their host, dressed" – Here, Miss Hoddy gestures to Robert and begins to speak theatrically, rolling her r's – *"for the occasion as Bacchus, god of wine and the harvest, who welcomed them to 'the forum'."* They are alone in the Hoddys' house. Robert had intended to pay a brief call and drop off the *Chronicle*, thanking Miss Hoddy for her frescoes, but Oswald asked if Robert wouldn't mind if he stepped out for an hour – he would be doing him a great favour – and there was not a part of Robert that wanted to refuse.

"The ancient Rome created at Cooke's Pleasure Gardens was a romantic ruin. The bandstand became an amphitheatre and the pavilion was transformed into a villa, with frescoes and mosaics depicting scenes inspired by Giuseppe Fiorelli's excavations of Pompeii. Couches were arranged in a U-shape around a central table, so that pleasure-seekers could experience feasting in the Latin style. But the success of Neptunalia was due as much to the guests as its host." Miss Hoddy breaks off from the newspaper column and with mock-indignation demands, "How dare they suggest such a thing?"

"How indeed?" says Robert, though he penned the piece himself.

"Much thought had been given by the dignitaries, businessmen and artisans who gathered together, each ensuring that the minutest particulars of his or her costume were accurate.

Mr and Mrs Jeremiah Colman made an impressive entrance dressed as Mark Antony and Cleopatra. To transform herself into the Greek queen who ruled Egypt, Mrs Colman had styled her hair in imitation of an image taken from coins minted in the year 37 BC. Her cape was designed to resemble the wings of a phoenix, embellished with thousands of bead-anchored sequins. Mr Colman wore an impressive breastplate depicting a roaring lion, mail armour topped with a scarlet cloak, and high Greek boots. What *does* a Greek boot look like?"

"I confess, my knowledge of Greek footwear is limited, but Mr Colman's looked rather like an elongated sandal with crossover ties."

"Mrs Benhilton came dressed as 'Aquarium' in a short-layered skirt reaching to the ankles. The ankles. Imagine! The underskirt was of satin, edged with brown plush to represent rocks, while the upper skirts were of sea-green tuille with fishes worked in floss silk. The bodice was cut low and trimmed with seaweed and the basque was formed of scallop shells. It sounds terribly uncomfortable. *As well as being god of the sea, Neptune has equestrian ties. This little-known fact was not lost on Mr and Mrs Berkeley James, who arrived on a pair of magnificent jet-black stallions and wearing antique riding habits from their private museum collection.* Hmmm," Miss Hoddy muses. "I wonder what I could have worn from my private museum collection. *Last to arrive was Mrs Harvey Carlisle, who outdid even Lady Dudley's famed costumery as a Roman empress.* Tell me, Mr Cooke. How many Roman empresses *did* you turn away?"

"Not one. I merely suggested some alternative identities they might like to adopt." Now that Robert's ordeal is over, it is possible to make light of it. In fact he feels strangely light-headed. He cannot be certain if he's taken off his mask and is revealing his true self, or if he has simply taken off one mask and donned another. Either way, it feels dangerous.

"Ah, here we are. Our one true empress. *Mrs Carlisle wore a broad, jewelled coronal, her hair beautifully ornate with ringlets framing her face, which was powdered white. Her stola (the dress that signifies the status of married women) was bordered with exquisite embroidery and affixed with silver brooches, and on her arm was a distinctive snake bangle, created especially for the occasion in the likeness of a piece displayed at the British Museum.* The British Museum, no less! *She was accompanied by Mr Carlisle, who came dressed as Gaius Julius Caesar Augustus Germanicus.* Am I right in thinking he was known as Caligula?"

"Indeed he was."

She closes the pages. "In which case, wasn't he mad?"

Their conversation is a clash of bright swords. "The story goes that he waged war against Neptune and won, then ordered his men to collect seashells as 'loot.'"

"Altogether the wrong choice for a festival held in Neptune's honour." He detects a glimmer of a smile.

"One might even call it tactless." What a relief it is to be able to laugh, not having to worry about doing or saying the wrong thing, with the wrong emphasis, at the wrong moment. Of appearing too self-important, or failing to put himself forward enough. To dance in time with Mrs Carlisle's music.

At the sound of unstable half-burnt coals collapsing, they turn to the fireplace. Embers spit from the flames like wayward fireflies.

"It seems we've angered the gods. Would you?" Miss Hoddy gestures to the fire irons.

Robert goes to work, pushing coals back from the hearth, making a tidy mound of them. "If I have learned one thing," he says, "it's that one cannot argue with the Carlisles."

"And I suppose *one* cannot do without them."

"I'm still waiting to find out how much the ingredients cost me. It must be a tidy sum. But the oysters!" His eyes close over in memory of them.

"Well, you did it. Your first big event since the Grand Opening and it was a great success."

We did it, his thoughts echo. *We proved the naysayers wrong.*

Miss Hoddy stretches out her arms as if yawning. "And I'm terribly glad I had a perfectly valid excuse not to go."

"Oh, and what was that?"

"I didn't want to."

"You might have enjoyed yourself."

"Among your stuffed shirts?"

"Stuffed –? I'll have you know, Mrs Jeremiah Colman climbed onto the fountain," at this, Miss Hoddy sits forward, "and sat astride one of Neptune's horses, then demanded wine, which she drank straight from the jug."

"Oh, how utterly delightful!" Miss Hoddy clasps her hands together and leans back in her chair. "What a sight that must have been!"

"I have one other small piece of news." Robert is a little puffed up. This is what he has been wanting to tell her.

"Let me guess." Air sucked sharply through her teeth. Should he ask if she is quite all right? But Miss Hoddy continues, "Do you know? I had never taken Mrs Colman for a hedonist."

"You were about to guess."

"I have it! You're to be appointed mayor."

"Something even *more* extraordinary. The Colmans are moving to Reigate and have asked if *I* would like to buy their family pew."

"But that would put you opposite..."

Something Robert didn't dare imagine two years ago. "The Carlisles!"

"I don't like to dampen your spirits, but –" Suddenly solemn, Miss Hoddy censors herself.

"What?"

"Surely you must see? That's an awful lot of noses you'll be putting out of joint."

Robert's smile dissolves. His world slows. He's made the decision to fund the purchase by selling off the Approach. After all, he's losing the battle to deter street-hawkers. They are still there with their jellied eels.

"And if not the families you'd leapfrog, then the Carlisles themselves. Robert, you weren't thinking of accepting... But you *were!*"

She called him Robert, but there's no pleasure in it. She's right, dammit. Mrs Carlisle may have him sit at her table, she may even seat him next to her so long as it's understood that this is a privilege. But she would look with contempt upon an attempt to buy his way into her echelon. He'll have to tell Freya he has thought better of the purchase, but the land, the land is gone. He signed the deeds of transfer two days ago.

CHAPTER TWENTY-SIX

OCTOBER 1895

He asks to be put in charge of turning out the lights, so that he might reclaim the gardens after the pleasure-seekers have left for the evening. The courting couples who have strolled under the arc of the rose walk. Men with copies of the *Sporting Times* tucked under their arms. Between the shadows Gerrard slips, extinguishing lanterns strung from branches, returning the night to its natural indigo or black, depending on the moon's cycle. But he is not alone. Foxes, bats, hedgehogs; once an encounter with a badger.

He squats down on his haunches. "Lost your bearings?" The animal snuffles about the tennis court. His father won't welcome any damage to his perfect turf, though the badger, its eyes gleaming beetle-black, has most likely returned to an old feeding-ground and discovered it altered.

Often, only distant stars and the glowing windows of the cottage light his slow, lingering way back to the front door.

Later, he is woken by the percussion of rain on roof tiles. Back to back with his brother, in the sloped-ceilinged room, little separates them from the weather. When he was younger and woke to darkness, Gerrard would whisper, 'Are you awake?' until John replied, 'I am now!' Now he sends a thought out into the night: '*Are you awake?*' She doesn't sleep well, sometimes not at all. There's no need for her to explain. He understands what horrors a person who has suffered an accident such as hers might see when she closes her eyes.

In the early mornings, too, the gardens are his. There's a magic to the place before the gates are opened and in troop tennis players swinging their racquets, high-spirited children with their hoops, ladies from the big villas who've come to take their exercise, the watercress sellers spruced up in their Sunday best. Only one person increases the magic. She arrives with the dawn, smelling of rosewater and turpentine, a heavy shawl draped around her shoulders, a tartan rug over her knees. He takes the handlebars of her chariot, waves Oswald off, asks, "Are you ready?" and her eyes shine their answer. Off they set. It is the hour when cobwebs glitter, when petals are jewelled and the grass is fragrant. Though Gerrard pushes her, there is never any doubt who's in charge. "This way, Master Reynolds!" she commands.

Chin low, he puts his full weight behind the task – he's had plenty of practice mowing the lawn. Even so, the gravel offers resistance. It takes time to build up to a run. Speed is a way for her to feel in the places where feeling has gone. Once momentum carries them, it's as if he's racing to keep up. She whoops in a way his mother calls unseemly, but really, what is that? One of those words which sounds as if it knows what it's talking about, but when you break it down, it means next to nothing. And who is here to take notice?

She pays attention, wants to know everything. She sees not only what's there, but what's been removed, and what might be there if you had a mind to make alterations.

He calls them her gardens – but for her they wouldn't be as they are – and she calls them his, in honour of the generations of Reynolds who laboured here. In stolen hours, they share this feeling of illicit ownership, but they are never completely alone. Birds open their beaks in a crescendo. First the black-birds, then the robins, the wrens, chaffinches, warblers and thrushes, and finally the late risers – the finches. Later, after the ground has been warmed by the sun, the hum and the buzz of insects will begin, bumblebees and beetles walking drunkenly over blades of grass. But for now, songbirds flit from high perches or flurry from small hollows. They risk revealing themselves for a meal of scattered seed. Embold-ened, the small brown wren watches the cosseted parakeets in the way a person might gawp at caged monkeys. Miss Hoddy holds her hand to the wire mesh. "Fairfax takes sunflower seeds from my mouth," she dares them.

Sometimes they nibble timidly, but the robin is happy to sit on her wrist and eat from the palm of her hand.

Gerrard wishes he could take her inside the aviary, so she could join him at the centre of the whirlwind, but in the time it would take to lift the wheels of her chariot over the metal lip, the parakeets would make their escape. Part of him thinks of how magnificent it would be to see them streak across the sky.

Instead he tells her that the warbler may have met a par-akeet before. That it mimics other birds, showing off about where it's been over the winter. "All the way to India," he says.

"When I was a girl, nothing was known about migration. We were taught that birds hibernated. The parakeets – have they laid any eggs?" Like his, her curiosity is greedy. Her eyes gleam with it.

"Quite a few." He repeats the phrase Mr Cooke used: "They're enthusiastic breeders."

She laughs loudly, then covers her mouth in a way that makes him laugh too.

"What did I say?"

"Nothing." But when she removes her hand, she laughs some more. "What happens to the chicks?"

"There aren't any."

All of sudden, her eyes are serious. "Whyever not?"

"We take the eggs away."

"Oh." She falls silent in a way that compels him to explain.

"Too many birds competing for the same space, and they start to squabble. That's what happened with number twelve."

"He squabbled with the others?"

"Not him, he's too timid by half. The others pulled out his tail feathers. Plucked them straight from his body."

She makes a small noise in the back of her throat, as if she is not surprised. "I know people who would do such things," she says.

It is not only the aviary that is inaccessible to Miss Hoddy. She cannot enter the grotto, studded with seashell porpoises, starfish, an octopus and, at the centre of it all, a mermaid. He did the tail, he tells her. He followed her design. *She's rather like a mermaid in her own way.*

She catches him staring; lifts her chin. "What?"

Gerrard looks away. He knows a man with a wooden leg who manages to get about perfectly well. A year's rent, it cost. But to think of Miss Hoddy on wooden legs, he would have to imagine there is nothing underneath the tartan rug, and that thought is too ghastly. She's better off as a mermaid. "Nothing," he says.

"It was something."

Despite the morning chill, his ears burn. "I was thinking that you're like the mermaid."

She smooths out the ridges in the tartan rug.

Only a year out of school, the memory of being made to wear the dunce's cap is strong in him. It was a stupid, stupid thing to say. He moves back behind her chair so that she can't see his beetroot face.

"I never would have thought of that." Her blind right hand fumbles up over her shoulder to find his, and clasps hold. "Shall I tell you what I miss?" she asks fiercely.

He is very still, barely daring to breathe. "What's that?"

"The grass under my feet. Sometimes I dream of walking here, barefoot." Gerrard sees she has closed her eyes. There is a faint smile on her lips. It is a still, not-to-be-interrupted moment.

A moment later she breaks the spell, lets go her grip: "Shall we go and see Neptune?"

He takes her to the old chalk face where the Roman god towers above them in a chariot of his own, drawn by three rearing horses, eyes wild, nostrils flaring, ears pinned back against their heads. Her eyes narrow, challenging, *Do your worst.*

The first time she saw it – them – she asked, 'Where on earth did Mr Cooke find such a thing!'

'It was his father who bought it.'

'Thought it might come in useful, did he?'

But her delight is evident as jets of water cascade into the oval-shaped basin, catching the morning light. He checks the coins, leaving just enough to encourage people to make a wish, but not so many that they pose a temptation. Even his father won't trouble himself with farthings.

He shows her the new rock garden they are building, and she approves.

"Your father's a clever man. Not everyone can take a plan and bring it to life the way he does. And now, it seems, he's turned designer."

"Mr Cooke –"

She cuts him short. "No, not Mr Cooke. Mr Reynolds."

His father ought not to be so proud that he fooled his schoolmasters into thinking he could read. He passed his school-leaver's certificate by reciting text he'd learnt by heart. The boy shrugs, says bullishly: "He just sees what needs doing and does it."

"He *sees,* that's the important thing. Not everyone does."

Gerrard is struggling to separate things, to make sense of them. *'I'll have that.'* The night of Neptunalia. And because bigwigs had been gallivanting, the money in the fountain wasn't just shillings, sixpences and the odd half-crown. It was half-sovereigns and sovereigns.

'This belongs to Mr Cooke,' he'd said. 'It's part of the takings.'

'Until it's written up in that book of yours it's fair game.'

'It's Mr Cooke's book and it's Mr Cooke's money!'

'What's all this carry on?' His mother, looking from one of them to the other. 'Well?'

'My father's after Mr Cooke's money.'

'It's only a few coins the rich folk made wishes on.'

'Show me.' A long brooding silence. 'Give your father a half-crown.'

'But –'

'I *said,* give him a half-crown.'

Hours later, heavy tread on the stairs, a thud as his father stumbled against the wall, and the cursing that followed. Then the noise Gerrard doesn't like to hear, the noise that travels through thin walls. "You make him sound like an artist," he says, and there's regret in it.

"The roof of the bandstand is a work of art. If he can do that, then who knows?"

He wonders if he might also be clever, the particular type she admires.

As if reading his mind, she says, "Joseph Paxton was only a gardener when he met the Duke of Devonshire. Sometimes that's all it takes."

He scoffs, "We don't get too many dukes around here." With that one sentence, he betrays his ambition.

She smiles, knowing, satisfied. "Come on, let's go and smell the roses."

Gerrard's skin seems altered where her hand clasped his.

He pushes her chair under the curving trellises and she cups a single bloom, brings her head close, inhales. "In five years' time they'll be at their best," he tells her. In five years' time Gerrard will be seventeen. When she clasps his hand, he'll respond.

PART THREE
1900 ~ 1902

CHAPTER TWENTY-SEVEN

MAY 1900

i

Robert walks the edge of the field. On each poppy stem is a single bud, which will nod until ready to bloom. Each white flower's glory lasts for thirty or forty hours, no more, before the petals fall away to reveal the part that interests Robert: the seed head. Smithers finds him resting his elbows on a gate. The older man is breathless. Can Robert come and see? Now, if it's not too much trouble. Someone's pasted a bill-poster about a meeting of the Society for the Suppression of the Opium Trade on the farmyard gates.

"Do you think it's a threat?" Smithers asks as they stand looking.

"No," says Robert. "The society's a Quaker organisation. Letter-writing and protest is what they do – though I admit I don't like it." But opposition is not only coming from the Quakers. It's a rare Sunday when Reverend Mears doesn't opine that the twin evils of alcohol and gambling are at the root of man's spiritual malaise. Recently he's identified a third culprit, more destructive than the first two: opium. While Englishmen will protest at the first sign of incursion into their personal liberties, when the message is thundered from the pulpit it's a different matter entirely. Robert can afford no more of his ostrich attitude. "We ought to hear what they have to say."

ii

John is ankle-deep in the fountain, feet bare, trouser legs rolled up, scooping out coins with the kind of net that Estelle has seen used for butterflies or tadpoles. "So many wishes," she says, the sound of her voice making his shoulders jerk.

He takes his time straightening up, reaching for the brim of his cap and falling just short. "Even you must have something you want, Miss Estelle. Have a go."

So many things she wants! From her pocket, she takes two farthings. She shows him the one that is damaged at the edges. "Will this do?"

"The older the better."

She's about to throw her coin when he catches her wrist. She gasps, "Did I do it wrong?" But she doesn't pull away.

"Throw it over your shoulder." He lets go his grip (she is rather sorry when he does that), turns around, the water swimming around his ankles, and mimes for her. "Like this."

"Why?"

"I don't know why, it's just what people do."

She turns her back, but knows he's looking. She can feel his gaze.

"And close your eyes."

She bites her bottom lip, aims over her shoulder. A splash. Too small for her wishes.

"Just the one today, Miss Estelle?"

"What do I get for two?"

"Two's for love."

Her breath hitches. "And three?"

"Three's for wedding bells."

"I think I'll stop at one."

"Pity," he says, getting back to his work, but Estelle has concealed the second farthing in her fist, and again she closes her eyes. A second splash and away she walks, biting her lip, smiling. She doesn't look back. Looking back would cancel the wish.

iii

The scrape of chair legs; the smell of wet wool. The meeting of the Society for the Suppression of the Opium Trade is well-attended, with few seats spare. Neither Robert nor Smithers expects to be recognised at the Croydon meeting house, equidistant from Mitcham and Carshalton as it is. All the same, they're conscious that these plainly dressed men and women believe their trade is morally indefensible. Smithers pulls his brown derby low as they shuffle into a row of severe wooden chairs. Responding to a nod, Robert is reaching for the brim of his own derby when he recalls that Quakers don't remove their hats indoors and is caught in an awkward half-salute. They sit. While Smithers folds his arms, Robert takes out his notebook and scores a line under his last entry.

He doesn't catch the name of the first speaker to take to the podium. Perhaps the man doesn't give it. What he does do is describe in considerable detail his association with Sir Joseph Pease, the society's president. "Gentlemen." Finally the speaker seems to be coming to the point. Robert readies his pencil. "I'm a plain-thinking man. I approach the subject of the opium trade on general principles. The time to discuss specifics will be when we come to legislate."

Robert and Smithers exchange furtive glances.

"In the eyes of the world, the manner in which this country conducts the traffic of such a dangerous commodity is of supreme importance. Great Britain's responsibility in India is a heavy one. If there are chinks in our armour, you may depend upon it, no people are more capable of locating them than the Indian people. In China, again, we have a nation eminently capable of sifting and considering our relationship with them. They will very quickly uncover our selfishness in pushing trade for the purpose of our own gain." So ingrained is the view of the Empire as a profoundly moral undertaking that even in this company, the comment deepens frowns. "This evening, like you, I am here as a willing disciple, to listen to those who have a far better right to speak on the subject than I. Mr Hughes, will you take the stand?"

The next speaker begins to add meat to the bones. "It is impossible to exaggerate the misery and degradation that has resulted from the opium trade. The responsibility for this rests entirely with the British Government, however well-meaning their intentions were. All right-thinking persons must agree that Great Britain has no right to derive income by inflicting a wrong upon people who have never done us harm." He raises a hand to silence an outbreak of murmurs. "Let me be clear: it is not an anti-British sentiment I'm expressing. It's *because* I value my native land so dearly that I wish to see this dark blot on its reputation erased."

All about, nods. *Better.*

"Indulge me if you will while I explain how the Indian trade operates – a system that the House of Commons condemned this April last. The East India Company – with whom I'm sure you are familiar – created the Opium Agency. Two thousand five hundred clerks working from one hundred offices administer the trade. The Agency offers farmers interest-free advances, in return for which they must deliver strict quotas. *What's so wrong with that?* you may ask. What is wrong, my friends, is that the very same Agency sets the price farmers are paid for raw opium, and it isn't enough to cover the cost of rent, manure and irrigation, let alone any labour the farmer needs to hire. And Indian producers don't have the option of selling to higher bidders. Fail to deliver their allocated quota and they face the destruction of their crops, prosecution and imprisonment. What we have is two thousand five hundred quill-pushers forcing millions of peasants into growing a crop they would be better off without. And this, *this,* is the Indian Government's second largest source of revenue. Only land tax brings in more."

More muttering, louder. The shaking of heads and jowls.

"I propose a motion. That in the opinion of this meeting, traffic in opium is a bountiful source of degradation and a hindrance to the spread of the gospel." Quakers are not the types to be whipped up into a frenzy of moral indignation, but their agreement is enthusiastic. "Furthermore, I contend that the Indian Government should cease to derive income from its production and sale."

Robert looks about. Surely he can't be the only one to wonder what is to replace the income the colonial government derives from opium? Ignoring this – and from a purely selfish perspective, provided discussion is limited to Indian production – his business will be unaffected. Seeing his neighbours raise their hands to vote, Robert lifts his own to half-mast. Beside him, Smithers does likewise.

A woman dressed in a plain brown dress and bonnet walks up and down, pointing her pencil at each raised hand.

Having secured a majority, Mr Hughes grows in confidence: "Now is the time to bring an end to this detestable traffic, and not just in India. Let us call on the government to limit the cultivation and export of poppies in *all* territories that come under its influence to strictly medicinal requirements."

Robert can say with absolute confidence that his poppies

are used for medicinal purposes – as an anaesthetic, in sedatives, for the relief of headaches, migraines, sciatica and numerous other painful conditions. As a cough suppressant and to treat pneumonia, and for the relief of abdominal and bowel complaints and women's cramps. But there is danger here. His poppy-seed oil has numerous uses besides medicine. Hold his tongue and the legislator may employ the reference to *strictly medical requirements,* severing a valuable income stream.

"If we throw away this God-given opportunity, let us beware lest we never be entrusted with another."

Robert raises a hand, not to cast a vote, but to put a question.

"Yes, the gentleman with his hand raised. Mister –?"

Robert stands. "Cooke. Mr Cooke." He feels himself colour.

"Mr Cooke, you have the floor."

"Can I firstly say how wholeheartedly I support any proposal to curtail the distribution of opium for recreational purposes. My question relates to the proposal to ask the government to limit the growth and distribution of poppies strictly to medicinal use. With all deference to my learned friend, I wonder if this meeting is aware that oil derived from poppies is used in all manner of domestic products. Everything from paints and varnishes to soaps and liniments."

"Do I take it, Mr Cooke, that you have a financial interest in such matters?"

Robert feels rather than sees his neighbours looking at him. "I'm involved in the manufacture of paints and varnish, yes." They need not know the whole of it.

"In which case my question for you, Mr Cooke, is this: is it possible that another type of oil – one sourced from a plant less likely to do the populace harm – might be used in its stead?"

"But if poppies continue to be grown for legitimate

purposes, would it not be wasteful if their by-products were not put to good use?"

"We must all weigh up the terrible evil opium represents. My personal belief – and I make no secret of this – is that other medicines which even now are being developed, and which carry far fewer risks, will do away with the need for poppy-cultivation entirely. And so my recommendation to you, Mr Cooke, is that you look for another source of oil. Does that answer your question?"

Robert understands. This is no debate. The speakers don't expect to be challenged. "It does, thank you." He sits, scraping his chair legs as little as possible.

The meeting concludes. By silent consensus he and Smithers refrain from speaking until they are certain they won't be overheard. As they walk towards the point where Abbots is waiting with the carriage, the regular scuff of their boots – at first two sets and then, as they fall into step, one – is their only accompaniment. Robert's breath forms a fog in the night air. Only when they are settled in the cabin does Smithers say, "What did you make of it?"

"It won't stop here. These people believe they have right on their side. One vote will lead to another."

"And what will that mean for the business?"

"If foreign growing ceases, and there's a reasonable chance it will, then competition will drop and –"

"Prices will rise!"

"In which case, rather than diversify, we'd do well to turn more land over to poppy-cultivation."

"It wouldn't be without risk."

"No, no it wouldn't. But I'm confident the British public feels more at ease with British produce, and the name Mitcham is the best guarantee of quality they have. What's impossible to predict is how long our heyday will last."

"Then you agree that other medicines will replace opium?"

"Opinion's already turning. It's the public rather than the legislators who hold our future in their hands."

"Just how much land would you turn over to poppies?"

Dithering will only compound their predicament. "All of it." Though Robert says it impulsively, it is not without sense.

Smithers hoots. "It's a bold plan."

With no one yanking his chain to make him dance, Robert feels as though he's his own man once more. "The question is, how soon to act."

CHAPTER TWENTY-EIGHT

MAY 1900

i

"The roses are marvellous this year," his mother says. "They smell divine. Do smell, Estelle, they're like Turkish Delight."

Estelle obliges, if only half-heartedly. Robert sympathises. Hettie hardly gives the appearance of someone whose judgement on matters of taste can be trusted. Things she was once so fastidious about – dressing appropriately for the occasion, for example – no longer concern her. Here she is at the gardens in country clothes and stout shoes. In contrast, his daughter has taken great care over her appearance. He's proud to have Estelle on his arm. She's now the age Freya was when she came to Carshalton to take a spring-water cure. Six months later they wed. Freya has mentioned this several times of late, and seems to expect him to react in a very specific manner, but Robert would not push his daughter in that direction, not when she rolls her eyes at any sentence that mentions 'the future wives and mothers of England.' Robert has heard her say it to her sister: 'Of course, we, the future wives and mothers of England...' with any number of endings and, ridiculous though they sound, they stray very little from the nonsense aimed at young ladies by popular magazines.

His mother inspects another peach-coloured bloom. "Have you considered distilling your own rosewater, Robert?"

"Mrs Reynolds has suggested it."

"And?"

His distillery is busy enough with poppy and peppermint oil. "I've said I'll think about it."

"I'd be interested to see how she goes about it." His mother clearly thinks Mrs Reynolds means to do it herself, as if she has time to spare! "What about you, Estelle? Rosewater must be something you make regular use of."

There are matters more pressing than the distillation of rosewater. It all began with the Reverend, who is up to his usual tricks, sending Mrs Mears to call on Freya. A certain amount of gambling has been tolerated these past few years. Draughts is a harmless game and, unlike the horses, requires a degree of skill. 'But now I understand we have *lady* parishioners placing bets. You do see why we must speak out against it?'

Freya was completely unaware of their little sideline. 'I was utterly humiliated,' she told Robert. 'On and on she went, like a Greek chorus.' As she spoke Freya massaged her temples. 'Every mention of the word *gambling* was accompanied by a reminder that those who accept bets are unscrupulous monsters.'

Robert felt his eyebrows lift. Since the gambling that has come under the Reverend's scrutiny concerns the tennis, Robert conceded that Freya *should* perhaps have been informed. Cooke's Academy has produced not one but two talented players. Their tutor, Miss Baskin, feels each has the potential to compete for a place at Wimbledon, and the pair have drawn to play each other this coming Saturday. That Cooke's candidates are young ladies has proven irresistible to the women of the parish. 'I must admit, I assumed you knew,' Robert said. 'Several of your friends were among those who asked John if he'd offer odds.'

Freya looked offended. 'I knew nothing about it.'

Unsure if this was because her friends had left her in the dark or because he thought she condoned women gambling, Robert asked, 'How did you leave it with Mrs Mears?'

'I agreed to raise the matter with you. What else could I say?' At this, Freya took a small brown bottle from a pocket. He assumed they were her 'women's friends', but the two pills she shook into her palm were white. 'Oh, and she made it very clear that the matter doesn't sit well with your position on the Parish Council. I know I shouldn't say so, but Mrs Mears really is the most appalling woman.' She placed the first of the pills on her tongue.

Scarcely able to believe what he was witnessing, Robert demanded, 'What are those?'

'Something new, I forget...' Freya wrapped her fingers around the label. 'The pharmacist recommended them.'

He thrust out an impatient hand. 'Let me see.'

'I know I shouldn't have...' Reluctantly, Freya laid the bottle in his open palm.

Aspirin!

She shook her head, tearful. 'Mr Burgess says he's coming under pressure to stop stocking opium-based products.'

Robert knows Burgess's game. He is targeting wives, the ones who decide which drugs to purchase for domestic use. 'I doubt even *he* knows what's in half the products he sells, or in what concentration. Until manufacturers are forced to list their ingredients on labels, they won't come clean. There are substances that do far more harm than opiates.'

'I dare say you're right.'

'Return the bottle. Tell Mr Burgess they had no effect and that you'd like your money back. I've no shortage of powdered opium. We'll make our own laudanum.'

Freya's cheeks were bright spots of colour, her mouth a thin tight line. 'And what will you tell Reverend Mears?'

'That he's a hypocrite. He saw nothing wrong with betting on the tortoise races – on a Sunday, too.'

Freya looked appalled. 'Please, Robert, have a care.'

'Fine. I'll remind him that once a bet is placed, there's a binding contract. I can only return the money if the match is cancelled.'

After their conversation, Freya sent her maid to the pharmacy in her stead and retired to her room. And so she is not with them at the gardens. Not there to interpret Estelle's glance at the cottage as the front door opens inwards. To watch her hope fade as Mrs Reynolds appears, stirring up dust clouds as she shakes out a rug.

Hettie waves a hand in greeting. "Good day to you, Mrs Reynolds!" She thinks nothing of raising her voice and striding through the middle of Nettie Easter's tennis practice. "We were just saying how beautiful this season's roses are."

Robert steers Estelle around the court muttering, "Your grandmother left her manners in the Scottish highlands."

"Mrs Reynolds," Estelle says brightly. She even manages a smile.

"Miss Estelle. Mr Cooke. Do mind yourself with the dust. I'm afraid you've caught me at my chores."

"Mrs Reynolds was just telling me," says his mother, "Mr Reynolds thinks this year's roses might be competition-standard."

"Of course, it's as much a question of timing as anything, but it *would* be rather nice for Mr Reynolds to have a win to his name." She blushes and nods to Robert. "For the publicity it would bring to the gardens, is what I mean."

The evidence of Frank's gardening is all about. The flowerbeds in front of the cottage weren't part of Miss Hoddy's design, but every cottage deserves a garden – dahlias, fuchsias and chrysanthemums – and if Mrs Reynolds thinks of it as her own, what of it? Robert touches the brim of his hat. "If it were a win for Cooke's, the credit would be his."

"That's very gracious of you. I'm so glad the way it's turned out. The chalk would have killed him, just as it did his father, God rest his soul."

"Work is the cause," Robert concedes, "often as not."

Mother, mother, I feel sick.

Send for the doctor, quick, quick.

Doctor, doctor, shall I die?

Yes, my dear, and so shall I.

"It's only John I have to worry about now."

"John?"

"Oh, Mr Cooke, I assumed you knew." Realisation that it's too late to backtrack is writ large on Mrs Reynolds' face. "He's taken it on himself to join up with the Third Surrey Rifle Volunteers."

A catch in his daughter's breath. Without thinking, Robert tightens his grip on his daughter's arm and shores her up. It is only a moment before she rights herself, but that moment cements what he thought he already knew.

"What a war being fought on the other side of the world has to do with my John, I don't know, especially one that seems to be over diamonds, but John's headstrong, as you know yourself, Mr Cooke."

Unsure how to respond and with his mind still on Estelle, Robert settles for, "He's always known his own mind."

Every bit as upright as her mother would have her be, it is Estelle who finds the right words. "Well, they can certainly use good men."

"He's never even seen the sea," says Mrs Reynolds. "Now he'll have to cross an ocean."

And who knows what John will face when he arrives? The newspapers do their utmost to make the war in South

Africa sound like a holiday, describing quayside crowds waving bowler hats, umbrellas and handkerchiefs as ships loaded with young men, horses and boxes of ammunition set a course for Cape Town. Last December's defeats came as a rude awakening to Britons taught in schoolrooms about their nation's might; assured of it by priests and politicians. Many volunteers signed up and shipped out in January, and now John.

His mother turns to him. "What do you know of the Boers?"

Savages, if you believe what you read in The *Times*. But what his mother expects are words of solace. "Farmers," Robert replies. "Each with his own horse and rifle, but no military training to speak of. They elect their own officers but are under no obligation to obey them."

Hettie takes this information; offers it, mother to mother: "There you are, Mrs Reynolds. Chaos!"

"Well," Mrs Reynolds hugs her rug to her chest, "it does provide some comfort to hear you say that. And don't you worry, Mr Cooke. Mr Reynolds and Gerrard will take up the slack."

"We'll manage, I'm sure." What is a pleasure garden when a war is being fought? It is selfish even to think of it.

Later, his wife seeks him out in his study, where he is at his paperwork; asks if he knows what could have caused Estelle such distress. "Nothing happened today, did it?"

He recalls the moment when his daughter's knees gave way. How quickly she rallied and how admirably she conducted herself. "Not that I can think of."

"I can't imagine what the matter is."

The clock on the mantlepiece strikes the hour. Almost without thinking, Robert takes out his watch, his father's and his grandfather's before him. It would have gone to Thomas. "Leave her to it. She'll sleep it off."

Freya smiles wanly. "I suppose so."

He adjusts the time, winding the crown between finger and thumb. "How is your head?"

"Much recovered after a rest."

She does not credit the aspirin. Robert does not apologise for his sharpness. "I'm glad to hear it. Do we need to run over the details for Saturday's match?"

"Everything's in hand." At the door she turns. "You will remember that we're to dine with the Benhiltons tomorrow."

"I had not forgotten."

ii

A Ladies' Championship to Rival Wimbledon

Rarely has more striking proof been offered that women are claiming the game of tennis as their own than Saturday's match between Miss Nettie Easter and Miss Lilian Dixie. A carnival atmosphere and fine weather attracted a large gathering at Cooke's Pleasure Gardens, where the dull shades of the workday week were abandoned in favour of bright waistcoats for the gentlemen and waves of fluttering silk for the ladies.

Both young ladies are pupils of the tennis academy based at the same establishment. Miss Nettie Easter is seventeen years of age, the daughter of a London hotelier. Her choice of apparel for the occasion was a white, ankle-length skirt with a small bustle, a long-sleeved silk jersey blouse and a sailor hat in the style of her heroine, Miss Maud Watson. Her opponent, Miss Lilian Dixie, though her junior by a year, is no stranger to the world of competition. She hails from nearby Epsom where her father is a renowned trainer of Arabian racehorses. She chose a full skirt, this time in navy, and cut to clear the ground by a full four inches. This she paired with a high-collared white blouse with ruched sleeves and a navy and white striped tie. Her choice of headwear was a straw boater with a plain white ribbon. Today's younger players go by the maxim, 'For freedom of movement, the simpler the outfit, the better,' the proof of which is in their game.

From the first serve it was apparent that the players were evenly matched, and the contest proved to be a tight one. In the excitement of the hour, riotous applause greeted the execution of any particularly good stroke. Better play than that which was shown by the young ladies is seldom seen even at Wimbledon. The service, the rhythm of the swing, the quick returns and the sharp volleying were breathtaking, and this was coupled with impeccable footwork, balance and weight distribution. Miss Easter captured the first set, astounding the crowd with the sheer artistry of her game, but, exhibiting greater accuracy in her strokes, Miss Dixie fought back to an eventual win. Her prize was a silver and glass hand mirror and silver-backed brush valued at ten guineas, donated and presented by leading socialite, Mrs Harvey Carlisle.

iii

"Gerrard!" Miss Rotherham says when she finds him reading the headlines outside her tall thin post office and bookshop. "I've been saving unsold copies of The *Sporting Times* for John, but he hasn't been by to collect them."

"He's gone, Miss Rotherham."

"Gone?" She turns her angular face towards him. "Where?"

"To South Africa. He joined the local volunteers."

She looks to the headline Gerrard was reading. "I had not heard." He doubts Miss Rotherham is a slow reader. She must read it several times over, because a few moments pass before she speaks again. "In that case, follow me. I have something that might interest you."

She is surprisingly brisk for someone of her age. It's impossible for Gerrard to say he must get back to his work, so he goes after her. Already behind her counter, Miss Rotherham is untacking a map of South Africa from the wall. "The *Daily Mail* published this, it must be two years ago now. I've been pinning flags to track the troops' movement." She spreads the map on the counter. "Do you see?"

Gerrard scans the routes, recognising a couple of place names he's read in the headlines: *Paardeberg* and *Bloemfontein*. Names he spelled out in his head, but hasn't been sure how to pronounce.

"I think you should have it, don't you?" She begins to roll the map.

"But, Miss Rotherham, all your flags…"

"I've a terrible admission to make, Gerrard." She pauses to look him in the eye. "And I hope we can keep it between us. I only kept the map going because it helps to sell newspapers. But your brother is risking his life."

Gerrard swallows. It is not that he doesn't think the same thing every day. But to have someone say it.

"And so you *must* take it." She passes him the rolled map. "We'll just find some string to tie it with." She cuts a length, makes a neat bow around the scroll and then pushes the string down to the centre. "That should do it. And I shall put the tacks in the box with the flags." He watches as she slips a couple of lemon drops in with the tacks. "There. Come and see me when you're here for the headlines. You shall have your pick of the unsold newspapers. That way you can stay up to date."

He finds he is gawping. *Thank you* doesn't seem adequate. "I –"

"Enough." She waves him away. "You'd better get back before your father misses you."

CHAPTER TWENTY-NINE

SUMMER 1901

"Gerrard would never say so, but he misses his brother dreadfully." Florence isn't painting, not at this hour. All the same, her attention is divided. Hettie must share Florence with Fairfax, and this poses a strange contradiction. Hettie willingly gave the parrot to Florence, but she can't help feeling jealous when Fairfax shuns her. "Before John went to South Africa, I don't think they'd ever spent a night apart."

"When someone you know is actually there, fighting," Hettie shakes her head as if it is almost beyond comprehension, "it must bring the war closer to home."

"Do you think he's trying to prove himself?"

The room at the rear of the Hoddys' house, the bright room overlooking the garden, is a place where problems are taken apart at the seams and re-stitched. Hettie considers the question. (What would Robert consider proof of John's worthiness? A Queen's South Africa medal?) While she does so, Florence puts a striped sunflower seed between her lips and turns towards Fairfax, who sidesteps along his perch, extends his neck, and takes the seed delicately in his black beak. The pair are intimate in a way that she and Fairfax never were, because Hettie was a different person then. She sighs, feeling the press of her ribcage against her corset. "I don't even know for a fact that John cares for Estelle."

"I *knew* it!"

Caught out, Hettie says flatly, "You weren't talking about Estelle."

"I wasn't, but *now* you must tell me everything."

"There really isn't much *to* tell. All I know is how my granddaughter reacted to the news that John had signed up, and Robert's response to her reaction." It was a year ago and still she pictures how he shored up her granddaughter.

Florence turns back to Hettie. "He responded?" There's a precision to the way that Fairfax nibbles at the edges of the seed, as if he's opening a can of condensed milk. "And there was I, mistaking him for a man who blunders through life." Florence's throwaway manner suggests she doesn't expect to be taken seriously.

Still, Hettie is moved to defend her son. "My Robert isn't nearly as insensitive as you think." Sated, Fairfax fluffs himself out. His neck feathers sit like an Elizabethan ruff. "His business puts him under tremendous strain. I tried to talk to him about poppy-production when the anti-opium brigade was first making its voice heard. Well, you can imagine how *that* went down! And now, I don't know, I fear it's the turn of the gardens." Hettie finds herself nodding, the smallest of movements, resisting what instinct is telling her.

"What makes you say that? I doubt many local tennis clubs can boast that they produce players fit to compete at Wimbledon."

"That's *precisely* what I'm thinking of. And the trouble is, I can't think of any other reason why Robert should have been so desperately upset when Nettie Easter was knocked out in the first round." He stood up from his seat in the stands and excused himself, saying he needed some air. About to point out that they were already outside, on seeing how pale he looked as he lumbered past, Hettie held her tongue.

"Give the poor girl a few years. Time's on her side."

"I don't know that Robert *has* a few years."

"What did he think would happen had she won?"

Hettie rolls her eyes. "Publicity, I imagine. *Cooke's Academy: training ground of champions.*" It feels as though she's describing someone who is clutching at straws.

"You don't think he placed a bet on the outcome?"

She shrugs. She has pondered exactly that. It was as if he'd wagered everything on the belief that a slight seventeen-year-old girl would be his salvation. And ever since, Hettie has been possessed by an unaccountably morbid feeling, the kind she last experienced before Walter died. "I can't help him because he won't appreciate his ancient mother interfering, but you..."

"Oh, no! I know nothing about finance. It's your daughter-in-law you should be speaking to."

Somehow, Hettie imagines Robert would shield Freya from bad news. "But *you* translated his vision."

Florence makes a small noise, as if this is a responsibility she would refuse. Her right hand comes up to cover her mouth and her darting eyes suggest that, beneath it, an internal struggle is taking place.

Hettie moves to the edge of her seat. "What is it?"

"Perhaps now is the time to tell you." There is a softening in Florence's voice, a kindness that can only spell bad tidings. Hettie swallows. *This* will be the cause of the morbid feeling. *This.* "For some time now, I've been having trouble with my circulation." It is a controlled and dignified performance. "It's quite a job to manage it when I have such limited movement."

"It must be."

"I've put it off for as long as possible, but what is recommended is that," there is a tremor at the corner of Florence's mouth, "I lose one of my legs."

"Oh, my dear!" The words rush out.

"It's not as if they're much use to me. But I am dreadfully afraid."

"Of course you are." Hettie's instinct is to ask if she's sought a second opinion, but Florence seems to have reconciled herself as to the necessity, which can't have been easy. "And here am I, burdening you with my woes."

"To be honest," an attempt at a smile, "I enjoyed the distraction."

Already, the wall within Hettie is reasserting itself, wanting to rebuild itself from the rubble, brick by brick. *It is only the old fear,* she tells herself. *The fear that means you don't allow yourself to love, or where it cannot be helped, not completely. Well, it's far too late for that.* She goes to Florence's side. Takes both her hands. "Tell me what I can do."

Fairfax chooses this moment to begin tut-tutting. He peers at Florence as if he, too, is invested in her response. She removes one of her hands from Hettie's; strokes a single scaled toe. He steps from the perch to her shoulder; huddles against the side of her face. How Hettie wishes she might do the same!

"I'll have no need of a wooden leg, but thanks to you I already have the parrot." Brave words that bring Hettie one step closer to tears. "It's Oswald I worry about. It's far worse for him than it is for me, and all we have is each other." Florence's breath catches. "That must have sounded most terribly ungrateful. You've been such a dear friend to me."

"Not at all. You two are as close as any brother and sister can be."

"You will look out for him, won't you? Keep him occupied."

Hettie refuses to listen to talk of things in the past tense. "After the surgery, would you like me to come and stay?"

"Would you? Oswald wouldn't leave my side after the accident. He didn't sleep for months on end, poor dear."

"There's no reason why Annie couldn't come too if more hands are needed –"

"Only people I know." She is resolute. "And none of the vultures. Promise me you won't let Mrs Mears come and peck at my bones."

"I'll bar the door, I promise. When will it be?"

"Soon I hope. I meet with the surgeon next week."

"Quite right," Hettie says, though a horror rises up in her. "Best not to have too much time to dwell on it."

"Will you tell dear Ida? Do you think she'll take it badly?"

"She loves you very much, but she's a practical child. Of course, I'll tell her."

"And Mr Cooke? Do you know, my grandmother prophesied that I was going to be lucky in life because I was born with a star-shaped birthmark on my back."

Hettie fights to maintain her composure. "You *will* be lucky."

"For years, I'd stand in front of the mirror and look over my shoulder so that I could see my star, and think, *I'm special*." Florence says this in a mocking way, accusing her younger self of naivety. "And then, I don't know, I suppose I must have forgotten about it." She widens her eyes. "Maybe I was caught looking at myself in the mirror and told to stop it."

"Oh! Most probably!"

"But when I next looked, the star seemed fainter, and I thought to myself…" Florence nods.

Hettie knows what comes next. The star is barely visible. It is possible that after Florence's accident it disappeared entirely.

But Florence's expression brightens. "Would it be too awful if we were to have a little farewell party for my leg?"

"That's a marvellous idea." In this moment Hettie would agree to anything. "How many of us will there be?"

"The three of us, then there's Ida and Gerrard and Mr Cooke."

"Six," Hettie says, unaware even of the exclusion of Freya and Estelle. "I'll go and make sure Oswald won't object if I order champagne and a cake."

In the hallway, reality comes at Hettie with a sickening rush. *Scalpels and incisions, saws and muscle and bone.* She cups her mouth and slumps sideways against the wall. She can hear Oswald laying down preparations for the evening meal.

First her father, then Walter.

Well, she'll have no more of it.

As Hettie enters the kitchen, he looks up from his bowl of flour and suet. "Florrie told you." Carefully, he wipes his hands on his apron. "It's a thoroughly wretched business."

Barely knowing what to do with herself, Hettie rests both hands on the table for support and lets her head drop. Questions race to the front of her mind and she pushes them away. Of course, Oswald wouldn't allow the amputation were it not absolutely necessary. And it would be unthinkable to tell him she's heard of surgeons who recommend unnecessary procedures simply to gain experience of the operating theatre. "I take it there are signs of necrosis?" she says at last.

He looks at her anew. "You're familiar with the condition?"

A reluctant acceptance begins to take hold, but Hettie wishes – how she wishes – it were otherwise. "My husband was a doctor."

"I didn't know."

"He's been gone a long time." *Listen to me, Walter, so dismissive.* "You've done well to keep it at bay for so long."

"We've worked hard at the massage. It hasn't been easy for Florrie, to have her brother do these things for her, but she never complains. Not a word."

Hettie never had a brother. Even if she had, she doubts he could have been as loyal or true. A long time has passed since Hettie held anyone, but her arm goes out to Oswald. He doesn't shrug it off.

"Will this be how it is from now on? First one leg and then..." Oswald bites down on his lip. Hangs his head and shakes it.

Oswald has faced losing Florence before. Hettie senses he came closer to it than he'd ever admit. And now the thought of what his sister will have to endure in order to live. "We cannot know that. We must be strong for Florence. But you and I, we may shed a few private tears together." She angles her head as Fairfax would, slides her hand around Oswald's stooped shoulders and dares to pull him to her side. "I have said that after the operation, when Florence is home again, I'll come and stay." She stands there, holding him. "I warn you, I'm no kind of cook." She can feel his shaking, his thinness, his stoop. After a moment, his forehead comes to rest against hers. "We'll manage," she says, and then silently, vehemently, to the God she still takes issue with, *You shall not have Florence, not if I have anything to do with it.*

Hettie has walked, she knows not how far or for how long. She walked until it struck her that it matters not what words she might use to deliver the news. She cannot shield her son and granddaughter from the blow. The surgeon may recommend that Florence's surgery shouldn't be delayed, in which case it could be as early as next week.

At this hour Robert ought to be at home, and if he is not, then she'll ask her daughter-in-law to be with her when she tells Ida.

Outside the front door she closes her eyes; acknowledges that she feels sick to her stomach. She tugs on the bell-pull. Lifts her chin.

A brief wait and the maid opens the door.

"Good evening, Kate. Is my son at home?"

"Oh, Mrs Cooke." From the way that the girl takes a step backwards and stares, Hettie knows she is windswept. Well, who gives a fig? She has on a bonnet and gloves. That will have to do. "I – I expect he'll be in his study." The girl glances over her shoulder. "I'll tell him you're here."

"No need." Hettie walks briskly past. Down the hallway with a clump of hobnail boots, a swish of underskirt. "Good evening, Robert." He is behind his desk. "No, stay seated." He looks tired, more than tired, but she cannot allow herself to be distracted. As Hettie says what must be said, what little colour he has leaches from his face. She knows only too well the thoughts he must work through. He fights what she says and what does not need to be said. *The anaesthetic. The barbarity of the operation. The blood and the bone.* And if Florence survives all that, she may still succumb to infection.

"I must go to her." Robert stands, patting down his pockets, looking about for things he might need. She recognises her son's need to do something, anything, but the helplessness of his actions contradicts the decisiveness of his words.

It is now that Hettie knows. She has sensed it, of course, but it becomes irrefutable. She wonders if her son allows himself to acknowledge it. Who, having come to know Florence, would not love her?

She does not say, 'You must not', but when Robert moves towards the door, she stands in his way. "I promised Florence we'd tell Ida."

"Of course. She has to know." His voice is jittery. "How will she take it, do you think?"

"It's a difficult thing to hear, but far better that it comes from us." Shaking, Hettie gestures to the decanter. "Will you have a brandy? I know I'd welcome one." Without waiting for permission, she pours two glasses, passes one to her son. "Drink. Then we'll tell Ida." She feels a great tenderness towards him. "Together."

CHAPTER THIRTY

SEPTEMBER 1901

The buzz of flies; hands that bat them from faces. The whole of the day following the Boers' ambush, John's regiment has lain in the dust. All of them on their bellies, khaki tunics taking on the brown of the veldt, rifles resting on anthills of earth. In this open endless landscape no one can pinpoint where the farmers are shooting from.

"Water." The plea is a dry refrain that barely expects an answer. "Water."

It is not his own voice, though it might as well be. John has been dreaming of rain. A single raindrop clinging to her eyelashes as she shelters under the eaves. The pitter-patter on the cottage roof, growing heavier, more percussive. Rain enough to fill a barrel, and his father, pale in the early morning light, whistling, dipping his cut-throat razor to shave.

"Shell-proof?"

"Yes, sir." The act of speaking prises his tongue from the roof of his mouth. It is automatic. Someone says your name – or, in John's case, the nickname he's somehow earned – and it's *Yes, sir.* The messenger (just a boy, not someone he need address as *sir)* is flat on his belly, looking at him sideways on.

"Captain Goff wants you." The messenger has crept up on

him. Boy he may be, skin pock-marked and pimpled, fuzz on his upper lip, but he might have been anyone.

There is no spit John can swill around his mouth in the place of water. "Where to?" His skin itches with the dust, his sweat, the infested seams of his flannel underwear.

"Reconnaissance."

John follows the trajectory of the finger that points, and as with many things in this godforsaken landscape, it appears like a mirage.

A hot air balloon, prepared for flight.

The kind of thing Mr Cooke talked about.

At a distance, the dark sphere of the balloon's outline stands out starkly.

'Do you see? Do you see?'

He looks behind him, intending to tell his skinny rake of a brother to keep it down. All his life, they've worked alongside each other. His absence still catches John out.

John (pray God he lives up to his nickname) finds the dry dust of the ground with his stockinged feet – bootless because didn't the army-issue supplies fall apart? And little wonder, the shoddy way they were put together. Overconfident and underprepared, that's his summing up. (Yes, his father Frank's a drinker and yes he likes a bet, but he taught them to do things properly.) Now crouching, he reaches into his pocket, where the gold horseshoe pendant she gave him is pinned by a nappy pin, of all things. *For luck,* she said, touching it to her lips. Now he touches the horseshoe, kisses the hand that touched it and brings that same hand to the earth. Careful now – stay low. Here, no one stands unless they have to. The Boers pick them off, one by one.

They go in sprints, John clutching his rifle, checking his pith helmet, his direction. A sound like a scythe cutting through grass; a near-miss. At one stop, John sees a body; counts seven bullet holes. He is worth more than many sparrows, but he's seen more dead men than he has dead sparrows, and every time he comes across a riddled corpse, he asks, *Was I worth more to the Almighty than you?* This dead man has no need of his water canister, lying in the dust, top off. There is no spillage, no trickle, but even a drop would do. John upends it over his open mouth. *Nothing.*

"Decent pair of boots on him," he says.

"I'm to deliver you to Goff," says the messenger. "You'll have to come back for them."

"I'll do that." No sooner are the words out than he thinks, *If I can get my hands on a draughts board, I can* win *myself a pair of boots. I can win anything I damn well please.*

Thoughts can't survive the searing temperature, not when you're running for your life. After a volley of bullets, John reaches for the horseshoe again, brings his hand to his lips and touches the earth. He cannot know whether this ritual keeps him safe, but now isn't the time to find out. If he survives this day, he'll write home to Gerrard. *Tell E I asked after her.* But the fact is he's no letter-writer. He knows that much about himself.

"Are you coming?" asks the boy.

John checks their direction once more. The balloon is a restless thing that moves as if underwater, a living creature from the deep. Now that they're closer, he sees that its basket sits in an ox-driven cart. "Right behind you."

Alongside the cart he comes to a breathless halt. *Water. I don't care where it comes from. A river where men have washed. A river which has carried dead cattle in its current.*

On the other side of the cart, a tall moustachioed officer cranes his neck. "Ah, Shell-proof."

He stands to attention. "Sir."

Goff approaches. "They tell me you have keen eyesight."

"That's what they say, sir."

"Ever flown in one of these things before?" The captain pulls on one of the tethers.

"Never, sir." One more thing in a long list of firsts. No point worrying about not staying low. Go up in the balloon and no one will mistake him for a cloud.

"Wilson here's our pilot." A second man nods a greeting. No distinguishing features. Men in pith helmets all look much the same. Only yesterday John struggled to recall the face of a man he fought alongside after being told he'd been shot. "Do as he says and you'll be fine. In you get."

John clambers onto the cart and grabs the ropes. The basket is smaller than it appeared from a distance. He hauls his feet over the side.

Wilson climbs nimbly to the basket's rim. "I'll ride the rigging."

Goff comes last and stands back to back with John. There is only one pair of binoculars and the captain has charge of it. Men move about, untying tethers. There is a moment when the basket lurches. John braces himself, then they lift clean from the cart. All he has below his feet – all there is to protect him – is wicker, like his mother's shopping basket.

Up, up. He looks over his shoulder, tries to catch Wilson's eye, but Wilson is also looking out. No one shares his elation.

The plain makes itself known. Dense clumps of yellow grasses, occasional barbed shrubs, lonely trees: all blur. Men on their bellies in the dust, and from this height it is impossible to tell the living from the dead. What you're left with is the vast unendingness of it. This is the angel's view Mr Cooke spoke of. And there, what must be the hill they've been trying to take, elongated and exposed.

"We have you," the captain taunts from behind him. "We have you."

Back at home the ground gives up chalk and coal. Here it is diamonds and gold. John scans the top of the hill, its sides, but can see nothing.

"Dammit!" says the captain.

This country humbles you, makes you realise how insignificant you are. The moment John was off the ship's gangplank, legs unsteady, he asked himself how he would ever get out of here. They may well be drifting into enemy sightlines.

Then, a glint. A spark. Something captured by the sun. (Did their brass buttons give them away?) John squints to be sure. This time a puff of black smoke. "There!" He thrusts out an arm.

"Step aside." The captain raises his binoculars. "My God! They were right about your eyesight, Shell-proof. The dirty women killers have dug themselves a trench."

John leans out of the basket. He sees them now: the barrels of the rifles – British-made .450 Westley Richards – laid across the top, sights trained on the men on the plain, waiting for the slightest movement, a hand batting away a blowfly.

CHAPTER THIRTY-ONE

SEPTEMBER 1901

i

A knock at the cottage door. "Coming!" Gerrard clatters down the staircase, tucking in his clean shirt. He glances into the kitchen. No sign of his mother.

The door stands open. *Roll up, roll up! Come take a look at the Reynolds!* Anyone who chooses to can peer inside their private lives, see the clothes his mother has ironed, the pan of soup they'll have for supper. Go around the back, as people tend to when looking for the outhouse, and you'll find their tin bath propped against the wall.

On the doorstep stands Mrs Mears, as pinch-faced and dour as he remembers, dressed as if in mourning. "Gerrard, we rarely see you these days." That same curt manner, designed to put any boy harbouring secret aspirations back in his place.

"I'm about my work much of the time." Much of the time, but today he has a party to go to.

"I pity you. When employers fail to observe the Lord's day, their workers' spiritual well-being always suffers." His status revised to that of a stray lamb, Mrs Mears comes to the purpose of her visit. "Is your mother in?" Over the threshold she steps.

"See for yourself." Gerrard has little choice but to back out of the way. "She must have nipped out."

Mrs Mears scans the kitchen, then clamps her lips and nods as if considering some important matter. "Will she be gone long? I hoped to offer her some comfort."

Gerrard's small world is knocked from its axis. He had registered Mrs Mears' black garments and made the association with mourning, but hadn't made the leap. "W-what have you heard?"

"Oh, dear, no." She smiles a smile that pretends benevolence. "You mistake my meaning. I come only as one mother to another."

He would like to collapse onto the bottom stair, to say, 'The mistake is yours, not mine. You should take more care over your choice of words.' She was always so particular about everyone else's.

"To give a son to the service of the Queen is the next best thing to giving a son to the service of God."

Anger rises in Gerrard like sap. Mrs Mears has only this minute raised John from the dead and she would strike him back down! "My mother had no say in the matter," he says. "She gave nothing."

"But we are all called on to make sacrifices."

He grips the newel post because what he wants to do, what Gerrard really wants to do, is to shove Mrs Mears out of the front door. In his mind, he does just that. He sees the shock on her face, hears her protest that she taught him his letters when his schoolmasters had all but given up on him. And to this he replies: 'There'll be no more talk of sacrifices. Do I make myself plain? I won't have you upsetting my mother.' John will come home and Gerrard will hand over his biscuit tin and say, 'I kept your winnings safe, like I said I would.' Nothing else is acceptable.

But Mrs Mears is the vicar's wife. The most Gerrard can

do is say his small piece. "I wouldn't tell my mother that, Mrs Mears. If you must say anything at all, tell her you'll pray for John's safe return. Now, if you'll excuse me." He sits his cap on his head and strides out, leaving the Reverend's wife to do as she will.

ii

Robert, Hettie and Ida arrive at the white weatherboarded house on West Street to find Miss Hoddy and Gerrard already outside in the garden. To Robert, still carrying the hamper he hauled in from the carriage, the scene from the window is extraordinary. Miss Hoddy is sitting on the tartan rug that is usually spread over her knees. Gerrard kneels on the lawn and seems to be directing proceedings. Neither has stockings on. Miss Hoddy's bare feet are off the edge of the rug, on the grass. Her hands too. She is leaning back, her face lifted to the sun. Her lips are moving, as if she doesn't have a care. His world narrows to her; only her. For a moment, Robert imagines painting Miss Hoddy. Capturing the light on her face. Her lack of inhibition. Her perfect concentration.

Oswald clears his throat, bringing the room back into focus. "You're just in time to witness a very important experiment," he announces.

On the way here, though dressed for a party, Ida said she was unsure if she could find it in herself to celebrate. Hettie reached for her hand, said, 'Nobody expects anything from you. Take your lead from Florence and all will be well.'

Now, Ida catches Oswald's mood, latches onto it. "What kind of experiment?"

"Oh, it's terribly scientific. Florrie told Gerrard that she missed walking barefoot in the grass. *That* isn't possible, but this…"

Ida looks on with apparent wonder. "She's transmitting the feeling through her hands!"

Admiration and envy converge as Robert considers Gerrard anew. He thought of this, this bright, sensitive lad, who could be so much more than his father given the right opportunities. But also this boy can sit close to Miss Hoddy and not be criticised for it.

"I want to try," says Ida. "Can I, Father?"

"I don't know that your –" But Freya is not here to disapprove, and here is his own mother, stooping to unlace the stout shoes she wears for her wanderings.

Hettie catches him staring. "What? Don't tell me *I* need your permission." At the sound of her voice, Fairfax leans forward and lifts his wings as if about to take flight. She goes to him and he straightens up, bobbing his head up and down. "So." She narrows her eyes. "You still recognise me."

Robert finds himself contemplating the bird. The fish-scale feathers about his head; his beak parted to reveal a black tongue. *His mother will have to have him back,* he supposes. A careless thought. He swallows it down guiltily.

Oswald plants one foot on a chair to untie his shoelaces. He turns his head towards Robert and grins. "I believe we promised my sister a party."

There is only one response. There is this one bright afternoon, and if that is all that there will be, a memory to sustain them, not a moment must be wasted. Robert sets the hamper on a table, then goes down on one knee, takes hold of his daughter's left boot.

"Shoe shine?" she asks.

"Not today." He unbuttons it. She laughs, delighted, and offers her right boot.

Out they troop, barefoot, to the terrace: Robert with the hamper, Oswald with clinking glasses, Ida a pile of china plates layered with lace-edged napkins, his mother the cutlery, turning as she goes to shut the French windows so that Fairfax cannot escape. They find a cake already set out on the card table Oswald has moved outside.

Robert looks to his mother. Hopes she isn't too disappointed.

She doesn't miss a beat. "Two cakes, how marvellous! I believe I detect Mrs Reynolds' handiwork. Caraway seed, if I'm not mistaken."

Ida sets down the plates and, placing her feet carefully, delicately, between the planks that are laid over the stone steps, walks down and onto the grass.

"Ida!" Miss Hoddy reaches out a hand, as if encouraging a swimmer who is taking their first strokes. "Come and join us."

Gerrard clambers to his feet, brushing the knees of his trousers, a slight squint against the sun. "Miss Ida."

"None of that Miss and Master nonsense, not between two of my very closest friends." She takes their hands, forming a conduit between them. Robert has a feeling she is trying to tell them they may need each other in the coming months. Then she releases them. "How is the grass?"

Ida curls up her toes and rocks back on her heels. "Delicious."

"Come now, you can do better than that."

His daughter begins a timid tour of the perimeter of the rug. "It tickles at first." She takes a few more steps. "Cushioned. Springy."

"I have a feeling my hands aren't as sensitive as my feet used to be. Gerrard thinks his are about the same. Will you try for me?"

"All right." Ida sits down on a corner of the rug, tenting her skirt over her knees. She brushes her hands over the blades of green.

"Try leaning back on your hands," Gerrard prompts. "It has to be as close to walking as possible."

Ida lets her hands take her weight. "I think you're right." She turns to Miss Hoddy. "My feet are more sensitive. I suppose they see less sun."

"What about you, Hettie?" Miss Hoddy calls out.

"I'm not sure what help I can be. These old feet are tough as leather."

"Try!"

His mother steps away from the sanctuary of the terrace. "Cooling."

"Anything else?"

Hettie holds her skirt so that the hem is just above her ankles; dances a small jig. "Liberating."

"Oh, very good!" Miss Hoddy claps. Robert is just thinking that his mother has had quite enough liberation when Miss Hoddy says, "And you, Mr Cooke?"

Always, he feels that slight lurch when he finds himself addressed by her, coupled with a yearning to be spoken to as a familiar. She did it once when she thought him vulnerable. He'll show her, he is not so formal as she thinks. "There *is* one way to test our hands." Robert turns to Oswald. "Did you ever play wheelbarrows?"

He pantomimes indignation, thumbing his chest. "Am *I* to be the barrow?"

"I'm far too heavy for *you*."

Oswald makes a play of linking his fingers together then stretching out his arms. He dives down on his front, palms flat on the grass, and braces. "Ready!"

Robert picks him up by the ankles, taking Oswald's lead as he walks the length of the garden on his hands, gaining speed as they weave in and out of the pear trees, boughs heavy with ripening fruit.

Laughter and applause on the return journey. Miss Hoddy calls out, "Well?"

"I'm not sure. The blood's gone to my head."

"Let him down, Robert!" calls his mother, who has seated herself in Miss Hoddy's invalid-chair.

Red-faced, Oswald struggles to his feet and corrects the arms of his spectacles. "Right, who's for champagne?"

"Everyone!" Miss Hoddy slaps her thighs, then reaches again for Ida's hand. "Have you tasted champagne before?"

"Never," says Ida.

"And you?" she asks Gerrard.

He shakes his head. "I've tried ale."

"Ale?" scoffs Miss Hoddy. "Ale's for every day. Champagne is for parties. Isn't that so, Mr Cooke?"

Ida presses her palms together, mouths, *"Pleeease?"*

CHAPTER THIRTY-TWO

AUTUMN ~ WINTER 1901

i

In quiet moments, Gerrard finds himself praying for Miss Hoddy. As he digs well-rotted manure into flowerbeds. As he breaks open pods and shakes the seeds into brown paper bags. When he plants daffodil and tulip bulbs, he prays she'll be home to see them bloom. He prays for Miss Hoddy at the expense of praying for his own brother, that's the truth of it. He lies in the bed he shared with John, not knowing where his brother is sleeping at night, and prays for someone else. Perhaps it's connected to his sense of fair play, but Gerrard cannot rid himself of the notion that it will be one of them or the other. John would put money on himself. *He's been away such a long, long while, bravely fighting in the rank and file.* With Miss Hoddy, all manner of complications could arise. Perhaps the surgeon decided she wasn't well enough to withstand surgery. Eyes scrunched, hands clenched, he pleads, *Save her, dear God, you have to save her.*

In his brother's case, no news is good news. That's what the Reynolds tell each other over cups of tea and bread and dripping, conscious of his empty chair at the kitchen table.

John never was one for his letters, not like Gerrard. Gerrard watches his father closely, his good eye bloodshot, its white yellowed, the appearance of broken capillaries on his nose, the tremor in his hands. He assuages his guilt by writing to his brother, letters that will go unanswered, assuring John his winnings won't go on ale, not while he has anything to do with it. This much is within his control. Only this.

ii

Robert cannot settle. The question *What news?* isn't to be asked lightly. Oswald's sister in the women's hospital. Frank's son God knows where. Gerrard caring about both. As for Estelle... Asked or unasked, the question is ever-present. It won't go away until, by one means or another, there's a conclusion, and the thought of that conclusion is agony. With nothing at the gardens that the Reynolds cannot see to, Robert has Abbots drive him to Mitcham. The workers in their aprons and smocks look up from the soil, surprised at first to see his carriage; waiting to learn if his presence is bad news or good; suspicious when he joins them in the fields. This is the first time they have seen him in mud-caked boots. He drives his spade into the soil, throwing himself into the task.

His body occupied, Robert's mind travels back to the scene in the Hoddys' garden, an afternoon with a pulse and heartbeat of its own. It's as if he's seeing magic lantern slides projected on a screen. The six of them, the feeling that they're a kind of family. Not only does Miss Hoddy possess a painterly preoccupation with light, but light seeks her out, dapples her in gold. He remembers a giddiness as the afternoon wore on, as the champagne blurred edges. There was laughter, the clink of glasses. 'Florrie,' he found himself wanting to say. To lean close and call her, 'Florrie.' Just that.

His spade hits flint, jolting him back to the soil, the field, the drizzle that greys all edges. Here is better. Robert doesn't have to wait and see. He can *do*. Rid the fields of the tattered remains of camomile, liquorice and wormwood; dig out great tangles of roots. (The mint, he suspects, will come back no matter what they do.) If the men and women who turn the soil, working bonemeal into it as they go, have opinions about what he asks of them, they keep them to themselves. He is operating without a safety net. And as they watch from the sidelines, the Carlisles, the Benhiltons, even the Reverend and Mrs Mears, will happily wager that Robert Cooke will lose his precarious footing and fall from a great height. Humbug-popping Loax may already have his obituary drafted.

iii

October, and the alders and oaks begin to shed. The borders have less colour, but they chose hardy chrysanthemums in reds and oranges because their season is long. Now is the time that the crimson glory vine lives up to its name. November arrives, cold and damp. In the pleasure garden, Gerrard rakes sodden leaves. Once he has a decent mound, he scoops it into a barrow and empties the barrow into the wire pen they use to make next year's mulch. He was itching for news, yet now that Mr Cooke is striding towards him, waving what appears to be a letter, he tightens his grip on the rake, light-headed and nauseous all at the same time.

John or Miss Hoddy. Who is it to be?

"Mr Hoddy has written," Mr Cooke announces. "His sister has come round after her operation."

Breath forces its way out of Gerrard. *Her poor legs.* He pushes away the image that comes to mind. "That *is* good news." He supposes this is the outcome he prayed for, yet it's hard to be certain.

"She was able to speak to him." Mr Cooke is clutching the letter, almost rattling it. "The doctors are cautiously optimistic, he writes."

Gerrard would like to see the words for himself, but the offer is not made and he doesn't see how he can ask. "When will she be home?"

"That may be some way off." A yelp carries from the tennis courts. "Oswald writes that he'll come home while his sister convalesces. No doubt he'll tell us more on his return."

Gerrard's legs are shaking. "But she spoke."

"She spoke," Mr Cooke echoes.

He will have to be satisfied with that. "When you reply, will you send Miss Hoddy my best."

"Why don't you write? I'll make a note of her address. Now, I must go and tell Ida," he says. He seems not to know what to do with himself.

"You told me first?"

"The letter was sent here. It was probably the only address Mr Hoddy had."

His poor mother's nerves. What must she have thought when the postman arrived at their door? "Will you take a look at the books while you're here?"

"Next time." Mr Cooke claps him on the arm then turns to go.

Something must be said. "The receipts are down, sir." Gerrard braces himself for the inevitable questions. People still come for the tennis, but not with the same enthusiasm since Nettie Easter's defeat. It knocked her confidence so badly, her game isn't what it was. And with John away, men have no reason to linger in the pavilion over games of draughts. He can't remember when he last lit the Chinese lanterns.

Mr Cooke stops. A moment passes before he turns. "The receipts always take a tumble come the winter."

"Should I be doing something?" He wants to. Has wanted

to for some time, but wasn't certain it was his place. Guy Fawkes night has been and gone. They should be posting notices about the Frost Fair.

"That's my responsibility, not yours."

Then do something, Gerrard wants to say. *Don't just stand by and let it all go to rot.*

Mr Cooke retreats, head bowed, hands clasped behind his back, the precious letter crumpled in them.

Alone, Gerrard lifts his eyes to the pewter sky. Miss Hoddy would know what to do. Then: *She spoke.* He has that to hang on to. Abandoning his rake, he heads towards the aviary. No one has mentioned the nesting boxes, the neat row he hammered together. If asked, he'll say that the parakeets need boxes for the winter. January last, they lost a bird. No sign of illness; it was simply lying on its side in the sawdust, talons curled. He lets himself inside and stands amid a flurried blur of green. "She spoke," he tells the birds. Tears pool at the corners of his eyes. "She spoke!" He lifts the lid of the first nesting box. On the straw, four perfect white eggs. In the wild, birds stop laying when the days shorten and food supplies dry up. Cooke's parakeets are strangers to hunger. As a result they're early nesters, laying between January and June. Though the odds are stacked against winter chicks he'll give them their chance. It's what Miss Hoddy would want. This is one thing he can do for her.

CHAPTER THIRTY-THREE

DECEMBER 1901

i

A good pair of boots on his feet, John strides through the camp towards the officers with their card tables and their pipes. Not a vest in sight. These men wear their khaki tunics even when about their leisure. In front of a tent the camp mascot, a white terrier in a feathered headdress, sits up on his hind legs.

In his drawstring bag are draughts pieces cut from a single branch. He stained the black discs with what passes for coffee in these parts; sunk to the bottom of his enamel mug, weighed down by stones. He begins as he always does, using a stick to score the lines of a chequerboard in the powdery soil. He says nothing; doesn't explain what he's about, not even after he captures the officers' attention. "What the devil?" he hears, and, "Blithering idiot." Many a game he has won lying on his side in the dust, but not with men of this rank.

When he's finished, he stands tall and salutes. "Who'll play me?"

There is laughter, most of it dismissive, but that's fine. He only needs one bite at the bait.

He doesn't move, not even to duck the buzz of a fly. Just stands there, eyes front, chest out, heels together.

It isn't long before an officer ambles over, thumbs tucked into his metal-buckled belt, moving his head from side to side, pursing his lips. "You need to get yourself a proper board."

"Sir!" he agrees. To fit in here, he'd need to raise a moustache and keep it neatly waxed.

"Goff has one on his tabletop." John feels a lift in his chest, hopes it doesn't show. The officer shouts over his shoulder. "Goff?"

John risks a glimpse. Goff is in a camp chair. Head back, towel laid across his chest, feet up on an ammunition chest, he's being shaved by his batman. John's father would never go to the barber's, never mind that they might not have accepted his custom. *'Never trust a man with a sharp blade that close to your Adam's apple.'*

"What?" comes Goff's reply.

"Will you play this man at draughts?"

"Which man?"

"What's your name, soldier?"

"Shell-proof, sir."

"I said your name, man!"

Eyes front. He will not spoil his chances now. "Captain Goff knows me as Shell-proof, sir."

The officer frowns, but it is an intrigued frown. "Says he's called Shell-proof," he yells over his shoulder.

"Why the devil didn't you say so?" Ignoring his batman, the captain kicks up his boots. He brings the towel up to his chin, wiping away whatever lather remains, wincing at what may be a nick. "Send him over!" He drops the towel, leaving his man to retrieve it.

The officer looks John up and down (eyes front). He can smell the sandalwood of his hair oil. "It appears you have yourself a game."

270

ii

As Gerrard gently lifts the lid of the nesting box, something in his chest catches. The hen is fussing over near-transparent hatchlings. Count them: two, three – all four eggs, hatched! He laughs for the sheer joy of it. The chicks are huddled, blind, bald, a sickly grey, their wings little more than raised shoulder blades. Though they look helpless, they've broken through shell, kicked and wriggled free. How ugly they are! There's an ancient reptilian quality about them. He can well believe that birds and lizards started from the same strange being. Do they hatch knowing what they are, that they'll fly?

Somehow their fates seem linked with Miss Hoddy's. John's. It's imperative they all survive. In the wild, chicks are vulnerable to plunder by woodpeckers and crows. Not his. But the cold is biting. He'll begin by bringing in straw.

Though it pains him, Gerrard removes the eggs from the other box. "I'm sorry," he tells the mother as she attacks his retreating hand. If more chicks were to hatch, he would have a problem on his hands. Already, it will be a devil to explain to Mr Cooke.

The third box: he lifts the straw. Still there. His brother's battered tin of winnings, moved from its hiding place in the cupboard under the eaves after Gerrard came home to find his father in their bedroom on his hands and knees, searching under the bed. Frank's head made quite a thud as he emerged.

'There you are,' he'd said, one hand rubbing his head, raking his hair flat.

'Did you think I'd be hiding?' That was as much as Gerrard dared say. Enough to make a point. 'That man can sniff out money,' his mother used to tell Gerrard, as she hid what he'd handed over for housekeeping. Short of burying the tin, the aviary is the safest place Gerrard can think of. His father has never taken the slightest interest in the parakeets.

The Cottage,
Cooke's Pleasure Gardens,
Hill Road,
Carshalton

15th December 1901

Dear Miss Hoddy,

I promised to write when there was news, but you are the only one who will know it. The parakeets have had four chicks! I stopped removing the eggs, then left everything to chance. Sometimes caged birds do not breed and nothing can be done about it. It is so late in the year, I still think it might be a miracle. They were born grey and completely blind. Until now, they have looked much the same as a baby songbird. You could almost see through their skins. They were so sickly-looking I did not think they would live through their first night, but when I went to check in the morning, there they were, looking like plucked chickens (although you would need more than four for the pot).

At four days old, their feathers are already starting to show. It gives them a stubbled look. At first they could not lift their heads but they have begun to stretch their scrawny necks. Their necks are all loose skin, like the neck of a witch. They knew what their mouths were for from the moment they were born, but now they latch onto things with their beaks.

I cannot stop checking on them. I do it when I should be about my other chores. They are changing so quickly that if I stood there long enough I might be able to watch them grow, though I dare not put that theory to the test. At some point Mr Cooke will notice, but he has been busy over Mitcham way and we see far less of him than we did.

It is very strange here, first without my brother John who I never thought I would miss and now without your visits. I cannot say it is quiet. The parakeets make sure of that, and we have the tennis lessons and club matches. Mr Cooke's mother brought Miss Ida to the gardens one afternoon when the weather was not too bitter. They sat on the bench under the eaves to have their tea and my mother was there, so I was able to ask Miss Ida about her painting. She has been to your house just as you asked. She was modest as usual and only said she has done her best, so I imagine she has produced a masterpiece.

I have read that chicks fledge at six or seven weeks. You should see their poor little excuses for wings! I do not know when you expect to be back among us, but I would like nothing better than for us to watch the chicks take their first flights together.

Your friend,
Gerrard

iii

"Father?"

Robert looks up from his desk to see Estelle standing in the doorway.

"I came to say goodnight."

He takes off his spectacles, rubs his eyes with palms that should really be bandaged. "Come in. Let me look at you."

"It's late." She nods towards his ledgers. "Can't whatever you're working on wait until the morning?"

"It will only keep me awake if I don't finish." His hope was that the days he spent in the fields would leave him so spent he might sleep. January days may be short, but they work all the harder to keep warm. There are people, he's told, who fall asleep the moment they lie down to rest. Blameless people.

He has a plan of which he is certain by day, yet something in Robert wakes when he closes his eyes, some churning thought or gnawing doubt. Sometimes it is Miss Hoddy, sometimes John. Sometimes the fear of all he has being taken from him. And, as Robert thinks this thought, last night's dream comes to him. Two men were standing over him, quite respectfully, aprons over their waistcoats and shirtsleeves rolled up to their elbows. Firstly, they applied something to his face, something with a greasy feel, paying particular attention to his eyebrows and moustache. The attention wasn't unpleasant, rather like a trip to the barber's. But then they laid a broad band of something heavy across his eyes and smoothed it into place, and he realised: the next strip would cover his nose. If he didn't speak up, he would be smothered. It was then that he knew: they were making his death mask.

'I'm not dead,' he tried to tell them, 'Tell Mrs Carlisle I'm not dead,' and it was that echo he woke with.

"Do you read much about the war?" his elder daughter is asking, and she is here, she is real.

Robert loosens his cravat. "Gerrard's the one to ask. He plots the army's progress. You might ask to see his map when you're next at the gardens."

Estelle seems to be waiting, expecting a question about the nature of her interest. A small, urgent part of him wants desperately to know, but the greater part of him thinks he has no right to ask. "I haven't had time to read today's newspaper." He holds out the folded broadsheet. "Take it." Seeing her hesitation, he holds it higher, as if trying to tempt a deer to take food from the palm of his hand.

She comes closer. "If you're sure." There is a gentleness about her, an uncertainty. Perhaps she's afraid of what she may read, but that doesn't give Robert the right to shield her. Not if what he thinks he knows is true. When John comes back, he may not be the same confident young man who left.

Estelle clasps the newspaper to her chest. "Ida says she's going to be a nurse."

He smiles at this. "That would please my father." Somewhere, perhaps in the attic, he still has Walter's old Gladstone bag. "And you?" When Estelle was younger, she seemed superficial, a little vain. He realises now that this was all she was ever allowed to be. *We, the future wives and mothers of England.* He barely knows the young woman who stands before him. He isn't even sure how she spends her days now that she's finished school. Transcribing family recipes into a household book and pressing flowers can only occupy so many hours.

Estelle is hesitant. "I don't know yet." Quietly, she says it.

"Well, there's no rush." Between them there exists simultaneously an unbreakable bond and an unbridgeable distance.

"Mother doesn't agree. She thinks I ought to have my future all mapped out." His daughter's attempt at lightness fails. There is a small quiver at the corner of her mouth.

Now would be the time to ask, but all Robert can think to say is, "If you have any ambitions about bookkeeping, you must let me know."

She stands there, just stands there, and his heart could break with all that is not said between them. He does as he has been taught; fills the awkward silence. "You mustn't mind your mother. She only wants your happiness."

Estelle lifts her chin just a little. "How is Miss Hoddy? Is there any news?"

"Oswald tells me she's still very weak, but that's to be expected."

"She must be very brave."

"I'd say she is." But what choice does a person have when they must face what she's had to face? Robert pictures Miss Hoddy in the convalescence home on the south coast, sitting at a window and looking out as grey waves break against the rocks. A poor substitute for her pear trees. Catching himself drifting, he takes Estelle's hand; kisses it. An apology of sorts. He thinks his daughter brave too, though he does not say it. He wouldn't know how.

iv

Gerrard scavenges potato peelings and cabbage leaves from his mother's kitchen. He forages for dandelions (thanks to his efforts, there are few at Cooke's). Collects earthworms as he digs. At three weeks, the chicks' constant chirruping begins to change. For some time now, they've been poking their heads out of the hole at the front of the nesting box, beaks open wide, necks straining. His little family has outgrown its home. Gerrard has made another, double the size, and now he must move them into it. Handling the chicks isn't a decision he takes lightly. Their parents may reject them, then he'll have all four to hand-rear. What would his mother, with her horror of squawking, have to say about that? But the alternative is that the chicks may push a sibling out of the nest.

He raises the lid. Slowly, slowly, he lowers a gloved hand. As soon as the mother realises the hand doesn't contain food, she raises the alarm, lifting her wings defensively. The chicks huddle and cower. "You know me, don't you?" he croons. "I'm not going to hurt your babies, see?" He clicks his tongue. As his hand comes closer, the female attacks – what mother wouldn't? – latching onto the leather with her beak. This same bird who has only ever nibbled, who has taken seed from his hand. "You have to trust me," he says, "I've made you a new home." But she calls out in panic, creating a great stir. Gerrard must be as determined as the mother. He nudges her aside; makes a loose cocoon of his hand around the first chick, imagines he can feel the rapid beat of its tiny heart. He lifts gently, smoothly, all the while making reassuring sounds. An adult male – most likely the father – flies at his face, furious talons foremost. He has taken one of the chicks, he will not have another. Gerrard closes his eyes (he has no wish to end up like his father, with only one good eye). Operating blind, he cannot transfer the chick to its new box as he intended. Instead he bends his knees; feels for the floor, releasing the chick in the triangle made by his feet. He risks a quick glimpse, sees it scuttle drunkenly. Eyes clenched tight once more, Gerrard straightens up; spits tail feathers from between his lips. "Go and see. Your chick's fine." For his trouble he receives a score the length of his right cheek. When he dares open his eyes a second time, it is to look down between his feet. Delighted with all the space at its disposal, the chick is a lanky thing, talons out of all proportion, green colouring beginning to show. Tap-tap-tapping, the mother holds out her wings and, with a dance not unlike courtship, shepherds him. A good mother, she won't leave her chick on its own where adult birds may pick on him. Perhaps Gerrard will fare better with her attention elsewhere. "Shall we try number two?" He lowers his hand into the box again.

v

Men lying on the veldt amid grassy tufts, lying where they fell; men who don't look like soldiers. Waistcoats and straining buttons, braces, a jacket hitched up. Not a pith helmet in sight. One on his back, an arm raised above his head as if he were taking a nap during haymaking. Another on his front, pale blue eyes turned towards John, reaching out as if drowning. When a man reaches out John's habit is to lend a hand, so that is what he unthinkingly does. This, then, is the enemy. A man not unlike himself, white-skinned, blond. *Even the very hairs of their heads are numbered.* It is suddenly clear to John. This is not his land, yet here he is, fighting over it. And this poor fellow has given his life.

"What are you waiting for, Shell-proof?"

He drops the dead man's hand. "Nothing, sir." It is drummed into them. *Every rifle left behind is a rifle that can be used against you.* Gently, he unburdens the man of his ammunition, the farmers' own, he assumes, but British-made. These are light duties, he reminds himself. Today he has not been asked to set fire to a man's homestead, salt his fields or poison a well. He has not been asked to take women and children captive. The women plead with them in Afrikaans.

Verbeel jou ek was jou vrou. Imagine if I was your wife.

Stel jou voor dit is jou kind. Imagine this is your child.

Not for the first time, he's glad his little squirt of a brother hasn't seen the things he's seen. He hopes Gerrard's belief in the undefeatable British Empire remains intact. How other men write home with news he doesn't know. Anything his family would want to hear would be a lie.

"Will there be a draughts tournament on Sunday?"

John grins. "There most certainly will." He, at least, is undefeatable.

"Save me a seat at the table."

"Can you afford one?" It is then that John sees it. The red ribbon. The lion astride the crown. *For Valour.* "Well, well," he says. "A Victoria Cross." He's heard talk about men who have left imperial regiments and ended up fighting in local South African units. "D'you think he's a defector?"

The Lieutenant looks down at the corpse, spits. "I'd say the bastard's wearing it as a trophy."

vi

January has turned to February. At forty-five days old, the chicks are flapping their wings. They'll fledge any day now – with or without Miss Hoddy.

CHAPTER THIRTY-FOUR

FEBRUARY 1902

"Gerrard! *Gerrard!*"

Mr Cooke's mother comes, huffing and puffing. She puts the flat of one hand to her chest as she sees him heading towards her, but she's smiling broadly. "They're coming." In response to his unspoken question – *She's home?* – a nod. "Her doctor advised bedrest, but she says she's had quite enough of that."

"Then she must be feeling better."

"Either that, or she's incredibly stubborn!" He notes the shadow in Mrs Cooke's eyes, sees how she blinks it away. "We have her bundled up as best we can."

She may have more to say, but Gerrard sees movement beyond the gates towards the top of the road. "Excuse me, Mrs Cooke." He breaks into a run, stumbling, throwing out his hands fully expecting to fall, yet somehow managing to right himself. *Look only at her face*, he cautions himself, as he clangs through the gates. Finally he comes to a halt, panting, pushing the hair back from his forehead.

"Dear Gerrard," she says, and it is enough. Her face has a waxen sheen, a slight yellowish tinge. Behind the laughter, there is a new expression. He would say it's the look of someone who's known tremendous pain, but Miss Hoddy doesn't feel pain. Perhaps it is only the reflection of the sea.

Afraid she may read his thoughts, Gerrard hugs his torso and doubles over. "I've given myself an awful stitch."

When he glances up, hands on his knees, she beckons him, closer, closer, until he is by her side and his ear is near enough for her to whisper, "Am I too late?"

Gerrard allows himself a glance beyond the swaddling. He feels he must, so he knows what to expect. He was wrong to imagine that one side of her lap would be flat. A square frame must have been rigged up beneath the tartan rug. "Your timing's perfect." And because he doesn't know how much she's told Oswald, he adds, "The snowdrops and the crocuses are showing their faces, and the magnolia's about to blossom."

She presses her hands together, brings the steeple of them to her lips. Pale though she may be, he can feel her glee.

Mr Hoddy stands aside, so that Gerrard can take the handles, and as he begins to push, Miss Hoddy's hand reaches up to find his and pinches it.

He pulls his hand away. "Ouch!"

She looks up over her shoulder, smiles. "I'm just making sure you're real."

"You could have asked."

"Ah, but you might have lied!"

He likes that they're sparring. It feels just as it was before.

They are passing in front of the cottage, where Mrs Cooke is speaking to his mother, when Miss Hoddy calls out. "Oswald?"

"I'm only a step behind you."

"Will you fetch my box easel? Oswald bought me a box easel, thinking I might use it while I was convalescing, but I found I'd lost interest in painting." It is her brother's hand she reaches for now. "Until today." She lifts her face, inhales. Nearby, one of the tennis tutors is adjudicating a disputed line call. "I'm going to sit here and paint."

Oswald frowns. "Is that a good idea?"

"I thought I might try my hand at painting a game of tennis. *En plein air.*"

"I was referring to the temperature, with particular reference to your doctor's instructions."

"Oh, I am *sick* and *tired* of being cooped up!"

With his hands on his hips, her brother looks even more angular than usual. He closes his eyes, sighs: "Lord preserve us."

Gerrard tries to think of something useful to say. "I don't know if the players will stay still long enough to be painted." The courts are scuffed, earth showing through the grass. He looks about for his father, but what's the use? If it isn't a rose, a horse or a pint of ale, Frank shows no interest.

"Look," Oswald is saying, "Why don't Hettie and I make ourselves scarce for an hour and the pair of you can do whatever it is you so clearly want to do."

"You're an angel," Miss Hoddy says sweetly, and then to Gerrard, "Quick – before he changes his mind!"

A parakeet is at the hole in the nesting box, nibbling its own toe, lime green plumage and blush-red beak, a smaller version of its parents.

Her breath catches and her gloved hand finds his. Holds it. He can feel no heat coming from her.

"Are you sure you're warm enough?"

"Not *you* as well!"

He pulls down his jacket sleeve so that it covers both of their hands. "I'll be the worst of all of them."

"I think I believe you. Oh –"

Another head emerges above the first, neck craning, movements jerky, as if listening intently. The first bird is displaced. The second tries the edge of the hole with its beak, rubs its neck against it. One talon appears over the edge and is withdrawn. Two heads pop out, eyes alert.

"You can come out now." *Do it for Miss Hoddy,* he wills them. "One of you."

Two talons at the edge of the hole. Balancing. Wings lifted, fluttering.

She tightens her hold on his hand. "I think he's –"

But no. The bird backs up. They both release the breaths they've been holding.

"It's been like this for the last couple of days."

"How can you stand it? It's agony. No, wait…"

The baby bird is back on the edge, leaning forwards, teetering. Miss Hoddy grips Gerrard's hand tighter still. Then a flurry. "Did you see, did you see?" she cries out, and she is grinning madly, they are both grinning madly, and John, John is quite forgotten.

CHAPTER THIRTY-FIVE

MARCH ~ JUNE 1902

i

John pockets his winnings. Innumerable unpronounceable insects that appear at nightfall flit in and out of the lamplight. Of all the wildlife South Africa has, for all the warnings about snakes and crocodiles, the *muskiet,* the mosquito, is its most dangerous.

"Another game!" Burrell slaps his hand on the tabletop.

John circles the draughts pieces with an arm; drags them towards him. "Not tonight."

"What if I were to make it worth your while?"

He gives a small laugh. "You've *already* made it worth my while." All evening, the stakes have grown higher, officers trying to outdo each other, taking a perverse pride in how much they can afford to lose.

"Wait!" Burrell stands, upending his camp chair. "I have something I think you're going to like." A slight stumble, then he rights himself. He tips the dregs of a champagne bottle into his mouth, tosses the empty bottle into the scrub and heads towards the row of tents.

John shakes his head, looks around at the company, pipes

in mouths, bemused expressions. They all know this is madness. He slaps at an imaginary *muskiet*. There is a type you can barely see that carries yellow fever, and yellow fever only has one outcome.

Moments later, Burrell is back, thrusting a scroll of paper at John like a baton.

The spectators shift forwards in their camp chairs, elbows on knees.

"Don't do it, Burrell," one of the party urges, perhaps the only one who knows what the scroll is, perhaps recruited to bluff.

John cocks his head. *What have we here?* A legal document of some sort. He unties it, moves himself inside the halo of lamplight and begins to unroll it.

"Shares." The officer grins. "In a gold mine."

"For God's sake, think about it." The cautious friend grabs Burrell, but Burrell flings his arm out and shakes him off. "On your own head…" The friend stalks off into the shadows (John is inclined to think he's genuine) with the white terrier trotting after him.

Burrell slaps the tabletop. "My shares against tonight's winnings."

John scans the page, frowning. He can hardly sit here and read the entire document while the others look on greedily. "What are they worth?"

On hearing the figure, John whistles through his front teeth. If true, this is a once-in-a-lifetime opportunity. He scans to the end and sees a signature that looks like Burrell. The war can't go on much longer. Here, living is cheap. The British have done what he's been told the British always do. They've built little Londons, with London houses, shops and churches, but without London's overcrowding, crumbling tenements and open sewers. The NCOs have been around asking if anyone would like to stay. The more British subjects the better, that's the thinking. John could set himself up and wouldn't have to worry about living hand to mouth. He'd have something to offer her.

All eyes are on him. Dammit, he'll take a risk. He reaches down between his feet for the drawstring bag, spills his winnings onto the table. "Blacks or whites?"

"Good man." Burrell offers his right hand. "Whites."

John clasps it and finds it clammy.

He reaches into his pocket, where the gold horseshoe pendant is pinned to the fabric.

God proves once again that he values John more than he values many sparrows.

ii

At the bottom of the cottage path, Gerrard feels strangely disorientated, as if something's amiss. *The biscuit tin.* The fact is, he hasn't checked on it these last few days. His father didn't come home for two nights, and then Gerrard's older brothers brought him, one on either side, and Frank looked and stank like the devil himself. "Got himself into a tap-room brawl," they said, setting him down in a chair. There is no room for complacency when his father has a thirst.

Look, there he is, making a wigwam for the sweet peas. If Mr Cooke were to arrive now, he would think, *There's Frank, hard at it.* Gerrard goes at once to the aviary, latches the door behind him, feels the familiar draught of air displaced by wingbeats. He opens the lid of the third nesting box. *Huntley & Palmer's Superior Biscuits.* As he lifts the tin, its contents shift. Gerrard crouches, makes a tabletop of his thighs, prises off the rusty lid. No silver, no gold. He swirls the contents around and around. Bronzes and coppers, no good for anything except wishes. Something in Gerrard, perhaps the last boyish part of him, fractures. "No!" The cry wrenches itself out of his gut, stirring up a lime-green whirlwind, but the answer comes back: *"Yes."* He launches the tin away from him. It clatters down. The birds circle from one high perch to another and coins spill, scaling the floor of the aviary, ha'pennies rolling to the far reaches. Gerrard, folding in on himself, throws down his cap and grabs fistfuls of hair. His tail feathers have been plucked from him.

"Son!" Frank is on his knees at the edge of a flowerbed. "Get yourself over here and lend a hand."

Fists balled, Gerrard stomps in the direction of the gates then about turns and strides back. Chest heaving, he stares down at Frank. Capless and with his hair wild, Gerrard breathes fury. "Don't *son* me!" His prayers may have scuppered John's chances of coming home safely (because that is Gerrard's growing belief), but this, this is a far worse betrayal.

Frank lumbers to his feet, taking his time about it. He's been puffed up with self-importance ever since Mr Cooke agreed that his roses should be shown at the Surrey Flower Festival. What would Mr Cooke say if he knew about this? What would he say if he knew about all the coins his father's had out of the fountain?

"You'll speak to me with respect," Frank growls.

Gerrard isn't so easily cowed. "Did you drink it? Did you?" He raises his fists and dances into Frank's blind side. "Or did you lose it? Did it go on a horse?"

"I'm warning you, you do *not* want to pick a fight with me."

But Gerrard does. He doesn't care that he's a featherweight to his father's heavyweight. Even fighting his brother, Gerrard pummelled away in the knowledge that he'd lose. So long as he gets a couple of punches in. He jabs at his father's chest.

"That's enough now."

He jabs harder, aims higher, straight for his father's bad eye.

"Don't say I didn't warn you."

In his head, his mother's voice. *"Shout. It'll take the sting out of it."* Then only stars.

The stench of ammonia. Gerrard recoils, the back of his head hitting the ground. There is pain, pain that refuses to be pinpointed. He feels for his face, follows a warm dribble of blood to a spot that makes him wince. His mother is bent over him, blurred, but her outline is unmistakable. "How?" Gerrard asks, the only word his mouth can form. How long he was out for? That's what he wants to know.

The look she aims at his father's disappearing back glistens with fury. "We'll not see him again before nightfall."

There is Gerrard's answer. He was only out for a moment. Unless it was Frank who fetched his mother. Unless he waited to see him come round.

His mother frowns. "Let's get you inside before anyone sees."

He raises his head, groans.

"Up you get." Her hand under his armpit does no good. Gerrard has to roll onto his front and push himself to kneeling before he can hoik up one knee, then the other. Even then he's hunched over.

Once she has him at the kitchen table, his mother upends the small, ridged bottle and says, "Shout."

Remembering the voice in his head, Gerrard gives a snort. The sting makes him suck in air through his teeth.

"Are you going to tell me what the pair of you were fighting about?" His mother dabs iodine on the cut above his eye, adding fire as she goes. Gerrard punched to provoke. His father punched to prove. *I can still knock you down with a single blow, boy.* "Well?" she demands.

He looks into his mother's eyes as she inspects his face; thinks about the scattered coins on the floor of the aviary. First he prayed for Miss Hoddy instead of John. Now he's allowed his brother's winnings to be stolen. "What did *he* say?"

"That you were trying to mark his face."

"And why would I do that?"

"To ruin his chances at the flower show."

Gerrard laughs mirthlessly. "His precious flowers!" Only when she turns away to put the stoppered bottle back in its place on the high shelf does he come out with it: "He helped himself to John's savings."

Her reaching hand freezes.

"I was supposed to keep them safe." Gerrard hangs his head. The cut above his eye throbs. "It was the last thing John said to me. 'I'm trusting you.'"

His mother's disappointment expands until it fills the kitchen and spills out into the hall. She must push happier things aside to accommodate it. "Let me guess. He replaced the silvers with coppers."

Gerrard's head jerks upwards. His mother isn't shocked. It's what she expected.

Her chest rises and falls, rises and falls, until she arrives at a decision. "Don't give me any housekeeping until you've replaced the money. Your father can live on broth, see how he likes it." She puts two fingers under Gerrard's chin. Looks him in the eye. "But you *must* find somewhere safe to hide it, do you hear?"

May. The Treaty of Vereeniging is signed. The *Daily Mail* prints photographs of a victory parade in Cape Town. Miss Rotherham leaves her counter to bring the paper to Gerrard. In the privacy of his bedroom, he searches the faces for John's.

There is no official record that John has been killed or is missing in action. From what little he's been able to discover, regular soldiers are shipped first, not home, but to their next posting. Only then will volunteers be processed before being sent to a transit camp where they'll wait for a homeward sailing.

The sun rises at half past five and he rises with it, knowing that Miss Hoddy will come. Along the tree walk he pushes her. The oaks are in leaf, the bunches of leaves almost stalkless. The alder's leaves are dark, leathery, heart-shaped.

"Still no word from your brother?" Miss Hoddy asks as they weave between the trunks, the low sun lancing through laden branches to find a passage to the ground.

Her words confirm it. They should have heard *something* by now. "Not yet." And though they talk about the oak's yellow catkins, the taste of pollen, the fearsome jaws of a shiny black stag beetle, Gerrard's heart isn't in it.

By the next week, Miss Hoddy's question is shortened.

"Any word?"

To have her keep asking this. When she is here. Alive. "No," he says.

"Anything?"

Families of other volunteers have received letters. There's no answer to why the Reynolds haven't. "Don't you think I would have told you?" he erupts. "Don't you think I would have run all the way to your front door?"

She reaches for his hand then, but he doesn't take it in his. "I'm sorry." Her voice is as quiet as he's ever heard it.

His heart thumping. "I'm the one who should apologise." He hangs his head. "I don't know where that came from."

"Letters go astray," she says. "Perhaps John's signed up to serve with the peace-keeping police force."

Perhaps, but it's an agony knowing what Gerrard knows. When he prayed, he had no idea that God would be listening.

iii

The first reckoning since they implemented Robert's plan to specialise, and the poppies are magnificent. *I was right to act before others realise there's opportunity to be had.* Robert brings Freya and the girls to see the flowers in bloom. Together, they walk the periphery of the fields. One and then another and another. Each plant has three stems, petals pure white at the outside edges and flecked with delicate violet. Seen from a distance, the poppies appear as a sea of delicate lilac, rippling in the breeze. Estelle is subdued. She is more inclined to turn her head to the occasional figures who appear in the landscape – the field workers – but they seem to disappoint her.

"Poppies, as far as the eye can see," Ida marvels. She has a way of walking that kicks up clouds of dry earth.

Freya coughs an exaggerated cough and tells her to walk properly. "And use your parasol. You're catching the sun."

Too accustomed to her mother's rebukes to be dispirited, Ida turns to Robert. "If only Miss Hoddy could see the poppies. It would do her good, don't you think?"

Warmed by the thought, he's about to suggest that she might paint them, when he catches Freya's eyes, and the look she gives him, the temperature of it. He goes to his wife's side, falls into step with her.

"I thought this was supposed to be a family outing," she says.

"And so it is."

"Then why do we appear to have brought Miss Hoddy with us?"

iv

Cooke's Pleasure Gardens Breaks Jollivette's Winning Streak to take Best in Show

Cooke's Pleasure Gardens in Carshalton, Surrey, fought off considerable competition from plant nurserymen to take first in show at the Surrey Rose Festival. Unlike so-called 'professional' exhibitors, who participate in up to sixty shows a year, this was not only Cooke's sole outing, but their debut on the competition circuit. Mr E Jollivette of Winchester in Hampshire has enjoyed a winning streak, taking gold, silver and bronze these past three years. Competitors feared he was unbeatable, but this year he must settle for silver and bronze.

The purpose of the rose festival is to set standards of artistic and horticultural excellence and to broaden knowledge of horticulture, flower arrangement and conservation. Cooke's head gardener, Mr F Reynolds, is entirely self-taught and has, since the gardens opened in 1895, experimented with creating hybrids capable of flourishing in its chalk-rich soil.

Mr Reynolds combined a hybrid perpetual rose with a tea rose to create La Neptune, *a flower that retains the beautifully shaped buds of the tea rose, but blooms in a bright shade of yellow not seen before in the hybrid perpetual. He is not the first to achieve a bright yellow double-flowered* Rosa foetida var. *That distinction goes to the Frenchman, Pernet-Ducher, whose* Soleil d'Or *was first exhibited in Lyons in 1898 and introduced in 1900. However, hybrid teas are too tender to withstand British winters. Mr Reynolds believes he has overcome this with the introduction of* R.wichuraiana *to the mix. The judges called Cooke's highly-scented rose with its vibrant blooms 'exceptional'. If the hybrid is as hardy as Mr Reynolds claims (he has trialled it for two winters), he would do well to patent it.*

V

Robert and Smithers walk among the shoulder-high stalks, a few pale petals still clinging here and there. Swollen crown-topped seed heads, as far as the break of trees, the curve of the land, the cloud and the sky. The crowns cast their shadows on the green-grey orbs. Robert takes out his blade, scoring one he thinks dry enough, watching the milky-white latex ooze out. Leave them any longer and the crows will have their share. "Good enough."

"Good enough?" Smithers echoes. "I've never seen a crop like it, and most of it already promised. Ballantyne wants double his usual."

This will be our year, thinks Robert. "Have the men harvest the seed heads and two inches of stalk. Nice and clean."

PART FOUR
1903

CHAPTER THIRTY-SIX

JUNE 1903

i

They do not hear from Ballantyne in April or in May. Come June, with the opium harvest imminent, Robert enquires if his order might perhaps have gone astray. Ballantyne responds. Last year loyalty cost him dearly. He'd rather take his chances at the auction houses than pay Cooke's inflated prices. Robert protests. He hasn't raised his prices for three years. *'No. But the rest of the market have lowered theirs.'*

It is true. Prices at last year's auctions were at a record low. Cheap imports continue to flood the ports. And this, despite lobbying, despite what seems to be a seismic shift in public opinion.

"Quality no longer seems to have a value." Robert shares this much with Freya over the supper table.

"Ballantyne built his reputation on the back of your produce." She salts her soup. "He'll find he loses it just as quickly."

This is no comfort. All the time that Ballantyne was on board there was no need to court potential custom. Now, Robert must make use of his contacts. Mr Berkeley James knows a couple of chaps – good fellows – who might want to cut out the middle man and secure a fair price. Introductions are made. The result is that Robert effectively conducts his own auction, lowering his price to a level Ballantyne might willingly have paid. And now word will leak that he's open to negotiation.

"It is what it is," Smithers says of the ledger.

"Damnation!" Robert utters.

The columns of figures say what both men are reluctant to. A healthy camomile harvest might have recouped a loss of this size. Instead the workers' pay must be reduced. How could any honest man consider this solution just? They've done all he asked and more, yet if he doesn't do as the tally dictates, they'll all be out of a job.

"I'll gather the men." Smithers seems resigned to it. "They've an idea of what's coming."

Robert stands grimly by as his overseer rings the handbell. The cobbled yard fills with the men, women and children who rely on him for their livelihoods. How round-shouldered they are, how worn down. Their brooding silence confirms that bad news will come as no surprise. But look at Hilda who has worked for him these past ten years. Her downturned eyes find their focus on her blistered palms.

He nods at her; sees how inappropriate she thinks his smile and alters his expression. "All here?" he asks.

"All here."

They are waiting. Looking to him.

Smithers clears his throat, a cue.

He cannot do it.

Jericho Walton, one of the old stalwarts, part of an almost-extinct breed, steps forward, touching the brim of his burlap cap. "If there's something needs saying, Mr Cooke, we ask that you do it now." He reaches into the wire of his beard to pull on an earlobe. "Least then we'll know where we stand."

Murmurs of agreement; shuffling feet.

The price will rise, it must.

He just needs to hold his nerve a little longer.

He *could* lose a little more land without compromising the gardens. But he won't sell to the railway company. More railway workers' cottages would set the wrong tone. As it is, with the distance they are at, they are just about tolerable, though he'd rather they were not there at all.

Robert assured Frank that the Reynolds' land wouldn't be built on. But Frank's a family man. He'll understand.

"I won't insult you by pretending not to know what you're asking," he begins. "But I have a way to weather this." *The tree walk is sacred. I'll never touch that.* "No one's wage will be less tomorrow than it is today."

The crevasses of Jericho's frown deepen. Robert sees he was prepared to sacrifice himself. "And no one loses their job?"

If Robert can't offer Jericho work, it will be the workhouse for him, and his sunken eyes already haunted. "Not today, nor any other if I can help it."

ii

A year after the war in South Africa finished and almost two years after her surgery Miss Hoddy comes to the gardens daily, not only at dawn, but to paint. These are warm days. Days when she can shed her cape. Possessed with an urgency she didn't have about her person before, she comes to capture a moment, to distil it into brushstrokes, and in a way no photographer could: in colour. Some days, rather than add to her canvas, she sketches tennis players, children on the see-saw.

Gerrard comes to check on her progress. "I like this little fellow." He points to a brown and white dog she has added to the scene.

She no longer asks questions. "Whenever you have something to tell me, I'll be here," she says.

iii

"There we have it, Frank," Robert says. "It's a case of robbing Peter to pay Paul."

Frank sits with his hands on his knees, looking towards the gates. Robert wonders if he ought simply to leave, to give Frank time to get used to the idea, but he delays. Eventually Frank says, "So that's that."

Robert can smell the liquor on his breath. Perhaps, he too, sensed what was coming. "My solicitor will draft a clause so that I have the final say in how the houses will look." He stands and makes as if to leave.

"You wouldn't be having to do it if more money was coming in."

"No," he concedes. At the back of his mind he may have thought Frank would find a solution. Build a wooden frame and pour concrete in it. Construct a perfect octagonal and roof it with dragon's scales. Transform a bandstand into an amphitheatre. Graft hardwood from one rose onto another.

"The locals still show their faces. It's the day trippers who don't come in the same numbers."

"I need to advertise more."

Frank purses his lips. "Gerrard doesn't think that's the answer."

"You've discussed it?" Of course they have.

"The boy talks to people, Londoners especially. They still want to get out of town and visit gardens, but public parks are opening up – parks with no admission charges."

Robert has been failing for some time, hoping for a small miracle, but that grace is not granted him. Here it is then. Not a final defeat, but a defeat nonetheless. Now that it can no longer be concealed – Freya has to be told – it doesn't feel quite as Robert thought it would. If it is humiliation, it feels like a penance. "We never reached the glorious heights of being the first, but neither will we be the last – not by a far stretch."

Freya takes the news without reproach, the reduction in her household allowance in her stride. "We've had lean years before. We'll manage." She mentions several small economies she can make. They will not be enough.

"The carriage is an extravagance we can no longer afford," Robert tells her. There's a pause and during that pause he holds his breath.

"I will not miss it so very much. Though I never *have* got round to taking the trip to visit my sisters." She is referring to Edith and Hilda, the sisters who live together, one widowed, the other never married.

"Go now. A few weeks will be neither here nor there."

"But you're busy and it would be too much of an imposition to take both of the girls." She raises her chin. "The sale of land can always be explained as a business decision. No one batted an eyelid when you sold the Approach." Robert doubts they realised it belonged to him. "But selling the carriage… All I ask is that the people we've courted shouldn't hear of it until the girls' futures are settled."

Robert laughs. "Surely Ida is some way from marriage!"

"As I recall, you thought that seventeen was an appropriate age for a wife. But I agree. Estelle must be our priority."

His mouth opens and closes. If he were to speak, it would be to protest. Estelle should not be part of any business transaction.

Oswald quickly grasps what needs to be done. In the Hoddy's kitchen, he draws up plans with a new boundary, using the wall of the cottage as his baseline. Robert would have liked Miss Hoddy's input, but Oswald will not have her taxed – and he's right, quite right. Recovered though she may be, she tires easily. And so she is in the room above, perhaps sitting at the window looking out at her pear trees.

"Not there," says Robert when Oswald lays his brass rule across the broad expanse of lawn. There is a tightness in his throat, the slow creep of panic. He fumbles with the knot of his cravat; loosens it. "Leave the cottage with a generous approach."

"Here." Oswald takes new measurements, re-positions his rule.

Robert's breathing eases. The Reynolds will keep a little privacy and the bandstand will remain, though it will no longer be central. "Better," he says. He looks up to see his mother in the doorway, her eyes focussed on the plan, the moment before she knows she's been seen.

"Robert." She smiles.

No matter. She would have found out soon enough.

"Florence thought she heard your voice, so I came to investigate. Why didn't you say you were coming?"

Robert glances at Oswald. "This is a business call."

"But you won't go without saying hello. I'll tell her you'll be up when you've finished."

He waits until Hettie's footsteps have retreated to ask, "Does your sister know?"

"I imagine she does." Oswald draws his spectacles down his nose and looks at Robert directly. "She has a talent for extracting information from people, and I doubt Gerrard is immune."

In a way it is a relief. He need not be the one to tell her what they're doing to her gardens.

CHAPTER THIRTY-SEVEN

JULY 1903

*A*NY *dwelling-houses or cottages to be erected on said land shall be erected in a position and according to plans and designs previously approved by the Surveyor for the time being of the Vendor.* His solicitor, Mr Braidwood's, wording. *THAT no other building shall be erected on any lot other than the buildings so authorised by the said Surveyor, and no alteration shall be made without consent in writing of the said Surveyor. And to ensure that nothing is done cheaply: THAT the houses to be erected on the said land be of respective values following in first cost of labour and materials at the lowest current prices that is to say £150 each in the case of a detached house and £250 in the case of a pair of semi-detached houses.*

Mr Ross balks at the last clause. "You make it impossible for a man to turn a profit!"

Robert, who knows more than he'd like to know about the difficulty of balancing the books, holds firm. "If you don't like my terms, I have other offers." He doesn't. Nonetheless he gets to his feet.

"Wait!"

Robert is surprised when Mr Ross takes up his pen, mutters

something about the world going to hell in a handbasket and beckons. Mr Braidwood slides the paperwork across the desk. All elbows, Arthur Ross, housebuilder, scratches his angry signature in Indian ink.

A fortnight is spent undoing. Lifting paving stones, untangling climbing roses from the arches, digging up root balls, preserving as much as can be preserved for replanting. Joyless work, the slow un-painting of a picture, their hands and forearms snagged with the evidence of it.

"This should be a job for spring," Frank says. "Roses are sensitive to shock." It is the only complaint he makes after all his experiments with cuttings, both the spring softwood and the autumn hardwood, grafting one stem to another, propagating new varieties. The damask, bourbon and china blooms he has protected from aphids; nursed through outbreaks of black spot.

"I know," Robert says plainly. *I know* as an apology, not only to Frank, but to Thomas, to Gerrard who will lose much of their lawn. It cannot wait. Not with Mr Ross impatient to take possession.

"On my count," says Robert.

The wrought-iron fence and gates have been dismantled and laid flat. It doesn't seem so long ago that they hammered the fixings into the ground. Then they were four, a man to each corner. Now they are only three. Oswald steps in to help, but Oswald is no John. He hasn't had a lifetime of Frank's tutelage. Robert would have suggested that Oswald was his opposite, but Gerrard claimed him, almost paternally, and Robert decided not to be the one to say no.

They carry the first section of fencing the length of the old rose walk. Robert goes backwards, taking small, stuttering steps, while he looks into the faces he has grown to know so well. Pained expressions, all three of them. Persistent drizzle dampens spirits further. Little is said that the task does not demand.

What Frank has already made of their salvage is a little miracle. A star of arches, a circular rose walk. And they do say that a severe cutting back encourages new growth. Now another miracle must be performed with wrought iron. The gardens always were a rhomboid, wide at the entrance, with Neptune towering at the narrowest point, the chalk pit that was. Moved inwards towards the bandstand, the fencing is too wide and the gates seem out of proportion. Yet somehow, they must be made to fit.

"Eventually, you will have to approve a building scheme," Mr Braidwood says.

"Not this one." These cheap semi-detached dwelling-houses have no place on Robert's land.

But it is *not* his land. Not anymore.

Truly, was he ever more than its custodian?

"Tell me what your objections are. Perhaps if I understood them."

It boils down to this: the designs do not match the handsome villas in his head.

I do not paint dreams, as far as I know.

Miss Hoddy was wrong about that. She painted his. He has a feeling that she might do so again, if only… But she must not be taxed. Oswald is right. Of course, he's right.

"Mr Cooke, I suggest you have your surveyor cast another eye over the plans, see if he can't suggest a compromise."

Surely in selling the land, Robert accepted the inevitable.

He took Mr Ross's money.

The endless *pop-bob-pock* of tennis balls.

The shrieking of parakeets.

At night, panic lies in wait for Robert. High above Mrs Carlisle's dining table, he is walking the tightrope. The eager predatory eyes of those seated, even those of the liveried servants, are fixed on him, waiting, willing him to drop his balance-pole.

CHAPTER THIRTY-EIGHT

AUGUST 1903

i

The handwriting on the envelope the postman passes through the wrought-iron fence is John's. Finally! Unlike a letter received while the fighting continued, sealed in an envelope his commanding officer required him to address before sending him into a bloodbath, this one can surely be trusted. It has travelled over land, over oceans and by rail – and his own name is on the envelope! *Who else would I write to, Squirt? Neither of our parents can read.* He breaks into a run shouting, "Mother! *Mother!*"

She appears at the front door, comes as far as the top of the path, hands on hips, scowling. "This had better be good."

He waves the envelope. "It's from John!"

Her hands fly to her mouth, then she reaches out as if guiding Gerrard home and puts one hand on either side of his face; tips his forehead into kissable range. There is an impatience about her, a trembling, dancing energy rising off her, but they remain in stillness for a moment, her hands hot against his cheeks, a prayer of thanksgiving. "Frank!" she calls out, then louder. "*Frank!*"

"*What!*"

"*Kitchen!*" She bustles Gerrard inside, shooing him, pulling out his chair. "Let's all sit ourselves down. Frank, there's a letter from John. He must be on his way home."

"Took his time," Frank says, as if he hasn't been itching for news.

"My hands!" They're shaking as Gerrard tears at the envelope.

"Hurry up." His mother can barely contain herself. "I want to hear what my boy has to say!"

There's a stowaway envelope inside the first. Gerrard ignores it, greedy to see what his brother has written. The fact is that Miss Hoddy needed his prayers and John did not. "*Dear Sprat.*" He reads and laughs out loud. His brother's voice is there, in the room.

"Ha!" His father breaks off from chewing on his pipe. "That's him all over!"

"Well? When does he arrive?"

"Hush, woman. Just be thankful he's safe."

"*I am writing to you from Johannesburg,*" Gerrard reads (not a name he stuck a pin in), "*where I have been living this past year.* That'll be the transit camp, I expect. *You will know that the war is over,*" Gerrard continues. "*I followed every instruction I was given to the best of my ability, but I am not proud of some of the things I have done. I cannot hold my head up high at home and say –*"

His mouth stops moving. Nothing John has written is for his parents' ears. But his eyes keep following the lines.

that I am proud to be an Englishman. I am not even sure what that stands for anymore. If anyone were to tell me I was a hero or tried to pin a medal on my chest, I would not care if it was the Queen herself, I would knock them down where they stood. If you could have seen the camps.

Gerrard has read about the camps. You don't *want* to

believe these things but they're here, at their kitchen table. Undeniable.

They told us that camps were needed to house refugees who had lost their homes, if you can say 'lost' when it was our lot who burnt them to the ground. Then to make sure there was no point in rebuilding them we salted their fields and poisoned their wells. The conditions the women and the children were kept in, the children in particular, would make you weep. If I tell you that there was not enough food to go round, and our orders were to leave the children of fighting men to starve.

Gerrard can feel it coming, like the moment before a nest of bees swarms.

It wasn't a case of money. I had money and would have bought food for them, but there was none to be had. I was of a mind to give them my own rations, but choosing who to give it to would have been like playing God and the risk was that I would be court-martialled.

"Well?" His mother, expectant, beaming. "Don't tell me he doesn't have a message for his old ma."

Gerrard shakes his head. Shakes away her interruption.

The sickly ones died first. We told ourselves that once they had died, there would be enough rations to go round and the death rate would slow. But the place was rife with typhoid and the bags of bones we had to bury, because that's all they were. Bags of bones.

Tell my parents... Here. Here it is *I am sorry but I have decided to stay.*

His mouth drops open. There's no hint of an apology for leaving them guessing all this time and now *Tell my parents.*

"Tell me what he says." His mother's voice is still sing-song, still playful, but pretence has crept into her tone. She reaches across the corner of the table, her fingertips not quite meeting the letter, as if they know what they'll find and are afraid to touch it.

Gerrard is shaking his head, or it is shaking him. *Sorry?* Sorry isn't good enough. He scrapes back his chair.

His mother's eyes are shadowing. "You're scaring me now. He's not injured, is he?"

The word shoots from him. "No!"

"Well, then. We've waited this long. I'm sure we can manage a few more months."

Gerrard doesn't intend to say it, but shock drags it out of his innards. "He says he won't be coming home."

"Of *course* he's coming home." Edged with wild laughter, his mother's voice demands he takes back what he's just said. She sees he cannot, but is unable to accept it. "Show me." She beckons, and the beckoning turns into grabbing, and the grabbing to flattening, until she has John's letter inside a right-angled frame of her fingers and thumbs. "Show me where it says that."

He points to the words his mother cannot read, though she has an idea of the length of them. *Tell my parents I am sorry.* She stares at the shapes he sounds out. *But I have decided to stay.*

Violently, bodily, his mother turns towards the range. Half afraid she'll snatch John's letter and throw it on the grate, destroying the evidence of why there's a burning rage in his chest, Gerrard pockets it.

"Well, that's that." His father begins to pack his pipe.

Outside. Outside will be better. Gerrard deadheads as he goes, crushing petals in his fist. Beneath the trees, gravel gives way to leaf litter. Pan. Puck. Down he goes, the half-spheres of his vertebrae grazed by bark. Repeatedly Gerrard knocks the back of his head against the trunk, harder, harder each time, to see if he can break out of his stupor. There is more he has yet to read.

I have enclosed a letter for E, if you could see your way to delivering it. I am asking if she will join me. I am already in business. There is opportunity that cannot be matched at home.

No trace of homesickness. No regret. And John must know the Cookes will never give Estelle their blessing.

If E agrees, I would like you to give her my winnings towards the fare.

Ha! Gerrard uses a sleeve to wipe the snot from his nose. What winnings? Now his mother knows that John doesn't plan on coming home, she'll hardly allow him to keep his wages. She may even have him hand over what he's managed to save this past year.

The Union-Castle Mail Steamship Company sails from Southampton to Cape Town and the cost is about £15/0/0 for steerage class.

Six months' earnings!

If E will come, I will send the rest. I make the same offer to you if you would like to come with her.

If he were to go too, his mother's fractured heart would surely break! And if what John's written is true, who's to say that Britons would be welcome?

I can scarcely believe it, but I miss lying there, you pretending to be asleep, both of us listening to the rain hammering on the roof. In case I forgot to mention, my business is gold. Gold!

ii

The bells of All Saints ring clear and true, calling the faithful to worship, but Robert remains behind his desk. On a working day, a splash of cold water will shake off any residue of sluggishness. Today, on what ought to be a day of rest, Robert feels enormously weary. Outside, the horses are whinnying, their hooves impatient on the cobbles, a mocking reminder that he's a man who can ill-afford a stable. Still, he has dressed in the carapace of success, the stiff white collar and the black frock coat. It's more important than ever that he shakes his fellow businessmen by the hand, talks the good talk. But something seems to have become unstuck.

His wife is calling, "Robert! Robert!" as if he's a dog that needs to be brought to heel. The clip of her heels on the polished wooden floor. "Robert, there you are! If we don't leave now, we'll be late." Freya glances from him to the button fastening of the glove she's working on.

Frank used to say that if Robert could convince the Reverend Mears to preach a sermon against something, it would be free publicity. Men build up a thirst as they sit through a tirade about the evils of alcohol, the devil bartering with God for their souls. Last week, poppy-growing took the brunt once again. *The opium slave, who is seldom unclaimable.* He sighs deeply and, with that sigh, his resolution is made. "I won't be coming with you."

This has Freya's full attention. She clicks the door closed, turns to face him. "What am I to say?" Meaning what is she to say to the Carlisles, the Jameses, the Benhiltons?

"Whatever comes to mind," he tells her. "I cannot stomach another of Reverend Mears' lectures on the three devil kings and my contribution to the moral dishevelment of the parish."

Freya does not exhort him not to take it to heart. Doesn't ask if he thinks Mrs Carlisle feels slighted when the Reverend says it's easier for a camel to pass through the eye of a needle than it is for a rich man to enter the kingdom of heaven. Instead, she stands there, her angry breathing, in and out, in and out, reminding him of the time he faced a bull in a farmer's field. Eventually she speaks. "Is this how it will be from now on?"

Robert experiments with honesty. "I don't know."

His wife's eyes flit to the clock. She clearly decides she can afford to give him another minute of her time because she says curtly, "We'll talk about this. And while we're about it, we need to discuss Estelle."

We, the future wives and mothers of Great Britain. "We ought to wait before deciding Estelle's future for her."

"Wait? For what?"

To say something when he isn't absolutely certain would be foolish, but Robert *is* sure, he *feels* sure, though he would not betray his daughter who approached him so gently.

Freya grows impatient. "I didn't tell you because I thought it would cause you distress, but Mrs Carlisle cut me the other day."

He casts his mind back. "She was at the gardens only last week."

"And you spoke?"

"We did, and she was perfectly civil." She wondered why Cooke's hadn't exhibited their hybrid roses at this summer's festivals. If anything, she thought this year's blooms better than last year's. "Is it possible she didn't see you?"

Freya comes close now. "No, Robert." She does not go as far as to lean on his desk, but she peers down at him. "She did it publicly. In the square. If we're on our way back down, Estelle's opportunities may be limited. The sooner she's settled, the better."

The girls' welfare has always been his wife's business, but now Robert wonders if he's done them a disservice, allowing so much emphasis on sitting up straight, pressed flowers, piano lessons, bonnets and gloves. He looks Freya in the eye. "We must wait to see if John comes home."

"Not the –" Her horror is palpable.

It was Estelle who remained close to her mother, clung to her, while Ida pushed for independence, but Freya has seen only what she wanted to see. "The Reynolds boy, yes. He's a fine young man." Robert not only says it. He means it.

"But not for our Estelle! Besides, the war's been over for more than a year. Who's to say he's even alive?"

"We'd know if he were dead."

"All right. For argument's sake, let's say he's alive. If he hasn't so much as written, he can't care for her terribly much." His wife's eyes flash. "He hasn't written to *you?*"

That would be the proper thing. A man asking for his daughter's hand. But first he'd have to make something of himself. "No, he has not written to me."

"Well then. If you have reason to believe Estelle's harbouring some romantic delusion, you must talk her out of it."

"No, Freya." His fist comes down hard on the desk. "I will not! The sin would be in committing herself bodily to someone else when she's already committed in her mind."

CHAPTER THIRTY-NINE

AUGUST 1903

Gerrard imagines ripping John's stowaway letter to shreds, throwing the pieces on the grate and watching them shrivel and burn. Instead he does as he promised. He goes to the Hoddys' and shows Miss Hoddy the letter that was addressed to him. The envelope.

"John's safe," she says with wonder.

He reads her the words written on the first page, and some of the words from the second. Watches as her expression changes. Her eyes hold the world as she looks at him. "Will you go and join him?"

Ratbag. Pigeon-liver. Halfwit. "Not me." He thinks he sees her expression relax.

"He'll be sorry about that. You with your bookkeeping skills."

"I doubt there's a shortage of men who can keep a ledger."

"Perhaps. But not ones he trusts."

Gerrard takes this on board. It may be true.

She turns to Fairfax, on his perch. "A *gold* mine, Fairfax! And John *won* it. If I had a gold mine, I doubt I'd have come back."

"Your chariot would be no good to you in a gold mine."

"True. I'd need something that runs on rails."

"A private train!"

"He's safe." She clasps her hands together. "It's what I prayed for."

"I –" What is it he wants to say? "I had no idea you prayed." Gerrard means in general, not only about John. While he prayed for Miss Hoddy, she'd been praying for John, their prayers forming a triangle.

"I had a lot of time on my hands." It seems to anger her, the memory of that time. "A *lot* of time." But Miss Hoddy is one of the few people he knows who can be angry and smile at the same time. "Apparently neither of us thought to pray that he should come home." She thinks he's told her everything. That there are no secrets left between them.

He cannot tell her about the dilemma of the stowaway letter. He cannot risk going to Mr Cookes' house, not even to present himself at the kitchen door. Miss Hoddy would deliver the letter if Gerrard asked, but it would be unfair to involve anyone else in this unholy mess. The right thing to do would be to give John's letter to Mr Cooke, but what then of loyalty between brothers?

Dulcie comes at the weekend. She arrives at the cottage unannounced.

"You should have let us know," his mother says, "I've got nothing in."

"I've had a letter from John," she says.

"Then you know."

Her manageress hasn't required a note from home, begging that she be excused. Apparently having a brother who was presumed dead (that was Dulcie's thinking) but is now known to be alive qualifies as 'special circumstances.' Gerrard's sister doesn't come home often. Says it's because she can't get away, but he suspects she likes her weekends in London. She acts all breezy, but Gerrard knows why she has come and it is not so that they can celebrate the 'good news'. On Saturday night, Frank moves into Gerrard's bedroom so that Dulcie and their mother can top and tail. It is not a happy arrangement. Frank is a great rumbling furnace. He tosses and turns, and the bedsprings creak. Gerrard doesn't sleep a wink and his sister fares no better. Through the thin wall, he hears his mother ask time and time again why John has chosen to remain in a godforsaken country on the other side of the world. What did she do that was so very wrong? A refrain he's heard many times already. Then he hears his mother say she doesn't want anyone to know about John's decision, as if it's something they should be ashamed of. *Well, it's too late for that.* He hears Dulcie ask their mother if she'd prefer people to go on thinking that John is dead. If there is a response, Gerrard doesn't hear it. Dulcie's presence is no more comforting than his own. On Sunday, the sunny pretence is gone.

"She doesn't want me," Dulcie tells him before she goes to catch her train. "She wants John."

A number of days pass before Gerrard catches sight of Miss Estelle approaching the gardens. Ida is not with her. His mind drifts back to the afternoon in Miss Hoddy's garden, when Miss Hoddy held both his and Ida's hands, and Ida had looked at him, not shyly but directly, her eyes so clear and intelligent that he realised for the first time that she was her own person. He couldn't say what it meant, but it meant *something*. Now, now Gerrard will never know.

If Estelle is alone, she won't linger. He intercepts her at the gates. "Miss Estelle," he says, bright as you like. "Here on business?"

"I've to pin up a notice about the tennis fixtures."

"The lemons are a great success this season. I could show you if you like." Then he lowers his voice. "I have a letter for you."

A small gasp breaks from her. *John!* She looks at him with a kind of startled wonder – *he's alive!*

Not here, he warns with his eyes. To all intents and purposes, it must seem that Miss Estelle is simply going about her business. "Shall I meet you at the glasshouse?"

Gerrard pauses by the vine-covered trellis to nurse his misgivings. *Too late to worry about it now. You've told Miss Estelle about the letter.* From the foot of the stairs he calls to his mother, "I forgot something," and takes two steps at a time, not waiting on her response. These last few days they have communicated in stunted sentences. Gerrard cannot bear to see the change in her.

He retrieves the envelope from underneath his mattress, tucks it into an inside pocket. He'll be glad to have it gone, but still he battles to reconcile himself with what he's about to do: deceive the man who's given his family a home and paid their wages. Halfway down the stairs he hesitates, listens, and it is as if the house is listening back.

Estelle is at the glasshouse before him. She has removed her right glove and is passing the fronds of a cinnamon fern through her fingers. He likes her slightly more for this.

"Did you see the lemons, Miss Estelle?"

Her hand flies to her collarbone. "Gerrard!" She laughs at herself. "I didn't see you there. I did, yes. I counted fifteen."

"They do very nicely as long as they get their eight hours' sunlight a day." He pinches off a leaf that has scalded at its edges. "Have you smelt them?"

She bends her head to the plant and cups one of the fruits to her nose. "Mmm. Lemon sherbet." He can feel all her unasked questions, her happiness, her impatience.

No one is close enough to see, but Gerrard takes no chances. "I found a cutting about growing citrus fruit under glass. I thought you might be interested." He passes her his brother's letter but, for a second, finds he cannot let it go. *Think of all it will mean for Ida, if you go in secret,* he thinks. *Even if Ida knows nothing of your plans, your parents will assume she did. Then she'll be watched and all her decisions taken for her. Because the Cookes will not have a second daughter go wrong.*

"How thoughtful." A small tug of war and he relinquishes his hold.

Miss Estelle slips the envelope into the drawstring bag that hangs from her wrist. Miss Estelle, whose destiny may seem to have been charted from the day she was born, does not know it yet, but she has been offered something unexpected. Choice.

"You'll let me know – if you find it interesting." In her place, Gerrard might be tempted. He might just go.

CHAPTER FORTY

AUTUMN 1903

"Mr Cooke!"

Robert is at the gates when he turns to see Frank hurrying after him. Strange. Robert isn't sure he can remember Frank ever using his surname. Whippersnapper. Schoolboy. Robert. Those are the names he has called him over the years of their acquaintance.

"If you have a moment, I'd like a word."

"Frank?" The gate gives a long sigh as he lets go of it.

The man dips his eyes. "It's best we go about this formally."

"I see." Robert gestures towards the bench under the eaves, where they've spent so many evenings. "Shall we?" It is not the walk from the gates that it once was.

Frank seems disinclined to sit, so Robert also remains on his feet.

"I always said I'd stay on as long as I could be of use."

Robert folds his arms, wraps them around his chest, needing the feel of something solid. "So you did."

"There isn't work for all of us here. Not any longer."

Uncertain what is being asked of him – would Frank have Robert dismiss his wife and son? – he says, "There's *less* work, but I'd not thought to make any adjustments." He is about to add that it suits him to have someone trustworthy living on site when Frank cuts in.

"Well, I have."

Seeing the man's discomfort, Robert prompts, "Go on."

"Mrs Carlisle has offered me a position as her head gardener, and I'm minded to accept." His eyes flit (his good eye and his bad), unable or unwilling to settle. "That is, I *have* accepted."

This is why Freya was snubbed that day in the square. Not because Mrs Carlisle thinks them too low to associate with, but because she intended to poach his right-hand man. "I'm sure you'll make a fine job of it." He forces a smile.

"You're not upset?"

"The Carlisles have an orchid house, vineries and six and a half acres of gardens. What kind of a friend would I be if I were to stand between you and an opportunity like that?"

"Mrs Reynolds said you might be relieved."

"I wouldn't go as far as that. You will not be so easy to replace."

Frank looks up sharply, his good eye and his not-so-good eye. "You'll replace me?"

"This place won't run itself. I take it there's accommodation for you at the Carlisles'?"

A twitch of a smile. "Their dogs have larger kennels, but Mrs Reynolds informs me it's serviceable."

He will lose not only Frank but Mrs Reynolds. It might not be such a disaster. Robert could simply let it be known that street-vendors will be admitted. He's been fighting them long enough. "And Gerrard?" He tries to say the words lightly.

"If you can't make use of him, his uncles will look out for him."

Gerrard, a knackermen? What a waste that would be. And what of John, arriving home after all this time to find his parents gone? "When do you leave?"

"Whenever you let me. I've said I'll send notice to Mrs Carlisle by the end of the week. She'll understand if there's a short delay."

Robert squares his hat on his head. "I'll be sorry to see you go, Frank. This place has always seemed as much yours as it was mine." He finds he cannot meet the man's eyes. Instead, Robert reaches for the top of Frank's arm and grips it.

At the bottom of the path, he looks towards the gates and the carcasses of half-built dwelling-houses then towards the stand of trees. He would prefer time to mull things over, but Gerrard will be waiting to hear if he'll keep his job.

Robert finds him by the fountain, scooping up leaves in a net, leaves which are the same colour as the farthings that litter the basin. One of the many jobs that is done before Robert gives it a thought.

"Not so many coins as there were." Gerrard plunges a hand into the water, picks one out and turns it over. "See here. An old half-farthing. Eighteen fifty-six."

"They were still in use when I was a boy."

Gerrard looks closer. "Someone's given the Queen a pipe."

"Leave that for a moment." He sits and pats the broad rim of the basin. "Sit."

The net drips as Gerrard lays it down. "My father's spoken to you," he says flatly.

"I have not had time to think it through, so I'm asking you to be honest. Tell me what you want to do."

"Do?" Gerrard looks towards the cottage. To him, this is not just a job. It's home. The land his family worked.

"I put that poorly. We may have scaled back but I still need someone to manage things. I ask myself, would that be expecting too much of you?"

"I've *been* managing things. Ask my mother. *She'll* tell you."

"I'm asking you."

The boy stares straight ahead. Robert can feel anger coming off him in waves. "Gerrard?"

"It's why she made him take the job. Mrs Carlisle won't allow her head gardener to drink or gamble."

"I'd no idea things had become so bad."

"The roses have been beautiful. That's all people see. *Hasn't Frank worked wonders?* they say."

Robert has been one of those people, making excuses when he smelled liquor on him. He *admired* Frank's ability to hold his drink. "Do you think he'll be able to hold down the job?"

"My mother says he'd better." Gerrard's smile is miserable.

Robert struggles to remember the last time he'd asked a question and the answer wasn't *Gerrard is seeing to it, Gerrard knows about that,* or *Ask Gerrard.* Everything between opening up and locking up, the receipts, the books. Eventually he says, "You wouldn't mind if I had to bring someone else in to live at the cottage? I'm not suggesting there won't be room for John, when he comes home."

Gerrard nods at this, and Robert senses something behind the nod. Something almost dismissive. "You mustn't give up hope," he says. "If anyone can fend for themselves, John can."

CHAPTER FORTY-ONE

AUTUMN 1903

i

Early morning. The sun has climbed as far as the upper branches of the third sycamore, but a bracing frost still chills the air. Gerrard clasps his hands as if to make the call of an owl. Instead, he blows a stream of warm air which buffets his mouth and chin. Even at this hour, labourers are on site. They are building on the middle plots now, moving steadily closer. *You're on our lawn,* Gerrard thinks. He thinks it maliciously.

One of the brickies must sense something – perhaps Gerrard has more power than he knows. The man nods. Straight-mouthed, Gerrard nods back. They are not the enemy, he knows that, but whole days pass, days of hammering and sawing, and the grinding wheels of carts delivering more and more materials; days when it feels as if the workmen will plough through everything generations of Reynolds built, and will then invite the swells to come and stare through the bars as his family go about their business.

It is not personal. It just feels that way.

Soon he'll be the only Reynolds left here.

Foreshortened though it is, the lawn needs aerating, and if Gerrard doesn't do it, nobody else will. Now that his father has accepted the position at Mrs Lah-di-dah's house on the hill, he's lost what little interest he still had in Cooke's. As for his poor mother, she doesn't know what to do with herself.

He has just driven his fork into the turf when he hears her. "I've decided to go."

Gerrard turns, sees Miss Estelle standing there. Her walk across the grass has darkened the hems of her skirt. "You'll go," he echoes as he straightens his back. There are no visitors within eavesdropping distance.

"Will *you?*" she asks shyly.

He gives a slow headshake.

"The decision's easier for me. I've nothing to leave behind."

"Nothing?" He feels indignant on behalf of Mr Cooke and Ida. *Perhaps if you could hear my mother crying at night.*

"I don't mean *nothing.*"

Gerrard should hope not. "It's three years since you last saw my brother, and I'm assuming that was his first letter to you."

Her look is defiant, as if she anticipates resistance. "He didn't think it was his place to write until he had something to offer me."

Gerrard clamps his mouth shut. He can't be certain what might come out were he to open it.

"Believe me, I've been over the objections. It's true. I don't know exactly what I'm going to. But the alternative isn't staying here, in the one place I know. My mother will have me married off, and if not marriage, she'll find me a position as a governess. Either way, I'd have to make a new start."

"But you wouldn't be leaving in secret. It wouldn't come as such a blow to your parents." There. He has spoken his mind.

She nods, and it is a sad little nod. "I've listened to my father these past few years, telling me that my mother only wants my happiness. I don't think even *he* believes it."

"If it's being a wife that you object to –"

"Oh, it's not *just* being a wife!" Miss Estelle has surprising spark! But then she concedes. "You *are* right, though. Do you know the monument to Dame Mary Scawen in All Saints?"

Gerrard shifts his weight, unable to make the leap. "I don't believe I do."

"That in itself speaks volumes! I imagine you remember the reclining gentleman with the skull."

"I remember the skull well enough. It stares straight through you."

"Ida always hated it." She smiles for a moment, then shrugs the smile aside as if it's something she regrets. "The man is Sir William Scawen, Governor of the Bank of England. He chose to honour his wife's memory with a sculpture of himself."

"Seems reasonable."

"There he is: full wig, ruffles at his sleeves. The inscription describes Dame Mary as his wife. It gives her father's name and tells us she was thirty-three when she died. But the only other thing it tells us, the *only* thing Sir William could think to say about his wife, was that she was *dutiful.* I don't want dutiful to be the only thing my husband can think to say about me when I'm gone. To John, I won't be an ornament or a glorified servant. I'm not as clever as Ida, but there's more to me than I'm given credit for. I *will* make myself useful."

It's hard to imagine Miss Estelle with her sleeves rolled up. Her beauty is of a demure kind. And does she realise she's just defined what it means to be dutiful? The difference, Gerrard supposes, is that this will be her choice. "Do you think it will be safe for you?" He means for a woman, a white woman. "After all the British have done?"

"I don't believe John would suggest I go if he thought I'd be in danger."

"And you don't worry that, when your parents discover you've gone, they'll take it out on Ida?"

326

"Ida? No one's ever been able to tell my sister what she can and can't do. Ida's going to be a doctor. My father's all for it. So, no, I have no fears for Ida."

He wonders how she can be so certain. "Well. You seem to have thought it all through."

"I have." Her chin is high. "John wrote that he left some money with you for safekeeping. He said he's asked you to give it to me."

Gerrard's hand goes to the pouch strung on a cord around his neck. "There was more." He hangs his head. "But I couldn't keep it from my father." For modesty's sake he turns away before reaching inside his shirt and passing the cord over his head. Does he grudge giving the money away? For this purpose, he does. But he passes the cord over Miss Estelle's head as if awarding her a medal. "I've been paying it back from my wages."

She closes a hand around the pouch. "Then it's yours. I can't take it."

He steps away, barks, "It's yours," more harshly than he intended. He drops his gaze. "I'm afraid it won't cover your fare."

A small noise comes from the back of her throat, acknowledgement of her predicament. "Perhaps if I tell my mother I'll consider marriage, she might give me money for a trousseau."

"John wrote that he'd send whatever else you needed."

"But a letter will take twenty days to get to him, and his reply twenty more."

"Is that too long to wait?"

Her eyes suggest yes. "You think me selfish and perhaps I am. But *you* think too much of others. My father's businesses are failing. I've seen the books. The gardens may not be here much longer, and then what will be left for you?"

"I hope there's time to turn it around. If there isn't…" He shrugs. "Perhaps then I'll think about South Africa. But I won't leave like a thief in the night."

She looks at him sharply. "You want to distance yourself from my departure."

Glad his meaning is clear, Gerrard says, "It's bad enough that I know as much as I do."

"I *had* hoped you'd help me."

If it is meant as an appeal, it is a weak one. "None of this sits easy with me. I'll write to tell my brother of your plans, but no more than that."

"I understand." She seems less certain of herself as she turns to go. "I'll trouble you no further."

ii

Mid-afternoon. Robert arrives at the gardens having ridden from Mitcham with the intention of continuing his conversation with Gerrard. On his way to seek him out, he sees Miss Hoddy at her box easel, takes in the blue tinge of her hands, the white ridge of her paint-speckled knuckles, the angles the joints of her fingers make. "Look at you. You're shivering." It is not just shivering, but a violent shaking. His instinct is to raise her hands to his mouth and blow warmth into them, as he used to with his girls, but the memory of that intimacy – the giving of your breath to another – prevents him. Instead, he says, "We must get you into the warm." He goes to lift the easel from her lap. He will push her home and come back for her belongings.

"Leave that!" There is no cloud of frozen breath – it is not that kind of an autumn day – but Miss Hoddy's circulation isn't all it should be.

"You'll catch a chill." A chill will be the least of it. Robert can hardly blame the tennis players, whose dashes from side to side are keeping their cheeks rosy. Where the devil is his mother? And Gerrard, where is he?

"If you're worried, fetch me another blanket."

He wonders that she isn't in pain. "I am not happy about this."

"Dear, dear." A pout. "Mr Cooke is displeased."

He strips off his jacket and drapes it about her shoulders. Then he unties his cravat and knots it around her neck.

She raises her chin, unrepentant. "How do I look?"

"Gloves." He peels his own from his hands and holds them out for her.

"How will I paint if I can't feel my brush?"

Robert would like to shout. *How can you paint when your brush is shaking?* "My God, you are impossible." He looks to the stepped path to the cottage. It is no use imagining he'll be able to push her chair up there. "I'll see what Mrs Reynolds can lend us."

Miss Hoddy turns her attention to her canvas. She looks serene. As Robert strides off, he glares in the direction of the tennis players, glares at their tutor, knocks but does not stop at the cottage door, which stands open.

The heat from the kitchen range hits him. He receives no satisfactory reply from Mrs Reynolds to his enquiries. His mother and Mr Hoddy often leave Miss Hoddy to her painting. Somewhere close by a dog is barking, the same regular sound, repeated and repeated and repeated, the animal making itself hoarse. "Not without adequate clothing, surely?" Although the fact is that Miss Hoddy is wearing a thick cape.

"What can *I* do?" Mrs Reynolds bustles about, picking anything up that looks as if it might be of use. If she's troubled by the barking, she shows no sign. "Miss Hoddy accepts no help from anyone."

His temples throb. *Will someone shut that wretched animal up!* "Well she must!"

Mrs Reynolds gives him a look that tells him he can't expect every living breathing person to jump to his bidding. And *she* doesn't appreciate being accused.

"I apologise." He massages his temples. *Think!* "Do you have a pair of scissors I can use?"

She points to a basket on the dresser. "In with the darning."

He moves aside balls of wool, finds the scissors, takes them to his good gloves. One by one, the fingers tumble onto the bleached tabletop like so many kidskin thimbles. He looks up into Mrs Reynolds' incredulous eyes, asks, "Is there water on the boil?"

She thumps a mug down on the table. "I'll make tea."

"Just water."

She glares. She won't be obliged to do his bidding much longer.

"If you please."

When the water is poured, Robert takes out his hip flask and adds a generous measure. A dash more.

Back down the path. This time he won't take no for an answer. Robert sits the mug in the grass and wrestles the brush from Miss Hoddy's hand. "You can have it back in a moment." He holds out a glove. "Left hand." Small mercies, Miss Hoddy doesn't resist. She wriggles her fingers in their too-large envelope. "An excellent fit, I'll take half a dozen pairs."

"I'm glad you find this amusing."

Once the right glove is on, Robert wraps her hands around the mug, covering them with his own.

"It's making my eyes water." Her voice swims. "What is it?"

"A hot toddy. To warm you up from the inside."

"You can let go." She nods towards their layered hands.

"If you're sure." Slowly, he releases his hold. "Sip slowly."

Her glassy eyes remain fixed on his as she raises the mug to the level of her mouth and blows, creating ripples.

Here is Mrs Reynolds with what looks like Frank's great-coat. Robert steps towards her and lowers his voice, "Would you mind watching Miss Hoddy while I send for her brother?"

"She won't thank you. Oh –"

He turns to see what Mrs Reynolds has seen. The mug fallen on its side, steaming spillage seeping into the grass; next to it a buckled tube of Prussian blue. What else has changed Robert cannot say, but he can delay no longer. His heart galloping, he removes the easel, the blanket and the metal cage, not caring what else topples to the ground. "I am going to lift you, do you hear? We must get you inside."

"Oswald?"

He looks to Mrs Reynolds but she does not correct Miss Hoddy.

"I'll make sure the coast is clear. I'd suggest the parlour but the kitchen's warmer."

"If you can," Robert tells Miss Hoddy, "put your arms around my neck."

She lolls against him, her bonnet knocked askew, awkward against his shoulder. He bends, reaches one arm around her back and, closing his eyes, searches with the other for the place he expects to find a knee.

"Mind your back," she murmurs.

No. It will be better if he lifts from the other side. There will be more to hold on to with her good leg on the outside. Robert repositions himself. "I have you." He lifts, feeling her lightness as her body settles against his.

iii

"Doctor Stanbury," Hettie says in a contrite tone on opening the front door. She cannot – will not – forgive herself. Dereliction of duty, that's what they call it. It's what she will call it.

"Mrs Cooke." The doctor touches the brim of his hat. This is the young Dr Stanbury, the son of the Dr Stanbury who took over Walter's practice. No longer in his youth, the doctor is bearded and balding. "Where's the patient?"

Hettie gestures towards the back of the house. "Go through." She follows in his footsteps.

Swaddled in the coat Robert brought her home in and covered in blankets, Florence is lying on the settle in front of a roaring fire. Robert keeps sentry. He has marked out his territory as a dog would. Hettie can feel his fury still. A man, even a son, can let his rage be known. He has no need to fold it into a neat square and lock it in a drawer.

The doctor sets down his Gladstone bag, allowing its gate-mouth to fall open. He applies the back of his hand to Florence's forehead, her cheek. She flinches from his touch and opens her eyes, but only briefly.

The doctor lifts one of her eyelids, then the other. "Her pupils are dilated. The cause isn't too much laudanum. That would have had the opposite effect. Has she remained conscious?" He puts his question to Robert, whose mouth dropped open at the mention of laudanum.

"I tried to keep her awake," he recovers himself, "but all she wants to do is sleep."

Hettie thinks she may cry. She should have watched over Florence. She failed.

Doctor Stanbury picks up Florence's hand, exposes its white palm and presses two fingers to her lower wrist. A frustrated sigh, he tries the left side of her pale neck. Out comes his pocket watch. *How does she seem?* Hettie wants to demand, but she has forfeited that right. There is no need for anyone to berate her. Guilt courses through her veins. That her dearest friend should have recovered from her operation, and now this.

After what feels like more than a minute, the doctor frowns. "Did she seem confused?"

Hettie cups her mouth. It surprises her how cold her own hand is when the fire is stoked so high. She has not and will not make excuses for herself. Robert won't remember that it is her mother's anniversary. They are not in the habit of marking the day together. When Hettie saw that the weather was fine, and with Florence wanting to paint – it wasn't as if she would be on her own – she decided on a small pilgrimage. She had Gerrard cut a few late roses and caught the train, then walked the short distance to Brompton, where Decima had been laid to rest. Fifty years ago, when the cemetery opened, Brompton was in open countryside. Even now that the city knocks at its gates, the cemetery is a fine place to wander around, trunks of oaks punctuated by stone angels and crosses and the tree canopies russet and gold. It took Hettie longer than she envisaged to locate her mother's stone urn, but she should not have lost track of time.

"She mistook me for her brother," Robert tells the doctor. He seems a little dazed.

"Her pulse is very weak. The day wasn't particularly cold, but of course Miss Hoddy's tolerance is far lower than yours or mine. Where is her brother? He should be here."

"In the city. Working. I – I've sent word."

Prompted to break her silence, Hettie asks, "Is there nothing more we can do for her?"

"Keep her awake, if at all possible. Give her warm drinks, a little broth if she's able, and of course her laudanum for relief. I will look in again this evening."

Robert shows the doctor out. Hettie does not need to eavesdrop to know what is being said. Florence's poor heart may give out. And Hettie cannot help thinking of how, at the cemetery, she saw a stone palette and brushes and thought, *That is what dear Florence will have on her headstone. The artist's accolade.* She had not even considered it morbid, the sky so blue, the russet leaves against it, and the birdsong.

iv

When Robert finally arrives at his own front door the house is in darkness. Rather than wake a servant he uses his keys, hangs his hat and coat. He lights a candle to take upstairs and treads as carefully as an intruder.

"Robert, is that you?"

His wife's bedroom door is ajar when normally it would be closed. *For better or for worse.* A sigh of a thought. He stares into the candle's flame for a moment then pushes the door wide.

Freya is sitting up in bed. "Where have you been all this time?" Her voice is sharp and high.

He turns and closes the door with a soft click, lights the candle on the mantle from the flame of his own and puts his alongside it. "Miss Hoddy was taken ill."

"And it had to be you who dealt with it?"

He plants himself in the chair by his wife's bed and rests his head in his hands. The hour is late. He has no desire to rake over his anger again by troubling with particulars. "I was the one who found her."

"Found her? Where?"

"At the gardens. You know how poor her circulation is. She wasn't dressed appropriately." In this version of events, Miss Hoddy's collapse is her own fault. She knew what was at stake and was reckless. "By the time I got her home she was barely conscious. The doctor said she shouldn't be left."

His wife's tone grows even tighter. "And where was her brother?"

"I sent word. He came as soon as he could."

"And yet you didn't send word to us."

Robert feels his brow furrow. Looks up. "I did not –"

"No, you didn't think. And your mother? Where was she?"

"She was…" She arrived at the house soon after Robert but

334

he doesn't know where she *had been*. The answer didn't seem to matter a great deal. "She was elsewhere."

"Because we, *we* had a crisis of our own, and you were nowhere to be found."

He sits up straight. "What kind of crisis?"

"Estelle." Freya seems so closed up with anger, she can barely get the word out.

"Is she unwell?"

"Oh, she's quite well. I caught her packing."

"Packing –?"

"As if embarking on a journey. She would not tell me where. When I pressed her, she took everything out of the trunk and hung it back up in her closet. And then she raised her voice to me."

"To say what?"

"That she hoped I was happy."

He suspects Freya of talking about marriage again, the importance of making a good match. But this is not the moment to say anything that suggests criticism, not when his wife is so clearly at the end of her tether. "That was all?"

"*All?* She was hysterical. I didn't know what else to do, so I locked her in her room."

Robert flinches, but he wasn't here. Who can say what he might have done in his wife's stead?

"She doesn't confide in me. I do not –" Freya is distressed, her face contorted. "I do not feel that I know Estelle's mind anymore."

You know it as well as you know your own. It is simply that it no longer aligns with yours. "I'll see what she has to say for herself. Do you have the key?"

Freya indicates a small porcelain saucer on her bedside table. Her voice is pleading as she says, "Where do you think she was going?"

"I honestly couldn't say." He squeezes her hand. "But I will find out."

CHAPTER FORTY-TWO

AUTUMN 1903

i

Gerrard thanks his mother for the supper of pork chops and boiled potatoes. The last meal they will eat together around this table, and it feels as if something should be said.

She says nothing.

"I'll wash the dishes, shall I?"

His father growls, "You'll do no such thing."

Gerrard clears the plates and the cutlery, takes them over to the sink.

Movement behind him. The scrape of a chair. A shifting tide of coins, the sound of a lid being prised off a tin. "Right," his father announces. "I'm off to the Hope for a farewell drink."

Footsteps. Gerrard feels the breath go in and out of his chest. He fills the sink from the simmering kettle. Just the two of them now.

His mother says nothing, but he has heard her muttering when he isn't in the room.

My poor heart.

It beggars belief.

It's absurd, that's what it is.

When he has finished the dishes and pans, Gerrard wraps two of the plates in newspaper and adds them to the wooden crate. The other plate he puts back on the shelf. He wraps the cutlery, leaving a knife and fork for himself. (He assumes she won't begrudge him a knife and fork.) He had thought his family was tied together, but first John and now his parents are cutting themselves loose.

"I'll empty the ash-can, shall I?" He doesn't wait for a reply, but does what needs to be done. It will be his job from now on.

His mother still hasn't moved. Gerrard nods at the door. "Do you remember when we first came here how I used to swing on the door handle? And you used to say, 'Don't do that. The cottage isn't ours. We've to look after it.'"

His mother clasps a hand over her mouth. Gerrard has erred. He has taken her back to a time when John was with them.

ii

When Hettie dreams, she dreams of Glencoe. She understands her father's itch because it is part of her now. When Mr Grey writes – even after all these years, he's good enough to write whenever he stays at the Clachaig – her lungs become home-sick for Glencoe's bracing air, her eyes for its bleak beauty, her feet for its rocky terrain, but duty keeps her by Florence's side. The fact is, she may not live to see the place again. And if she does, what will that mean?

She looks at Florence, lying on the settle, resting.

Imprinted on Hettie's memory, two ruined croft houses backed by a single stand of trees, all with their crowns bent by the prevailing wind in the same direction.

Oswald must work, and his days are long. He goes where the grand building projects are. Railway termini and hotels to accommodate new arrivals, a redevelopment of Regent's Quadrant, The Mall and Kingsway. Hettie doubts she'd recognise them now.

"London's creeping ever closer," he tells them. "It will be on our doorstep soon enough."

The women talk, often at length, though Florence is quick to tire. Most days after lunch, Hettie reads aloud to her. *Daisy Miller, The Woman in White, The Well at the World's End.* Poetry. Scientific essays. Anything from Mudie's Circulating Library that takes their fancy. Fairfax preens and puffs out his feathers, sidesteps along his perch. *Tut-tut-tut.* (He's a harsh critic.) They rarely mention her sketchbooks unless Florence brings the subject up, but Ida comes often to paint the scene from the back window, the slant of the light, and sometimes Florence watches Ida at the easel.

"I believe you could fill my commissions," she says without a hint of envy. "No one would be able to tell the difference. Dear Ida." When she smiles, her smile is distant. "You're quite the artist."

"I'm no match for you." Like Florence, Ida is single-minded when she has a brush in her hand. She doesn't turn her head to acknowledge whoever's speaking. "Besides, you'll want your easel back soon enough, and I want to go into medicine."

"Medicine! Medicine will try to keep you in your place – unless you dress as a man. You know, it turned out that the great surgeon, Dr James Barry, was a woman. No one realised until they were preparing her body for burial. By then her gravestone was already engraved and it seemed a shame to waste it, so Dr James Barry she'll be for all eternity."

"I've applied to the London School of Medicine." On one cheek, a bright fleck of vermilion. "They only accept women. I won't be at a disadvantage there."

The news ambushes Hettie. "I thought you'd settled on the Red Cross."

"I have… made some enquiries." Ida does not need to look in Hettie's direction for Hettie to feel her granddaughter's discomfort. Money, or lack of it, will be the issue.

"Don't think that you need to wait for me to die." Florence's eyes dance, but her pupils are pinpricks, as laudanum users' so often are. "I may go on for quite some time."

Hettie reaches for her friend's hand.

"They say that there's a man – an American – who had a mausoleum built for his wife to look exactly like their parlour." The stories Florence tells betray her growing preoccupation. "It had a stove and a mantlepiece and pictures hanging on the walls. He took his wife's parrot there to keep her company, and when it died he had it stuffed and nailed to the perch."

"Hear that?" Hettie addresses Fairfax, trying to make light of it. "She's going to have you stuffed."

"Don't turn him against me! The man's dedication was legendary. When family and friends wanted to visit, there was no point in calling on him at home. They knew to look for him at the mausoleum. Complete strangers kept vigil with him, women especially. Three Buddhist monks came all the way from Burma."

A diversion is needed. Hettie chances upon a volume of poetry in olive binding. "Shall we have a little Tennyson?"

Florence turns her gaze to the window. "Must we?"

But when the book falls open on *In Memoriam* Hettie snaps it shut. No more mention of death. Not this afternoon.

Hettie remembers being reborn in Glencoe, the crisp clear air that filled her lungs a second baptism of sorts. Here the air is stale and the smell of the oil lamp is strong, but Florence must be bundled up tightly before the windows can be opened. Hettie would do almost anything for her dear friend, but she cannot bear to see her like this.

iii

"And it's to be all poppies again next year?"

Robert understands why Smithers puts the question to him. The soil, he knows, will be all the better from a couple of seasons of poppy-growing. They make an excellent break crop, ideal if you plan on planting first wheats. But Mitcham isn't known for its wheat, and poppies are sensitive to disruption. Sow an alternative crop and they may never come back. "All poppies," he says.

The price *will* increase.

That's what his instinct tells him.

Relent now and the sacrifices he's made will have been for nothing.

Right now, another sacrifice weighs on Robert's mind.

CHAPTER FORTY-THREE

AUTUMN 1903

i

Father and daughter. They are clutching each other's hands, almost as if they are the ones who are eloping. As the train passes through England's patchwork fields, the euphoria of their escape wears thin. Through Estelle's hands, Robert can feel her certainty ebbing. Perhaps she's been struck by the enormity of what she is doing. Robert had wondered if Estelle was attracted by the *idea* of eloping. Her answer was to show him John's letter, which made no attempt to paint a rosy picture of what their life together would be. *I am about my work much of the week and the gold mine is no place for a woman.* Because of that letter, Robert knows that Johannesburg is a new town and has many of the problems new towns suffer from when they expand quickly, along with other problems that are peculiar to South Africa, its recent history in particular. The English governor has decided the best solution is to segregate the blacks from the whites. When she gets there Estelle will know no one, but she and John will have their Sundays together. *I will understand if your answer is no, he wrote, but I must ask.*

Why, thought Robert as he read it. Why must he ask her to make this terrible decision? But he was there. He saw the pair of them together, and there have been many times since when he sensed something. After all this time, it is no comfort to discover that his instincts were correct.

He looks at her sideways. Her face is turned to the carriage window and in profile it is both familiar and new.

He will not say it again. He said it once, while he stood in her bedroom. 'You mustn't be embarrassed to say if you've changed your mind.'

'Have *you* changed your mind, Father? Is that what you're trying to tell me?'

'No.' He said it quietly. 'No.'

It was then that she cut a lock of her hair and gave it to him, and this memento made her decision final. Still, even now, he wills the thought to transmit itself from his hand to hers. *It is not too late to say you've had a change of heart. Right up until the announcement that the ship will depart.*

She turns to him, her eyes full and heavy. She smiles slightly, ever so slightly. Then she leans her head on his shoulder and this moves him to a degree he hadn't thought possible. He will do it now, while farewells are not a distraction. Robert reaches into his breast pocket and takes from it his watch. He closes her hand around it. "It was my grandfather's. It would have gone to Thomas."

He hears her intake of breath. She knows what this is. An object with a history, one that would have had a different future, but might now go to her sons – if she has sons.

ii

The gate sings louder after dusk has fallen. Under the sheltered eaves of the porch, Gerrard's whittling knife stills in his hand. The shape of a hunched man approaches, head down, a large bag slung over one shoulder. The lit windows of the new houses create an artificial twilight, a yellow glow rather than the white of starlight, not enough to see clearly by. Is it his father, come to scrounge some coins? Perhaps come to spend the night, having been warned by his mother not to show his face when he's in his cups.

No. This shadow-man isn't as broad as his father.

He takes to his feet. *Who, then?*

Gerrard could holler and someone in the new houses would hear him. For now, he tightens his grip around the knife handle and braces himself. It is only when the man is on the steps of the path that Gerrard recognises Mr Cooke.

Here it is then. Comeuppance. Estelle's plans will have been discovered. They'll force her to marry, a widower most likely with children who need to be cared for, and the fault will be his. Gerrard swallows, then realising how he must appear, sets his knife down on the bench. "Mr Cooke," he says.

His employer gives a start. "Gerrard! I didn't see you there in the dark."

"It's never completely dark, not anymore." *Hold your tongue. Let him tell you what he knows.*

"I find myself in a… a somewhat embarrassing position. I'm in need of somewhere to lay my head."

Gerrard picks up the saucer with the stub of two candles melded to it. This is not what he expected.

Mr Cooke nods to the bench. "Do you mind if I…?"

Gerrard uses his cap to sweep the pale curls of wood onto the black and white tiles and steps aside. *I was only the messenger,* he will say: a feeble excuse, and beneath him.

Mr Cooke sets down his bag, sits, and takes out a hip flask. He is about to put it to his mouth when he hesitates. "Will you take a drink with me?"

Gerrard is half-flattered. No one, not even his father, offers liquor to a boy, but he has uncles and brothers enough to know that drinking is a family trait. "I don't drink, sir," he says. It is not quite true. He drank champagne when Miss Hoddy offered it to him. He drank it because she wanted them all to have a good time. And Gerrard did. He had a fine time.

"Of course." Mr Cooke drinks deeply then puts one hand to his chest. "My heart is racing. I can scarcely believe what I've done."

Nervously, Gerrard ventures, "And what's that?"

"Something there is no taking back." Mr Cooke is laughing now, a wild unsettling laughter. "I've just told Mrs Cooke that I put Estelle on a ship to Cape Town."

"*You* put her on the ship?" It is out before Gerrard remembers he is supposed to avoid incriminating himself. Thankfully his face is in shadow. He can hear the smack of Mr Cooke's lips against the neck of the flask.

"Estelle would have gone with or without my blessing, so I made the only decision possible. I took her to Southampton and saw her to her cabin. And I paid a stewardess to look in on her on the voyage and see she has everything she needs." He pats the bench beside him. "Sit. You must have been relieved to hear that John's safe. As was I."

Gerrard sits. "I'll take that drink now, if you don't mind."

Mr Cooke hands him the flask. He sips tentatively. Sharp enough to make him gasp. He gladly hands the flask back.

The bench rocks slightly as Mr Cooke turns towards him. "Estelle told me you tried to talk her out of going. I appreciate your loyalty." Mr Cooke raises the flask as if about to propose a toast. "I… well, I was *not* so loyal. Had I told Mrs Cooke of my intentions, she would have put a stop to it." He begins to laugh again. "I don't think what I did was wrong, but from my wife's point of view, I understand that it's unforgiveable." His shoulders shake. His head drops. "I only hope to God that Estelle is safe at sea."

Do something. Say something. "I'll go for your mother."

"My mother?" Mr Cooke looks up startled, his glassy eyes reflecting the flicker of the candles' flames. "Yes, do that. Go for my mother."

iii

Oswald's hand on the bedroom door's edge. "Gerrard is asking for you."

"At this hour?" Hettie glances at Florence, who was short of breath earlier this evening but now appears to be sleeping, her lips slightly parted.

"I'll sit with Florrie," Oswald says. "You're needed else-where."

Good news doesn't arrive at this time of night. Hettie sets her knitting aside, gets to her feet, smooths her hair and heads downstairs.

"Mrs Cooke," Gerrard says, while she is still making her descent. "I'm sorry to call on you so late, but Mr Cooke needs you."

Something in Hettie's chest lifts and settles. Until now she didn't know this is the sentence she's been waiting to hear. Yet if it's true, the reason must be serious. "Has he been taken ill?"

Gerrard hesitates, then says, "Not exactly." One of his arms is raised, ready to shepherd her out of the house. "But he's not himself."

She threads her arms into her coat sleeves. Flaps her hands dismissively at her bonnet. "You were right to fetch me." Hettie is first down the path.

"Not that way, Mrs Cooke," Gerrard says. A sudden shriek pierces the night; perhaps a fox, perhaps some poor soul. Most people abroad at this hour are the worse for wear, either in their cups or through lack of a place to lay their heads.

She halts and turns.

"He's at the cottage."

Gerrard walks in the rutted mud of the road, Hettie on the narrow footway. They go quickly down West Street, stepping in and out of the pale haloes cast by street-lamps. "Estelle is gone," Gerrard explains. "Bound for South Africa to join my brother."

"She's eloped?" *No wonder Robert is beside himself.*

"I don't know that *eloped* is the right word. Mr Cooke put her on the ship."

The news stops Hettie in her tracks. "Without my daughter-in-law's knowledge, I assume."

"That's my understanding."

This rebellion will have repercussions. Hettie walks on, finds more speed. There are few lights in the windows of the new houses at this late hour. The wrought-iron gate sings and Gerrard holds it open, allowing her to pass through.

He is not himself.

Her son is a shadow, no more. The boy brings fresh candles and sets them down, enough for her to see what there is to be seen. Robert with his head in his hands, defeated, broken and entirely human. *I told him he had to be the man of the house. He was twelve years old.* Whatever Robert has done will have been out of love, of that Hettie is certain. He lost two sons and now there is every possibility he won't see his daughter again – no doubt Freya will say that was his choice, a choice he robbed her of. Freya who has seen so little of her own family since she married. And the fact that they will both be right may be irreconcilable.

"I must be about my rounds," says Gerrard, and Hettie lets the lie go unchallenged because it is a kindness.

Perhaps what has been done cannot be mended. Perhaps it can only be carried. "Son," she says, a short word and inadequate for what she feels at this moment. She sits. The night folds itself around them and Robert shudders silently beside her. But when his head comes to rest on her breast, she puts her arms about him and says fiercely, "I have never been prouder of you than at this moment."

"Proud?" The word is cloyed, disbelieving.

She rests her chin on the top of his head. "Never more so."

CHAPTER FORTY-FOUR

OCTOBER 1903

The headache Robert woke with is with him still, but it is the first day he's felt strong enough to ride to Mitcham and look the facts squarely in the face. He and Smithers go to the auction house to seek out Mr Bloodforth, the chief auctioneer. If anyone has inside knowledge it will be him. Mr Bloodforth's opinion is that although the price of raw opium has failed to recover, it must rise. "But who can say if it will be next year or ten years from now?"

Robert needed to hear this. The opium-growing year has acquired a new cycle. Optimism each spring, bountiful harvests, bleak reality. Robert thought he couldn't face the prospect again. Now he realises: he doesn't have to. He thanks Bloodforth for his honesty. Shakes his hand.

"Ten years!" Smithers raises his voice above the shouts of barrow boys and the clatter of cartwheels. Chickens in wooden crates. Apples and plums piled in high pyramids. Competing smells of baking and straw and blood and dung. "It's one thing, Indian farmers producing crops at a loss but…"

"We can talk ourselves blue in the face about the guarantee of British quality, but all businesses have shareholders to answer to." *All the hard years, the years when his endeavours* did little more than pay other men's wages, were for nothing. There were profitable years, but they have receded to a far corner of Robert's mind. "I've arrived at a decision. I won't renew the lease on the farm when it expires."

He can hear the squeal of animals at the nearby piggery. Next year, Mitcham marketplace will be his place of bartering no longer.

They walk on without speaking until they reach the farm-yard. "Will you gather everyone together? I'd better tell them."

"Actually…" Smithers shifts his weight from one foot to another, purses his mouth.

"You look as if you're in two minds."

"I am." He brings a hand to his mouth and paces. Then he repeats himself: "I am."

Robert waits for the overseer to come to a standstill, and while he waits he massages his right hand. No one insists he works cold cream into it at the end of each day. It is a labour-er's hand.

"Would you object if I were to take on the lease?"

Robert frowns. "You think you can make the land pay?"

Smithers winces. "Not with poppies."

"Was I stubborn to hold out as long as I did?" Stubborn? Stubborn is something you say to a child. A man who refuses to admit his own mistake is a fool.

"Your reasoning was sound. Imported poppy *will* be banned, of that I'm certain." Smithers shrugs. "But I don't have the financial backing you have."

"*Ha!*" Robert snaps back his head. "All I ever had was the names of twenty people I thought I might persuade to buy from me."

It is Smithers turn to frown, as if he's trying to remember something that eludes him. "You talked yourself up when I took the job, I have to say."

Then, Robert had the vim and energy of a young man. A

confidence born of naivety, without the experience to realise what he was doing was hard and that many before him had failed in the trying. "Will you return it to a physic garden?" he asks.

"A *market* garden. Fruit, vegetables, that's the way I see things heading."

"Should we tell the men?" Robert says 'men', though he has women working for him. Always has done.

"Can you give me a week? I need to work out how many hands I can afford to keep."

Robert nods. Jericho Walton will go. Smithers will place more reliance on seasonal workers. And women. Women will work for less. You do things differently when it's your own money you're spending.

"Have a drink with me," he says.

"I won't if you don't mind. I'd like to make a start on the calculations."

Robert nods. Smiles. It's probably for the best. His mother has acted as a go-between, brokering a truce so that he and his wife can have a civilised conversation. That is what he has planned for this afternoon and he'll be better off sober. Robert offers his hand and Smithers takes it. Two calloused hands, hardened skin acting as a barrier between them. He unties Buzzard's reins. "Come along, old friend," he says, leading him out of the farmyard.

CHAPTER FORTY-FIVE

OCTOBER 1903

His daughter answers the door. "Father," she says, and her face crumples.

"My dear, sweet Ida." Robert puts one hand on either side of her face, kisses her forehead, then wipes away her tears with his thumbs. He did the same with Estelle as they said their farewells in her cabin on board the SS *Galeka*. Those not intending to travel had been asked to leave. Departure would be at four o'clock sharp. Suddenly it was real – and they were unprepared.

'I don't know when I'll see you again.' Panic crept into Estelle's voice.

'Write to me.' Robert fended off sudden images of shipwrecks. John arrived safely. Estelle would as well. 'Promise?'

'The moment I arrive,' she said. And when he was at the cabin door: 'Thank you, Father. Thank you, thank you, thank you.'

Now he tells Ida, "I had to do it. I couldn't let Estelle go off into the world all on her own."

She nods, rapid little nods dismissing any alternative. "I know."

"But I couldn't be sorrier that this has landed in your lap. It's far harder to be left than it is to leave."

The way Ida tries so very hard to smile, and the weakness of that smile, breaks Robert's heart. He is aware of the familiar house all about them, the hall, everything down to the knots in the floorboards. Already, it has begun to feel different. Perhaps *in*different. "Have you heard from the medical school?"

"They'll have me, and there's a position for me at the Royal Free while I train."

"But that's wonderful!"

"Is it? It feels like the most awful timing. How can I possibly go when Mother…?" She turns her head in the direction of the parlour.

Looking at the closed door Robert realises he's ill-prepared for whatever the conversation with his wife will bring. "Your mother is precisely why you must go." He decides to attempt lightness. "She'll have a procession of suitable young men lined up for you before you know it."

"You've just said that it's harder to be left behind than to leave. If I go, Mother will have been left by everyone."

He doesn't lower himself by saying, *Your mother pushed Estelle away. And she asked me to leave.* "Come here." He opens his arms and Ida walks into the harbour of them.

"What if I can be of more use here?" She speaks into his shoulder. "With Miss Hoddy?"

"You must stop thinking of others. Medicine's a calling. Think only if it's what you want to do with your life. If your answer is yes, then grasp this opportunity with both hands."

She nods.

"Promise me."

"You ask too much."

"Then promise to think about it."

"I do little else."

Father and daughter look at each other. Robert has the strange impression that Ida is the adult and he the disobedient child. "Would you like to go to the churchyard and look for lizards?" he asks.

"There never were any lizards." She slaps him lightly on the arm. "And don't be such a coward." She slaps him a second time. "You must make things right with Mother."

And if I cannot? he thinks. *If things have gone beyond that?* It is impossible not to feel dispirited. "I'll do my level best."

Robert's best is no match for his wife's. "Let me see if I understand?" His anger is roused, something he wanted to avoid. "Am I accused of having an *affair?*"

"No, Robert." Freya stands behind the settee. Her pinched appearance suggests she's endured as many sleepless nights as he has. "Nothing so honest. Though I've no doubt that you transferred your affections to Miss Hoddy almost as soon as you met her. As did Ida."

"It's hardly fair to bring Ida into it." He had somehow assumed their conversation would centre on Estelle, but so far there has been no mention of her, or of his role in her departure.

"Whyever not? Miss Hoddy has stolen much from me. I learned to accept it." Freya holds herself upright. She is self-contained. Precise. "It was nothing I could compete with, and I was confident no scandal would ensue."

"For the love of God, listen to yourself!"

"Do you deny it?"

The clock ticks resolutely. "This is absurd. I've never given you the slightest cause for jealousy." What can Robert say about what he feels for Miss Hoddy? If it is anything, it's loneliness. Him here, her there, and nothing to be done about it. It is no different from the loneliness he feels now that Frank has gone to Mrs Carlisle's, and there are no more evenings under the eaves of the cottage, hours so amicable they frittered themselves away. The pipes they smoked, the plans they made, small and large. But there *is* a difference, Robert realises. He never once felt a burning desire to be understood by Frank. He pushes the thought away. "Let us talk about the real issue."

"Fine," she says. "Let's talk about your pleasure gardens."

He looks up, sharply. It's as if Estelle no longer exists. First Thomas and Gerrard, and now a third child whose name is taboo.

"You gambled with our family's future." Freya cannot look him in the eye. It is no truce his mother has brokered. Robert must consider the possibility that his wife has consulted a solicitor.

"You were quite happy all the time the gamble was paying off." He takes no pleasure in saying this. "While the invitations kept arriving."

"I wasn't happy. I was extremely concerned. Your mother will confirm it."

"My mother?"

"Who else was I to confide in? My own family was so far away."

"Your *husband!*"

She scoffs, and she's right to. For a moment he considers saying, 'You blame me.' Not for the fact that Freya will most likely not see Estelle again, not for Thomas who became ill first, but for Gerrard. Because it was he who insisted Thomas was only teething. He who said the boys need not be separated.

Freya goes to the corner of the parlour and stands with her back to him. "You think I should have confided in *you?*" She speaks as if addressing the vase on the side table. "What about all you kept from me? I had no *idea* of the risks you were taking!"

Robert did it for their sons, *their* sons. And *because* it was for their sons, he couldn't bring himself to cut corners. But Freya cannot know this. He did not tell her. Even while acknowledging this, he persists, "Let us be honest, you and I.

We wouldn't be having this conversation had I succeeded. The issue is that I tried and failed, and now that I've failed your inclination is to shun me, just as Mrs Carlisle shunned you. Because you don't want to associate yourself with failure."

"No, I do not!" Though Robert provoked Freya into saying this, her sharpness takes his breath away. His wife is a person he barely knows. "And what is so very wrong with that?"

There is an inevitability about what happens next, as if Robert is watching a scene play out, the lines already written. Freya does not want him to return. Though nothing in her demeanour suggested otherwise, to hear her say it comes as a blow.

What is she proposing? A separation?

Silence.

There are no grounds. He has never raised a hand to her.

Nothing.

The house must go, he tells her, not to inflame her further but because it is fact. She will move to what was his mother's cottage. At this Freya makes an aggrieved sound. He has already given the tenants notice. They leave in a fortnight's time. It was to have been his suggestion that they all moved there.

This is out of the question. Freya has been told that no one can make her leave the house.

Told by whom?

Silence.

Robert's mother had been adamant that Freya would prefer compromise to scandal; would hold her head up high and say it had all been pre-arranged. Because the alternative – to admit that her eldest had eloped – would invite the kind of spiteful gossip that cannot be survived in small places. It seems his mother was wrong. Robert looks at Freya anew and it dawns on him. "You *need* to stay here so it cannot be said that you left! You intend to claim I deserted you!"

The ticking of the clock.

"What good will an unofficial separation do you?" He can feel Freya closing up, shutting him out. He tries one last time. "It was you who asked me to leave, and I did as you asked. Now, I am willing to return – I could insist on it – but understand this: whether or not I return, we can no longer afford the house."

When the front door is shut behind Robert there is the sound of church bells. All the history in that tumble of notes. As if everything in this small rural backwater is exactly as it always was.

CHAPTER FORTY-SIX

OCTOBER 1903

They padlock the gates. Time enough to make a social call – perhaps long enough to have a decent meal, if Robert can persuade Gerrard to set foot in a tavern. Neither man's culinary talent extends beyond boiling an egg, and Gerrard is usually satisfied with a cup of Bovril. Their arrival at the Hoddys' front door causes curtains to twitch. Freya has the ear of a great many women of the parish. After everything else, now he's had her vacate her home. What further proof is needed that she is the wronged party?

Oswald shows them to the bright room at the back of the house.

Miss Hoddy looks up, demands, "Will the gardens have to close?" With colour in her cheeks, she looks better than she's looked for a while, and Robert would be glad of it – is glad of it – but for the fact that their friendship now seems tainted. He could not possibly be alone with her, not now.

"Won't you invite your guests to sit before you fire questions at them?" asks Oswald, gesturing to a couple of chairs. "I hope you won't mind if I leave you to it," he excuses himself. "I have a few things to attend to."

They sit. It seems strangely formal, Robert with his hands

357

flat on his thighs; Gerrard, cap off and hair flattened down, very upright. "Will my mother be joining us?" Fairfax flies from his perch to the curtain rail to Miss Hoddy's shoulder.

"Don't take it personally," she says, "but when Hettie heard you were coming she decided to take herself off on one of her great walks. I don't expect we'll see her until tea-time."

"I see."

"And now that you're seated," she sits forward, unrepentant, "will the gardens have to close?"

"As always, dear Miss Hoddy –" *too much, perhaps* "– you are nothing less than direct."

Gerrard is staring down at his hands. She will have her information from him.

"I ask the questions I want answers to." She pulls her woollen shawl tighter. "And the gardens have become quite important to me."

Now Gerrard looks up at her. A glance is exchanged between them.

"For a while I hoped that if we lost most of the lawn, the rest might be salvaged."

"Rather like a surgeon." Miss Hoddy smiles wickedly. She is the only person who can say this, and knows it.

It is difficult, now that Oswald has told him, to understand how he did not see it. Miss Hoddy is in pain, not just since her surgery, but ever since her accident. One truth, something Robert was certain of, fractured in that moment. *The laudanum wasn't Oswald's. The story she told was for Ida's benefit and the pretence – the courtesy of pretence – extended to Gerrard.* His mother knew, if not from the moment they met then soon afterwards. Miss Hoddy's life is only made tolerable by opiates, but all the time she painted she was strict with herself. Other artists take opium to enhance their creativity, but she wanted her eye to remain true. Now dust clusters on the caked oil paint in her palettes.

"How much more can you afford to lose and still call it a pleasure garden?" She is matter-of-fact.

"I've thought about it."

"And?"

Gerrard speaks out. "To run it as a tennis club would make the most sense."

She looks to Robert and he feels her impatience for a reaction.

It isn't the first time Gerrard has voiced this opinion – he may have already suggested it to Miss Hoddy – and it is as sound advice as any Smithers ever gave him. But Freya appointed herself president of the tennis club. She ran the tournament, found the tutors. And she is liked.

"Mr Cooke?" Miss Hoddy prompts.

Can't they see his dilemma? Must he spell it out? "What if the tennis crowd stays away?" he says, though what he means is, what if Freya finds an alternative venue for what she sees as *her* club?

"Where else would they go?" Miss Hoddy asks plainly. "Only a handful of people have gardens large enough to play at home, and they're precisely the sort who wouldn't risk damaging their own lawns."

Robert tries to think whether there are any other tennis clubs closer than Wimbledon and concedes that he cannot.

"*Oswald!*" Miss Hoddy leans sideways and calls into the hall. "*Bring me my designs. And the greaseproof paper.*"

He appears at the door. "We agreed. You're not to tire yourself."

"Then help me."

Oswald sets a board on top of the cage that sits over Miss Hoddy's legs.

Gerrard looks in wonderment as Oswald lays down the plans. "These are your original drawings." He takes to his feet and peers over her shoulder to better see.

The rose walk as it was. The broad stretch of lawn with its central bandstand.

"They are. And now I'm going to cover them up." Miss Hoddy takes a measure of greaseproof paper, creases it, then tears along the crease.

Oswald stokes the fire, then comes to stand next to Gerrard. This is too much for Fairfax, who flies to some high perch. As his sister traces everything, Oswald looks on. It is easy to imagine how she devised her original design, her deft lines under his critical eye. She draws representations of the new houses, the likes of which you'd see on an Ordnance Survey map. All from memory. "I think I have that right. Now, where to need to make our incisions?"

They all consider, Oswald included. The cottage, the tennis courts and the pavilion are to the left.

"I suppose we must extend the road." Without waiting for agreement, Miss Hoddy draws an unforgiving tract through the tennis courts, dissecting the copse, the alders and the oaks with their green canopies that spread fifty feet into the air – the trees Robert swore must never be felled. He hears them now, his shadow-sons, playing hide-and-seek among the gnarled and ribbed trunks. *Ninety-nine, one hundred. Coming, ready or not.* And then the sound of the woodman's axe.

"We'll need a turning circle," Gerrard chips in. "For carts and vehicles."

"I take it we lose everything to the right." Again, this isn't a question.

Within Robert is turmoil, a great churning disturbance. *This isn't final,* he tells himself. *It is simply what might be possible.* At the same time, he knows. It has to be done.

The plots Miss Hoddy draws mirror those at the developed end of the road, each wide enough for a pair of semi-detached houses or a more substantial villa. They extend from the turning point like the sun's rays. Neptune and his chariot find themselves in someone's back garden. "Eight plots. I can make it ten if you're prepared to lose the grotto."

The kilns that were. They all look to Gerrard. Miss Hoddy reaches up over her shoulder for his hand. "They're all that remain of your grandfather's legacy."

"My grandfather's legacy? You're forgetting *my* mermaid."

"I would never do that," she says, and the boy blushes, some secret meaning passing between them, but Miss Hoddy looks to Robert.

He nods; in that nod, permission to destroy. If he is to do this – and there is little choice – he must get the most he can from it.

"What are the measurements for a tennis court?"

Gerrard had the answer ready. "Thirty yards by twelve."

She draws the lines of six new courts. Flowerbeds filled with plants. A new terrace in front of the pavilion. A path leading to the aviary. (She has left that, he notes, and hopes Gerrard will be glad.)

She presents him with her plan. "This need not mean failure." Her voice is kind. "It can be something new."

But it is too early for positives. Robert has not yet reckoned with the loss of his small corner of the world, what it means, what it *will* mean. It feels like a betrayal of his sons, of old William, of Frank. He wonders that Miss Hoddy does not feel betrayed.

Later that evening, as they sit out on the porch, he with his pipe, Gerrard with his whittling, he says it lightly, disingenuously: "I don't think I ever told you that I once had a son called Gerrard."

Gerrard's knife stills. There is a heavy pause. Robert can almost hear him deciding how to respond. At last he says, "How old was he?"

"He was only a year old when he died." Robert hates the way this sounds. As if the loss was somehow less significant because Gerrard didn't have the opportunity to grow into himself. "I've imagined them here."

"Them?"

"Gerrard had an older brother. They died within a day of each other. I thought the older one was teething..." Robert lives all his days with the consequences of that singular mistake. His insistence that he knew better than his wife. How he overruled Freya's instincts. He decides to say it because he can tell Gerrard is wondering if the brother was a John. "The brother was called Thomas."

Gerrard nods. It doesn't seem to come as a surprise to him. "You called my brother Thomas once."

"You remember that?"

A shrug. "The name stuck for a while."

"I imagined I was creating a little Eden in memory of them, but..." He falters. "It became so full of other people that they were squeezed out. The tree walk was for them. And now..." Even as Robert gave the instruction for the trees to be felled he mourned their loss. Of all his questionable decisions, it is this final betrayal he hopes will escape the eyes of God.

Robert is on foot, on the return journey from the auctioneer's. The sound of hooves. A gleaming closed carriage draws to a halt and the cabin door opens.

"Mr Cooke!" The voice is unmistakable.

He prepares his face. "Mrs Carlisle." Though she tugs on his chains, there is no need to dance. He has little to fear from her now. "I trust you are well."

"I hear you are selling some land."

"How news travels. The notice has just gone up."

"You might have come to me."

"It's still available. Are you interested?"

"That is not what I meant." She looks wounded. "I've always thought that Cooke's was of immense value to the community."

362

"That was certainly my intention, and I believe we succeeded for a while at least, but I cannot continue to run it as a charity."

"I'm sure we could have seen our way to doing *something*."

Does she think he hasn't *tried?* "This isn't the end. Cooke's will continue as a tennis club. And if that's all, I'll bid you good day." He inclines his head, replaces his hat and walks on. It is hard to feel any triumph, but Robert does at least feel less like a shackled beast.

The plots go under the hammer. The winning bid is from a consortium: Mary Emily Duncan, William Stewart Forster and George Edgar Frere. The same clauses are added to the contracts – that Robert shall have the right of approval of plans – and the purchasers react in much the same way Mr Ross did. But they sign. They all sign, Robert included, his own backhanded scrawl not as bold as it once was.

Part of the money raised is for Ida's college fees, as certain an investment as Robert has ever made.

But old Neptune: what to do with Walter's gift? Robert spends an afternoon standing knee deep in water, hands on hips. He cannot fathom how to take the thing apart. The next day he finds Gerrard dismantling the pipework.

"I thought I'd better make a start," he says, then hesitates. "That *is* what you wanted?"

"Yes." Robert perches on the edge of the basin to remove his boots. None of this is what he wanted. He knows how he and Frank fixed Neptune to the plinth. They'll need to chisel him off.

The wrought-iron gates and fencing come down once again, and once again Oswald lends a hand.

Oswald has just said, "We could do with a fourth," when Reverend Mears appears, wheeling his high-wheel tricycle.

Is there no place on Earth where God does not cast a shadow?
"Reverend," says Robert. "Come to lend a hand?"

"I hoped I might have a word."

"As you can see, I have my hands full."

"Later, then. I'll come back."

"No need." Robert doesn't stop what he's doing. He is in mid-manoeuvre and the section of fencing is heavy and awkward.

"I beg your pardon?"

"I take it that you've come to ask me to consider returning to Mrs Cooke."

"I –"

"It was she who asked me to leave." With some difficulty, he pivots. "And she will not have me back. Granted, I could insist, but I see no purpose in it. We can be unhappy together or unhappy apart. There will be fewer regrettable words if we are apart."

He does not care to see if the Reverend is still standing there but, after a few moments, Gerrard says, "That saw him off." Robert twists his head to see the Reverend in retreat, but feels no relief. The reason he doesn't insist on returning to Freya is this: of the four children they were blessed with, two were left, only two, and now one of them is gone to the other side of the world and he – Robert – put her on the ship that took her there.

This time the fencing cannot be made to look right. It is too tall, too grand. He sells the pieces to a scrap-metal merchant, who agrees to deliver Neptune to Mrs Berkeley James.

Robert and Gerrard set to work erecting a wooden fence along the new boundary, then they dig a trench and plant laurel for a hedge. The owners and tenants of the new houses stand by and watch, asking what is happening. Some say they bought the houses because of the pleasure gardens.

"And yet," says Gerrard, "Not one of them's ever set a foot inside."

It feels to Robert as if they are barricading themselves in. Bracing themselves for whatever blow comes next.

CHAPTER FORTY-SEVEN

NOVEMBER 1903

"Father!"

Robert looks up from his weeding, turns. In place of his young daughter he sees an elegant young woman striding towards him. In a high-necked blouse, dark fitted jacket and a plain skirt, she already looks every inch the scholar.

"A letter." She waves it. His mother says Ida takes after Decima, and Decima was a strong woman.

"Is it –?" To his feet he clambers.

"Yes."

He peels off his leather work gloves, throws them down and wipes his hands on his jacket. "Shall we?" He gestures towards the bench under the eaves, but Ida's eyes drift towards the place where the tree walk had been. He watches them pool.

"I didn't think…" She swipes at their corners. "It is…"

He hadn't wanted her to see the stubborn shards of bark, the small twigs, the chips of wood the axe left behind. "It's shocking. There is no other word for it."

"Perhaps when you've finished," Ida attempts to smile, "it won't look quite so dreadful."

"Come." He needs this distraction as much as she does. "Let us see what your sister has to say."

He finds his hands are trembling.

Ida leans her head on his shoulder and tucks her hand inside his elbow.

"Are you cold?" he asks.

"Not one bit."

Dearest Father,

The fact that this letter has reached you will confirm that I have arrived safely, although a sea voyage is not an experience I am keen to repeat. My first real piece of news is that I am now Mrs John Reynolds.

There is a sudden tightness in Robert's throat. *Freya, our daughter is married.* "Your sister is married," he manages.

"Surely you realised that was what she intended."

"Yes, of course. But…" *We weren't there.*

Ida hugs his arm. "I didn't get to be a bridesmaid."

He kisses her forehead. "I have a new son-in-law."

"Only one? I am fairly certain I have *two* new brothers-in-law."

"Where *is* Gerrard? We should tell him."

"We should all celebrate!" But Ida's face falls. "We can't *all* celebrate, can we?"

"Has your mother mentioned Estelle yet?"

"Scarcely. She may be happier now they're wed. No one will be able to say that her unmarried daughter has run off."

A sigh tears through him. "I've thought it through, and I honestly don't see how I could have done things any differently."

"You were supposed to have stopped her."

366

"She's an adult. How long can you keep an adult daughter locked in her room?"

"I'm rather afraid my mother will try it with me."

"Have you threatened to go to medical school?"

"Not threatened. I've told her that I'm going and she said you can't afford it. I thought better than to mention that you've already paid my fees, so I told her I'll pay my way by nursing at the Royal Free Hospital. She is not happy."

"I doubt she is. But *I* am. I am very happy."

With each strike of the house-builders' hammers, the parakeets fly circuits of the aviary. They settle, but only for an instant, then the next strike brings the next green tornado of wings. "I know, I know," Gerrard assures them and, "It won't be for long," but they fly and fly about his head.

"The stress will kill them," he tells Robert, who sighs.

"It may kill us all."

"This can't go on. I can't bear it."

Robert is about to say that perhaps the birds have earned their freedom, but Gerrard already has the latch undone.

His hand reaches. *"Wait!"*

Gerrard turns.

"If we are to do it, then let's at least make a ceremony of it. I'll go and see if the Hoddys will come. And my mother."

"And Miss Ida?"

"And Ida, of course."

They are assembled. His mother, questioning the need for such urgency. Miss Hoddy grasping why they cannot wait for Oswald, cooperating with their attempts to bundle her up. Ida.

Gerrard, who has not left the aviary, unlatches it from the inside. For a moment, everything is as it was, then a hammer strikes and, in a blur of lime, the birds commence another desperate anti-clockwise circuit. At the centre of the spiral, Gerrard spins in the same direction as the parakeets, to see what they will do. For his part, Robert tightens his grip on the handles of Miss Hoddy's chair. It seems they will all pass the open door, but one alights on the edge of the frame and peers out. Behind this one bird, the parakeets fly, the movement of their wings too fast for the human eye to register.

Gerrard scoops a handful of seed, opens his palm and steps outside. Seeing him, the hesitant bird follows, beak and claw, beak and claw, to the edge of the open door. It is outside, but still it clings to the cage. Born to captivity, perhaps it doesn't seek freedom. It may not know what to do with it.

"Come on," Gerrard croons, backing away, sideways on to the party. "Come on."

"A little further," Miss Hoddy says. "Be brave." And her hand reaches over her shoulder for his. His body goes rigid. *I've no doubt that you transferred your affections to Miss Hoddy almost as soon as you met her.* But his mother steps closer and takes Miss Hoddy's other hand, and seeing this, meeting his mother's eyes for a moment, knowing passing between them, he reaches for Ida's hand, and they are not two people but part of a chain.

Folded, the bird's wings are smooth. An experimental ruffle. Then it displays its silk lining, the lime green, the yellow and the grey.

They all watch the one bird, certain it will be the first to fly free, when the parakeet leading the whirlwind swoops through the opening with the flock in pursuit. The watchers tilt back their heads. Ida's free hand reaches up to shield her eyes from the low sun. How they soar! More space, more sky than they imagined, their first intoxicating experience of the Angel's View. Robert remembers it as he tightens his hold on the two hands in his: the patchwork fields, the network of streets, the snaking Thames. But Cooke's parakeets aren't long-distance flyers. They complete a short circuit and settle on the roof of the aviary. Then another hammer strike. All take to the air, with the exception of the mite who seemed so brave but still clings to the wire mesh. Gerrard wiggles the door back and forth. "Stubborn so and so."

"I take it he is one of ours," says Miss Hoddy.

"Last to fledge, last to fly free." Gerrard tips the seed into a pocket and offers a forefinger. The bird nibbles it, then clambers aboard, suspended for a moment with one talon tightly wrapped around Gerrard's finger, the other hooked onto the wire mesh. "On you get," Gerrard tells it, moving the door closer. He waits for the flock to make another circle and settle, waits for the next hammer strike, then jerks his arm down and then up, trying to trick it into flight. It flaps its wings but still it clings.

Robert unrolls Miss Hoddy's plans. He considers the ground. "It is some time since I marked out a tennis court." The fact is, back then Frank took the lead as he did in most practical matters.

"Pegs and rope," Gerrard says, the parakeet on his shoulder. "That's how we did it."

Robert reads from the yellowed rules that have been pinned in the pavilion all these years: *"The ground shall be a right-angled parallelogram, thirty yards long by twelve yards wide and divided into two right and two left courts."* He skims the part about the net. *"The ground may be marked by any means the players think proper, either by whiting or by cord or tape. The objection to whiting is that it disfigures the lawn and wears the turf by confining play to the same spot. A common hempen cord is ugly and apt to trip the players, therefore a white tape, such is used in marking the ground for croquet, is recommended."*

Gerrard nods in agreement. Like his father, he can measure an accurate yard by using the length of his stride.

Robert's shoulders jar with every strike of the hammer. Even when he can hear birdsong, he's on edge, waiting for the next blow. It would be good to shout at the workmen to stop, but how can he when he signed his name under the purchasers' signatures?

Tennis lessons resume, but it is immediately apparent that the arrangement is going to be an unsatisfactory one.

Miss Baskin manages to be both apologetic and forthright. "I cannot make my instructions heard over the builders, and the noise puts my students off their games."

"I'll see what can be done." At least now Robert has reason to complain. He approaches the foreman, who doesn't like to be mistaken for one of his men. He wears a bowler, a little on the small side, and has a silver watch tucked into the pocket of his shabby waistcoat. The man doesn't deny there is shouting – indeed, he has to raise his voice to be heard above the din – but tells Robert it's a necessary part of the job. The workers must respond to commands to confirm they have heard them (Robert can hear the commands, the responses). It's for their safety.

Up on a high parapet, only a brick's width, stands a man holding a plank of wood that is a good four and a half yards long. From where Robert is standing, he might be a roped-ancer.

As for the noise generated by the work itself, the foreman *supposes* they could build one house (or pair of houses) at a time, but the project would take longer and would most likely cost more, and who's going to pay for that? His profit-margins are next to nothing as they are. Sometimes it feels as if he's in business just to keep this rabble – he thumbs over his shoulder – in work.

Robert appreciates his dilemma.

"And your tennis players might still find the noise disagreeable. No, my feeling is that we press on and get the job finished."

"And if you press on, how long then?"

"Well, that will depend on the weather."

Robert comes away, having sold Buzzard to the foreman. He couldn't continue to keep him tethered behind the cottage. The next tennis lesson has begun, but the players who would ordinarily have stayed to take refreshments have gone elsewhere. At this rate there will be no spectators for their tournament.

"I am very sorry, Miss Baskin, the foreman tells me they can't reduce the noise."

"That is most inconvenient."

"Can I perhaps reserve the courts for you in the evenings?"

"That won't do. I can only teach one couple at a time!"

He can see her thought process. She is clearly unhappy (*seething* might be a more accurate description), but if Miss Baskin had other options she would be exercising them. "Perhaps I could offer you a discount," he suggests.

"*Robert!*"

He turns to see Oswald approaching at what is more of a limp than a run, though clearly he has been running.

"Do excuse me," he says, heart in his throat. "Gerrard! Will you help Miss Baskin with her bookings? Change them to whatever times she would like, and apply a fifty per cent discount." He strides over to Oswald who is hugging his sides.

He drops his hands to his knees and looks at the ground, shoulders heaving. "Go on ahead. The front door is open."

Robert takes one of Oswald's arms. "Is it Florence?"

He lifts his head only slightly. "No, Robert. I'm afraid it's your mother."

CHAPTER FORTY-EIGHT

NOVEMBER 1903

It is the Hoddys who stop the clocks and drape the mirrors, since the cottage at Cooke's has neither. Robert is moved to see how they observe even the smallest rituals. The curtains are closed, photographs turned face down. Robert's suggestion was that his mother's body be taken to her former home – now his wife's – until the burial, but Florence insisted, 'Our home was her home. It's the least we can do for her.'

'It will be no small undertaking.' No small undertaking for such private individuals to have a constant stream of people calling to pay their respects.

'I think it's what she would have wanted.'

Robert's contribution is the laurel from which a wreath for the door is made and armfuls of flowers from Cooke's, this at Gerrard's prompting.

'I must admit,' said Miss Hoddy. 'I'm curious so see who calls.' She meant who will come now that Hettie is dead when they did not think to call on her while she was alive.

She is laid out in the Hoddys' front parlour, a room Robert had never before set foot inside. He does not know how the furniture is arranged ordinarily, when a coffin is not its focal point, how it is lit when not by candles. Somehow, between them, Ida and Florence have managed it. Ida mainly, because how much help would Florence have been able to give? They have her in her best dress, but Ida lifts the hem to show him her terrible walking socks and her stout shoes. Her walking staff is at her side. She has her map of Glencoe. A grey feather has been laid on her chest.

"She's ready for her journey," says Miss Hoddy, stroking Hettie's forehead, which is just within her reach.

Robert takes his mother's hand in his and it is cold, and the feeling that he has forgotten something is with him, all the things he didn't say or has put off saying. All the things he thought could wait. Then he draws up a chair and sits.

People come and go.

The professor shambles in, removes his hat and sits heavily. "Good day, to you Mrs Cooke," he says. "Do you mind if I smoke?" He pats his pockets then, not finding what he needs, removes a candle from its holder and uses it to light his pipe.

"It's good of you to come," Robert says.

"My wife was most insistent. But you know," he draws deeply, then eyes his pipe approvingly, "I admired your mother. Sometimes I think I worry too much about what people think of me."

Miss Rotherham comes quietly. Robert doesn't notice her arrival, and she does not announce herself. She just lays one hand on his shoulder and lets it rest there. "We were the same age," she says.

"I did not know that."

There is nothing from Freya. If she wishes to avoid him, she could call when he is elsewhere. This neglect is unforgivable. It is his mother, not Robert, she insults.

The day before the funeral, Oswald comes to the gardens to find him. No urgency, but a letter of condolence has arrived. Something Florrie says he should see.

It is from a Scottish innkeeper's wife named Aileen. Miss

Hoddy's hands are trembling. "I wrote to tell her about your mother's passing. Hettie always spoke of her with such fondness. Read it," she says, as if she may at any moment overflow.

When his mother stayed at their inn, she asked Aileen if they kept old guest books and though they did, Aileen couldn't locate the older books. It was some time after Hettie's departure that she stumbled across them (they were at the back of a closet) and by then, Aileen had mislaid Hettie's address. Of course, Miss Hoddy's letter put that right. Perhaps, now, her family would like the entry. A second envelope is inside the first.

Miss Hoddy's eyes are shining. "I haven't looked," she says. He hands it to her.

"Are you sure?" She opens it. Unfolds what is a single page, yellowed, as old paper is. She scans the page. "Here he is. *Ernest Winstanley.*" She looks up at him. "Your grandfather."

Hettie's request was that she be laid to rest with her mother. People will say it isn't proper. That even in death, a wife's place is with her husband (perhaps they remark on it as they leave the Hoddys' with their heads bowed, having discovered that there will be no funeral service at All Saints). But Walter has his grandsons for company, while Decima has been alone all these years.

They are a small party of mourners. Ida, Oswald, Florence and Robert himself. Gerrard has volunteered to stay behind so that the tennis players do not miss their lessons. Robert had wondered about sending a telegram to Estelle, but typed words seemed so impersonal. It will be another three weeks before the news reaches her in Johannesburg, a place further from Cape Town than Glencoe is from Carshalton. He tries to picture it, this new town, with its new town hall and its new post office, so that he can picture Estelle there with John and the child she is expecting. It will be sunny there. Hot perhaps, as spring moves towards summer. It's a struggle to visualise a place with no past, no ghosts. He dare not entrust the locket he is having made to the mail boat – perhaps one day he'll take it in person. For now, he has sent the plaited lock of hair it was designed to hold.

Only two carriages make up their cortège. The glass-sided hearse is drawn by a pair of magnificent Flemish stallions, coal-black with long flowing tails, their heads bedecked with ostrich plumes. Their carriage follows behind. Shortly after they depart, a whinny. The blinds have been drawn to give them their terrible privacy. They can only look at one another and with the silence the occasion demands. The horses take a little convincing that their destination is not All Saints. After that, nothing but the rocking of the carriage. Ten miles, painfully slow. Robert imagines figures on the footways pausing as they pass, removing their hats, crossing themselves. Veiled, Ida and Florence are shoulder to shoulder, black-edged handkerchiefs held in black gloves. In heavy crêpe (Freya's, he assumes) Ida looks older than her years. Save for gloves, she said she needed nothing new. *If Ida has borrowed her mother's dress, what is Freya wearing for the mourning period?* Freya, so concerned about appearances, and this leads Robert to think of all of the lost gloves of Ida's childhood. Somehow he must transmit this thought (perhaps he is staring at her hands) because, without looking at him, she removes the left one. On seeing her do this, perhaps thinking it some peculiar family custom, Miss Hoddy does the same. An act of solidarity. But Robert cannot return Miss Hoddy's gaze, even through the safety of her veil. He suspects Freya would turn her being here into something it is not. *He had Miss Hoddy attend his mother. Miss Hoddy took my place.*

When the time comes, Ida goes with the men to the graveside. It breaks with convention but her mother isn't here to remark on it. Florence alone remains in the carriage, but Oswald pulls up the blind so she can see out. As Robert stares at the rectangular hole dug by the gravediggers, he is comforted to have one of his daughters by his side.

The gravestone has yet to be engraved with a tribute to his mother. The lives it honours are those of Decima and Ernest, who is not buried here, or anywhere else. It was Florence who told him this. She had the story from Hettie, whose given name was Aonach. That is what her Scottish trip was all about. Following in her father's tracks. Finding the mountain trail she was named for.

It is incredible to Robert how little he knew of his mother's life.

'You only need ask,' Florence said. 'I have stored all of Hettie's stories.' And she pointed to the side of her head.

How can he know *what* to ask? And he doesn't feel it would be right to suggest that her store might be transferred onto paper, because of all that might imply.

"Have I ever been here before?" Ida asks of Brompton.

"I very much doubt it. *I* have never been here before," Robert admits. His mother will be flanked by an Egyptian column and a Celtic cross.

"You didn't attend your grandmother's funeral?"

"If I did, I have no memory of it."

"It feels very peaceful."

But Robert does not feel at peace. The stone urn and its shroud; the veil between the world of the living and that of the dead. But what about the veil that separates two people in life? He clasps his gloved hands and looks about to see if Freya has relented and made her own way. He begrudges his wife's absence because it distracts him from the service. Perhaps she thinks that attending funerals is something only women of the poorer classes should do. Perhaps, because he accepted the Hoddys' offer, Freya feels slighted and doesn't wish to bring her anger to an occasion such as this. But as the graveside service progresses and the vicar's low drawl washes over him, moments claim Robert.

His mother's refusal to watch his ascent in the hot air balloon (although he knows now that she did).

'Close the curtains!'

How she strode across the lawn on the day of the opening looking like the Wild Woman of Borneo.

And that dreadful evening at the Carlisles' when he allowed a story to be told about her.

How he resented her interference in his business affairs.

But *"I've never been prouder of you."* She left him with that, and it will have to be enough. And now the coffin, straps straining, is lowered into the grave, the earth. His mother, carrying her father's signature, returning it to Decima, and if all else is wrong, there is at least a rightness about that.

EPILOGUE

1910

Victory for the anti-opium movement as Britain agrees to dismantle the India-China opium trade.

As he reads the headline, a hollow laugh erupts from Robert's throat. He wonders if the news has reached Smithers. The Reverend had been so vehement, the anti-opium movement so confident. Ten years, it took them! Now is the time that home-grown poppies will be in demand. Now, prices will soar. But it is too late, too late for Robert, too late for the fields and those who worked them, too late for Cooke's pleasure gardens.

Three years, he stuck it out, good years for poppies. Come June, great rippling seas of white petals and what a sight they were! Each head as big as a man's fist and the juice more plentiful than he could ever remember it. Now tobacco addiction is the new evil, cigarettes 'the opium of the people', a drug that has no useful medical purpose, but leaves users lazy and lethargic.

The occasion should be marked, somehow. He'll send a note to the Hoddys. Propose they crack open a bottle of champagne in commiseration. It's easier now that they live in the city. It may be a train ride away, but curtains don't twitch when he arrives at their front door. And it was the right choice. Oswald needs to be where the surveying work is, Florence where she has better access to medical care. Ida sees them as often as she can manage, when she can get away from the hospital. Robert… not nearly as often as he'd like.

He goes to take out the ash-can, bids good evening over the garden fence to the new neighbours to his left, a couple with a young family. Boys. Robert likes to hear their laughter. He hears it and he remembers, not a true memory, but a memory of two imagined childhoods. The husband is watering their yellow roses, unaware of their pedigree. Perhaps the worst part was signing the deeds for the final plot. If his neighbours are too close, if Robert feels encroached upon, the fault is his, not theirs. Selling the narrow strip of land ought not to have been as upsetting as the decision to close Cooke's, auctioning off all that remained, but Robert's whiskers were greyer by then. With Gerrard gone to South Africa and Ida busy with her studies, he had less optimism. Defeat seemed absolute when, with great reluctance, he dipped the nib of his pen. In realising his dreams, he took too many risks. He was as Freya correctly put it, pig-headed. And he lost sight of what it was all for.

"Have you lived here long, Mr Cooke?"

A horse chestnut sits almost on the boundary, a lone trunk, planted by God or one of his smaller creations. It stretches its branches out over the fence as if to reclaim lost territory. Come autumn, half of its leaves will be shed in his neighbours' garden, half its haul of conkers will fall, armoured cases splitting, hatching, to be collected by their boisterous young sons. Pan sits to one side of its trunk, Puck to the other. "I had this cottage built," he says.

"We heard it was the gate house for an estate."

"Did you?" To leave this uncorrected, knowing that it may in time become received wisdom, is part of Robert's penance.

He has Miss Hoddy's design and there are, of course, her paintings. He might invite his neighbours into his parlour to show them the scene with the tennis players in front of the pavilion and the edge of the cottage. The chimney, the dormer window, the eaves. Better still, he could take the painting down from the wall and take it outside to show them. Point out that the road runs through the very spot where the game of tennis was being played. But that would be dangerous. The road continues through the place where the tree walk was. His sacred tree walk.

No. He'll let the story of the gate house stand. Eventually his neighbours will get around to asking one of the couples who've lived here since the semi-detached houses were built. Some of them still remember when the place was a pleasure garden, how they once watched the Baddeley brothers play, and how those brothers played! Some, he knows, did their courting under the rose walk or in among the alders and the oaks. *You should have seen them on a warm summer's evening, lit by Chinese lanterns.* Their grandparents told them how, before that, it was a chalk pit, one of those small family concerns that fell victim to progress.

But when those residents move on, Robert's small contri-bution to the history of the place will go unacknowledged. The road is not named after the Cookes, or the Reynolds, but Mr Ross, the housebuilder. There is no name on a signpost and there will be no heritage plaque. It is as if Ida has torn the final chapter from one of her mother's novels.

It was an act of foolishness, of youthful optimism, and for one brief, shining moment, he thinks as he takes his seat on the porch under the eaves, as his neighbour's sons run rings around their garden, as a lone parakeet flits down from a high perch to see if Robert has any seed in his pockets, it was magnificent.

NOTES

Who can really say what first attracts us to the things we later feel that we were destined to own? Think of all the ideas that don't stick, all the times you window-shop and walk on by, the person for whom you acknowledge a passing attraction but fail to act on it, and then the moment you see something and think, *That's mine.* It has absolutely nothing to do with practicality. If practicality were a consideration, we would have taken one look at Rossdale cottage and laughed. It has little to do with affordability. When we want something, we want it regardless of how much it costs. In the case of the cottage, we had viewed more than a hundred properties and knew we could buy a five-bedroomed house for less. If anything, anything at all, it is a willingness to throw caution to the wind. A sudden and decisive impulse to act boldly. To scratch an itch, if you will.

And so it was that on 1 June 2000, we took up residence. The cottage intrigued us. Why did it stand alone when all of the other houses had been built in pairs? Why was the neighbouring house with the datemark 1935 squeezed into a tight plot? Why, when we dug, did we uncover old footings and steps that led nowhere? Why were there old upright gas pipes that seemed to serve no purpose?

Old Ordnance Survey maps revealed part of the history – our cottage had been built by a Mr E Cooke and sat in his pleasure garden, laid out in an old chalk pit. Each subsequent map showed the creep of new houses, hemming in what was left of the gardens I have named Cooke's, because no name has been recorded in its history. I suspect that the First World War was a factor in its demise, but I decided to shorten my timeline. Had I allowed Cooke's to remain in business, I would have had to send Gerrard to war, and I preferred to have him join his brother in South Africa. The real gardens limped along until 1923, when Grove Park (originally part of the grounds of Stonecourt Manor) opened, providing the community with a free alternative.

It was here, in the cottage, that I would first entertain the thought that I might one day write a novel, and I would live with that notion for a long time, turning it over and over, before I finally dared to say the words out loud. Because it has been a rule of mine since childhood: once you say something out loud, a bargain is struck.

ACKNOWLEDGEMENTS

In writing this story, I am indebted to a number of sources, including *Inventing the Victorians* by Matthew Sweet, *Elegant Etiquette in the Nineteenth Century* by Mallory James, *How to be a Victorian* by Ruth Goodman and *The Victorians* by A. N. Wilson, as well as local photographs, including a picture of elephants in Carshalton's ponds. But my main source of inspiration was the cottage I have called home for the past twenty-one years, built (as far as we have been able to ascertain) as the ticket office for the pleasure gardens which opened at the turn of the century and had closed by 1923. What led a man to embark on such an endeavour after the last of the London pleasure gardens had failed isn't written in any local history books. The little we know comes from Ordnance Survey maps, census records and a reproduction of a woodcut which hangs in our hall, depicting Edwardian ladies playing a game of doubles on a tennis court, just in front of our cottage. Of course, if our research had been more successful, there would have been no story to write.

I found one of my grandfather's sketches with the inscription on the back: 'If you study something long enough and don't try to dictate what you think it ought to say, eventually you'll find it speaks to you.' We believe these were his own words, rather than a quote. I have given them to Miss Hoddy.

Incidentally, I am related on my father's side of the family to Annie Adams, the music hall star and Great Britain's first international star.

Heartfelt thanks to my beta readers, for their generosity and insightfulness, especially Carol Cooper, Beth Allen, Karen Begg, Anne Clinton, Kath Crowley, Helen Enefer, Mary Fuller, Dawn Gill, Bronwyn Kotze, Lynn Pearce, Sarah Marshall, Matthew Martin, Delia Porter, Will Poole, Julia Powley, Julie Spearritt, Sheila Christie, Sarah Hurley, Amanda Osborne, Sally Salmon, Peter Snell, patron saint of indie authors and bookseller extraordinaire (allegedly retired), and Trevor Stubbs.

The Sanctuary, the best online writers' group a writer could ever hope to belong to. To JJ Marsh and Jean Gill for their cover quotes and to Carol Cooper, Jean Gill, Debbie Young, JJ Marsh, Clare Flynn, Jessica Bell, Alison Morton, Linda Gillard, Helena Halme, Amie McCracken, Karen Inglis, Laura Morelli, Roz Morris, Jane Dixon-Smith and Liza Perrat for input into the cover blurb, help with technicalities and so much more.

Extra special thanks to my editor, Lorna Fergusson (https://www.fictionfire.co.uk/) and Andrew Candy of Tentacle Design for his fabulous cover design.

And not forgetting proofreader Perry Iles (contact him at chamberproof@yahoo.co.uk), JD Smith Design for typesetting, and, last but by no means least, all of the team at Clays.

ABOUT THE AUTHOR

Hailed by *The Bookseller* as 'One to Watch', Jane Davis is the author of ten novels.

Jane spent her twenties and the first part of her thirties chasing promotions at work, but when she achieved what she'd set out to do, she discovered that it wasn't what she wanted after all. It was then that she turned to writing.

Her debut, *Half-truths & White Lies*, won the Daily Mail First Novel Award in 2008. Of her subsequent three novels, Compulsion Reads wrote, 'Davis is a phenomenal writer, whose ability to create well-rounded characters that are easy to relate to feels effortless'. Her novel, *An Unknown Woman*, was awarded Writing Magazine's Self-published Book of the Year in 2016 and was shortlisted for two further awards. *Smash all the Windows* won The Selfies (Best Independent Fiction Author) Award in 2019.

Jane lives in Carshalton, Surrey with her Formula 1 obsessed, star-gazing, beer-brewing partner, surrounded by growing piles of paperbacks, CDs and general chaos. When she isn't writing, you may spot her disappearing up a mountain with a camera in hand. Her favourite description of fiction is 'made-up truth'.

A personal request from Jane: "Your opinion really matters to authors and to readers who are wondering which book to pick next. If you love a book, please tell your friends and post a review on the site you made your purchase from."

OTHER TITLES BY THE AUTHOR

At the Stroke of Nine O'Clock

Half Truths and White Lies

I Stopped Time

These Fragile Things

A Funeral for an Owl

An Unchoreographed Life

An Unknown Woman

My Counterfeit Self

Smash all the Windows

Can a camera capture the truth?

For further information, visit https://jane-davis.co.uk. Sign up today at https://jane-davis.co.uk/newsletter to be the first to hear about future projects, pre-launch specials, discounts and competitions. You'll also receive a free ebook of reader favourite *I Stopped Time.*